THE TEXAS
HILL COUNTRY

THE TEXAS HILL COUNTRY

WILLIAM W. JOHNSTONE
AND J.A. JOHNSTONE

KENSINGTON
PUBLISHING CORP.

kensingtonbooks.com

All Kensington titles, imprints, and distributed lines are available at special quantity discounts for bulk purchases for sales promotion, premiums, fund-raising, and educational or institutional use.

Special book excerpts or customized printings can also be created to fit specific needs. For details, write or phone the office of the Kensington Sales Manager: Kensington Publishing Corp., 900 Third Avenue, New York, NY 10022. Attn. Sales Department. Phone: 1-800-221-2647.

KENSINGTON and the K with book logo Reg US Pat. & TM Off.

ISBN: 978-1-4967-5281-9

ISBN: 978-1-4967-5282-6 (e-book)

First Trade Paperback Printing: October 2025

10 9 8 7 6 5 4 3 2 1

Printed in the United States of America

The authorized representative in the EU for product safety and compliance is eucomply OU, Parnu mnt 139b-14, Apt 123
Tallinn, Berlin 11317, hello@eucompliancepartner.com.

"I must say as to what I have seen of Texas it is the garden spot of the world. The best land and the best prospects for health I ever saw, and I do believe it is a fortune to any man to come here. There is a world of country here to settle."
—Davy Crockett

Texas, 1875

The old man threw himself out of the saddle. He hit the ground hard and rolled over a couple of times, losing his grip on the Winchester as he did so. He grabbed the rifle as he scrambled to his feet. A bullet screamed past his head. He ran several steps and then dove to the ground, landing behind a pile of rocks. It wasn't much, but it was the best cover he could reach in time.

The horse galloped away, leaving him there a-foot. That was his own choice, he thought, as he squirmed around and thrust the Winchester over the rocks. If these were to be his last moments on earth, he'd rather spend them fighting. Continuing to flee wouldn't have gotten him anything except an ignominious death from a bullet in the back.

Some of his thick gray hair had fallen over his eyes. He blew it up out of the way and squinted over the rifle's sights as he snugged his weathered cheek against the smooth wood of the stock. One of the men who'd been chasing him seemed to leap into focus. He might be old, but his eyes were still good.

He stroked the trigger.

The Winchester cracked. The old man controlled the recoil easily and worked the rifle's lever. He shifted the barrel without even looking to see if his first shot had found its target. There was another of the varmints! Again, the rifle spat fire and lead.

This time, he watched long enough to see the attacker fly backward, arms flung out to the sides, driven from the horse by the bullet slamming into his body. The old man's tightly clenched jaw jerked in a curt nod. That was two of them down. He could tell because he saw another riderless horse, made that way by his first shot. Yep, two down.

It was a blasted shame there were ten more of the would-be killers.

However, losing two of their number was enough to give them pause. If they continued galloping right into the teeth of the old man's rifle fire, they would lose more. They hauled on their reins and swung their mounts to the side, peeling off and circling until they were headed back toward the trees from which they had emerged for their ambush a few minutes earlier.

The old man watched them go. He knew better than to believe they were giving up. They were just falling back to catch their breath and figure out what they wanted to do next.

He rolled onto his side and did some breath catching of his own. His lips quirked in a grimace under the drooping mustache. He was too ancient to go around jumping off horses and crashing to the ground. His muscles already ached, and he knew he'd be so stiff and sore by morning he would have trouble getting around—assuming he was still alive in the morning, which meant jumping to a mighty big conclusion.

But as he lay there dragging air into his lungs, he felt his racing pulse began to slow a mite. It wasn't hammering inside his head quite so loudly anymore. Things could be worse. The odds were only ten to one now.

He looked around and spotted his broad-brimmed brown hat lying upside down on the ground about ten yards away. It had flown off when he dove from the horse. The sun was hot and he could use the hat's shade. He pushed himself up and looked toward the trees. The riders who wanted to kill him had disappeared in there.

The range was pretty long, even for a rifle. The old man considered for a moment longer, then gathered himself and surged to his feet. He dashed toward the hat, bent down, and reached for it.

The hat jumped and the flat crack of a rifle came from the trees at almost the same instant. The hat landed several more yards away. The old man jerked back and dove behind the rocks again.

He lay there cursing under his breath, directing some of the invective at the rifleman hidden in the trees—who was a mighty fine shot, by the way—and some at himself for risking getting ventilated over a hat.

If nothing else, this incident had confirmed that he was pinned down here good and proper. Somebody in the trees had a powerful, well-sighted rifle and the skill to use it.

His friends would be coming along to look for him if he was stuck here long enough. That was the only sliver of hope to which he could cling. He would just have to hold off these fellas until help arrived.

In the meantime, he looked around. He was in an open valley about half a mile wide, flanked east and west by wooded hills with rocky outcroppings here and there. A creek ran north to south through the valley in meandering fashion. It was about a hundred yards to the old man's right. Might as well be a hundred miles for all the chance he stood of reaching it and taking cover in the trees that grew along it. The trees where his enemies were hidden were to the north.

At least with so much open ground around, they wouldn't be able to sneak up on him.

If things worked out so that he died today, he would have beautiful scenery around him when he left this world. Nowhere was more beautiful than this Texas hill country. He had visited many places in his long, eventful life, but nothing matched Texas. Even though he had been born on the other side of the world, he had thought many times over the years that Texas was his destiny, the place where he was meant to be.

Otherwise, why would he and the rest of his family have come here all those years ago? It was fate. There was no other word for it. . . .

Book I

Chapter 1

Grand Duchy of Alpenstone

The clash of steel against steel created a clamor that echoed from the chamber's ancient tapestry-hung stone walls.

The saber-wielding men lunged back and forth. The blades darted out, darted back, thrusted and parried, sent sparks flying when they came together. Each time when it seemed as if one of the men was tiring and might make a fatal slip, he found a reserve of strength and stamina somewhere inside and continued the battle.

His opponent was growing frustrated and impatient, Athelstan Braxton sensed. Charles Edgerton considered himself to be the finest swordsman in the Grand Duchy of Alpenstone. Granted, it was a very small country, but to be the best of anything was an achievement to be desired.

Charles wouldn't like the idea of losing to one of his cousins. Especially not to a poor relation such as Athelstan Braxton.

Just as Athelstan expected, the frustration boiled over inside Charles and prodded him into acting rashly. He charged, swinging the saber in wild, chopping blows. Athelstan twisted aside and brought his saber down on top of Charles's. As Charles's momentum carried him forward, his sword's point rammed against the stone floor. The impact jolted the weapon out of his hand.

Charles stumbled and might have fallen, but Athelstan gripped his upper arm and steadied him. Charles glared and pulled away.

"You've been practicing," he told his cousin, with grudging admiration.

Athelstan smiled. "That's the only way I can hope to compete with you and not be terribly outclassed."

"I'll beat you next time."

"I have no doubt of it," Athelstan said.

Soothing Charles's ruffled feathers was grating, but it was the smart thing to do. Although the Edgertons and the Braxtons were both noble families, descendants of the English adventurers who had founded the Grand Duchy of Alpenstone in a corner of the mountains where France, Germany, and Switzerland all came together, the Edgertons possessed a great deal more wealth—and therefore, a great deal more power and influence.

This castle in Lornsburgh, the capital, belonged to the Edgertons, who owned a large estate outside of town. The Braxtons owned one of the neighboring estates, but it was smaller and much less ostentatious. Athelstan lived there with his brothers, Jeremy and Perry, and their sister, Bodicia. The siblings were the last of their line, for now. But Bodicia was the youngest at nineteen and Athelstan the oldest at twenty-eight, so they still had plenty of time to add to the family heritage.

Athelstan sleeved sweat off his face. It was cool year-round here in the mountains, but the two men had worked hard in their duel. He picked up Charles's saber and held it out to him.

"Another bout next week?" Charles asked, as he took the sword.

"Of course. How else will I get better?"

Charles whipped the sword around and rested the blade's tip against Athelstan's chest, just above where the shirt hung open to reveal a bit of curly brown hair. He didn't press hard enough to break the skin, but Athelstan definitely felt the point against his flesh.

"Just don't get too good," Charles said. For one grim moment, Athelstan wasn't sure if his cousin meant the warning seriously.

Then Charles grinned and pulled the saber away. He clapped his free hand on Athelstan's shoulder and said, "Come, let's have some brandy."

Their steps echoing against the high ceiling, the cousins left the hall and stepped into a small library. It was their custom to step in there for a bit of refreshment after a spirited round with the sabers. One of the servants already had left a tray with a decanter and a pair of snifters on the heavy inlaid table in the center of the room.

Charles tossed his saber on the table and poured the brandy. He handed one of the snifters to Athelstan and lifted his.

"To Alpenstone," he said.

"To Alpenstone," Athelstan echoed, happy to drink to their homeland.

As they drank, a new voice said, "You drink to a bit of land when you could be toasting a person instead."

The two men turned as a young woman strolled into the room. Charles asked her, "In that case, to whom should we be drinking, Claudia?"

"Your beautiful sister, of course," Claudia Edgerton replied with a smile.

"That seems quite reasonable to me," Athelstan said. He lifted his brandy snifter in salute to the lovely fair-haired young woman.

Charles said, "If you have to goad people into drinking to you, I'm not sure how much of a tribute it really is."

Claudia came closer and rested a hand on Athelstan's arm. "You're sincere in your admiration of me, aren't you, Athelstan?" she asked.

"Of course," he answered without hesitation. Only a blind man could fail to admire Claudia's lithe beauty, effectively displayed in a light blue gown with a square-cut, daringly low neckline. And even a blind man could enjoy the lilting music of her voice.

Charles snorted and said, "Our cousin admires you because he didn't grow up with you bedeviling him at every turn."

Claudia turned to him. "Actually, we did grow up together. Practically. Alpenstone is a very small country, after all, and our family estates are next to each other."

"Yes, yes." Charles drank the rest of the brandy in his snifter. "What do you want, Claudia?"

She lifted her hand and stroked the tight line of his jaw. "Can't I simply desire to enjoy the company of my dear brother?"— a quick smile toward Athelstan—"and my darling cousin, of course."

"There's a time for the company of women," Charles snapped. "The aftermath of a brisk contest of swords between two men isn't it."

"Oh?" Claudia reached down and closed her hand around the grip of the sword her brother had tossed on the table. She picked it up and turned quickly, raising the blade until the tip was poised in front of Charles's face. "Perhaps you'd care to test my skill with a sword?" She whipped the saber toward Athelstan, who took an involuntary step backward. "Or you?"

Athelstan grinned and held up his empty left hand, palm out. "Not me," he said. "I'll readily admit your superiority, Claudia."

"Oh! I know you, Athelstan. You're just indulging the whims of a little girl. Have at you!"

She brandished the saber again and sprang at him, cutting the air back and forth. Athelstan had to give ground. Instinctively, he brought up his saber and blocked Claudia's attack. The blades rang together.

The saber wasn't a lightweight weapon, but Claudia handled it with relative ease. Athelstan knew her to also be a superb rider, and when they were young, she had been able to outrun all her male cousins and outwrestle some of them.

Despite how she referred to herself, she was no longer a little girl but a woman in the vigorous prime years of her youth. A wicked smile appeared on her face as she pressed the attack and Athelstan retreated across the library. Unfortunately, he didn't have much room to withdraw. His back struck the shelves full of thick leather-bound volumes. The saber in Claudia's hand darted at him. He barely turned the thrust aside with his blade.

Was she actually trying to hurt him?

Athelstan had a hard time believing that, but he didn't have a chance to find out one way or the other. Charles grabbed his sister from behind, his left arm going around her waist while his right hand reached around her to grab the saber. He pulled it out of her grip and said, "That's enough! What's wrong with you, Claudia?"

"Wrong with me?" She twisted in his grip and glared at him. Her lips pulled back from her teeth in a feral snarl. "There's nothing wrong with me, dear brother! You boys just don't know how to handle me."

"I'll put you over my knee, that's what I'll do," Charles threatened.

"It's all right," Athelstan said. This unexpected confrontation made him uncomfortable. "Claudia was just having a bit of sport with us, Charles. I'm sure she meant no harm."

"She could have hurt you, waving that saber around like that."

"Please," Claudia said, contempt dripping from her voice, "if I'd wanted to hurt either of you, you couldn't have stopped me. And I'd have done it with something other than a blade."

Somehow, Athelstan had no trouble believing that.

Without turning around, Charles tossed the saber onto the table behind him again. Then he let go of Claudia, who gave him a withering look and said, "The next time you lay hands on me, Charles, you'd best be serious about it."

"Believe me, I will be."

She turned back to Athelstan. "I've not offended you . . . ?"

"Of course not," he told her. "I know you meant no harm."

He wasn't completely convinced of that, but he saw no need to express that thought.

Claudia started to walk away but paused and looked back at the two young men.

"That's the trouble with you boys," she said. "You play at swords and fail to realize there are much deadlier weapons in the world."

With that, she was gone.

Charles waited until his sister's footsteps had dwindled away in the corridor outside the library. Then he said, "I apologize for Claudia. I have no idea what possessed her to act that way. I swear, sometimes I think madness must lurk somewhere in our family, and it comes out now and then in Claudia."

"If your family is mad, then so is mine," Athelstan pointed out.

Charles shook his head. "No, the Braxtons are very different from the Edgertons. The blood may be linked, but your family is the solid, hardworking stock that allowed England to spread an empire around the globe."

"You make us sound dreadfully boring. Don't forget, the Braxtons came here along with the Edgertons, the Fitzwarrens, and the Bucklands, to found Alpenstone."

Charles clapped Athelstan on the shoulder. "True. You're daring adventurers at heart, I suppose. And it's your family that has the closest connection with the Habsburgs, and without that, Alpenstone most likely wouldn't exist. We owe you a great deal, Athelstan."

"Not me, personally. It was my grandfather, and yours, and all the others who left England—"

Charles laughed. "One step ahead of the law, no doubt! I've never heard the full story of how the grand duchy came to exist, have you?"

"No, not really. But I hardly think our ancestors were outlaws who fled the country."

"Perhaps someday we'll find out. In the meantime, allow me to apologize again for Claudia's outlandish behavior."

"You didn't really mean that, did you, when you threatened to put her over your knee?"

Charles looked solemnly at Athelstan and said, "Cousin, I meant every word of it."

Chapter 2

The Huntsman's Rest had a sign hanging over its entrance that depicted a man wearing old-fashioned clothing, including a peaked cap with a feather in it, and carrying a blunderbuss. The figure sported a sharply pointed goatee. He was supposed to be a huntsman stalking his prey, Jeremy Braxton supposed, but the patrons of this tavern—himself included—spent very little time tramping around the woods in search of wild game.

The only game Jeremy was interested in at the moment was *vingt-et-un*. He studied the cards in his hand, looked across the table, and nodded to the dealer, who lofted another card in front of Jeremy.

Only a heartbeat was required for Jeremy to recognize the cluster of pips on the card as being too many. He rolled his eyes in disgust before tossing his other cards away. The dealer's gaze moved on to the player on Jeremy's left. His eyebrows rose inquisitively.

Jeremy didn't care what the hand's outcome was. He wouldn't be raking in the pile of coins in the middle of the table, so he didn't care who did. He shoved back his chair, stood up, and headed for the bar that ran across the back of the smoky low-ceilinged room. Only a few lamps burned in the tavern, and the smoke made the lighting even dimmer.

One of the serving girls turned away from the bar with a tray in her hands laden with a pitcher and several tankards. When she saw him, she said, "You're not playing anymore, Jeremy? Did you grow tired of the game?'

"Yes, that's it, I'm tired of it," he said. As good an explanation as any and better than admitting that he was—momentarily, to be sure—without funds.

"Well, if you're in search of some other way to pass the time, I can make a suggestion," she said with a bawdy smile, as she passed him, carrying the tray. "Just let me deliver this to that table over there."

"Another time, Sophie," he told her. "I wouldn't be very good company right now, I'm afraid."

"Suit yourself," she said breezily, over her shoulder.

He went to the bar and nodded to the burly, white-haired tavernkeeper. "A pint, Fred."

The man squinted piggish eyes at him, making them even more swinelike. "On the family account, I take it?"

"Of course," Jeremy responded stiffly.

As he was drawing the pint, Fred said, "You know, lad, you're the only one of the Braxtons I've ever seen in here, so it's a reasonable thing to believe the family account is *your* account."

"Athelstan handles the finances. I've explained that to you."

"And you've informed him as to the amount you owe the Huntsman's Rest?"

"Of course," Jeremy said. That was a barefaced lie; he had told his older brother no such thing. But Fred didn't have to know that. Jeremy was certain his situation would improve shortly. Any day now, in fact.

Fred looked like he didn't know whether to believe him or not, but finally the tavernkeeper nodded in acceptance of Jeremy's answer.

"That brother of yours had best get around to handling his responsibilities before too much more time passes," Fred said with a frown. "Otherwise, I might have to go see him myself."

"There's no need for that."

"Just remember what I said, lad."

Fred moved off down the bar, and Jeremy lifted the tankard to his lips. He drank deeply of the ale and tried to bring his anger and resentment under control. A man like Fred had no right to talk to him like that.

Sophie came back to the bar with the now empty tray under her arm. She leaned closer to Jeremy and said under her breath, "You need to meet me in the back."

"I told you, I'm not in the mood for—"

"Not that. I have to talk to you." Her eyes cut toward a corner where three men sat at a table.

Jeremy followed her gaze without appearing to do so, studying the men from the corner of his eye. They were strangers to him.

"I don't know them, if that's what you're trying to tell me," he said.

"You may not know them, but they know you," Sophie said. "I overheard them talking about you just now. And it didn't sound like they were your friends."

Jeremy took another drink from the tankard to give himself time to think. Then he said, "Go on in the back. I'll join you shortly."

"All right." Leaving the tray on the bar, she disappeared through a narrow door at the end of it. Jeremy knew there were a couple of private rooms in the rear of the tavern, as well as a storage area.

He stood there drinking slowly from the tankard, trying to give off an air of not having a care in the world. Handsome and dark-haired, he looked to be an indolent young man, which was exactly what he was.

He swallowed the last of the ale and placed the empty on the bar. Down at the other end, Fred saw that and looked a question at him. Jeremy shook his head and turned to stroll toward the door to the back.

Fred made a face but didn't interfere. Sophie and the other girls who worked for him made their own arrangements with the customers, if such arrangements were to be made. Fred had no desire to mix in with any of that. He owned a tavern, not a brothel, he had been known to declare.

Jeremy stepped through the door into a hallway. At the far end was a window coated with a thick layer of grime. It let in enough light for him to see the two doors on the right that opened onto the private rooms and the single door on the left to the storage area.

Sophie stood in the first open doorway on the right. She beckoned to him in the gloom.

Jeremy closed the door to the tavern's main room and joined her.

"What is it?" he asked. "Did you overhear those strangers plotting against me?"

"One of them asked the others if they were sure that was you at the bar. They said it was, and he told them to go ahead." Sophie looked worried. "That sounds pretty ominous to me."

"It doesn't sound good," Jeremy agreed. He looked at the filthy window. "Perhaps it would be a good idea to leave. I can always come back later after those men are gone."

"Before you go—" Sophie reached up and put her arms around his neck. She pulled his head down and pressed her lips to his in a hard, hungry kiss.

For a second, Jeremy felt a surge of impatience. He had no idea who those men were or what they wanted from him, but he owed money to more than one man in Alpenstone. A few others held grudges against him involving wives and daughters. With so much potential trouble hanging over his head, the details didn't really matter. He needed to get out of there, and she was delaying him.

But the urgency of her embrace, the pliant softness of her body as his arms went around her, the hot sweetness of her mouth, all those things were too much for Jeremy to ignore. He clasped her more tightly to him and returned the kiss.

The crash of a door slamming open shattered Jeremy's preoccupation. He let go of Sophie and jerked around to see two men entering the gloomy hallway. He couldn't make out any details, but he was sure they were two of the men the serving girl had overheard talking about him.

For a second, he thought that perhaps she was working with them and had distracted him and delayed his flight so that they could catch him.

Then Sophie gave him a shove toward the window. "Get out of here! I'll slow them down!" She ran toward the two men and waved her hands in front of her as she cried, "You can't be back here!"

With his suspicion of her dispelled, he dashed to the window, which had a brass handle at the bottom for lifting. He grabbed it and thrust the pane up, then threw a leg over the sill.

The alley behind the Huntsman's Rest was almost as dark and gloomy as the corridor Jeremy had just left. His boots had barely landed on the hard-packed dirt when a rush of footsteps came from nearby.

He twisted toward the sound and spotted a large indistinct shape charging toward him. Two of his enemies had followed him into the rear hallway, but the other man had left the building and circled around to cut off this means of escape. It was a sound strategy.

Jeremy glanced at the other end of the alley where numerous crates were piled up. He might be able to navigate through them, but they would slow him down and the attacker would overtake him.

Faced with that obstacle, Jeremy turned the other way and threw himself toward the ground. His shoulder rammed into the man's legs. The stranger, carried forward by his momentum, yelled as he hurtled over Jeremy's back.

The man landed on Jeremy's legs, weighing them down and pinning them to the ground for a moment before Jeremy kicked his way free. The man rolled and grabbed at him, but Jeremy landed a kick to his face and knocked him away. Jeremy scrambled up and ran for the street.

Behind him, someone shouted, "Gustav! Gustav, get after him!"

Jeremy threw a look over his shoulder. In the thickening shadows, he couldn't make out anything clearly, but he thought the two men who had burst into the tavern's rear hallway had climbed out the window after him. One of them was tending to the man Jeremy had kicked while the other lumbered after him.

The man chasing him looked big enough to tear him apart. But to do that, he'd have to catch him, and Jeremy was faster. When he reached the cobblestone street, he darted right, away from the tavern.

Lornsburgh, although not as old as many of the towns in Europe, had the same air of antiquity about it: the narrow, twisting streets; the heavy, imposing stone buildings; the dark passages between looming structures. Jeremy ran into one of those openings and was swallowed up instantly by shadows. He stopped a few yards in and pressed his back to the wall as he struggled to control his rapid breathing. He didn't want his pursuer to hear him gasping.

The big man huffed and puffed past the alley and never even glanced toward Jeremy. Jeremy waited in the shadows to make sure the man didn't come back and that no one else came along looking for him. He thought about going the other way in the alley, but the gloom was so thick, he couldn't see a thing. He decided not to venture in that direction.

Finally, he eased up to the alley mouth and leaned out just far enough to look up and down the street. A few people were still out and about since it was only early evening, but no one appeared to be searching for him. He stepped out and, with his head down, walked swiftly toward the next street. He wanted to get back to the stable where he had left his horse when he rode into town from the family estate earlier in the day.

He hadn't gone very far when he heard the scuff of shoe leather on the cobblestones behind him. An instant later, something hard and round pressed against the back of his head, causing him to stop short and freeze in his tracks.

"Please try to run, Herr Braxton," a man said. "I would like nothing more than to blow your brains out."

Chapter 3

Braxton Manor was a rambling, one-story stone house with a gabled roof located in the middle of five thousand acres several miles north of Lornsburgh. The estate also included stables, a blacksmith shop, storage sheds, and a number of cottages to house the workers who tended the fields to the south of the manor house. To the north of the house lay thick, practically untouched woods. A few trails had been laid out through the forest, but other than that, the area looked very much as it had for hundreds of years.

Perry Braxton rode along one of those trails. He held the big gray stallion down to a lope. The horse wanted to run, but this was no place for it. The trail was too narrow and twisting. A hard run risked a stumble and fall. Besides, a few low-hanging branches extended out over the trail, and Perry didn't want to risk bashing his head into one of them.

A voice called from behind him, "Perry! Perry, wait for me!"

Perry reined in and looked over his shoulder. The branches were so thick overhead that they cast the trail into deep shadow, but beams of light slanted through gaps here and there and reflected off the blond hair of the rider hurrying after him. That hair tumbled in waves around the shoulders of his sister, Bodicia.

For years, their mother had tried to civilize Bodicia and turn her into a proper member of respectable society. That effort had failed for the most part. Bodicia and her cousin, Claudia Edgerton, had seemed to be in some sort of competition for most of their childhood to see which one could act most like a boy.

Despite that, both girls had grown into lovely young women.

Genevieve and Alexander Braxton were both gone now, taken by the sickness that had swept through Europe, including Alpenstone, two years earlier, leaving their four children to carry on. Athelstan, the eldest, was the head of the family now. It would be up to him to find a suitable husband for Bodicia, and since she was nineteen now, the sooner the better.

Perry didn't envy his older brother that job.

He turned the gray and waited in the trail. Attempting to get away from Bodicia would be a mistake. That would just goad her into trying harder to catch up. Better just to let her ride with him.

It didn't take long for her to join him. The chestnut mare she rode was nimble and fast. She smiled as she drew even with him.

"I told you to let me know if you went for a ride and I would join you," she said. "Did you forget?"

"That's right," Perry said, making an effort to keep the dry tone out of his voice. "It slipped my mind."

Bodicia made a scoffing noise, but she didn't seem upset. She was full of life, excited by practically everything that happened, and she seldom got angry about anything. To her, each day was a new adventure.

Her mother wouldn't have been pleased to see her now with her hair loose, wearing a man's shirt and trousers, and riding astride. But she was happy and healthy, and that was what mattered to Perry.

He was three years older, but anyone who didn't know about the difference in their ages might take them for twins. They had the same golden hair, slender build, and dark blue eyes.

One difference was that Bodicia was unarmed while Perry carried a flintlock rifle across the pommel of his saddle. Wild boars roamed these woods, and encounters with them, though uncommon, did happen.

"Where are you going?" Bodicia asked.

"Nowhere in particular. It's just too fine a day to stay cooped up inside."

"You're not going to Edgerton Hall?"

Perry frowned as he looked over at her. "Why would I do that?"

His sister wore a sly smile as she said, "I thought perhaps you might be paying a call on Claudia."

For a moment, Perry didn't respond. Then he laughed and shook his head.

"If you're trying to insinuate that I might be interested in courting our cousin, you can put that completely out of your mind. That's the most insane idea I've ever heard."

"I'm not sure why you'd think that. She's beautiful, and the Edgertons have a great deal more money than we do."

Perry's jaw tightened. He couldn't dispute either of the things Bodicia had said. Claudia, undeniably, was beautiful. Perry also had thought more than once that she was a bit mad—perhaps more than a bit.

The Braxton family's financial situation was precarious, too, although no one would ever know that from Athelstan's demeanor. The oldest of the Braxton siblings didn't like to display any signs of weakness.

But Perry had overheard Athelstan talking to Jeremy a few days earlier, and Athelstan hadn't been happy. He had laid into Jeremy about the gambling debts he was running up, not to mention the drinking and carousing he did in the taverns of Lornsburgh. According to what Perry had heard Athelstan saying, Jeremy's behavior was a threat not only to the family's social standing but to their financial well-being.

Jeremy, of course, had promised to do a better job of controlling his impulses, but Perry had his doubts about that happening.

"Well?" Bodicia prodded, breaking into Perry's thoughts. "I think it's a wonderful idea."

"Courting Claudia?" Perry shook his head. "I know the two of you were as close as sisters when you were young, Bodicia, but things have changed—"

He was spared the necessity of going into detail about his current opinion of their cousin because, at that moment, a gunshot blasted not far away.

Perry and Bodicia had been riding along the trail at an easy pace. They stopped short and sat straighter in their saddles as the clamorous echoes drifted through the forest. Bodicia said, "Who's shooting out here? No one should be shooting in this forest, should he?"

"No, they shouldn't," Perry agreed. "Aside from our game-keeper, and I happen to know he's back at the estate right now." He lifted his reins. "I'll go find out."

The obvious answer had already suggested itself to him: a poacher. The estate was beset with them from time to time. A large number of deer could be found in these woods, and they were tempting targets.

As he heeled the stallion into motion, he called over his shoulder, "Go back to the manor!"

He hoped Bodicia would listen to him and do as she was told—but he couldn't make himself believe that was likely to happen.

Holding the rifle in his left hand, he rode as fast as he dared along the trail, leaning to one side and then the other to balance himself as the stallion took the turns with nimble-footed ease. There was no way to disguise the swift rataplan of hoofbeats on the earth. Whoever had fired the shot would know someone was coming.

He might be riding into an ambush, Perry thought, but he wasn't going to turn back. Family honor demanded that he protect their estate and everything on it.

He rounded another bend in the trail and saw a clearing up ahead on the left. A shallow bluff rose on the far side of the clearing, and from it, a tiny waterfall trickled down to feed a small pool. Perry and his brothers had splashed around in that pool many times as they were growing up.

It also served as a watering hole for the wildlife in this forest, so it wasn't surprising to see that a deer had come to drink. Clearly, a pair of poachers had waited, silent and motionless in the nearby brush, to see what animals might come along. One of them had downed the deer with a single shot, and now both men were trying to lift the carcass and drape it across the back of a draft horse they had brought with them. They were hurrying, no doubt because they'd heard a rider approaching, but the draft horse, probably spooked by the smell of blood, wasn't cooperating. It sidled away without warning.

With a despairing cry from one of the men, the pair lost their hold on the carcass. It slipped back to the ground at their feet as the horse danced skittishly.

One of the men whirled toward Perry and dragged a pistol from where it was tucked in the waistband of his trousers.

"Elbert, no!" the other man shouted as the pistol rose in the first man's hand.

Perry yanked on the stallion's reins and swerved the big gray to the side as powder smoke blossomed from the pistol and flame spurted from the muzzle. He sensed as much as heard a hum like a bee and knew that sound was the wind-rip of the pistol ball passing close beside his head. He hauled back on the reins, and the stallion twisted to a stop.

Perry brought the rifle to his shoulder, earing back the hammer as he raised the weapon. With the stock pressed hard against his shoulder, he aimed at the poacher who had just tried to kill him.

His finger froze on the trigger as he squinted over the rifle barrel and saw the face of a boy staring at him, wide-eyed with horror and fear.

"No!" the other man cried. "Don't shoot! Please, *mein Herr*!"

Although tall and huskily built, the lad was no more than fourteen, Perry saw. At that moment, he could have shot the boy where he stood and would have been within his rights to do so. Elbert and the other man—his father?—were poachers and had slain that deer illegally. Also, since Perry didn't recognize either of them, he knew they were trespassers and had no right to be anywhere on the Braxton estate. He could press the trigger right now, blow a hole through young Elbert, and no one could say that he had done anything wrong.

But instead, he took his finger out of the trigger guard and lowered the rifle.

With an inarticulate yell, Elbert charged at him, crossing the distance between them before Perry could raise the rifle again.

The other man shouted at him to stop, but Elbert ignored that. He leaped up and grabbed Perry's arm. Perry had been so shocked by the unexpected attack that he didn't react quickly enough to pull the stallion away.

Perry came out of the saddle and crashed to the ground. The rifle slipped out of his hands. At such close quarters, it wouldn't have been any good to him anyway. Although shaken by the fall, he tried to get up, but Elbert was on top of him now, pinning him to the ground with a knee on either side of Perry as he hammered frenzied punches at the young nobleman's face.

Chapter 4

As he rode up to the stable on his family's estate, Athelstan was still thinking about the look he had seen in his cousin Claudia's eyes when she came at him with that saber. He hated to think that Claudia was deranged, but madness had lurked in her gaze. That thought deeply disturbed Athelstan.

No, he was the one who was mad to think such a thing, he told himself sternly. He had known Claudia all her life. He remembered when she was born. He had been a boy of almost ten years and had little or no interest in a female infant. There was already one of those in Braxton Manor—his sister, Bodicia—and one wailing baby was enough.

Even so, he had watched Claudia grow up and felt a certain loyalty to her because they were related. Her brother would take her in hand and soon enough would be marrying her off to some suitable match. Randolph Miller, perhaps, Athelstan mused. He would make a good husband for Claudia. Just the sort of boring, levelheaded man she needed to settle her down.

As Athelstan swung down from the saddle, one of the boys who worked in the stable hurried out to take the horse and tend to it. But as the youngster reached for the reins, Athelstan noticed a worried frown on his face.

"What's wrong, Griggs?" he asked.

"Nothing, sir," the boy answered quickly. But after a second's hesitation, he added, "It's just . . ."

"It's just what?" Athelstan's tone held a crisp note of command.

The stableboy swallowed and said, "Master Perry went for a ride earlier, and Mistress Bodicia followed him not long after, and neither of them have come back."

"How long ago was this?"

"An hour, sir. Maybe a bit longer."

"Which way did they go?"

"North, sir."

Athelstan nodded. "There are thousands of acres of woods up there for them to roam around in. I'm sure they're fine."

Young Griggs made a face and said, "It's just that . . . well, a few minutes ago I thought I heard a gun go off somewhere in that direction."

Athelstan caught his breath. "Was my brother armed when he left?"

"Oh, yes, sir, Master Athelstan. He took a rifle with him. In case he ran into any wild boars, he said."

It was entirely possible that was what had happened. Perry wouldn't go looking to shoot one of the boars, but he would defend himself if the creature attacked him.

Or Bodicia was in danger, he added to himself. The fact that their sister was out there somewhere in the forest added to the uneasy feeling stirring inside Athelstan.

"The two of them didn't ride out together, you said?"

"No, sir, Master Perry was first to leave, and then Mistress Bodicia followed him a short time later."

It was just possible that Bodicia had failed to catch up to Perry. She might have even gotten lost. Even though he was confident that nothing serious was wrong, Athelstan knew he wouldn't rest easy until he was certain his younger siblings were all right.

"Never mind about putting the horse up," he told young Griggs.

He didn't want to take the time to switch his saddle to a fresh mount. This one would be all right for a while yet; he had taken it easy riding back over here from the Edgerton estate, and it wasn't a long journey.

He stepped up into the saddle, asked Griggs which trail Perry and Bodicia had taken, and trotted off in the direction the lad pointed.

When Perry had told her to go back to the manor, Bodicia had considered obeying the order.

She had considered it for a good ten or fifteen seconds before jabbing her boot heels into her horse's flanks and galloping after her brother.

Perry knew her quite well, she reasoned. Surely, he was aware of how unlikely she was to flee in the face of danger—especially when he was charging right into it.

Because of the way the trail twisted and turned through the woods, she lost sight of him several times, but following him was no problem because she could still hear the stallion's hooves hammering the ground. Of course, her own mount's hoofbeats were louder, so it was easy to get confused, and she hadn't realized that Perry had stopped until she rounded a bend in the trail and saw him reining the big gray to a halt.

Bodicia's keen blue eyes took in the scene instantly: the clearing, the waterfall, the pool, the two men, and the slain deer. She recognized the place. Unknown to her brothers, she had followed them here several times when they were all younger. She had never spied on them when they stripped off their clothing and plunged into the water, but it was easy enough to know what they were doing just by listening, what with all the laughing and splashing.

They didn't know she had trailed them out here, and they certainly didn't know that she had enjoyed swimming in the pool as well when they weren't around, reveling in the cold bite of the water against her bare skin.

As Bodicia's horse skidded to an abrupt stop, one of the men fired a pistol at Perry. She gasped, fearing he would be hit.

The ball missed him, though, and Bodicia gasped again as a low-hanging tree branch near her jerked and broke. The pistol shot had struck the branch, she realized—which meant it had come within a couple of feet of striking her.

Her head spun dizzily and she had to clutch at the saddle for support as the knowledge of how close she had just come to dying sunk in on her. She had lived a pampered, protected existence, and she knew it. The closest she had ever been to death was when sickness claimed her mother and father. Certainly, she had never faced such violence as this.

Perry was aiming his rifle at the man who had just shot at them, and for an instant, Bodicia felt a fierce surge of anger and wanted her brother to shoot the man.

Perry hesitated, though, and lowered his rifle, of all things, and sure enough, the man attacked him again, charging across the clearing and dragging Perry out of the saddle. He straddled Perry and began slugging away with his fists.

The sight of her brother being assaulted like that broke Bodicia out of her frightened immobility. Anger replaced that fear. She leaped off her horse and ran toward them.

She recalled too late that there were two men. Before she could reach Perry to help him, the second man lunged forward and intercepted her. He grabbed her around the waist and swung her so that her feet flew off the ground.

Bodicia yelled and kicked her feet and squirmed in the man's grip. She managed to twist her body enough that when she brought her right elbow back sharply, it cracked into her captor's jaw. He staggered and his arms loosened around her waist. She tore free from him.

As she stumbled forward, she saw Perry buck up from the ground as he shot a fist straight up. It caught his attacker under the chin and rocked his head back. The blow knocked him off Perry, who threw him to the side.

The man who had grabbed Bodicia snagged her left arm. She balled her right hand into a fist and whipped around to strike him on the nose. She had wrestled with her brothers and cousins when they were all children, but she didn't have any experience with this sort of fighting. Luck and instinct guided her blow and blood spurted from the man's nose as Bodicia's fist landed squarely on it.

He staggered back, groaning, and held up both hands as he said, "Please, milady, stop! I've no wish to hurt you—"

"Get away from her or I'll kill you!"

The angry shout came from Perry, who had rolled to the side and snatched his fallen rifle from the ground. He was on his feet now with the rifle leveled. He backed off a few steps and moved the weapon from side to side so he could cover both men.

The man and the boy, rather, Bodicia saw now. The one Perry had been struggling with was tall and husky, but his face wasn't that of a full-grown man. He was four or five years younger than she was, she estimated.

"Bodicia, are you all right?" Perry asked.

She was breathing hard from fear and exertion, but she could tell she wasn't injured.

"Yes, I'm fine," she assured her brother, as she moved closer to him. "What about you?"

"Other than some bruised dignity, I'm not hurt."

The man held a hand to his bleeding nose. It muffled his voice slightly as he said, "Please, *mein Herr*, we meant no harm. My wife and my little ones are hungry. My son and I thought we might find a boar and hoped you would not care if we took one of those beasts—"

"That's not a boar," Perry interrupted. "That's a fine deer."

"When we saw it come up, I told my son we could not shoot it, but I—I—"

"I shot it!" the young man burst out. He had climbed to his feet. "Punish me if you must." His chin jutted out defiantly. "And I would shoot it again to feed my brothers and sisters!"

Bodicia put a hand on Perry's arm. "Perhaps we should just let them go."

He glanced at her, but not long enough to tempt the two poachers to try anything. Then his gaze was fixed on them again and he said, "They tried to kill us, and you think we should just let them go?"

With a sullen expression on his face, Elbert said, "I apologize for shooting at you, Herr Braxton. I didn't think—"

"Evidently not."

The sound of more hoofbeats approaching along the trail made all of them fall silent for a moment. Then, without taking his eyes off the poachers, Perry asked, "Who is it, Bodicia?"

She felt relief go through her at the sight of the tall, straight-backed rider coming around the bend in the trail.

"It's Athelstan," she said.

"Good. He can sort this out. As the head of the family, it's his responsibility to do so, anyway."

Chapter 5

Athelstan wasn't sure what he expected to find when he caught up to Perry and Bodicia, but it wasn't the sight of Perry pointing a rifle at two strangers while the carcass of a slain deer lay near the pool at the foot of the waterfall. That was enough, however for him to form a reasonably good theory of what had happened here.

He dismounted before his horse had fully stopped moving. Perry was the only one who appeared to be armed at the moment, although Athelstan spotted a pistol lying on the ground near the dead deer. That meant he didn't have to act quite as urgently as he might have otherwise, if the strangers represented an imminent threat.

Even so, he wasted no time stalking forward and demanding, "What's going on here?" His tone softened slightly as he added, "Perry, are you and Bodicia all right?"

"We're fine, Athelstan," Bodicia answered for herself and her brother. "That boy killed the deer and then tried to shoot us."

Athelstan faced the two strangers. He saw the resemblance between them and supposed they were father and son. They had the look of German farmers. Although Alpenstone was ruled by the descendants of the English families who had come here and been granted land by the Habsburgs, its position, tucked away between France, Germany, and Switzerland, meant that numerous citizens came from families originating in those other nations.

"Who are you?" he asked these two.

The father had taken off his cap and held it in front of him in a subservient pose. He looked down at the ground as he answered, "Franz Schiller, *mein Herr*. This is my son Elbert."

"You're not tenants on our estate," Athelstan said with confidence. He prided himself on knowing everyone who worked on his family's land, although he supposed it was possible there might be a few with whom he wasn't acquainted.

"No, *mein Herr*, we have a farm nearby. It is our own land—"

"We are not serfs," the boy, Elbert, interrupted to declare defiantly.

"Of course not," Athelstan said. "There are no serfs in Alpenstone. We are a sovereign state of free men."

"Free but not equal, eh?"

"Elbert, that is enough!" the boy's father said. "Have you no shame?"

"Shame?" Elbert repeated. "Why should I be ashamed?"

Athelstan said, "By killing that deer, you make yourself a thief, lad. By taking a shot at my brother and sister, you declare yourself a would-be murderer. For either offense, you might be hanged."

Schiller paled. "Please, *mein Herr*, I beg of you—"

Athelstan held up a hand and said, "There's no need to beg." He turned to Perry and Bodicia. "You're certain that neither of you was harmed?"

"We're all right," Perry said.

Athelstan nodded and turned back to the two poachers. "Take a quarter of that venison and leave. Take care not to set foot on the Braxton estate again. Things won't go nearly as well for you if you do."

Schiller looked vastly relieved. "Of course, *mein Herr*, of course," he said hastily as he backed away, bowing. "Thank you. Elbert, come along."

Perry stared at his oldest brother and said, "You're going to allow them to get away with what they've done?"

"They're not getting away with much," Athelstan said. "They're still poor and hungry, aren't they?"

"They're not our tenants. We're not responsible for their well-being."

"No, but I'm no mood to be responsible for a boy being executed."

Bodicia said, "You might feel differently if that pistol ball had been a few inches closer to me."

"You were almost hit?" Athelstan asked sharply.

"I can show you the branch the ball broke. It wasn't far from where I was sitting on my mare."

Athelstan looked toward the poachers, who had moved over to the slain deer to dress it and claim the portion of the meat he had allowed them. The boy sullenly ignored the Braxtons, but his father kept glancing nervously at them.

"Knowing that might have changed things had I been aware of it before," Athelstan said, "but my decision stands." He turned toward the poachers. "Schiller."

The man jerked around. "Yes, *mein Herr*?"

"I'm going to send my gamekeeper out here to fetch the rest of that venison. I'd advise you not to take more than I've allowed you, and to be gone from this place by the time he gets here, as well."

"Yes, of course," Schiller said, bobbing his head quickly.

"You're making a mistake," Perry told Athelstan.

"It's my mistake to make."

Neither of the others could argue with that.

Athelstan inclined his head toward the horses and went on, "Let's go back to the manor."

"That's where I told Bodicia to go when we heard the shot," Perry said as they mounted.

Athelstan smiled at his sister and said, "Let me guess. You didn't do what Perry told you."

She tossed her head. "Why should I? He's my brother, not my keeper."

"Speaking of brothers," Athelstan said as the three of them rode back along the trail, "where is Jeremy?"

Bodicia shook her head, and Perry said, "I have no idea. But there's one thing you can count on: wherever he's gotten off to, he's likely in some sort of trouble."

"I'm not sure you have much room to criticize our brother, considering how I just found the two of you," Athelstan said.

"This trouble wasn't of our making," Perry insisted. "We were just riding along peacefully when it found us."

"I'm sure Jeremy would claim the same thing—if, indeed, you're correct about what he's doing right now."

But despite playing the devil's advocate on Jeremy's behalf, Athelstan knew Perry was right.

No matter whose fault it was, trouble had a definite habit of finding Jeremy Braxton.

In the shadowed alley in Lornsburgh, Jeremy stood very still, not wanting to spook the man with the gun at his head into pulling the trigger. He had lifted his hands about halfway to his shoulders and kept them there in plain sight.

"I'm not going to run," he said. "I have no reason to run, because I don't know what this is about. If you intend to rob me, you're going to be thoroughly disappointed. I have a few small coins on me, that's all."

"You're a fine one to accuse someone else of robbery," the gunman said. "You who steal by failing to honor your debts."

"I still don't know what you're talking about," Jeremy insisted.

"I work for Jacques LeCarde. Now do you know?"

Jeremy stiffened at LeCarde's name. He was acquainted with the Frenchman, all right. LeCarde ran a gambling house where Jeremy was a regular patron.

"There's been some misunderstanding," Jeremy muttered. "I have a line of credit with M'sieur LeCarde—"

"It has been revoked. M'sieur LeCarde is calling in all his debts. You already know this, Herr Braxton. He sent word to you three days ago that he expected your payment in full by today. But you have not honored his demand."

"He had no right to do that. We have an arrangement—"

"You wish to take the matter to the grand duke? You would have him judge the right and wrong of it?"

Although the gunman behind him couldn't see his face, Jeremy grimaced. Grand Duke Alistair was his second cousin twice removed, and he had always been a bit cool toward the Braxtons. Alistair would be furious if he had to sort out something as crude and common as a gambling debt. Not only would he be likely to decide against Jeremy, but he might even consider it fitting to dole out some sort of punishment.

"There's no need to involve the grand duke," Jeremy said. "If Jacques will just give me a few more days—"

"He already gave you time. No more."

Jeremy's mind whirled. He and LeCarde had always been on decent terms, probably because Jeremy represented a steady source of funds for the gambler. For LeCarde to take such a hard line with his regular customers, someone else must have been pressuring him for money.

Regardless of the details, Jeremy knew that LeCarde could be ruthless when he wanted to be.

But the man was smart, too, and knowing that prompted Jeremy to say with newfound confidence, "You won't shoot me."

"You sound awfully certain of that."

"I am certain. Dead, I'm not worth anything. My brother Athelstan controls the family finances."

"Perhaps M'Sieur LeCarde will present your notes to your brother and persuade him to settle them to preserve the family honor."

"Gambling debts?" Jeremy had to laugh. "Athelstan would throw him out and tell him to do his worst. Either that, or he'd realize that LeCarde was probably responsible for my death, in which case he'd run him through with a sword." Jeremy shook his head. "No, there's really only one avenue that LeCarde—and by extension, you—can pursue. Give me a day, and I'll see what I can come up with. I'll do my best to obtain the full amount, but if I can't—well, Jacques may have to satisfied with what he can get."

For a long moment, silence reigned in the alley. Then Jeremy tensed as he heard heavy footsteps coming closer.

The gun finally went away from Jeremy's head. The man who had been talking to him said, "Very well. You may have a day, Herr Braxton, but it would be in your best interest to settle your debt in full. To demonstrate to you exactly what I mean . . ."

His voice trailed off, but Jeremy didn't have to hear anything else to know what was about to happen. He wasn't worried about the man shooting him now, so he lunged forward and tried to run.

He had taken only a couple of steps when someone caught him from behind.

Helpless in the powerful grip of whoever had grabbed him, Jeremy flung up his hands and barely got them lifted in time to keep his face from being slammed against the wall of one of the buildings. His body crashed against the bricks with enough force to knock the breath out of his lungs. He kicked behind him but didn't hit anything.

An instant later, a fist struck him in the back, pounding his right kidney. Jeremy arched his body and cried out in pain. Another blow landed on the side of his head and hammered him to his knees. Thick-fingered hands took hold of his coat and jerked him back up. His attacker spun him around and hit him in the belly, doubling him over. Again, Jeremy fell to his knees.

A vicious kick to his ribs knocked him on his right side. More kicks thudded into him. Two huge shapes loomed over him.

Once, at a traveling circus, Jeremy had seen a trained bear. These two reminded him of that bear.

That thought didn't last long before a sea of pain washed it away. The men continued kicking and stomping him. Finally, sounding as if his voice came from far, far away, the gunman said, "Gustav, Detzer, that is enough. Remember what M'sieur LeCarde told us. Herr Braxton is not to be killed. But he has been taught a very good lesson, I believe."

The man hunkered on his heels next to Jeremy, a shapeless mass in the alley's shadows.

"When you feel up to riding again, go home and tell your brother you need money," the man said. "Tell him that if you fail to pay what you owe, next time will be worse. Do you understand, Herr Braxton?"

"I—I understand . . . that," Jeremy wheezed. His assailants had concentrated their punishment on his body, not his face, so his lips weren't swollen and his jaw worked. "But I don't—don't understand . . ."

The man leaned closer to him. "What is it you fail to comprehend?"

"Whether you're a . . . French *fils de pute* or . . . a German *arschloch*—since you use . . . both languages. Or maybe you're just . . . a bloody git . . ."

The man stood up and drove the tip of his boot into Jeremy's stomach, making him curl into an even tighter ball of agony. Jeremy heard the man spit and felt the wetness strike his face.

Then several sets of footsteps went away, and he was left alone in the alley with his pain.

Chapter 6

B y the time Athelstan, Perry, and Bodicia got back to Braxton
Manor, the encounter with the father-and-son poachers, if it
had not been forgotten, had at least faded in significance. Athelstan knew that Perry and Bodicia each possessed a reckless streak
that came out from time to time, but they had never been as rash
as Jeremy often was.

Athelstan forgot about that, too, as the three of them rode up
to the house and he saw a carriage with its fine pair of horses and
luxurious silver trappings parked in front of the manor. A roughly
clothed driver leaned against the carriage, smoking a pipe. He
straightened respectfully from that casual pose as the three riders
dismounted.

Griggs, the stableboy, hurried to take the mounts' reins. As he
did so, he said under his breath, "You have company, Master
Athelstan."

"I can see that," Athelstan said, "and I believe I recognize the
carriage. It belongs to Baron Herbert Mandeville, doesn't it?"

Griggs bobbed his head. "Aye, sir."

"When did the baron arrive?"

"A quarter of an hour ago, I'd say."

"Did you know he was coming to visit?" Perry asked.

"I did not," Athelstan said. "If I had, I would have made certain to be here and greet him."

But if he hadn't come along and found Perry and Bodicia confronting those poachers, the outcome of that situation would have been very much in doubt. He was glad he'd been able to settle things without anyone being seriously hurt.

"But I'll deal with the baron," Athelstan went on. "Thank you, Griggs."

As the three siblings walked toward the entrance, Perry said, "I wonder what that old—"

Athelstan silenced his brother with a firm hand on his shoulder. He wasn't sure what Perry had been about to say, but he had a strong suspicion it wouldn't have been anything good about Baron Mandeville. "Prig" would have been about the best Athelstan could have hoped to come out of Perry's mouth, and Mandeville's coachman was close enough to overhear.

"We'll find out why the baron has come to call," Athelstan said. He glanced toward Bodicia. "You go on to your room and change your clothes."

"Because I'm not dressed suitably for a young lady from a respectable family?"

"You said that, not I."

Bodicia sniffed and gave him a resentful look, but when they reached the manor's foyer, she turned right and headed along the corridor toward her bedchamber.

Symmes, the Braxton family's elderly butler, was waiting for Athelstan. The wizened, balding servant said, "Baron Mandeville is here to see you, sir. I've put him in the library and provided him with refreshments."

"How does he seem?" Athelstan asked.

"Annoyed, sir, that none of the family was here to greet him." Symmes sniffed. "Even though he sent no word that he would be arriving."

Athelstan smiled. "Well, I'll greet him now."

Symmes cocked an eyebrow as he looked doubtfully at Athelstan's boots, whipcord trousers, and simple shirt. "Without dressing for the occasion, sir?"

"I don't know what the occasion is, so this will have to do."

Athelstan would only humble himself so much for Baron Herbert Mandeville. True, the man held a title and was considered an important and trusted advisor to the grand duke, but Athelstan didn't like him and never had. He suspected that the feeling was mutual.

"Should I come with you?" Perry asked. He was dressed in an equally informal manner but didn't care any more about that than his brother did.

Athelstan nodded and said, "Come along."

He didn't think he was deliberately trying to irritate Mandeville by treating this visit in such a casual manner—but the prospect didn't particularly bother Athelstan, either.

The brothers walked into the library and found their guest sitting in an armchair and holding a snifter of brandy. Baron Mandeville stood up, set the brandy on a small side table, and said, "There you are, Braxton."

"Baron Mandeville," Athelstan greeted him with a respectful nod that stopped well short of being a bow. "How are you?"

"Too busy to waste my time waiting like this." The baron's bushy gray eyebrows drew down in a frown as he stared at the way Athelstan and Perry were dressed. "Have the two of you been out working in the fields with your tenants?"

"No, we were taking a ride in the forest on the northern section of the estate. It's always wise to keep an eye on the grounds. We try to inspect them regularly."

Mandeville said, "Hummph." He was a short, broad, mostly bald man with a face like a bulldog. Although his garments were expensive and the latest styles from London, he always somehow managed to look like a shopkeeper. But he had a keen mind, Athelstan knew, and a reputation for financial acuity that the grand duke put to good use.

"What can we do for you, Baron?" Athelstan asked.

"For me, nothing. But there is a service you can perform for your grand duke and your homeland."

"You know all the Braxtons are devoted to Alpenstone and will always do whatever is necessary to defend her and further her interests."

"Of course." Mandeville's frown deepened, which made him resemble a bulldog even more. "In this case, it actually isn't you or your brothers who are required to step up and perform that service for the crown I mentioned."

"I don't understand," Athelstan said, shaking his head. "If there's not something Perry or Jeremy or I can do—"

Mandeville interrupted by clearing his throat. "You, ah, have a sister."

Perry stiffened, caught his breath, and then burst out, "What in the name of—?"

Athelstan silenced him with a curt gesture. Frowning now as darkly as Mandeville was, he said, "I'm afraid I don't understand what you mean, Baron."

"Your sister, Bodicia, has caught the eye of a visitor from England. Well, the son of a visitor, actually. Lord Scrimshire is visiting Grand Duke Alistair for discussions of a financial nature, and his son Leslie accompanied him. Young Leslie noticed your sister on the street in Lornsburgh the other day and made inquiries about her. Now he, ah, wishes to make her acquaintance in person."

Athelstan struggled to tamp down the anger he felt rising inside him. With an effort, he kept his voice calm and level as he asked, "Lord Scrimshire is one of the directors of the Bank of England, isn't he?"

"He is, indeed."

"And as such, he would have a great deal to say about any loans that might be arranged between the grand duchy and that institution?"

"Certainly." Mandeville cleared his throat. "But this is a personal matter—"

"The devil it is!" Perry said. "You and Alistair want us to trade our sister to that English lout in return for financial favors!"

Mandeville's eyes got larger. He sputtered, looking horrified at that blunt accusation. Athelstan was upset himself, both at what Mandeville was suggesting and Perry's crude reaction to it.

"How—how dare you, you young—"

Athelstan held up a hand to stop Mandeville's words. "My brother is much too plainspoken at times, Baron, and I apologize for his rudeness. But I fear that the basic concept of what he says is accurate."

"Nonsense!" Mandeville insisted. "While it's true that Alistair would like to introduce your sister to Leslie at a ball the grand duke plans to give in honor of Lord Scrimshire, he wishes her to provide no more than pleasant company and stimulating conversation for the young man."

"Just how *stimulating* should that conversation be, eh?" Perry asked with a sneer. "Or does that depend on the size of the loan Alistair thinks he can negotiate with the Bank of England?"

"Perry, that's enough," Athelstan said sharply. "Baron Mandeville is our guest, and I won't have you speaking to him like that." He turned to the visitor. "But I'm not the least bit comfortable asking Bodicia to—"

"Asking Bodicia to do *what?*"

The question came from the library doorway where Bodicia stood, now attired in a simple but elegant light blue gown with lace trim.

"Nothing," Athelstan told her. "This discussion doesn't concern you."

"Clearly it does," she returned. "You just mentioned my name." She smiled at Mandeville. "Baron."

"Miss Braxton. A pleasure to see you again. My apologies if I'm intruding—"

"Not at all," Bodicia said as she came into the room. "Now, if one of my brothers would be so kind as to explain what your visit has to do with me. . . ."

"Go back to your room, Bodicia," Perry said. "You don't need to hear this."

"On the contrary, I think I do."

Athelstan considered for a moment and then said, "Baron Mandeville was delivering an invitation to a ball being given by Grand Duke Alistair."

"Really?" Bodicia smiled. "I love to dance, you know that. When will this ball take place?"

"Ah, tomorrow night," Mandeville said.

"I'll have time to prepare properly, then."

Perry said, "You don't know what he's actually asking you to do, Bodicia."

"No? Then why don't you explain it to me."

Perry glared and looked embarrassed. Speaking plainly to the baron was one thing. Repeating to his sister what he'd said was something else again.

Athelstan looked at Mandeville and said, "This invitation you're delivering includes all of us, doesn't it, Baron?"

"Of course."

So he and his brothers would be there to keep an eye on Bodicia and make sure that nothing improper happened. Under those circumstances, what Mandeville was asking wasn't quite so scandalous and unacceptable. Athelstan supposed it wouldn't hurt anything for Bodicia to smile at the young man from England, laugh at whatever jests he might make, even dance with him. He and Perry and Jeremy could make certain nothing went any further than that. The idea still rubbed him the wrong way, but cooperating would help Alistair and, in turn, Alpenstone, and wouldn't really besmirch the family honor, so Athelstan supposed it might be acceptable.

He was about to say that and explain to Bodicia what they were talking about when unsteady footsteps sounded from the corridor just outside the library. Athelstan heard Symmes's reedy voice objecting, "Please, sir, not right this moment, please just come with me—"

The new arrival ignored the butler's entreaties. Jeremy appeared in the open doorway and lurched to the side, almost falling.

He rested a hand on the jamb to brace himself as he looked around the room.

Baron Mandeville exclaimed, "Good heavens!"

Jeremy's clothes were disheveled, and his dark hair was tangled and askew. He was pale and breathing heavily. His face was unmarked, but the way he held himself hunched over with his other arm pressed across his midsection showed that he was in great pain.

Athelstan took a step toward him and began, "Jeremy, what in the world—?"

That was as far as Athelstan got before Jeremy's eyes rolled up in their sockets, his knees buckled, and he collapsed in a heap on the library's polished wooden floor.

Chapter 7

Jeremy remembered almost nothing about the ride from Lornsburgh to Braxton Manor. He recalled stumbling out of the alley where his assailants had left him and somehow making it back to the stable. The man running the place had stared at him with huge, horrified eyes but had helped him climb up into the saddle after Jeremy insisted on having his horse brought out.

The next thing Jeremy remembered after that was trying to dismount in front of the manor and falling flat on his face. The stableboy, Griggs, had assisted him to his feet, although the youngster was much smaller than Jeremy and had to struggle to lift him.

The looks on the faces of his brothers and sister and—who was the other man who'd been in the library? Baron Mandeville, Jeremy remembered now. All of them had looked at him with surprised, dismayed expressions on their faces. He wasn't sure why. He hadn't looked that bad, had he? He wasn't bloody or anything. Not outside, anyway. There was no telling what damage that beating might have done to him inside.

As awareness seeped back into his brain now, he slowly realized that he was dressed in a nightshirt and lying in a soft bed between cool, clean sheets. The feeling was soothing, almost heavenly.

Until he tried to shift his position slightly and an ache welled up within him and swallowed him like the gaping maw of a great beast.

After that, breathing hurt. Even opening his eyes was uncomfortable, although he hadn't been struck there.

"You're awake."

The voice belonged to his brother Athelstan. Even in his pain, Jeremy knew that. A blurred shape moved above him. Jeremy tried to focus on it, and after a moment his vision sharpened enough for him to make out the expression of angry disapproval on his brother's face. Athelstan stood beside the bed with his hands clasped behind his back as he leaned forward slightly.

"It's good . . . to see you . . . too," Jeremy said. His voice sounded raspy and far away in his ears. But at least now he could move his lips and blink his eyes without it hurting so much that it made him gasp. The pain had receded that much, anyway.

"What in the world happened to you, Jeremy?" Athelstan asked.

Before answering, Jeremy moved his head just enough to look around the room. He recognized the wallpaper and knew that he was in his own bedchamber, as he had thought, and he and Athelstan were alone. No sign of Perry or Bodicia. That was good. Jeremy didn't see any need for his younger brother and sister to hear any of this.

"I had . . . a bit of an accident."

Athelstan frowned and shook his head in obvious skepticism. "What did you do? Fall off your horse thirty or forty times? Symmes and I undressed you and wrestled you into your nightshirt, Jeremy. Your body is one giant bruise between your shoulders and your knees. Clearly, you were beaten within an inch of your life."

"I don't think it was . . . quite that close." A tiny *heh* of laughter came from Jeremy's lips. "But close enough, no doubt . . . about that."

"Was this assault because of your gambling debts?"

"How do you know—?"

"That you have gambling debts?"

"I've never told you . . . never asked you . . ."

"I have friends who tell me things, Jeremy," Athelstan said. "I've heard plenty of rumors about how you frequent the establishment of that Frenchman, LeCarde. It stands to reason that you must be in debt to him, as much time as you spend there." He paused, then added, "And if our friends are aware of this, you can be sure that our enemies are, too."

"Why should we have . . . enemies? We're related to . . . the grand duke."

"That's reason enough right there. Have you ever heard of any family of nobles and aristocrats that's not riddled with resentment and hatred?" Athelstan sighed. "What's it going to require to set this right?"

"It's none of your affair—"

"It is indeed my affair, every bit of it. I'm the head of this family. If you're being attacked because you've failed to pay what you owe, I have to do something about it." Athelstan glared. "I can march into that den of snakes and put a pistol ball through Jacques LeCarde's head."

"No!" Jeremy tried to push himself up, but he was too weak and still in too much pain. He slumped back on the bed and breathed hard for a few seconds before he was able to say, "You can't do that . . . Athelstan. His men would kill you. I'll pay him back—"

"How? How much do you owe him?" When Jeremy didn't answer, Athelstan went on, "You've all but admitted that's what's going on. It serves no purpose for you to refuse to answer my questions now."

Jeremy knew his brother was right. He closed his eyes and whispered the amount he owed to Jacques LeCarde. When he opened his eyes again, he saw that Athelstan looked shocked by the answer he had demanded.

"You don't have that much, do you?" Jeremy asked.

"Not to hand over to the likes of Jacques LeCarde."

"Not even to save your brother's life?"

Athelstan sighed, lifted a hand, and rubbed his forehead. "Do you think LeCarde would accept a smaller amount in lieu of nothing at all?"

"I don't know. He might."

Athelstan nodded. "I'll send word to him, then, and ask for a face-to-face meeting with him to discuss the matter."

"Have him come here," Jeremy suggested.

Athelstan looked shocked by that, too. "To our home? A man like that?"

"What would you do instead? Go to his gambling house? If you set foot in there, Athelstan, he might just decide to keep you until he gets what he wants."

"That's absurd! He wouldn't dare."

"You can't put anything past a man like LeCarde when money is involved."

Athelstan just stood there. After a tense moment, he shook his head.

"Other things are going on, things you don't know about, Jeremy. I can't deal with this right now. But I will send word to the man and inform him that I'll discuss an arrangement with him later. Until then, you're to remain here on the estate, do you understand? I think it would be a good idea if you didn't even leave the manor. You'll be safe here."

Another dry, husky laugh came from Jeremy. "I don't think old Symmes would be able to fight off the sort of men who work for LeCarde, if they should decide to come calling."

"Some of our tenant farmers would be capable of that, though. I'll put together a group of them to stand watch and protect the place. Also, Perry and I will be around part of the time." Athelstan made a face as if he had bitten into something that tasted bad. "Not tomorrow evening, though. Tomorrow we have to attend a ball given by Grand Duke Alistair."

"A ball? I've heard nothing about it."

"Rather a spur-of-the-moment thing, from what I understand."

"I don't believe I'll be in good enough shape to attend." Jeremy managed to laugh again. "I don't believe I'm up to dancing a spirited waltz right now."

"That's all right," Athelstan told him. "It's probably better that way, to be honest."

Jeremy couldn't suppress the bitter edge that crept into his voice as he said, "You wouldn't want your disreputable brother there, is that it?"

"There would be no point in adding to the rumors going around about you. I don't mean to offend you, Jeremy, but that's simply the truth of the matter."

Jeremy closed his eyes again and nodded. "I know," he said. "I'm sorry for getting the family in such a devil of a mess, Athelstan. Truly, that was never my intention."

Athelstan leaned over and gave Jeremy an awkward pat on the shoulder.

"We'll get it sorted, you can be sure of that. Right now, just rest and get your strength back. Let those bruises heal. There'll be time to worry about Jacques LeCarde later."

Jeremy didn't open his eyes as he listened to Athelstan leaving the room. The door closed quietly behind him. Jeremy hoped that his brother was right, that some sort of arrangement could be worked out with Jacques LeCarde.

He hoped as well that Athelstan wouldn't wait too long to make his move—because the gambler almost certainly would not.

Chapter 8

Alistair I, Grand Duke of Alpenstone, was a member of the Ormiston family and spent most of his time at Ormiston Castle, the family's ancestral home located atop a picturesque hill several miles east of Lornsburgh. But his official residence was the Grand Ducal Palace in Lornsburgh, and that was where functions such as the ball he was giving were held.

The palace was an ornately impressive three-story building in the heart of the city. It featured spires and towers and gables and balconies, and, like many of the other structures in Lornsburgh, conveyed an air of antiquity even though it wasn't even a hundred years old yet. Compared with other European royal edifices, it was positively recent.

As the sun sank below the mountains to the west and evening settled down on Alpenstone, a steady stream of carriages converged on the Grand Ducal Palace. The men and women who disembarked from the vehicles were beautifully dressed and stately in their demeanor as they made their way inside. Even on relatively short notice, this evening's ball had attracted almost every member of the grand duchy's aristocracy.

One who wasn't there was Jeremy Braxton, but his siblings Athelstan, Perry, and Bodicia were. Bodicia had Athelstan on her right and Perry on her left, her arms linked with theirs, as the three of them entered the huge, high-ceilinged ballroom. Although she had been there before, the lavishly decorated room was so beautiful that the sight of it took Bodicia's breath away for a moment as she looked around.

"Every time I come here, I always think this must be what it's like in England," she said quietly. Athelstan was the only one of the siblings who had visited the mother country.

"The palaces in England are even more ostentatious," he told her. "The country has had a long time to get used to being the center of empire."

"And we're just an outpost," Perry added.

Athelstan shook his head and said, "Alpenstone is a sovereign nation, not a colony. I don't consider us part of the British Empire."

Perry laughed. "France and Germany would be more than happy to absorb us," he said. "The only place without any designs on our little grand duchy is Switzerland."

"True," Athelstan admitted, "but as long as both of them have their eyes on us, each prevents the other from trying to move in and take over."

With a note of annoyance in her voice, Bodicia told them, "We're in a fancy ballroom full of beautifully dressed people, and you two decide to have a political discussion? We came here to dance!"

As if they had been waiting for her cue, the musicians at the far end of the huge room began playing. The notes of a bright, sprightly waltz filled the air. Athelstan turned to his sister and said, "I'd be honored to have the first dance with you."

"Very well."

He took her hand. They arranged themselves in the familiar position and swirled off into the mass of dancers moving around the parquet floor. Perry watched them go with an amused look on his face.

Athelstan was an excellent dancer, but he was her brother, after all, and Bodicia didn't intend to spend the entire evening swooping around the floor with him.

It didn't take long before they almost bumped into another brother and sister couple. Charles and Claudia Edgerton stopped beside Athelstan and Bodicia, who halted as well. Charles smiled and said over the music, "A fortuitous encounter. We'll change partners, eh, Athelstan?"

"Of course," Athelstan replied. He took Claudia in his arms while Charles clasped Bodicia's hand and slipped his arm around her waist.

Athelstan looked a little nervous as he and Claudia rejoined the dancers, almost as if she made him wary, Bodicia thought. But then she lost sight of them in the crowd as she and Charles began following the tightly prescribed steps of the waltz.

"You look lovely tonight, Bodicia," he told her. "I've always said that I have the prettiest cousin in all of Alpenstone."

"I'm sure Athelstan thinks the same thing about Claudia. She's stunning, as always."

Charles smiled. "I'm not sure Athelstan is as taken with her as you believe. They had a bit of a clash yesterday when Claudia decided to demonstrate her skill with a saber and chose poor Athelstan as her victim."

"Are you serious?" Bodicia asked. "They fought with sabers?"

"It was less of a fight and more a case of Athelstan trying to defend himself without hurting her."

"I wish I could have seen that!"

"It was entertaining, to say the least. Although probably not to Athelstan."

"I take it Claudia emerged victorious?"

"Claudia always wins"—Charles paused and then added—"no matter what it takes."

Bodicia didn't know what to say to that. She and Claudia had been best friends when they were young, but over time they had grown less close.

After a moment, Charles changed the subject by saying, "I saw you come in with Athelstan and Perry, but I didn't notice Jeremy. Is he not in attendance tonight?"

"Jeremy is not well. I'm afraid he didn't feel like coming."

"I'm sorry to hear that. Give him my best, will you? I hope he recovers quickly."

The speed of Jeremy's recovery would depend entirely on what Athelstan did, Bodicia thought.

She didn't know the details of what had befallen Jeremy. All Athelstan had told her and Perry was that he was dealing with the matter, and his attitude clearly conveyed that as far as they were concerned, that was the end of the discussion.

It didn't take much effort for Bodicia to figure out what had happened, though. Jeremy had been set upon in Lornsburgh and beaten badly. The attack was no mere robbery attempt; if it had been, Jeremy and Athelstan would have had no objection to saying as much. Their silence meant it was something more sinister than that, and Bodicia knew that Jeremy had a definite weakness when it came to gambling.

In all likelihood, someone to whom he owed money had sent ruffians after him to frighten him into paying his debt. That explanation made the most sense. However, Bodicia didn't know what Athelstan could do about it other than pay whatever Jeremy owed. He could have gone to the grand duke and asked Alistair to step in, but Bodicia knew her eldest brother was too proud to bring such shame onto the family.

Besides, Alistair had never been that close to the Braxtons. It was entirely possible he would have refused to help.

Bodicia put those thoughts out of her head. Athelstan didn't want her involved and there was nothing she could do, anyway. She concentrated on dancing with Charles until the music ended and another of Alpenstone's young aristocrats moved in to claim her for the next dance.

The evening continued that way for a while until Athelstan came to her and took her arm.

"You've been summoned," he told her.

"By His Royal Highness?" Athelstan had explained that the

grand duke wanted to introduce her to some visitors to Alpenstone who were being honored at tonight's ball.

"By Baron Mandeville on Alistair's behalf."

"All right. Lead the way, Athelstan."

He had a rather grim expression on his face as they made their way across the room to the raised platform where Grand Duke Alistair and his wife, the Grand Duchess Eleanora, sat in beautifully carved chairs. Baron Mandeville stood next to the grand duke, who was talking to a slender, gray-haired man. Also nearby, standing with his hands clasped behind his back, was a younger man, slightly built, with light brown hair and a narrow face that reminded Bodicia of a fox.

She disliked him on sight, especially when he turned toward her and his eyes lit up with unmistakable avarice and lust. She repressed a shudder as his unpleasant gaze raked her from head to foot and back again.

Alistair broke off the conversation he was having with the older man and said, "Ah, here they are." He nodded toward Bodicia and Athelstan as they stepped up onto the platform. "May I present my cousin Athelstan Braxton and his sister, Bodicia?"

He went on, "Athelstan, Bodicia, this is Lord Scrimshire from England and his son Leslie."

"It's a great honor to meet you, Lord Scrimshire," Athelstan said, as he shook the visitor's hand. "And you, Leslie."

"The honor is ours," Leslie said, as he quickly dropped Athelstan's hand and reached with both of his to clasp Bodicia's hand. "And the very great pleasure. How are you, my dear?"

"Fine," she murmured. She wished he would let go of her hand, but she was too polite to pull it away.

Finally, he released her, but the smug smile remained on his face, and he stood much too close to her. She felt hemmed in and wanted to flee.

Athelstan cleared his throat and asked, "Are you enjoying your visit to the grand duchy so far, Lord Scrimshire?"

"Beautiful place," the Englishman said. "Quite lovely scenery."

"It is, indeed," Leslie said, still staring at Bodicia from close range.

Lord Scrimshire, Alistair, and Athelstan continued chatting, but Leslie quickly got bored. He took Bodicia's hand again and said, "Shall we dance?"

"Of course," she said, not knowing how else she could respond. "That would be lovely."

The confident light glittering in his eyes bordered on arrogance. He seemed to know that she had to go along with whatever he wanted.

But only to a certain extent, she vowed. Athelstan had told her to be polite and pleasant to this guest, but there were definite limits to her willingness to go along with that.

It didn't take long for Leslie Scrimshire to test those limits. They twirled around the floor several times, and then he said, "I'm told there's a garden behind the palace. I'd love to see it. Perhaps you'd be so kind as to show me, Miss Braxton?"

"Oh, no, I'm sorry," Bodicia said. "It's dark back there—"

"Grand Duke Alistair assures me that there are lights in the trees along the paths. I'm sure we'll be fine."

Anger tightened Bodicia's jaw. It was obvious what Leslie expected. He wanted to take her into the garden and paw her like she was some sort of tavern girl. And Alistair, no doubt, had guessed that was what he was up to when he asked about the garden.

Alistair didn't care, either. Bodicia didn't know who Lord Scrimshire was, but he had to have something Alistair wanted. Money, more than likely, since Baron Mandeville was lurking around so attentively. Bodicia had no proof of any of that, but her keen mind had no trouble putting it together.

No wonder Athelstan and Perry had been angry and upset during Mandeville's visit to Braxton Manor the day before. The baron had asked—no, he probably had demanded—that Bodicia trade her favors for whatever Alistair wanted from the English visitor.

"I don't want to go to the garden," she said bluntly to Leslie Scrimshire.

"Oh, I'm sure you do," he said with a little laugh, passing off her refusal as meaningless. He took her arm. "Come along and show me more of the beauty Alpenstone has to offer."

"I'm sorry. I don't feel well. I think I'd like to leave now."

His grip tightened on her arm. "You're not going anywhere," he told her quietly, "except with me."

Speaking under her breath just as he had done, she said, "You need to let go of me right now."

He shook his head. The smug smile on his face disappeared, replaced by a look of irritation and anger.

"No woman tells me what to do, not even one as lovely as you, Bodicia. Now come with me. I'll make certain that you enjoy yourself."

What did he think he was going to do, drag her out of a ballroom full of people and have his way with her in the garden?

Yes, she realized. That was exactly what he thought he was going to do. More than likely, he had done similar things many times in the past—and always gotten away with it.

Not this time. She took a deep breath and turned to face him squarely, lining herself up so that she could ram her knee right into his groin.

She didn't have to because at that moment Perry appeared beside them and said, "Excuse me, you need to let go of my sister's arm."

Leslie regarded him with a smirk. "I don't believe we've been introduced."

"I'm Perry Braxton, Bodicia's brother."

Leslie sniffed and said, "Run along, boy. This doesn't concern you."

"I believe it does. I know my sister very well, and I can tell that she doesn't want to have anything else to do with you, *sir.*"

The last word dripped with the contempt that Perry obviously felt for Leslie Scrimshire.

"What she wants doesn't matter. My father and I are guests in this miserable little colony of yours—"

Repeating what Athelstan had said earlier in the evening, Perry snapped, "Alpenstone isn't a colony. It's a sovereign nation. And I don't care if you're the bloody king of England. Get your hand off my sister."

Leslie regarded him for a long moment and then said, "Very well." He let go of Bodicia's arm and stepped back.

That gave him room to close his hand into a fist and drive it into Perry's face.

Chapter 9

The blow landed with enough force to make Perry take a step backward. He didn't think about how he reacted. The facts of the situation never entered his mind as he set his feet and swung a right that slammed into Leslie's jaw.

The punch knocked Leslie back into the mass of dancers that had continued to swirl around the confrontation, which had gone unnoticed until now. That finally disrupted the ebb and flow of elegantly dressed guests. Women screamed and men let out startled cries as Leslie crashed down on his back. The music stopped abruptly and so did the dancing as people drew away to form a circle around the fallen man and the two Braxton siblings. Perry's right hand was still clenched. He put his left arm around Bodicia's trembling shoulders and pulled her against him.

Leslie pushed himself into a sitting position, stared at Perry in a mixture of shock and rage, and said, "You—you . . ."

For a second, he couldn't find the words to go on. Then as he scrambled up, he spewed a torrent of obscene venom directed at both Perry and Bodicia. He charged them as he cursed.

Shouts filled the ballroom, but Perry was under attack and that was the only thing that mattered to him at the moment. He pushed Bodicia to the side to get her out of harm's way. The next instant, he ducked under a wild, looping punch that Leslie threw at his head and stepped in to hook a left into the young English-man's midsection. That doubled Leslie over and put him in position for the swift right cross that Perry landed on his jaw.

Leslie went down again. Before he could get up, two of the grand duke's guardsmen, resplendent in tight white trousers, red coats, and black shakoes, rushed in and grabbed Perry from behind. With strong grips on both his arms, the guards jerked him backward.

The horrified crowd parted. Grand Duke Alistair, even more resplendent than the guards in his medal-bedecked uniform, strode through the opening and planted himself in front of Perry with a furious glare on his face.

"How dare you attack one of our guests?" he raged. "Do you know what you've done?"

Normally, the natural respect Perry felt for the grand duke, along with not wanting to bring Athelstan's disapproval down on his head, would have tempered Perry's answer. But he was too angry now to hold back as he said, "I defended my sister against that lecherous British boor you tried to sell her to!"

The buzz of excited conversation in the room vanished instantly. Dead silence fell as everyone stared in disbelief at Perry.

Alistair had gone white with fury. His mouth opened and closed as he tried to find the words to express his feelings, and Perry was struck by the ludicrous thought that at this moment the grand duke bore a certain resemblance to a fish.

Finally, he was able to exclaim, "How dare you? How dare you speak to the grand duke like that?"

Athelstan came up alongside Alistair. "Your Grace, please forgive him. You know how hot-blooded young people can be—"

"Youth and hot blood are not excuses for such behavior!" Alistair turned his glare on Athelstan. "Get him out of my sight. All three of you, get out of here, now!"

Lord Scrimshire stepped forward as well. Leslie, looking sick, was on his feet again and stood behind his father.

"I say, there must be repercussions for this brutal, unwarranted attack on my son," Scrimshire said. "Your Grace should take action and do so immediately."

"I agree," Baron Mandeville put in as he came up to join the angry knot of people in the middle of the dance floor. "This is reprehensible behavior." He sneered at Perry. "And totally unworthy of a nobleman."

"Nobility doesn't always extend to the way people act," Alistair snapped.

"That's certainly true, Your Grace," Bodicia spoke up. She pointed at Leslie. "That man treated me in a very disrespectful, ungentlemanly fashion."

"That's a damned lie," Leslie said. "She offered herself to me like a . . . a common tavern slattern, and I rebuffed her!"

Perry struggled against the grip of the guards still holding him. "Let me go!" he shouted. "I'll pound those lies back down the scoundrel's throat!"

"Get him out of here," Alistair ordered the guards. "Escort him out now." He turned to Athelstan. "You and your sister should leave as well. We'll speak of this tomorrow."

Athelstan looked like he wanted to say something else, but after a heartbeat, he nodded and turned to Bodicia.

"Come on."

"But Athelstan—" she began.

He took her arm. "Not now."

The silence enveloped them as they followed the guards hustling Perry out of the Grand Ducal Palace. When they reached the street, the guards released Perry but planted themselves between the Braxtons and the entrance.

"You don't have to worry," Perry told them in a scathing voice. "I wouldn't go back in there if somebody paid me!"

They had to wait for their carriage to be brought from where it was parked. That took several minutes, and while they were waiting, Charles Edgerton came out of the palace.

"Thank goodness you haven't left yet," Charles said as he started toward them.

One of the guards moved to get in his way. Charles fixed a cold stare on the man, who stopped and then stepped back. Charles was also related to the grand duke, and unlike the Braxtons, he hadn't been ordered to leave the palace, so the guard couldn't justify interfering with him.

"If you've come to harangue me, too—" Perry began.

"Not at all," Charles broke in. He glanced at the guards and lowered his voice. "To be honest, if it had been my sister, I would have dealt just as severely with that English lout. Although Claudia probably would have made him regret his actions before I could get there."

"I was about to," Bodicia said. "He got off easily compared to what I was going to do to him."

Charles laughed. "I've no doubt of that." He grew serious as he went on, "But I wanted to let you know what I overheard in there just now. Lord Scrimshire is so furious that he wants Perry arrested and thrown into prison."

Athelstan shook his head. "The grand duke would never do that. He wouldn't take the side of a stranger over one of his countrymen, and a cousin, at that."

"I'd like to think that's true, but I wouldn't be so sure, Athelstan. Baron Mandeville was also huddled with them, and he was pressing Alistair to go along with what Scrimshire wants. And I think Eleanora had his ear, too."

"That witch has never liked us," Bodicia said.

Athelstan sent a quick, exasperated glare toward her then turned back to Charles.

"You don't really think he'll have Perry arrested, do you?"

"I think it's a distinct possibility. At least until Lord Scrimshire and his son have left Alpenstone."

Perry said, "Let them arrest me. That will just cause more problems for Alistair in the long run. The people won't stand for it."

"You underestimate what people will stand for as long as they have food to eat and a roof over their heads," Athelstan said.

"We have to do something, Athelstan," Bodicia said. "We can't allow Perry to be locked up just for helping me escape that boor."

Athelstan sighed and shook his head. He glanced at the guards and said, "We'll have to think about this. I don't believe Alistair will do anything about the situation tonight. Here's the carriage. Let's go home."

As the carriage rattled to a stop on the cobblestone street, Perry understood his brother's reticence. Athelstan didn't want to discuss any options they might have in the presence of the guards, who would pass along anything they heard to the grand duke. It would be better to talk about it on the way back to Braxton Manor.

Despite his display of bravado, Perry didn't want to be arrested, and he certainly didn't want to be thrown into prison. But if Alistair was determined to appease Lord Scrimshire and lock him up, he'd have a hard time getting away. Alpenstone was a small country; there weren't that many places to hide.

Athelstan opened the carriage door and helped Bodicia in. Perry went next, and finally Athelstan pulled himself up onto the step and said to the driver, "Braxton Manor." He got into the carriage and closed the door after him.

The driver had a skilled hand with the team, so there was barely a jolt when the vehicle rolled into motion. Athelstan sat on the front seat, facing backward, while Perry and Bodicia were on the rear seat. Perry scrubbed a hand over his face and said, "I'm sorry, Athelstan. I acted rashly. I know that."

Athelstan surprised the other two by laughing. The sound had a bleak edge to it, but it was still a laugh.

"One of us was going to do something," he said. "It was inevitable. I had my eye on young Scrimshire and was about to head that way when you stepped in, Perry."

"And Perry barely beat me to it," Bodicia said. "I was about to introduce my knee to Leslie Scrimshire's—"

Athelstan stopped her by raising a hand. The carriage's interior was dim, but some light made its way inside from the windows of the buildings they passed.

"He would have richly deserved it," Athelstan agreed. "For now, let's try to figure out what we're going to do next."

"I'm not going to run away," Perry declared. "I did nothing wrong." He shrugged. "Besides, there's not really any place to run away to."

"I'm not so sure of that."

"What! You just said that one of us had to do something—"

"I didn't mean you were in the wrong," Athelstan interrupted his brother. "I just meant it might be wise if you got out of Alpenstone for a short time. Perhaps a brief tour of the French countryside. The Scrimshires will leave, Alistair will get over his anger, and you can come back."

"You're wrong," Perry said bluntly. "If Alistair doesn't get what he was after from that Englishman, he won't cool off. He'll be more furious than ever. And after what happened, it's not likely Scrimshire will give him what he wants, not unless I'm behind bars in a dungeon."

"This is insane!" Bodicia burst out. "None of us are to blame for this."

Athelstan said, "Lord Scrimshire is a director of the Bank of England and a titled nobleman. By definition, he can do no wrong, and I'm sure he believes that extends to his son, as well."

"It's not right!"

"There's no place in this world," Athelstan said, "where what's right matters more than who has the money—and the power."

A sense of gloom thicker than the darkness gathered inside the coach. None of the Braxtons spoke as they left Lornsburgh behind. The vehicle swayed slightly as the team of horses pulled it along the narrow road leading north out of the city.

Trees loomed close on both sides. The path led up slopes and down and twisted around the occasional bend. It would have been difficult to follow at night if old Theobald, the driver, hadn't been guiding carriages along this route for many years. He knew every turn, every dip.

And his instincts were finely honed for possible trouble. Without slowing down, he leaned over on the seat and called to those inside the carriage, "Riders coming up fast behind us!"

Athelstan twisted on the seat and leaned toward the window on one side. He stuck his head out and asked, "Who are they?"

"No way of knowing, sir! I can hear them coming up on horseback, that's all!"

"Perhaps they're just in a hurry and want to pass us. Is there a place where we can turn out and let them by?"

"Not anywhere close, sir."

"Well, keep going. That's all you can do."

"Aye!"

That wasn't all Theobald could do. The three inside the carriage felt the jolt as it began to go faster. They heard the pop of the whip as the old driver urged the horses to increase their pace.

Then, suddenly, Perry and Bodicia were thrown forward a little and Athelstan pressed against the front wall as the carriage began to slow violently. It careened from side to side as much as it could in the narrow lane. The Braxtons knew from the way Theobald was shouting in alarm that the old man was hauling back on the reins and trying to bring the vehicle to a stop as quickly as he could.

The boom of a pistol shot sounded as the carriage shuddered to a halt. Athelstan threw the door open and half stepped out so he could see what was going on.

Torchlight threw a garish glare across the road. Four men sat there on horseback, one of them holding the brightly blazing torch, the other three leveling pistols at the carriage.

Chapter 10

"What is it?" Perry asked as he leaned forward.

"Highwaymen," Athelstan replied. "And none of us are armed."

"Theobald carries an old pistol under the driver's seat," Bodicia said.

Her brothers looked at her, and Athelstan asked, "How do you know that?"

"He, uh, he's let me shoot it a few times—"

Athelstan heard Theobald cursing in German and felt the carriage shift. The old man had leaned forward, and that probably meant he was fumbling under the seat for the pistol Bodicia had mentioned.

"Theobald, no," Athelstan said sharply. He dropped from the step to the ground. "Don't fight."

"I can blow a hole in at least one of them—"

"No, I said! Leave that weapon where it is."

Theobald muttered his objections, but he straightened on the seat and stopped trying to find the pistol.

Athelstan heard the hoofbeats of horses coming up from the rear. They hadn't yet rounded the closest bend behind the carriage, a glance over his shoulder told him. The torchlight reached that far and revealed that the lane was still empty back there, although it probably wouldn't be for long.

"Be ready with the whip," he said quietly.

Theobald shot him a look. The old man seemed to understand what Athelstan meant.

Just to make sure, Athelstan added, "I'm going to cooperate with them—if I can."

The thieves were going to be disappointed; Athelstan didn't have many coins on him and assumed that Perry didn't, either. Bodicia was wearing some jewelry the highwaymen would no doubt steal, but at least none of the pieces were family heirlooms with sentimental value.

One of the gunmen and the rider with the torch urged their horses forward. Athelstan walked a few steps ahead to meet them as they approached the carriage.

"This is despicable behavior," he told them in a scathing tone as they reined to a stop again. "There's very little crime in Alpenstone, and you know it. Respectable subjects of the grand duke don't indulge in such reprehensible behavior."

"I don't care how full of fancy words you are, *mein Herr*," the gunman said. Like the others, he was masked, and the kerchief across the lower half of his face muffled his words.

Even so, Athelstan heard the German words and the man's guttural accent. They reminded him of what Jeremy had said about the attack on him in Lornsburgh. The leader of that trio working for Jacques LeCarde had been German, as well.

The realization made a cold fist clench on Athelstan's stomach. Many people of German descent lived in Alpenstone, he told himself. This man didn't have to be the same one—

"Tell your sister to get out of the coach," the man ordered as he pointed his pistol at Athelstan.

The words carried clearly to the two passengers still inside the carriage. Athelstan heard Bodicia's gasp of surprise and fear, along with Perry's low-voiced exclamation of anger.

"I'll do no such thing," he said in a chilly voice. "If you're bent on robbing us, take what little money and what few valuables we have and let us be on our way."

The gunman laughed. "What I want is valuable, all right, Herr Braxton, more valuable than any baubles or coins." The pistol jutted at Athelstone. "Now, tell your sister to get out of the coach, or I'll shoot you down where you stand."

"If you do that, Jacques LeCarde will never get a single centime from the Braxton family."

"I doubt that," the gunman said with a shake of his head. "I suspect that once you are dead, your brothers will pay whatever is required to get your sister back safely."

Athelstan met the man's cold stare for a long moment and then sighed as if in acceptance of defeat.

"Very well. I'll pay the blasted debt. There's no need for any negotiation, and you can leave my sister out of it. Tell LeCarde that I'll meet him tomorrow and deliver full payment."

"Don't be foolish, *mein Herr*. You know I won't agree to that. Bring the full amount to M'sieur LeCarde's establishment tomorrow night, and you can have your sister back then. She will be safe, I promise you." The man shrugged. "Perhaps a bit transformed by the experience, but nothing that cannot be borne."

With an effort, Athelstan tamped down the fury that threatened to explode inside him. He said thickly, "I'll pay now."

"You have that much with you?" The gunman sounded dubious. "Really?"

Athelstan turned toward the carriage's open door. "Perry, hand me my walking stick."

The gunman jabbed the pistol toward Athelstan and said, "*Nein!* No stick."

"Don't be a fool. There's a secret compartment in it. I have to unscrew the handle to open it. There are enough gems in there to settle my other brother's debt with LeCarde."

"You carry valuable gems around with you? Do you take me for a *Dummkopf*?"

Athelstan held out his hand. Perry tossed a walking stick of gleaming black wood with a silver head and ferrule to him. The gunman hesitated just long enough, reluctant to fire on the unlikely chance that Athelstan actually was telling the truth about having gems hidden in the stick.

Athelstan caught it deftly, whipped around, and swung the stick like a club, batting the pistol aside just as the gunman jerked the trigger. The weapon blasted as smoke and fire spewed from the muzzle, but the ball went well wide of Athelstan.

"Theobald, go!" Athelstan shouted as he leaped back to the step just under the door. He grabbed the side of the opening with his free hand as the team leaped forward under the lash of Theobald's whip and the old man's urgent shouts.

From this level, Athelstan was able to jab the stick's silver tip into the chest of the masked man holding the torch. The blow rocked the man back in the saddle. His horse, startled by the shot and the sudden burst of action, reared up and pawed at the air with its front hooves. With a yell, the man went over backward and the torch sailed into the air as he fell.

Athelstan hung on for dear life as the carriage raced toward the other two gunmen blocking the road.

Both men fired, but Theobald was bending low on the seat and Athelstan was pressed against the side of the open door. The shots went wild. The men had to jerk their mounts out of the way to avoid being trampled by the carriage's four-horse team of large black geldings.

Athelstan felt the carriage suddenly shift again on the wide leather thoroughbraces that ran underneath to support it. He looked across the roof and saw that one of the masked men had leaped out of his saddle and grabbed the carriage as it went past him. He clung to the silver railing on the other side of the roof and was trying to pull himself on top of the racing vehicle.

Athelstan still held the walking stick. He reached across the roof and struck at the man's hands with it. Because of the way the carriage was bouncing around, the blow missed and bounced off the railing on that side. The man let go with one hand and used it to grab the stick. Athelstan hung on to it tightly.

He realized a second later that he should have let go. That

might have caused the man to lose his grip and fall off. Instead, using the stick as an anchor, the man was able to pull himself higher and throw a leg onto the roof. He levered himself atop the vehicle. Once he was there, he came up on his knees and used both hands to wrench the stick away from Athelstan.

"Theobald, look out!" Athelstan shouted as the man beat at the driver with the stick he had taken away. Theobald hunched over on the seat to make himself a smaller target, but it was only a matter of time before the attacker landed a damaging blow.

Athelstan grabbed the railing around the carriage roof, braced a foot in the window, and heaved himself up and over. As he landed on the roof, the man twisted to slash at him with the stick. Athelstan ducked under the stick and tackled the man. They sprawled on the roof, writhing and kicking and punching at each other.

The man was large and powerful, and although Athelstan was a superb athlete, he didn't have much experience at battling hand to hand like this. The stakes had never been quite so desperate, either. If the man was able to stop the carriage, the rest of his group would gallop up and overtake them. They would carry Bodicia off to what was likely to be a terrible fate.

That knowledge fueled Athelstan's efforts. He hooked a punch to the man's face and scrambled on top of him. The swaying carriage tossed both back and forth. Athelstan tried to ram his knee into his opponent's groin, but the man twisted his body so that the blow landed on his thigh. He grabbed Athelstan's shoulders and flung him to the side.

Suddenly, nothing was underneath Athelstan except the open air beside the racing carriage.

His hands shot out instinctively and closed around the rail. He fell, and when his weight hit, it almost tore his grip loose and felt like it was going to pull his shoulders out of their sockets.

He cried out in pain, but somehow, he held on. After a moment, he forced his tortured muscles to work and began pulling himself up again. As his head came level with the roof, he saw that the attacker had lost the walking stick during their struggle, but that hadn't stopped the man from going after Theobald again. The man had his arm around the old driver's neck from behind and was choking him. Theobald had dropped the reins and the horses were running uncontrolled now.

Athelstan clenched his teeth and said, "Perry, help me!"

His brother leaned out a window, wrapped his arms around Athelstan's knees, and said, "I've got you!"

"Lift me up there!"

With Perry's help, Athelstan reached the roof and rolled over the railing onto it. He caught his breath for a second, then came up on hands and knees. From there he dived at the man choking old Theobald.

Taken by surprise and not braced for an attack from behind, the man pitched over the seat with a startled yell. Athelstan's momentum carried him forward as well, and they both toppled over Theobald and landed on the floorboards at the old man's feet.

The wild struggle continued there, but in the close confines, Athelstan's opponent quickly got the upper hand. He dug a knee into Athelstan's belly and clamped his left hand around Athelstan's throat. His right fist rose and fell and rose again.

This time, Theobald grabbed the man's lifted forearm and leaned over to bite his exposed wrist. The man howled in pain as the old driver's strong teeth dug into his flesh. He let go of Athelstan and reared up to hammer wild punches at Theobald with his other hand.

Theobald let go and fell back, stunned by the brutal assault. The attacker turned his attention back to Athelstan, who had used the brief respite to paw under the driver's seat until his hand closed around the grip of the pistol Theobald had stashed there.

Athelstan lifted the weapon and fired up into the body of the man looming over him. The pistol was so close that the tongue of bright orange flame licking from the muzzle scorched the front of the man's coat.

The man jerked back from the ball's impact and then swayed forward as he fumbled in horrified, futile desperation at the blood-spouting hole in his chest. He fell off the driver's box and landed between the two matched pairs of runaway horses.

The loose-limbed weight striking them made the horses run even faster. The man slipped on through and landed among the slashing hooves. The carriage gave a big leap as two of the wheels bounced over his body. Athelstan had to grab the tail of Theobald's coat to steady the old man and keep him from falling off.

Athelstan sat up and pulled himself onto the seat. He leaned forward and grabbed the reins Theobald had dropped. Luckily, they were still within reach. He handed them to Theobald and then turned on the seat to peer back at the lane behind them. It was too dark for him to see much, but he thought he made out the shapes of several riders galloping along behind them.

Feeling the carriage start to slow slightly, Athelstan exclaimed, "No! Keep going as fast as you can. If we stop now, they'll be on us within moments."

"Begging your pardon, sir, but with the team running away like this, 'tis the Lord's own miracle we haven't already crashed. I can manage this road fine in the dark as long as we're traveling at a more sedate pace."

"We have no choice," Athelstone told him. "Do you have more powder and shot for this pistol?"

"There should be a pouch under there with both in it."

Athelstan reached under the seat and located a leather pouch that contained a powder horn and a chamois bag with half a dozen more balls in it. He had reloaded plenty of pistols and rifles in his life, but never before on the driver's seat of a racing carriage with a gang of highwaymen bent on kidnapping his sister thundering along behind them. Even though he fumbled a bit, he soon had the pistol ready to fire again.

Twisting around on the seat, he held the pistol in both hands and braced his elbows on the roof. He caught sight of a shape not far behind the carriage and pressed the trigger. The pistol boomed and bucked and spewed smoke.

It was difficult to tell over the hoofbeats, but Athelstan thought he heard a man cry out in pain.

A second later, muzzle flame bloomed in the darkness like crimson flowers as the pursuers returned fire. Athelstan and Theobald both ducked low. As far as Athelstan could tell, none of the shots struck the carriage.

"Are you all right?" he raised his voice to ask the old driver.

"Fine, sir!" Theobald replied. "Are they still back there?"

Athelstan risked a look. "I don't see them, but it's hard to tell. Just keep going. It's all we can do."

Staying low, Athelstan stuck his head around the side of the carriage and called through the window, "Perry! Bodicia! Are you all right?"

He had started to worry that one of those shots the pursuers had fired might have penetrated the carriage's back wall.

He felt a surge of relief when Perry answered, "We're not hurt! What about you?"

"I'm all right," Athelstan assured his brother.

"Are they still following us?"

"I don't think so," Athelstan answered honestly. "I believe the shot I just fired at them may have caused them to give up the chase."

"There was another shot earlier—"

"One of them is dead," Athelstan answered. "That one, at least, won't be bothering us again."

The words he spoke made his guts clench coldly. He had killed a man. Ended another human being's life. True, the man had been intent on injuring or even killing him as well as subjecting Bodicia to captivity and quite possibly degradation. Athelstan had been fully justified in shooting him.

But he had never killed a man before, and the sheer enormity of it stunned him and left him mentally grasping for something to help him cope with it.

Instead, the situation seemed even worse the more he thought about it. Not only had he killed a man, but that man worked for Jacques LeCarde. The Frenchman was not noted for being forgiving, and now, to his way of thinking, the Braxtons would owe him more than money. It was a blood debt, and LeCarde would insist on it being paid, over and above what Jeremy owed him.

Tonight, the family had brought down the grand duke's anger on their heads. Perry was facing possible imprisonment. Jeremy had a vicious criminal after him, and now Athelstan probably did, too. Bodicia had played a part in creating dangerous political enemies, and she also was threatened by what LeCarde might do. When Athelstan thought about all of that, only one possible solution to all those problems came to mind.

Like it or not, no matter that the grand duchy was their ancestral home, it was time for the Braxton family to get out of Alpenstone.

Book II

Chapter 11

Hamburg, Germany

Two months had passed since the night the Braxton family fled Alpenstone. That flight, taking place in the middle of the night, still galled Athelstan. His first instinct was to stay and do battle against the web of trouble that had ensnared them.

But to do so would have been to place his younger siblings in danger, and as the head of the family, he had a responsibility to protect them.

It was a cold, overcast day. Earlier, a light mist had fallen, so the piers of the great harbor along the river Elbe were a bit slick and treacherous. Athelstan, Jeremy, and Perry wore overcoats and hats; Bodicia had a hooded cloak over her dress. Behind them, wheeling a cart that contained the bags, was Theobald, the old carriage driver. Young Griggs, the stableboy back at Braxton Manor, followed him.

Athelstan hadn't intended to bring either of the servants with them when they left the estate. Theobald had begged to accompany them, saying, "I have been serving the Braxton family my entire life, sir. I wouldn't know how to work for anybody else." Touched by that request, Athelstan hadn't been able to bring himself to refuse it.

Griggs was a different story. The lad had a craving for adven-

ture, and when he had heard that the Braxtons were going to em-
igrate to America, that sparked the desire inside him to go along.
He had no family, being an only child and his parents having died
several years earlier, so nothing was holding him in Alpenstone.

Athelstan had to admit that the trip across Germany had been
easier with the two servants along. He and his brothers and sister
had piled their belongings—as much as they could, even though
it was only a small fraction of the family's possessions—into a
wagon, and Theobold had done most of the driving. They had
started in the dead of night, following the road north into Germany as Alpenstone's border curved back to the east. They could
have headed west into France or Belgium or the Netherlands,
but all the seaports were approximately the same distance away
and Athelstan reckoned their chances would be better traveling
across Germany. Having grown up in the tiny grand duchy tucked
between countries, they all spoke German like natives.

Not only that, he knew that ships left Hamburg bound for
America on a regular basis, and putting an ocean between the
Braxtons and their enemies seemed like a good idea.

The ship that would carry them on that voyage loomed ahead
of them, a sturdy brigantine known as the *Apollo*. It belonged to a
group of German nobles who had arranged for immigrants to
journey to an unofficial colony in a place called Texas. Lacking
sponsors among that group, Athelstan had purchased their tickets with funds brought from Alpenstone.

The little group reached the foot of the walkway that angled
up to the ship's deck. Two sailors stood at the top, and one of
them called down in German, "What are you doing?"

"We've booked passage to Texas on this ship," Athelstan
replied.

The sailor waved a hand toward the cart. "Not with all that
baggage, you haven't. You're only allowed to bring a small amount
with you."

"No one said anything about that."

"Well, they should have told you when you purchased your

tickets, and I don't really care if they did or didn't." The sailor laughed. "Come aboard if you want, but you're going to have to leave most of those bags here."

Bodicia said, "Athelstan, we can't. We only brought the things we absolutely have to have."

Athelstan shook his head. "It appears that what we consider necessities and what the crew of this ship considers necessary are different."

Jeremy said, "You may have to bribe them, Athelstan."

"Not everyone can be bribed," Perry said. "Some people have moral standards."

"And I don't?" Jeremy snapped, with a glare at his younger brother.

Perry shrugged. "That's not what I said, but you can take it however you'd like."

In the weeks since leaving Alpenstone, Jeremy had recovered from the beating he had received at the hands of LeCarde's men. He also hadn't had a drink in that time. It had been a difficult habit for him to break, along with his propensity for gambling, and that had left him rather pale and haggard, not to mention short-tempered.

"This is no place for an argument, you two," Athelstan told them. He turned back to the men on the *Apollo*'s deck. "When does the ship sail?"

"Less than an hour from now," the second sailor replied.

Athelstan nodded to his siblings. "Let's go through our things and decide exactly what we have to have."

He had already seen that the brigantine's deck was crowded with people. Men, women, and children, most of them clustered in family groups, and there were even some goats, pigs, and chickens among the passengers. It would be an unpleasant crossing for them, living out in the open like that with nothing to protect them from the elements but temporary shelters rigged from blankets. He had been able to book a single cabin for himself and his brothers and sister; they would be crowded, with no privacy, but at least they would have a roof over their heads. Theobald and Griggs would have to make do on deck.

Each of them pared their possessions down to what would fit in a small carpetbag. The sailors waved them on up the walkway. One of the ship's officers saw them boarding and hurried over to meet them.

Athelstan gave the man their names. He checked a list he carried and nodded.

"Your cabin is belowdecks," he said. Pointing, he went on, "Go down those steps. You're in the fourth cabin on the right."

"That would put us in the middle of the ship," Jeremy said.

"That is correct, sir."

"No windows?"

The officer smiled. "No portholes, you mean. But no, there are none in your cabin."

"It'll be like being shut up in a box."

That brought an unconcerned shrug from the officer. "Someone with deck passage would be happy to trade with you, I imagine."

"No, that's all right," Athelstan said quickly. "Come on."

The corridor outside the cabin was dimly lit by a few widely spaced oil lamps. When the door was open, enough light spilled in for Athelstan to see that the room had only one lamp in it. He scraped a match into life and held the flame to the wick. When it caught and he lowered the glass chimney, the glow that spread through the cabin didn't do much to improve it.

The room was very small, with only two bunks and not much space between them. Athelstan said, "You can have your pick of them, Bodicia. Two of us can share the other bunk, and the third will sleep on the floor. We can take turns doing that."

"That's not fair to the three of you," she said.

"But it's the way we're going to arrange things," Athelstan replied, his tone making it clear that he wouldn't stand for any argument from her.

Perry said, "It's better than having to stay on deck like Theobald and Griggs."

"Only if you don't want to sleep between here and America," Jeremy said with a scowl.

"That's enough," Athelstan told him. "I don't know about you, but I'm grateful for what we have."

"For what we have?" Jeremy repeated. "We've lost everything! We had to flee our home, we're practically penniless, and we're on our way to a land that's completely untamed. You've read about this place they call Texas. It's full of brutes and wild animals!"

"The Indians can't be any more savage than Jacques LeCarde and his hirelings," Perry said. "Or had you forgotten about them—and what they tried to do?"

Jeremy sighed and shook his head. "No, I haven't forgotten. But I am getting tired of feeling like I have to apologize for bringing trouble to the family. Don't you forget, Perry, that you're the one who struck that Englishman."

"I doubt if I'll ever forget that night," Perry said coldly.

Athelstan's firm voice cut into the squabbling. "Enough. We'll leave our things here and go back up on deck to watch as the ship sails. That's not something you see every day, eh?"

"I've never seen it before," Bodicia said.

"Only Athelstan has," Perry added.

It was true. Except for his one trip to England, they had all spent their entire lives in Alpenstone other than brief visits to the nearby regions of France and Germany. The ocean crossing was going to be a whole new experience for them, just as settling in the new land of Texas would be.

They left their bags in the cabin and went up the stairs to the deck, which was even more crowded with emigrants than it had been earlier. As they made their way toward the railing, Griggs spotted them and squirmed through the press of people to join them, hanging on to Theobald's coat sleeve so he could tug the old man along after him.

"Isn't it exciting?" the youngster said as he stood next to Bodicia and clutched the rail.

"I'm worried about you and Theobald," she said to him. "Are you going to be all right?"

"We'll be fine, miss," Griggs assured her. "This is going to be a wonderful adventure."

Athelstan overheard that and hoped the boy was right. At any rate, it was taking them far away from any vengeance meted out by Grand Duke Alistair and Jacques LeCarde.

The Braxtons had earned the enmity of the highest and the lowest in Alpenstone, he mused. The sovereign ruler and a vicious little criminal. That was quite an accomplishment, he told himself with a wry quirk of his mouth.

A quarter of an hour later, the sailors cast off the lines, the sails were raised, and the damp breeze along the Elbe caught the canvas, billowed it out with a snap, and the *Apollo* eased away from the dock and started along the broad river toward the North Sea some 68 miles away.

Beyond the North Sea lay the rest of the world—and the Braxton family's destiny.

Chapter 12

Down the North Sea, through the English Channel, and then up through the Irish Sea to Liverpool at the mouth of the River Mersey sailed the *Apollo*.

One of the officers had told Athelstan, that normally, the vessel would have docked at Southampton to take on supplies for the Atlantic crossing, but on this voyage, the *Apollo* was stopping at Liverpool to pick up a German nobleman who had been in England on business. Baron Friedrich von Weilburg was a member of the group promoting migration to Texas and was going to make the journey to the new land himself.

From the *Apollo*'s starboard railing along the bow, the Braxtons had a good view of the English port city as the ship approached it. Having lived all their lives until recent weeks in the beautiful rustic surroundings of the grand duchy, the sprawling, rabbit's warren of buildings crowded close to one other and overhung by a smoky gray sky looked terribly unappealing.

Bodicia shuddered as she stood at the railing with her brothers and looked at the city.

"I don't see how people can live packed in so close together like that," she said with a shake of her head. "It won't be like that where we're going in Texas, will it, Athelstan? People and buildings everywhere?"

Athelstan laughed. "From what I've read about the place,

Texas is mostly wide open spaces, with very few settlements at all," he said as he stood beside her with his hands resting on the railing. "And most of the settlements that have been established there are small and primitive."

From the other side of Athelstan, Jeremy said, "You may wish you were back in Lornsburgh once we get there, Bodicia."

She shook her head. "No, I'm thinking about this voyage in the same manner that Griggs does, as a once-in-a-lifetime adventure to be enjoyed."

"It hasn't been all that enjoyable so far, though, has it?"

She had to admit Jeremy was correct about that. None of them had been accustomed to traveling on a ship, and the constant rocking, rising, and falling motion had sickened them for days.

The cramped, almost airless quarters hadn't helped matters, either. All too often, they found themselves bolting from the cabin and charging up on deck to dash to the closest railing, pushing their way through the horde of emigrants as they rushed to do so. Many of those traveling on deck were sick, too, so the rails were always crowded.

Thankfully, Bodicia's stomach had settled down for the most part, and she no longer suffered from such distress except on rare occasions.

Things would be even better once they reached their destination, Bodicia told herself. Even though Jeremy's complaints made Texas sound like a dangerous place, she knew it wouldn't be too bad. Judging by some of the descriptions Athelstan had gleaned from reading about it, parts of Texas even resembled their homeland with its rugged, thickly wooded hills and the cold, fast-flowing streams that twisted among them.

The *Apollo*'s crew skillfully docked the ship at Liverpool. Bodicia was surprised when some of the deck passengers disembarked, taking their belongings with them.

She turned to Athelstan and said, "I thought they were all bound for Texas. This is England, isn't it?"

He nodded and said, "It certainly is." Catching the eye of a passing crew member, he asked, "Why are those people getting off the ship?"

"You'd have to ask them," the sailor replied curtly, "but I imagine it's because they're already sick of traveling by sea and have decided this is far enough for them." The man shrugged. "We usually lose some passengers on our last stop before the crossing begins in earnest. But that's all right because we'll take on more to replace them."

"People from England are also emigrating to America, you mean? Not just Germans?"

The sailor looked impatient to get about his duties, but he lingered long enough to respond, "English, *ja,* and many Irish, as well. They say the Irish are starving because of some blight on the potatoes and many of them are fleeing to America to escape that."

"So you'll have an international cargo the rest of the way," Jeremy commented with a smirk.

The sailor ignored that and hurried away. The Braxtons remained at the railing, watching the hustle and bustle of passengers going ashore as others boarded. Crates and bags of supplies were carried aboard the ship and taken belowdecks. All that frantic activity surrounded Bodicia and her brothers, and everyone scurrying on and off the *Apollo* seemed to have some urgent goal to accomplish.

One group of new passengers caught Bodicia's eye as they came aboard the brigantine. Four men, ranging in age from their early twenties up to their middle thirties, clomped up the walkway from the dock with canvas bags slung over their shoulders and caps pulled low over their eyes.

The eldest, a burly man with curly brown hair already turning gray, led the way, followed by three more who bore a distinct resemblance to him. Bodicia could tell by looking at them that they were brothers.

One had raven-black hair and the other two had thatches of rust-colored hair sticking out from under their caps. The youngest of the quartet brought up the rear and was smaller than his brothers, slightly built, with a face that reminded Bodicia of a ferret. His pointed features were set in a sly expression.

All four men were shabbily dressed in patched, threadbare canvas trousers and woolen coats over homespun shirts. Heavy, well-worn work shoes were on their feet. Clearly, all they had in the world were their clothes and whatever was stuffed in the bags they carried.

Of course, that same description had applied to her and her brothers when they boarded the ship back in Hamburg, Bodicia thought wryly.

The Braxton siblings' position at the railing wasn't far from the opening where the walkway reached the deck. As the four men stepped onto the ship, the eldest glanced toward them and then looked away in disinterest.

The next man, the one with hair the color of midnight, paid more attention to them, running a cool, appraising gaze over them that made Bodicia a bit uneasy. He didn't look threatening, necessarily, but there was something about his face and eyes that was unreadable but somehow sinister, like the eyes of a beast that had its wildness tightly contained.

The two redheads were joking and laughing with each other as they boarded, but the youngest stopped short when he reached the deck to stare openly at Bodicia. After a moment, he jerked his cap off his head, ran his fingers through his tangled hair, and grinned as he took a step toward her.

"'Tis beggin' your pardon I am, miss," he said. "I don't mean t' stare, but ye may well be the loveliest colleen I've ever laid these poor eyes o' mine upon. Could I be askin' your name, perhaps?"

Before Bodicia could say anything, the oldest brother reached back, snagged the collar of Foxface's coat, and tugged him hard enough to make him stumble.

"Come on, Ceallach," he rumbled. "We've no time to waste

while you're botherin' the swells. We need to find a good place on deck to claim before they're all took up."

The black-haired brother grunted and said, "We don't have to worry about that, Ronan. When we find a place we like, we'll just take it."

The flat way he spoke left no doubt in Bodicia's mind that he meant what he said. The words made it plain he was the sort who took what he wanted, ruthlessly.

That reminded Bodicia of Leslie Scrimshire. Too much so, in fact. She frowned at the memory of the confrontation that had contributed so much to the Braxton family's woes. They might have been able to deal with the menace of Jacques LeCarde if they hadn't gotten on the grand duke's bad side, as well.

"Don't look like that, lass," Foxface called to her as his brother pulled him along. "Don't let me brother Eamon fool you. We're friendly folks, we are. You'll not find any friendlier than the MacLochlainn brothers!"

The crowd closed around the newcomers then, which was fine with Bodicia. She had seen enough of the MacLochlainn brothers, whoever they were. It would be fine with her if their path never crossed those of her and her brothers again during the voyage across the Atlantic.

But the *Apollo*, though it was a good-sized vessel, wasn't *that* big. Unless she remained down in the cabin for the entire crossing—a prospect that made Bodicia shudder at its unpleasantness—there was a very good chance she would run into the MacLochlainns again before they reached Texas.

Chapter 13

Once the Atlantic crossing began in earnest, the Braxton siblings found themselves plagued by a recurrence of the seasickness that had made the first part of the voyage so unpleasant. The waves were bigger in the vast ocean, lifting the *Apollo* to their crests and then plunging the ship down into the troughs between.

Every time that happened, Perry Braxton felt as if the vessel's violent motion was going to wrench his stomach right out of his body.

After so much of that torment, he almost would have welcomed such a development. At least that would have put an end to his misery.

He was at the railing one day, clinging to it as the *Apollo* bobbed on greenish-gray waves under a leaden sky. A short time earlier, he had emptied his belly, and now he was enjoying—if you could call it that—the brief respite that always followed such an occasion. The seas had smoothed out slightly in the past few minutes, and the ship was moving along at a good clip, its many and intricately arranged sails billowing with air.

A man lunged up to the rail beside him, clapped his hands on it, and leaned far over as he retched violently. Perry started to turn away, worried that the sight and sound of such distress might make him feel queasy again. Before he could leave, the sick man let go of the railing with his left hand, reached out, and grasped Perry's arm.

"Linger a moment, lad," the man said as he straightened, breathing hard from his exertions. He dragged the back of his other hand across his mouth and then went on, "I thought maybe havin' somebody to talk to might help both of us calm our roisterin' bellies."

Perry wanted to jerk his arm away, but he suppressed the impulse. He'd been raised to be polite, even to people who annoyed him.

"It's pretty bad, isn't it?" he said, trying to make himself sound sympathetic.

"Aye. I don't understand how the sailors manage to live like this."

"I suppose they get used to the motion and it doesn't make them sick after a while."

"Could be, though such seems impossible t' me." The man thrust out his hand and introduced himself. "Ceallach MacLochlainn is me name."

Perry hesitated, recalling that the man had used that hand to wipe his mouth, but then he gave a mental shrug and clasped it in a firm grip.

"Perry Braxton."

Ceallach MacLochlainn cocked his head a little to the side and grinned in recognition. "I remember you. Ye were standin' there at the rail lookin' on as me and me brothers boarded the ship at Liverpool."

Perry remembered Ceallach, too. Bodicia had mentioned later how he'd reminded her of a fox. Perry could see the resemblance in the man's prominent sharp-pointed nose and weak chin. They gave his face an animalistic look, like a snout, and the thick, tangled red hair sticking up, almost like ears, just added to the impression.

His sister hadn't liked the look of his man, Perry recalled. Neither did he.

Ceallach seemed friendly enough, though. He leaned on the railing and said, "You're an Englishman, ain't ye? Ye sound like one. Did ye board at Southampton?"

"I'm not English," Perry said, "although my family came from there, which accounts for the similar accent. More than a hundred years ago, my ancestors settled in a place called Alpenstone."

Ceallach frowned and shook his head. "Never heard of it. Be it in Scotland?"

"I'm not surprised you don't know of it. Not many people do. Alpenstone is a grand duchy established by the Habsburgs, in the mountains where France, Germany, and Switzerland come together with each other. Originally, it was part of Germany. A group of noblemen from England, my grandfather among them, were granted sovereignty over it."

Ceallach laughed. "Ye might as well be talkin' about the moon, Perry, me lad. I've heard o' some of those places, but I don't know a thing about them. Before me brothers and me left Ireland, I'd never been more than five miles from our farm."

He hawked and spat over the side before continuing.

"I'm glad to be out o' England. I hate the bloody Britishers more than anything in the world. I was prepared to make an exception for you because ye seem like a nice enough young fella, but to tell you the truth, I'm glad ye ain't one of them." Ceallach dropped one eye in a wink. "I'll forgive ye for your elders comin' from there. At least they had the good sense to leave!"

Perry was no snob, but he found Ceallach MacLochlainn crude and irritating. Even so, he was willing to make an effort to get along with the man, although Ceallach seemed to be getting the impression they were now friends, and that certainly wasn't the case.

The conversation might have continued in that manner if the Irishman hadn't grinned and said, "I recall a sweet, fair-haired lass bein' with you when me brothers and me came aboard. Would that be your missus?"

"My sister," Perry replied. He felt his jaw tighten as he spoke. He didn't want to discuss Bodicia with this man.

Ceallach's grin broadened even more into a leer. "Ah, so she's not wedded to you. What about the other two gents who were with you? Either of them married to her?"

"Hardly. Those are my brothers. Her brothers, too."

"Then the lass doesn't have a man, that's what you'd be sayin'."

Perry no longer bothered to keep the unfriendly chill out of his voice as he replied, "I don't believe that that's any business of yours."

"Oh, I mean no offense," Ceallach responded quickly. "I'm just sayin' that a girl as beautiful as your sister needs a husband to take care of her, that's all. I don't think anybody can argue with that."

"When the time comes, I'm sure she'll marry. There are sure to be plenty of good men in Texas. She'll have no trouble finding a suitable husband."

Ceallach's leer disappeared, replaced by a puzzled frown. "Wait, where did ye say?"

"She'll find a husband—"

"No, the other part. About . . . Texas?"

Perry nodded. "That's where we're bound. It's a place in America." Perry frowned, too. "Don't you know where you're going?"

"Me brothers and I thought this boat was bound for New York City."

Perry started to correct him and explain that the *Apollo* was a ship, not a boat, but he pushed that aside as irrelevant. Instead, he said, "No, we're going to a place called Texas. Have you heard of it?"

Ceallach scratched his head. "Th' name is vaguely familiar, I'll admit, but that's all I know about it."

"I believe it's part of the United States now, but it was its own country until recently, ever since winning its independence from Mexico."

"'Tis all news to me. Some of our friends and relatives from back home went to New York, and I thought we were headed to the same place. I reckon Ronan just grabbed the first boat he could get us on, though, and paid little attention to the destination." Ceallach shrugged. "I suppose it doesn't matter, as long as we go someplace we can get by. That's sure not Ireland anymore! 'Tis not a land fit to live in these days."

Perry started to mention what he'd heard about the potato famine and the problems in Ireland, but he decided not to. He didn't want to encourage Ceallach MacLochlainn to continue the conversation.

On the other hand, talking to the Irishman actually had gotten his mind off how terrible he'd felt a few minutes earlier, and he was surprised to realize that he wasn't sick anymore. Unlikely though it seemed, this encounter had served some purpose after all.

But he was ready to bring it to an end now. "I'd best be going," he said.

"Tell your sister hello for me. What's the lass's name, by the way?"

"There's no need for you to know that," Perry said, knowing that he sounded stiff-necked and unfriendly, but not caring. "You won't be talking to her."

Ceallach pushed out his lips for a second and looked surprised. "So I'll not be talkin' to her, eh? Because ye'll not allow her to be approached by such a disreputable human bein' as meself?"

"I just don't think it's a good idea."

"Well, I'll not be arguin' that." Ceallach smiled, but Perry saw anger lurking in his eyes. The redhead raised a hand and prodded a fingertip against Perry's chest. "But mayhap we'll allow the lass herself to make the decision about who she does or doesn't talk to."

"Stay away from her," Perry said bluntly, no longer caring about trying to be friendly or even pretending to be.

Abruptly, Ceallach stepped back and raised both hands, palms outward.

"I want no trouble. 'Tis beggin' your pardon I am, good sir. You can rest assured I'll keep me distance from you and yours. At least, as much as I can on a boat like this. Ye have to admit, there might be times we'll run into each other."

"That's fine, as long as you don't bother my sister."

Ceallach tugged on the bill of his cap and backed away, but Perry didn't believe his suddenly servile attitude for a second. He had seen the flash of hatred in the man's eyes and knew Ceallach harbored resentment against him.

That was fine with him. He didn't care if someone such as Ceallach MacLochlainn liked him or not.

Chapter 14

The lantern hanging on a chain over the table swayed back and forth with the ship's motion. The glow from it cast shifting shadows around the windowless room, but the light was consistent enough to illuminate the table on which a faro layout had been placed. The layout consisted of a suit of cards, all spades in this case, painted on a board, six each in two rows and the thirteenth card by itself at the left end.

Coins and folding currency were placed on the cards in the layout to show the bets. In most gambling houses, players bought chips with which to make their wagers, but here aboard the ship they just used whatever money they had. As a result, the currency was a mixed lot—German marks, French francs, and English pounds. There were even a couple of American gold eagles scattered among the other wagers.

Half a dozen men clustered around the table, five players and a banker representing the house. Today that banker was Eamon MacLochlainn. The MacLochlainn brothers owned the layout and the so-called shoe, the box from which the cards were dealt, so one of the three eldest—Ronan, Eamon, or Cathal—was always the banker.

Ceallach, the fox-faced youngest brother, never served as the banker, which made Jeremy Braxton wonder if the others didn't fully trust him.

Jeremy was seated directly across from Eamon tonight. He watched the dealer's face closely, but that was mostly just a matter of habit picked up from other games. Faro wasn't a game that involved any bluffing; it was more just the luck of the draw. A man had that luck or he didn't.

Of course, a dealer could still cheat by stacking the deck and making the cards come out of the shoe in a certain order. That possibility made close observation worthwhile.

However, as far as Jeremy had been able to tell, Eamon and the other MacLochlainn brothers dealt a straight game. The house was always ahead overall, as could be expected, but not by much.

Jeremy, himself, was also a little to the good. If things continued like this, he wouldn't be rich by the time the *Apollo* reached Texas, but he would have a nice little amount built up. Those winnings would help the Braxtons make a good start in the new land.

Eamon dealt two cards from the shoe, placing one to the right—the house's card—and one to the left—the players' card. Soft exclamations of satisfaction or disgust, depending on the outcome of their wagers, came from three of the players. The other two had neither won nor lost on this round.

Eamon settled the bets, including taking two francs from the pile in front of him and adding them to the pair of francs Jeremy had placed on the seven of spades on the layout. He pushed the notes across the table to Jeremy, who collected his winnings with a smile.

He considered for a couple of heartbeats, then picked up two of the francs and placed them on a different card in the layout, the jack this time. Faro's fast pace didn't give a man very long to make up his mind about what he was going to do next.

The door opened behind him, and someone came into the cabin. Jeremy didn't look around. He was watching the other players making their bets. As Eamon prepared to deal from the shoe again, Jeremy saw Ceallach MacLochlainn from the corner of his eye. The young man stalked over to one of the cabin's bunks and threw himself down on it as if he owned the place.

The man who had booked this cabin for the voyage, a red-faced German named Buchholz, glared and said to Eamon, "MacLochlainn, tell your brother to get off my bunk."

"Ceallach, behave yourself," Eamon snapped without looking at his youngest brother. "Get off of there."

"But he ain't usin' it," Ceallach responded in a surly tone.

"I don't care. Get off."

Ceallach looked like he wanted to argue, but at the same time, it was obvious that he didn't want Eamon angry with him.

"Beggin' your pardon, *Herr* Buchholz," he said as he stood up. The apology didn't have an ounce of sincerity in it, and everyone in the room knew it.

Buchholz didn't push the matter, though, and neither did Eamon. He dealt the next two cards, paid off the bets that won, and collected from the two losers.

Jeremy's card was neither of the two just dealt. He let the two francs ride where they were for the next round.

Ceallach wandered over behind his brother and watched while Eamon dealt a few more rounds. Then Jeremy became aware Ceallach was looking at him with great interest.

"Something I can do for you, friend?" he asked. He didn't actually consider Ceallach a friend—in fact, there was something unpleasant about him, provoking the same sort of reaction one felt when overturning a log and seeing the crawling things under it—but there was no point in antagonizing the rest of the MacLochlainn clan.

Ceallach poked a finger at Jeremy and asked, "Don't I know you?"

"I've played in this game a number of times since the ship sailed," Jeremy replied.

Ceallach shook his head. "No, that ain't it." He considered for a moment longer and then snapped his fingers. "I've got it. Ye and your brothers and sister were at the rail watchin' when me and me brothers came on board back in Liverpool. You're one o' them Braxtons."

"'Tis playing a game we are here, Ceallach, in case you hadn't noticed," Eamon said, clearly annoyed by his brother. "Why don't you go bother someone else?"

"I'm not botherin' Master Braxton there. Am I, Master Braxton?"

Jeremy waved a hand to dismiss the question. "It's fine."

"Y'see, Eamon? Master Braxton ain't upset wi' me."

Jeremy wished Ceallach would stop calling him that. He obviously didn't mean the term to be respectful. In fact, Ceallach sounded rather resentful and insulting.

"Just go away," Eamon said without looking at his brother. Jeremy silently seconded that sentiment.

Instead, Ceallach directed an ugly grin toward Jeremy and went on, "This fella is the brother o' that lass I been talkin' about ever since we got on this ship. Ye know the one I mean, Eamon. The one I'd like to—"

Jeremy had placed his hands on the table, and his face drew taut with anger as he was about to stand up. Before he could do so, Eamon MacLochlainn shot to his feet and grabbed his brother by the coat collar.

With seeming effortlessness, Eamon flung Ceallach into the corner. Ceallach struck hard against the wall and bounced off to fall to the cabin's wooden floor. He lay there and looked up dazedly at his brother.

"Next time I tell you to do something, you'd be better off doing it," Eamon told him. "Now get out of here before I boot you a few times in the ribs."

Breathing hard, Ceallach scrambled to his feet, cast a hate-filled glance at Jeremy, and hurried out of the cabin. Eamon took his seat again, muttered, "My apologies, Braxton."

"It's all right," Jeremy said. He had relaxed and sat back in his chair again.

"My brother can be a weasel at times." Eamon grunted, and even though his face was as expressionless as ever, Jeremy realized that what he'd just heard was as close as Eamon MacLochlainn came to a laugh. "I'd say that he means well, but 'tis doubtful I am that he actually does."

Jeremy knew the wisest thing would be to let the matter drop, but something prompted him to say, "He's been talking about my sister?"

"Don't worry. I'll have another word with him. Ceallach works his mouth too much, but I don't believe he'd actually bother her. I'll make sure of that."

"Thank you," Jeremy told him.

With an impatient glare, Buchholz said, "Are we going to talk or get on with the game?"

"The game, gentlemen," Eamon said as he reached for the shoe once more. "Always, the game."

The three Braxton brothers took a stroll on deck that evening, as much as anyone could stroll through such a crowded area, while Bodicia remained below in their cabin. It had to be a strain for a young woman to be shut up in such close quarters with three males, even her relatives, so they tried to give her a bit of privacy several times a day.

They stopped along the railing near the stern. The sea wasn't too rough at the moment, and the evening meal was sitting all right in their stomachs—for now. Perry hoped that condition would last for a while.

That thought made him remember what had happened earlier in the day. He clasped the railing, looked out over the waves that reflected tiny glints of light from the millions of stars in the black sky, and said, "I had a rather unpleasant encounter this afternoon."

Jeremy grunted and said, "As did I."

Athelstan leaned on the railing. "Neither of you said anything about any trouble."

"Oh, it wasn't really trouble," Perry said. "Just a conversation I didn't enjoy."

"That's what happened to me, too," Jeremy said. "Who was yours with?"

"Do you remember in Liverpool, those four brothers we saw come aboard? I know Bodicia noticed them because she talked about them later, especially one of them."

Jeremy said, "Ceallach MacLochlainn."

Perry looked over at him in surprise. "How do you know that?"

"Because that's who my unpleasant encounter was with." Jeremy cocked his head to the side. "Don't tell me you had trouble with him, as well!"

"I thought you said it wasn't trouble," Athelstan said.

Jeremy shrugged. "It could have been. MacLochlainn made some coarse comments about Bodicia, or at least, he was about to. I was on the verge of taking strong exception to it, but I didn't get the chance to. Ceallach's brother Eamon stepped in and chastised him before I had to do anything."

Athelstan frowned slightly as he said, "You seem fairly well acquainted with this family, Jeremy."

Jeremy shrugged and shook his head. "Not really. I've spoken to the older brothers a few times. Today was the first time I've had anything to do with the youngest one."

Athelstan looked at Perry and asked, "How did you happen to meet him?"

"I was at the railing up toward the bow when MacLochlainn came up and was sick over it. I was just recovering from a bout of that myself, so I suppose it was natural we'd commiserate with each other for a bit." Perry paused. "Talking to him was all right at first, even though we'd nothing in common. But then the man's comments took an ugly turn."

"About Bodicia, I suspect," Jeremy said. "He seems to be quite interested in her."

"That's unacceptable," Athelstan snapped.

"Of course it is," Perry agreed. "They're Irishmen."

"And poverty-stricken," Jeremy added.

"I don't care about either of those things," Athelstan said. "No matter where he's from or how much money he has, no gentleman goes around saying inappropriate things about a lady. Especially to that lady's brothers!"

In a dry voice, Jeremy said, "I think it's safe to say that Ceallach MacLochlainn is no gentleman."

"You mentioned that his brother spoke to him. . . ."

"Quite sternly," Jeremy said with a nod.

"You and this man—what's his name?"

"Eamon."

"You and Eamon MacLochlainn are friends?"

"No, not really," Jeremy said. "Acquaintances, at best."

Athelstan eyed his brother rather suspiciously and asked, "How did that come about?"

"We have common interests, I suppose you could say," Jeremy returned.

Athelstan looked intently at him for a moment, then said, "Damn it, Jeremy! You're gambling again."

Jeremy frowned and shifted his feet uncomfortably, but his voice held a note of stubborn defiance as he said, "I'm winning, Athelstan. I'm well ahead of the faro game the MacLochlainn brothers run. I know we brought what funds we could with us from Alpenstone, but with my winnings, we'll have an easier time making a fresh start in Texas."

"Are we supposed to find that admirable?" Perry asked. "You could also lose everything."

"I'm not going to," Jeremy insisted. "In fact, I think it may be time to leave well enough alone."

"That would be very wise," Athelstan said. His voice hardened as he added, "I insist on it."

Jeremy nodded. "Of course."

His brother looked and sounded sincere, Perry thought, but he couldn't bring himself to believe Jeremy's disavowal of gambling. The appeal of it was too strong for Jeremy. He had risked much in the past simply for the thrill of wagering on the turn of a card.

In the end, he had risked almost everything and had endangered the rest of the family. Perry hoped that Jeremy wasn't about to do the same thing again before they even reached their new home.

"There's something else to be considered," Athelstan said. "Bodicia."

"What about her?" Perry asked.

"You said this fellow MacLochlainn threatened her."

Jeremy said, "Well, he didn't actually threaten her, I suppose. He was about to say crude things about her before his brother stopped him."

"He wants to talk to her," Perry said. "He implied that he wants to . . . court her."

"Impossible," Athelstan said.

"I don't think he'll actually approach her," Jeremy said. "Eamon warned him to leave her alone. He and the others don't want any trouble."

"Do you think Ceallach will pay attention to what his brother said?"

"He's afraid of Eamon," Jeremy declared with conviction.

"He should be afraid of me," Perry said. "I warned him, too."

Athelstan thought for a moment and then nodded slowly.

"We're all going to be on this ship for another week or more," he said. "All we can do at this point is hope that Ceallach MacLochlainn won't cause too much trouble."

"Should we tell Bodicia what he's been saying?" Perry asked.

Athelstan shook his head. "There's no good reason to worry her over the matter. We'll make sure that MacLochlainn has no opportunity to bother her."

"How are we going to do that?" Jeremy asked.

"From now on," Athelstan said, "we're going to take our eyes off her as little as possible!"

Chapter 15

Over the next couple of days, Bodicia was puzzled by her brothers' behavior. They had always been tolerant of and attentive to her, of course.

Even when they were all youngsters and she had forced herself into their rough-and-tumble games, they hadn't pushed her away but allowed her to participate while still making sure she didn't get hurt—as long as she wasn't too obnoxious about it.

Now, though, every time she turned around one of them was there! They continually wanted to know what she was doing and where she was going.

It wasn't as if she wanted to wander all over the ship. As long as she got some fresh air and sunlight, she was willing to spend most of her time in the cabin. However, she wouldn't have minded an occasional stroll by herself, but Athelstan, Jeremy, and Perry seemed determined not to permit that.

Even when they left her alone in the cabin for the short intervals that were necessary, she had a feeling they were waiting right outside the door.

Inevitably, she began to feel smothered, and the situation grated on her nerves.

She didn't plan to deliberately defy their wishes, but one night when they left her alone for a while after the evening meal, as they normally did, the urge to get out of the cabin suddenly hit her. It was all right for her brothers to take an after-dinner constitutional, she thought. Why not her?

She put on her coat and drew the hood up over her fair hair. She would be just a dark shape moving around the deck. No one would notice her, including Athelstan, Jeremy, and Perry. She didn't intend to stay up there for any great length of time. Just long enough to move around and get some fresh air. She had been on deck for a while earlier in the day, but it hadn't been long enough to suit her.

If Texas was as spacious as Athelstan said, she was looking forward to it. To be able to roam where she wanted under an endless sky sounded heavenly.

She cracked the door open and checked the corridor outside the cabin. Footsteps sounded somewhere nearby. Bodicia drew back so she wouldn't be seen but left a tiny gap through which she could peer.

A man moved past outside. Based on the glimpse she had of him, she thought he was one of the sailors from the *Apollo*'s crew. The man hurried along the passage to the stairs and went up them to the deck.

Bodicia waited for a few minutes, listening intently. No one else was moving around outside. She eased the door open wider and saw that the corridor was empty, just as she had thought.

She stepped out.

The knowledge that she was doing something she wasn't supposed to made her heart pound faster. That felt good.

She didn't let the excitement make her reckless, though. She paused just below the top of the stairs and raised her head carefully to take a look around. She would feel foolish if her brothers were standing right there and discovered her immediately, she thought.

Some of the emigrants who were making the voyage on deck were not far away, huddled under a blanket shelter they had rigged to keep the spray and the night chill off to a certain extent. They didn't appear to be paying attention to anything that was going on around them. No one else was nearby.

Bodicia stepped out onto the deck and began to walk toward the stern.

It was cold here in the middle of the Atlantic. The same stiff breeze that filled the sails whipped at Bodicia's coat. She pulled it tighter around her and lowered her head. Salt spray pattered against her cheeks. It didn't feel that bad. It was invigorating, she told herself.

Despite that, she hadn't been on deck for very long before she realized she wanted to go back to the cabin.

She turned around and began retracing her steps. As she approached the stairs, she saw a man start down them. In the poor light, she couldn't make out any details about him except that he was smaller than any of her brothers. He had to be one of the other passengers who had booked a cabin for the voyage.

Bodicia slowed down, lingering long enough that she thought the man would be gone by the time she reached the corridor outside the cabins. When she went down the steps, she was surprised to see him outside one of the cabins to the left, several doors past the one shared by the Braxton siblings. He had his back to her, and in the dimly lit corridor, which was almost as murky as being out on deck, she couldn't tell what he was doing.

Perhaps he was trying to rob the cabins? She wondered briefly if she ought to turn around, go back up on deck, and locate an officer so that she could report that something odd was going on.

But whatever the situation, it was probably perfectly harmless, so she hurried to the door of her cabin instead and reached for the latch.

The man farther along the corridor turned and said, "Hello, lass."

Bodicia caught her breath but managed not to let out an audible gasp of surprise and fear. She didn't recognize the man's voice, but as he came toward her, she knew something was familiar about him. It took her only a heartbeat to realize where she had seen him before.

He was the foxlike man she had seen coming aboard the *Apollo* with his brothers back in Liverpool.

The hungry look in his eyes was visible even in the poor light. It made Bodicia's heart slug even faster. She reached for the latch again, but he was too quick for her. He glided forward and positioned himself so that his shoulder was between her and the door.

"There's no need to hurry off," he told her. "I mean ye no harm. A few minutes of pleasant conversation 'tis all I be askin' of you."

"We—we haven't been introduced," Bodicia managed to say.

"Aye, that's true. We have not." He swept his cap off his thatch of rusty hair. "Me name is Ceallach MacLochlainn. And I already know your name. 'Tis Bodicia Braxton. You see, I've made the acquaintance of two o' your brothers."

He probably meant that to reassure her, but she didn't feel reassured. His presence still made her extremely nervous.

She swallowed and said, "I'd be happy to speak with you some other time, Mr. MacLochlainn. Perhaps up on deck. But right now, I'd like to go inside, please. I've been for a walk and I—I'm rather chilled."

"Of course ye are. 'Tis not a fit night for a lass such as yourself to be wanderin' around topside. I'd offer you me coat to warm up, but what you're already wearin' looks better than what I have on." His voice took on an edge as he continued, "Everything about ye is considerably better than the likes o' me, ain't it?"

"I wouldn't say that—"

"Those brothers o' yours didn't mind sayin' it," he interrupted. "One of them told me to me face that I ain't good enough to breathe the same air as you, let alone talk to you. And the other one was about to say the same when circumstances intervened. But I know what he had in mind, oh, yes, I do. He was about to tell poor ol' Ceallach that he ain't fit to associate with a princess such as yourself."

Bodicia shook her head and said, "I don't know where you're getting all of this, but I'm sorry if my brothers offended you. And I'm hardly a princess. Now, please, let me past—"

She tried to move around him, but he reached out and took hold of her arms. This time she did gasp as he leaned toward her, grinning. She wasn't used to being handled roughly like that, especially by a stranger.

"Don't run off, lass. We're just gonna talk—"

A rush of footsteps sounded in the dim corridor, and an instant later, someone crashed into both Bodicia and MacLochlainn, knocking her loose from his grip.

Bodicia staggered, lost her balance, and fell to the corridor floor. She cried out as her shoulder struck hard. Grimacing, she pushed herself up on one hand and looked along the passageway to where two men had fallen and were now struggling with each other.

One of the combatants was Ceallach MacLochlainn. The other was Bodicia's brother Perry. The collision had knocked Perry's hat off, and she had no trouble recognizing him.

Perry was bigger and heavier than Ceallach and had landed on top when they both went down. Perry heaved himself up on his knees, straddled Ceallach's torso, and hammered punches at his opponent's face.

Even though the light in the corridor was dim, it was bright enough for Bodicia to see the sudden flash of steel in Ceallach's hand as he produced a knife from somewhere. The blade jabbed at Perry's side like a striking snake as Bodicia screamed a warning.

Chapter 16

Perry twisted away frantically from that deadly thrust. Bodicia saw the knife's glittering tip snag her brother's coat but couldn't tell if it had found Perry's flesh.

Whether the strike had wounded Perry or not, it loosened his grip on Ceallach enough that the Irishman was able to draw his leg up and scissor it across Perry's chest to lever him off. Perry rolled away, but the corridor was so narrow that he couldn't go far before he fetched up against the wall.

Ceallach scrambled onto hands and knees and went after him, slashing with the knife.

Perry grabbed the wrist of Ceallach's knife hand and held the blade off with both of his. He tried to twist Ceallach's arm enough to make the Irishman let go of the knife, but Ceallach rammed a knee into his belly that made him gasp and curl up around the pain. Bodicia could tell he was about to lose his grip on Ceallach's wrist.

If that happened, Ceallach would plunge the blade into Perry's body in a heartbeat.

Bodicia leaped to her feet and raced over to them. Lacing her fingers together, she raised her arms and brought her clubbed hands down on the back of Ceallah's head as hard as she could. The impact shivered up her arms.

Ceallach fell forward onto Perry. Again, Perry threw his strength into wrenching Ceallach's wrist around. This time, the knife's handle slipped out of Ceallach's fingers and the weapon clattered to the corridor floor. Bodicia kicked it and sent it spinning away, well out of reach of either man.

While Ceallach was still partially stunned from Bodicia hitting him, Perry grabbed him by the shoulders and flung him to the side. The knee to the belly had left Perry's face pale and drawn, but he forced himself up with a visible effort, clambering onto his feet and bracing himself with his left hand pressed to the corridor wall.

Perry could have kicked Ceallach in the head at that moment. Part of Bodicia wanted him to go ahead and do it. Ceallach deserved it.

But that wasn't the sort of man Perry was. He stood there, breathing hard and waiting with clenched fist, while Ceallach pushed himself part of the way up, paused to shake his head groggily a few times, and then straightened the rest of the way to his feet.

Ceallach swayed but managed to stay upright as vile curses directed at both Braxtons spewed from his mouth.

Perry stepped in and shut him up with a swift right-hand punch to the mouth.

The blow rocked Ceallach back against the other wall. Bodicia could tell that Perry was getting some of his strength back. He bored in on his opponent and hooked a left to Ceallach's belly. That made Ceallach lean forward and Perry hit him with another right, this one a crossing blow that jerked Ceallach's head to the side.

Ceallach sagged against the wall and tried to throw some punches of his own, but Perry's battering had knocked the strength out of him. His efforts were feeble and easily warded off. Even the blows that got through and clipped Perry did no real damage and didn't make him back off.

Bodicia knew it must be the rage surging through her brother that Perry drew on for strength now. He slugged Ceallach again and again, right and left, pinning him against the wall and hammering him mercilessly.

When Ceallach lifted his arms in a futile defense, Perry shifted his attack. His fists sunk in Ceallach's belly to the wrist, once, twice, three times. Ceallach doubled over and retched. Perry grabbed his collar and jerked him upright again, then drove a fist into the Irishman's mouth that flattened Ceallach's lips and left them bloody. Ceallach's head wobbled back and forth. He was almost senseless now.

Perry would have beaten him into unconsciousness or worse, more than likely, if his brothers hadn't appeared in the below-decks corridor at that moment and charged in to grab him. Athelstan took one arm, Jeremy the other, and between them, they dragged Perry back.

Ceallach's eyes rolled up in their sockets. His knees buckled and he pitched forward on his face. He appeared to be out cold, but his back rose and fell with his breathing. He was still alive, anyway.

"Perry, what in God's name are you doing?" Athelstan demanded. "When you didn't come back up on deck, we worried that something might be wrong, but you almost killed this man!"

"Athelstan, wait," Bodicia said as she stepped forward and lifted a hand. "That's one of the MacLochlainn brothers."

"I could have told you that," Jeremy said. "That's Ceallach."

Grimly, Bodicia said, "He attacked me. He put his hands on me, and he . . . he might have done anything if Perry hadn't come along and stopped him."

Athelstan's face hardened. He glanced down at Ceallach's senseless form and then asked his sister, "Are you all right?"

"Yes. He didn't hurt me. He didn't have a chance to—commit any indignities. But you can't blame Perry for losing his temper. He was just defending me."

A startled exclamation came from the other end of the corridor. Bodicia and Athelstan looked around to see one of the ship's officers hurrying toward them.

"What's wrong?" the man asked. "Has there been an accident? Oh, good heavens!"

The officer was close enough to see Ceallach lying face down. He dropped to a knee, grasped Ceallach's shoulders, and rolled him onto his back, revealing the bloody, heavily battered face. From there, the officer's shocked eyes went to Perry's hands. The knuckles were scraped raw. It was obvious he was the one responsible for the state Ceallach was in.

The officer straightened and demanded, "Why did you attack this man?"

"He had it coming," Perry snapped. "He took liberties with my sister."

The officer looked at Bodicia, whose face was flaming red by now. "Is that true, miss?" he asked.

Bodicia swallowed. "Yes. I mean, he spoke very rudely to me—"

"Is that all?" The officer's tone made it clear he found the idea of such actions justifying a savage beating unconvincing.

"He grabbed hold of me. He—he put his hands on my arms . . ."

Even as she spoke, Bodicia realized that what she was accusing Ceallach of, while improper, hadn't done any real damage to her. There was no telling what he might have done, but his actual behavior could be considered crude and insulting while not necessarily threatening.

The frown on the officer's face told her that was probably what he was thinking, too.

She spotted something further along the corridor and quickly pointed to it. "And he pulled a knife on my brother," she said. "That's it lying right there."

The officer sniffed. "I imagine he felt that his life was in danger. I'm not surprised he would try to defend himself."

"He wasn't defending himself," Bodicia insisted. "He was attacking us—"

From the floor, Ceallach let out a groan and shifted slightly.

"I'd best see about getting this passenger to the ship's surgeon," the officer said. "One of you men help me get him up."

"The hell we will," Jeremy snapped. "After what he did—"

"Let's just get this over with," Athelstan said. He let go of Perry's arm and stepped over beside Ceallach to help the officer lift him. Once they had Ceallach on his feet, the Irishman shook his head. Drops of blood flew from his nose and mouth.

"I'll be speaking to the captain about this," the officer said over his shoulder as he assisted Ceallach in stumbling along the corridor. They turned at the far end of it and went out of sight.

Athelstan looked at his youngest brother and said, "Perry—"

"If you want me to apologize for what I did, I won't," Perry said. "MacLochlainn had it coming. I'd never apologize to the likes of him!"

"You may have to, if the captain takes his side," Athelstan warned.

"What can the captain do?" Jeremy said. "Put us over the side in a small boat? He's not going to do that, Athelstan, and you know that. Certainly not on behalf of some penniless Irish immigrant who assaulted a young lady!"

"We're not exactly wealthy as we once were," Athelstan pointed out. "Besides, we're all on our way to Texas, and from what I've read of the place, every man is considered an equal there. No, you can't count on the captain supporting Perry in this matter because of where we're from or what we possess."

"But Perry is in the right," Bodicia said, "and I'll talk to the captain and tell him that if I need to."

"It may come to that"—Athelstan shrugged—"or it may not. We'll have to wait and see. And no, I don't believe he'll put us overboard." He looked at Perry. "But he could lock you up for the rest of the voyage. The captain's word is law on a ship, you know."

"Let him do his worst," Perry said. "I'm not ashamed of what I did, and in the same circumstances, I'd do it again"—he paused— "except that next time, I might grab that knife away from him and carve him up with it!"

Chapter 17

For the next few days, Bodicia stayed closer to the cabin than ever. Athelstan insisted on it.

He asked Perry to remain belowdecks as much as possible, too. He knew that should Ceallach or the other MacLochlainns catch sight of either Perry or Bodicia, it might stir up anger and resentment, and provoke even more trouble. There was no point in that if it could be avoided.

The fact that the *Apollo*'s captain didn't summon any of them came as a surprise to Athelstan. He expected at least a discussion with the captain or one of the other officers, warning him and his siblings to avoid causing any further problems.

When that warning didn't materialize, Athelstan began to relax a little. Perhaps nothing else unusual would happen during the rest of the Atlantic crossing.

He should have known better, he was to tell himself later.

Several days after the fight, the Braxtons had returned to their cabin from the ship's dining room following the evening meal. The brothers had put on overcoats and hats to protect them from the elements while they took their usual constitutional and allowed Bodicia some time alone.

Before they could leave, a knock sounded on the door.

When Athelstan opened it, he found a ship's officer standing there. The man's name was Muller, Athelstan recalled. He was the one who had come along in the aftermath of the battle and helped Ceallach MacLochlainn to the ship's surgeon. It was obvious from the surly expression he wore on his face now that he didn't bear any fondness for these passengers.

"Captain Steinbach wants to see your brother," Muller said. He pointed past Athelstan at Perry.

"What's this about?" Athelstan asked, while holding out a hand toward Perry in a signal to keep quiet for now.

Muller shook his head. "That's for the captain to explain to you. My orders were to fetch Perry Braxton, and that's what I intend to do."

He hooked his thumbs in the waistband of his white trousers and glared at Athelstan. Muller was a burly man, and Athelstan suspected that he wouldn't mind if he had to drag Perry to the captain by force—or at least attempt to.

And if Muller was unsuccessful in doing that, he would simply return with half a dozen or more crewmen, Athelstan knew. Putting up a fight was pointless.

"We'll come with you," Athelstan said.

"My orders are just to bring your brother—"

"You'll deliver him to the captain, just as you were told to do. Nothing was said about me and my other brother coming along, was there?"

Muller's prominent jaw tightened angrily, but after a moment he jerked his head in a curt shake.

"No, Captain Steinbach said nothing about that. I suppose I can't stop you."

Jeremy said, "You certainly can't."

"I don't like this," Perry said.

Muller sneered at him. "You should have thought about that before you—"

All four siblings looked at him curiously as he stopped short. "Before I did what?" Perry asked.

Muller shook his head and made a brusque gesture. "Come along. The captain will tell you all about it."

With his face set in angry lines, Perry walked out of the cabin. Athelstan nodded for Jeremy to follow and then said to Bodicia, "I know you want to come with us, but it would be best if you stayed here."

"But I might need to tell the captain about what happened with MacLochlainn," she objected.

"The rest of us can tell him. He'll accept our word for what you told us." Athelstan hoped that would be the case. "Besides, Perry saw him with his hands on you, treating you roughly. He can testify to that of his own knowledge. Captain Steinbach will have no choice but to believe us."

Bodicia didn't look convinced, but she didn't raise any more objections.

"Be sure to latch the door," Athelstan added. He put a hand on Bodicia's shoulder and squeezed encouragingly for a second before following Jeremy into the corridor.

Captain Helmut Steinbach was a stocky middle-aged man with the craggy face of someone who had spent decades exposed to the sun, sea spray, and wind. His hair was iron-gray, and he had a sweeping mustache the same color. His pale blue eyes were like chips of ice as he stonily regarded the Braxton brothers, who still wore their overcoats but held their hats in front of them.

"Which one is Perry?" he asked.

Perry stepped forward. "I am."

Steinbach looked at Muller and said, "I told you to bring this one."

"The other two insisted on accompanying us," the officer said. "My apologies, Captain."

Steinbach waved a hand dismissively. "It does not matter." To Perry, he said, "Do you know why you are here?"

"Here" was the captain's cabin. Even though it was small, as ship's cabins nearly always were, he was the only one who lived here alone, a privilege not afforded to any other members of the crew, who all had to share their accommodations.

"I assume it has to do with that fight I had with Ceallach MacLochlainn," Perry said. "I won't apologize for it, if that's what you want. He was rude and physically abusive to my sister, and he deserved what happened to him."

Steinbach, who wore his captain's uniform but had taken off his cap and loosened his collar, clasped his hands behind his back and said, "*Ach*, you think so, do you, Herr Braxton?"

Athelstan suddenly had a bad feeling about this. He said, "Perry, perhaps you'd best not say anything else—"

Perry interrupted to declare, "It's the truth. MacLochlainn is a grubby little weasel who had it coming."

Steinbach nodded slowly. "So you believe you had the right to deal with him—strenuously?"

"Absolutely."

Athelstan felt as if the deck had begun to sunk under him. He glanced over at Jeremy and saw that a sick expression had appeared on his face, as well.

Only Perry seemed to have no hint of what might be coming.

"So," Steinbach said, "you feel justified in killing Herr Ceallach MacLochlainn?"

"I certainly—" Perry stopped short as his eyes widened in shock. "What did you say?"

"I said that you believe you were justified in killing that man, MacLochlainn."

"No! I don't believe that! I mean—I didn't kill MacLochlainn or anyone else." Perry looked utterly confused. "He's dead?"

"That can't be," Athelstan said. "We saw him and his brothers earlier today. They were on deck near the stern, and my brothers and sister and I were up along the bow. He looked fine. They all did."

"Nevertheless, Herr MacLochlainn's body was discovered not long ago," Steinbach said. "It was hidden in a storage compartment adjacent to one of the belowdecks corridors. A member of the crew passing by spotted a small trail of blood leaking out from under the door and investigated."

"I had nothing to do with it," Perry insisted.

Steinbach went on as if Perry hadn't said anything. "Someone attacked Herr MacLochlainn with a knife. He was stabbed numerous times, and it appeared that someone hacked at his face with the blade, as well." The captain shook his head again. "A gruesome, terrible sight. I have seen bad things in my life, *mein Herrn*, but this was one of the worst."

"Damn it, I didn't do it!"

"You are the only one on board the ship who has had trouble with the man," Steinbach went on relentlessly. "And you were heard to say that if you fought again, you would take a knife and carve him up with it!"

Perry stepped back and looked as sick as if he had gotten a knee in the belly again.

"You said that, did you not, Herr Braxton?"

"I—I might have said something to that effect . . ."

"According to a witness, a passenger who was looking out a door open a crack after your previous clash with Herr MacLochlainn, that is exactly what you said. And now"—Steinbach spread his hands—"the man is dead, carved up with a knife. What am I supposed to think?"

Jeremy cleared his throat and said, "See here, Captain, my brother couldn't have done this. He's been with us, with my other brother and myself, all day."

"Every minute of the past hour?" Steinbach asked with a sharply aggressive note in his voice.

"Yes, the four of us had dinner together in the dining room—"

"One of the stewards saw Herr Perry Braxton leave before the rest of you," Muller said, clearly happy to be taking part in this confrontation at last. "I questioned the man myself. He said Perry Braxton left the dining room between a quarter of an hour and half an hour ahead of the rest of you."

Perry said, "I was feeling a bit under the weather. Lost my appetite. I thought a turn or two around the deck might help me, and it did."

"A few minutes isn't long enough to commit a crime such as the one you just described, Captain," Athelstan said.

"On the contrary, it could have been done," Steinbach insisted. "The *Apollo* is not so large that a man cannot get around it in a hurry, if need be. And the actual attack, savage though it was, could have been carried out in a matter of moments. A few seconds to open the door of the compartment and shove the dying man inside." The captain shrugged. "It is possible."

Jeremy said, "But if it was as violent as you claim, surely Perry would have gotten blood on him."

"That's right," Athelstan said. "Look at his clothing. There's no blood."

"Perhaps he changed clothes," Steinbach suggested.

"But I didn't!" Perry said.

"We would have known if he did," Athelstan added.

"I mean no offense, *mein Herrn*, but all I have to base my judgment on is the word of the accused's brothers, who would surely lie for him."

"We're not in the habit of lying," Athelstan said coldly.

"But your brother has never been accused of murder before, eh? So there is no way of knowing what you might do to save him."

"And since when is it your right to pass judgment?" Jeremy snapped.

Steinbach stiffened and glared at him. "Since I was made the captain of this vessel. And I am not passing judgment on your brother's guilt or innocence, only that he is the most likely to have killed Ceallach MacLochlainn. An actual legal determination is a matter for the courts."

"What court?" Athelstan asked. "We're on the high seas. No court has jurisdiction here."

Steinbach looked at him with narrowed eyes and asked, "Are you suggesting I go ahead and hold a trial, Herr Braxton? Hear from all the witnesses in a formal setting? We know what the outcome of that is most likely to be, and hangings have been carried out on ships in the past."

"Wait a minute," Athelstan said hastily. "I'm suggesting nothing of the sort—"

"Good, because I would prefer that someone else deal with this. I must tell you, the dead man's brothers pressed me to declare Herr Braxton guilty and pass a sentence of death on him to be carried out immediately, but I refused to do so. Instead . . ." The captain looked levelly at Perry. "Herr Braxton, you will be confined for the remainder of the voyage. I believe you and your brothers and sister are to disembark in Texas, at Karlshafen?"

"That's correct," Athelstan answered, even though the captain had addressed Perry.

"Very well. As I said, you will be confined until we reach Karlshafen. There I will turn you over to the local authorities and explain the situation to them. If they wish to undertake an investigation and hold a trial, they may do so. In that case, I will wash my hands of the matter."

"What if they don't want any part of it?" Perry asked.

"Then, regrettably, I shall be forced to exercise my authority. The crime was committed on my ship. A trial will be held, and I think it very likely, Herr Braxton, that before the *Apollo* sets sail on the return voyage, you will be hanged by the neck until dead."

Book III

Chapter 18

Karlshafen, Texas

This stretch of shell-covered beach was one of the most desolate places Athelstan had ever seen.

From every point inside the boundaries of Alpenstone, snow-capped mountains were visible, majestic in their rocky upper slopes and evergreen-covered lower slopes. Just looking at them could make a man feel cool and restful and surrounded by the glories of nature.

From the deck of the *Apollo*, the landscape that sprawled in front of Athelstan's eyes was the flattest he had ever seen. Gentle waves lapped on the curving beach. Beyond it was a sandy plain dotted with ugly tufts of grass broken up by ponds and narrow, twisting waterways. Farther inland, the plain turned into a grassy prairie with clumps of scrub brush here and there. That brush, which wouldn't come up even to Athelstan's chin, was the highest thing in sight other than a huddle of crudely built structures that looked as if a strong wind would blow them down.

"Oh, Athelstan," Bodicia said in a half-moan as she leaned against him at the railing, "this is what we have traveled so long to reach? This is where we will rebuild our lives?"

Athelstan shook his head. "No," he said with more confidence in his voice than he felt. "This is simply where we get off the ship. Our new home is waiting for us several hundred miles in-land. The Adelsverein colony is in something called the Hill Country."

Jeremy said, "Judging by what I can see, there are no hills any-where to be found in this Texas!"

"It's a large state. The largest, I believe, of all the United States."

The *Apollo* had eased in beside a long pier built out into the water. The deck passengers were disembarking and walking along the pier toward the shore, carrying all their worldly posses-sions with them.

Athelstan saw numerous tents set up on the sandy ground be-yond the shell beach. He stopped a passing crew member and asked, "Do the people stay in those tents?"

"The ones fortunate enough to get a place do," the man re-plied. "The others live out in the open."

"But I thought they were supposed to be taken to a colony in-land."

"There are only so many wagons and teams available to carry them," the sailor said. "They have to wait their turn. It's not too bad as long as a storm doesn't blow in."

Bodicia clutched Athelstan's arm. "Are we going to be forced to stay here for a long time?"

"I don't know," he told her. Before the sailor could hurry off, Athelstan asked the man, "Can people arrange for their own transportation?"

"I suppose so, if you can find someone willing to take you—and can afford to pay for it."

Jeremy said, "Perhaps we should have gotten off the ship when it stopped in New Orleans or Galveston. At least those are actual cities. Not like this place."

That was true. And yet, if they had stopped at New Orleans or Galveston, there would have been nothing there they could claim as their own. Athelstan had reached an agreement with the German noblemen who had put this venture together. They were to have an estate in the Hill Country. The man Athelstan dealt with in Hamburg had assured him that a settlement was being developed in the area. It sounded like an excellent place to live.

Theobald and Griggs came up behind them, loaded down with bags. "We have your belongings, Master Athelstan," Theobald said. "Should we take them ashore?"

"Yes, that would be good. Jeremy, you and Bodicia go with them. Wait for me at the end of the pier."

"What are you going to do?" Jeremy asked.

Athelstan's face and voice were grim as he replied, "I have to speak to the captain about Perry."

Their brother had been locked up in a tiny storage compartment for several weeks now, living a cramped, almost lightless and airless existence. Athelstan knew his brother well enough to realize that such confinement must have been torture to him.

The situation might not improve any time soon, either. Earlier, Athelstan had seen Ronan, Eamon, and Cathal MacLochlainn leave the ship and go ashore. He had also spotted a man coming aboard who had a metal star of some sort pinned to his vest. Athelstan assumed that was a badge of authority and the man had been summoned by Captain Steinbach to deal with the prisoner.

The mate on the bridge told him that the captain wanted to see him in his cabin. Athelstan knew the way. He was about to knock when the door opened and the man with the badge he had noticed earlier stopped just as he was about to step out.

"Ah, Braxton," Steinbach said from behind the Texan. "I was about to send for you."

Athelstan didn't waste any time getting to the heart of the matter. "What's going to happen to my brother, Captain?" he demanded.

Instead of answering directly, the captain said, "This is Marshal Calhoun."

"Will Calhoun," the Texan introduced himself. He was a tall, lean, leathery man wearing a hat with the biggest brim Athelstan had ever seen. "Marshal of Indian Point."

"Where is Indian Point?" Athelstan asked with a frown.

Calhoun jerked a thumb over his shoulder. "That's the name of the settlement back yonder."

"I thought this was Karlshafen."

"The beach is Karlshafen," Calhoun explained. "When the first few buildin's went up, folks talked about usin' that name for the town, but the area was called Indian Point already, so they decided to use that instead. Anyway, it don't matter. I'm the law around here, and I don't want nothin' to do with no murder that happened whilst the ship was out on the ocean. That's about as far outta my bailiwick as you can get."

"I kept my word, Herr Braxton," Steinbach said. "I tried to turn the matter over to the local authorities. Now I have no choice but to deal with it myself."

"By hanging my brother? You can't do that!" The wheels of Athelstan's brain turned over quickly and desperately. "You can't hold a trial. The MacLochlainns have already left the ship, and any other witnesses probably have, too. There's no way to hear their testimony."

"On the contrary," Steinbach insisted. "The others involved in this matter are only a few hundred meters away, just beyond the beach, and they will be for at least a week. I can send for them, have them brought back aboard temporarily. I have prevailed upon Marshal Calhoun to assist me in that."

Calhoun shrugged and said, "Seems like a reasonable request."

"It's not reasonable," Athelstan said. "My brother is innocent. Just because he said something in anger is not proof that he carried out any threat! No one saw him attack Ceallach MacLochlainn with a knife."

Calhoun rubbed his angular jaw and said, "I don't mean to interfere, Cap'n, but this fella's got a point. Here in Texas, we gen'rally don't like to put a hang rope around a fella's neck unless somebody actually saw him doin' what he's accused of."

Steinbach glared. "No matter what I do, this incident will not sit well with the Adelsverein. But very well. I will speak with Herr Perry Braxton again before I determine how to proceed in the matter."

For the first time, Athelstan saw a glimmer of hope. He could understand how the captain might believe Perry was guilty. But believing something and being able to prove it were very different things. From what he knew of the American legal system, it followed the example of the Magna Carta when it came to an accused man being considered innocent until he was proven guilty.

Perhaps the captain would let Perry go, after all. That wouldn't eliminate the possibility of more trouble from the MacLochlainns—in fact, it would make such a chance more likely—but at least Perry would be alive to defend himself.

"I'll send for your brother and have him brought up to the bridge," Steinbach went on. "Things will be settled there. Will you attend this proceeding, Marshal, as a representative of Texas authority?"

"Sure," Calhoun said. "I ain't any kind of authority except in Indian Point, and even there folks don't always pay me no never mind." A grin creased the weathered face. "But I'm a mite interested to see how this hand plays out."

Perry knew the ship had stopped moving, which meant it had reached its destination and docked. Out there was Texas, which was meant to be the new home of the Braxton family.

But in here was nothing, only the dirty blanket that formed his only bedding when he curled up on the storage compartment's floor. It wasn't big enough for him to stretch out. He had to sleep with his shoulders hunched and his legs drawn up.

A small louvered window was set into the door a little above head height. It let a bit of light and air into the cramped space. Twice a day, the door opened and a sailor handed in some meat, bread, and a flagon of water. He also took the wooden bucket that served for Perry's personal needs and tossed in a replacement.

It was a grindingly terrible way to live, and Perry had endured it for several weeks that seemed more like months.

In that time, he had become thin and weak. His hair was long and curled over his ears. His beard had grown bushy. He must look like a wild man, he thought. Not that he cared. It didn't matter what he looked like when he was soon to be hanged by the neck for a crime he hadn't committed.

If Ceallach MacLochlainn was aware of the fate that awaited Perry, he would be laughing hysterically in hell. Perry was certain of that.

He sat with his back against the wall and his knees drawn up, feeling the ship's gentle rocking as it sat at anchor. Perry wondered if he would set foot on Texas soil before he died. Would he even lay eyes on the place that had drawn his family here? It seemed unlikely.

Sunk in those depths of despair, Perry paid little attention to the footsteps that came along the corridor outside the storage compartment until they stopped just on the other side of the door.

He lifted his shaggy head as the latch rattled. When the door opened, the light that spilled in, even from the dimly lit corridor, was enough to make him wince.

"C'mon out, Braxton. The captain wants you up on the bridge."

Perry lifted a trembling hand and shaded his eyes. His vision adjusted fairly quickly. He made out the shapes of two sailors standing in the corridor.

"Are we in Texas?" His voice rasped from disuse as he asked the question.

"*Ja*, we have docked at Karlshafen," one of the sailors said. "Come along. The captain does not like to be kept waiting."

"You'll have to help me," Perry grated. "I haven't stood up for so long—"

Making an impatient sound in his throat, one of the men reached into the compartment, took hold of Perry's shoulders, and jerked him to his feet.

For one half-crazed instant, Perry considered attacking them and trying to escape. He discarded the idea almost immediately. He was too stiff and weak to overwhelm two burly sailors. If he tried, they would beat him into insensibility and drag him to the captain anyway.

But if he saw even the slimmest chance to escape, he would seize it, he vowed, as they pushed him along the corridor toward the steps at the end.

Even if he wound up losing his life in the attempt, that would be better than simply standing there and doing nothing while a sentence of death was pronounced on him.

Why wait for doom when you could at least strike back against it before the inevitable end?

Chapter 19

Athelstan, Captain Steinbach, and Marshal Calhoun left the captain's quarters, emerged onto the deck, and went up the short flight of steps to the bridge.

From there, Athelstan saw that all the deck passengers had left the ship and were scattered along the sandy ground behind the beach. The passengers who had been able to afford cabins had gone ashore, too, leaving the long dock empty except for a few sailors engaged in various tasks.

Athelstan looked along the dock to the point where it reached land. He spotted Jeremy, Bodicia, Theobald, and Griggs waiting there. Jeremy had a hand lifted to his eyes, shading them as he peered back at the ship. With any luck, Athelstan would be joining them soon, and Perry would be with him.

Once the family was reunited, they could see about finding some way to start for the Hill Country without waiting for one of the Adelsverein wagon trains.

But that would come about only if the captain was reasonable and released Perry.

As the three men waited on the bridge, Marshal Calhoun thumbed his big hat back on his head and asked, "Do you truly believe your brother's innocent, Mr. Braxton? You don't figure he killed that MacLochlainn fella?"

"I believe in Perry's innocence with all my heart," Athelstan said.

Calhoun tugged on his earlobe and frowned. "I reckon your heart feels that way 'cause he's your brother. I wouldn't expect nothin' less from a fella. But what does your brain say about the whole deal?"

The marshal seemed genuinely interested in Athelstan's opinion. He considered for a moment and then replied, "It's true that if you consider the bad feelings between Perry and Ceallach MacLochlainn, as well as the time that MacLochlainn was killed and the fact that Perry's whereabouts are unaccounted for at the time, I suppose it's a reasonable conclusion that he had something to do with MacLochlainn's death."

"You see?" Steinbach said. "This is what I have been saying all along. With those circumstances, I had no choice but to lock up Herr Braxton."

"More than likely, I'd have done the same thing in your place, Cap'n," Calhoun agreed. "But like Mr. Braxton here pointed out, and you just used the word circumstances yourself, that ain't exactly proof. If it was up to me—which it ain't, again, 'cause it didn't happen in Indian Point—I'd be leanin' toward lettin' the fella go."

Steinbach scowled, clearly not liking the way this conversation was going. To his stern way of thinking, Athelstan realized, he would rather hang Perry on the chance that he was guilty than release him on the chance that he was innocent.

Something else occurred to Athelstan. He asked Calhoun, "Is there any other law in this region? Some authority that might take an interest in the case?"

"Well, there's the Texas Rangers. They're law, of a sort, and their jurisdiction is the whole blasted state. But that don't extend out into the ocean, and they're more Indian fighters than lawmen, to be honest."

"I will adjudicate this matter," Steinbach said. "There is no other choice."

Athelstan nodded. He would plead Perry's case and appeal to the captain's sense of reason. And to his sense of mercy, if it came to that.

And what would he do if Steinbach decided against Perry and tried to mete out the harshest possible justice?

Athelstan didn't know the answer to that question, but he knew he could not simply stand by without doing anything and see his brother hanged for a crime he hadn't committed. He would not allow that.

His eyes went to the pistol that Calhoun carried in a holster at his waist. It was unlike any such weapon Athelstan had seen before, but he was sure he could figure out how to use it. It had a hammer, and there was bound to be a trigger to pull somewhere on it. The gun was in reach, and Calhoun wasn't trying to protect it. Athelstan believed he could get his hands on it and pull it from the holster before Calhoun or anyone else could stop him—

He stiffened as Perry emerged from the stairs leading below-decks, followed closely by two sailors. Athelstan caught his breath as he saw how Perry was stumbling along, evidently so weak that he could barely stay on his feet.

But he *was* on his feet, walking by himself. Whatever his fate might be, he was heading toward it on his own. No one had to drag him to it. Athelstan felt a surge of pride in his brother. Perry might be reckless and hot-tempered at times, but no one could say that he lacked courage and resolve.

Perry must have felt his brother's gaze on him. He raised his head and looked up onto the bridge where Athelstan waited with Captain Steinbach and Marshal Calhoun. Perry hadn't seen Calhoun before and wouldn't know who the marshal was, but probably he could figure out that the man was some sort of authority figure.

He might have even mistaken Calhoun for the hangman.

At that moment, as Perry raised his eyes to the bridge, something changed. Athelstan saw Perry straighten from his shambling attitude. Perry's back stiffened, his head lifted higher, his bushy-bearded jaw jutted out in defiance. Anger blazed in his eyes.

He believed he was going to his death.

Athelstan opened his mouth to shout at Perry and tell him to wait before he did something foolish. He didn't have time to get the words out before Perry summoned up strength from somewhere in his abused body and whirled around. One of the sailors exclaimed angrily and made a grab for him, but Perry rammed a shoulder into the man's chest and knocked him back. The sailor stumbled into his companion's path, and both of them tangled their legs and sprawled on the deck.

That opened a path between Perry and the railing along the port side of the *Apollo*—the side away from the dock and toward the open waters of the bay. Perry dashed toward the rail with surprising speed despite the awkward hitch in his gait. After the ordeal of being locked up for so long in such cramped quarters, it was a miracle that his muscles worked as well as they did.

Both sailors scrambled to their feet and lunged after him. Other members of the crew heard the commotion and came running to help, but they were too far away to stop him. Perry's arms and legs weren't tied; that was an oversight on the part of his captors. He was free to run for his life.

Up on the bridge, Marshal Calhoun blurted out, "Look at that boy go!"

"Perry, no!" Athelstan cried, but if Perry heard his brother's plea, he gave no sign of it. He certainly didn't slow down. When he reached the railing, there was no graceful leap and dive on his part. He clambered onto the railing and fell off the other side of it as the closest sailor tried to grab him but barely missed.

Athelstan rushed to the side of the bridge and leaned over the railing there in time to see Perry plummet toward the water, arms and legs waving, an involuntary yell floating up from him as he fell.

Perry hit the water with a splash and went under. Athelstan gripped the railing tightly and watched to see if he was going to come up. He was about to yank off his coat and boots and dive in himself when Perry's head broke the surface.

He started swimming away from the shore, out to sea.

Marshal Calhoun drew his pistol from its holster. He raised the long-barreled gun and eared back the hammer, which caused the recessed trigger to drop into position.

Instead of aiming and firing, Calhoun kept the pistol's barrel pointed skyward for a long moment before shaking his head and saying, "Nope. Ain't gonna do it. Fella ain't been found guilty of nothin', and I ain't gonna shoot him."

He lowered the gun and carefully let down the hammer before sliding it back into its holster.

The two sailors who had had charge of Perry ran to the bottom of the steps leading to the bridge. One of them yelled, "Captain, should we lower a boat and go after him?"

Athelstan waited tensely to hear what Steinbach was going to say. Finally, the captain shook his head and called to his men, "*Nein*. As the marshal says, Herr Braxton has not been found guilty, and he is no longer on my vessel, nor is he a member of my crew." Steinbach's brawny shoulders rose and fell. "Unsatisfactory though the outcome may be, my responsibility has been discharged."

"Thank you, Captain," Athelstan said with relief in his voice.

Slowly and solemnly, Steinbach shook his head. "Do not thank me, Herr Braxton. Your brother has escaped one fate only to embrace another." He nodded toward the figure struggling through the water in the distance. "Undertows are common in these waters, and I fear that one has him in its grip now."

Athelstan's eyes widened in horror as he stared out over the bay. He could tell now that Perry was struggling to stay afloat. His head went under, popped up, went under again.

"No!" Athelstan cried. "Someone help him!"

"I am sorry, but no one can reach him in time, Herr Braxton. The best we can do is recover his body when the tide carries it back in, if it does. There are sharks in this bay, and they may take him."

Athelstan's hands clamped harder on the railing as he hung his head. He couldn't bear to look again, and when he finally forced himself to do so, he saw no sign of Perry. Nothing moved on the gentle, endlessly rolling waves of the bay.

"Well, hell," Marshal Calhoun said softly. "That is just too bad. I'm sure sorry, Mr. Braxton. But I reckon your brother figured he'd rather go out tryin' to escape than let hisself get strung up."

"He didn't kill Ceallach MacLochlainn," Athelstan said. "I'll never believe that he did."

"And it is your right to believe so," Captain Steinbach said. "However, it appears that the issue will never be settled. Perhaps your brother's loss will be sufficient for the other MacLochlainn brothers to set aside their anger."

Athelstan didn't believe that for a second. Even though he didn't know that much about them, the MacLochlainns didn't seem the type to forgive and forget. More trouble from them might well lurk in the future.

But he would have to worry about that later, Athelstan told himself.

Right now, his chief concern was figuring out a way to tell Jeremy and Bodicia that their brother was dead.

Senselessly, needlessly dead.

Chapter 20

Almost numb with shock, Athelstan trudged along the dock toward the shore. His brother and sister saw him coming and hurried out to meet him.

"Where's Perry?" Jeremy asked.

"Is the captain going to release him?" Bodicia added.

From where they were, they hadn't been able to see what happened on the ship. Wordlessly, Athelstan motioned for them to return to the spot on shore where they had been waiting with Theobald and young Griggs.

"What is this?" Jeremy demanded. "Is the captain still determined to put Perry on trial?"

"There will be no trial," Athelstan replied, shaking his head. "Perry escaped from custody."

"Escaped!" Bodicia repeated. "Then where is he?"

"He leaped over the side of the ship and swam out into the bay." Athelstan had to swallow before he could go on. "An undertow caught him and pulled him down."

Bodicia's hand went to her open mouth. Jeremy breathed harder as he stared at his brother.

"Where is he?" Jeremy asked again.

"Gone."

"You mean he drowned?"

"He must have," Athelstan said. "He went under the water

several times and, finally, he never came back up." He paused, then added, "Captain Steinbach said that sharks are commonly found in this bay. It is—unlikely—that his body will ever be recovered."

Bodicia put both hands over her face and sobbed. Jeremy looked out over the bay as if searching for some sign of his lost brother, but there was nothing to be seen other than the endless gently lapping blue-green waves.

Griggs eased up to the siblings, took his cap off, and said to Athelstan, "Theobald and I couldn't help overhearing, Master Athelstan. We're so sorry. I—I can't believe Master Perry is gone. . . ."

"Neither can I, lad," Athelstan said. He squeezed the boy's shoulder.

Jeremy let out a long sigh and turned away from the water. "What are we going to do now?"

"Do?" Bodicia said. "What can we do? Perry is *dead*!"

"And we're on the other side of the world from our home, in a place that's nothing but a desolate wasteland!" Jeremy flung a hand toward the treeless prairie rolling inland. "I don't know why we ever thought we could make a new life for ourselves in this—this Texas!"

"Not all of Texas is like this," Athelstan said. He knew he ought to tamp down the anger Jeremy had roused in him, but he was so shaken by Perry's sudden and shocking fate that he couldn't restrain himself. "And your behavior is probably the biggest reason we're here, remember? Your inability to control your gambling placed our sister's life in danger."

Jeremy turned on him, face darkening in fury. "It was Perry and his hot temper that made the grand duke turn on us."

"I would have been able to deal with Alistair, sooner or later—"

"You don't know that. But if you had just paid off LeCarde, none of this would have happened. We would never have been on that ship, and Perry wouldn't have had trouble with Ceallach MacLochlainn."

"LeCarde tried to kidnap your sister, and men died," Athelstan said. "There was no paying off that debt, and again, it was your gambling that caused—"

"Stop it, both of you!" Bodicia cried. "Just stop it! Perry's dead, and we're marooned here. It doesn't matter whose fault it is."

She began to sob again.

Theobald took off his hat and edged forward. "Master Athelstan, I beg your pardon, but perhaps Griggs and I should take the bags and carry them into that settlement. I heard some of the other travelers saying that they were going to inquire about renting rooms, and we will need a place to stay."

Athelstan looked toward the cluster of crude buildings. Indian Point, Marshal Calhoun had called it. Theobald, practical as ever, was correct, of course. They needed a place to stay.

"Very well," he said. "We'll all go." He glanced at the ship riding at anchor. "There's no reason for us to remain here."

He slipped an arm around Bodicia's shoulders and turned her toward the path that led to Indian Point. The servants picked up all the bags except for two, which Jeremy took with ill grace. Athelstan and Bodicia led the way toward the settlement. She was still sniffling, but she had brought her tears of grief under control for the most part.

Athelstan knew his sister quite well. Bodicia was too stubborn to allow sorrow to overwhelm her. All the Braxtons had a strong practical streak running through them. It might even be called fatalism.

He had a hunch they might need that in order to survive in this place.

Athelstan hoped to find an inn or a hotel where they could stay, but he was doomed to disappointment. The closest Indian Point had to such accommodations were two ramshackle boarding-houses, both of which displayed signs indicating that no rooms were available.

"Where are we going to sleep?" Jeremy asked. "Should we go back to the beach and try to claim one of those tents, or perhaps erect a temporary shelter?"

Athelstan felt certain all the tents were spoken for already, and he wasn't sure what they would use to build a shelter since, evidently, there were no trees to be found in this region. They might be able to weave something out of the brush, but it wouldn't provide much shelter.

Besides, the last he had seen of the three MacLochlainn brothers, they were loitering on the sandy ground adjacent to the beach, and being around them would be likely to cause more trouble.

He was trying to figure out how to respond to Jeremy's question when he spotted a rangy, familiar figure walking along the other side of the dirt street.

"Stay here," he told his companions. "I'll see if the marshal has any suggestions."

Marshal Will Calhoun paused and nodded in recognition as Athelstan intercepted him. "Howdy, Mr. Braxton," he said. "If you figure on askin' me about your brother, I'm afraid I don't have any news for you."

"Captain Steinbach made it clear there was a very good chance Perry's body would never be recovered."

Calhoun nodded solemnly. "What the sea takes, it sometimes don't want to give up." He changed the subject by asking, "Have you and your folks found a place to stay yet?"

"No," Athelstan replied with a shake of his head. "I was hoping you might be able to suggest a place for us."

Calhoun rubbed his chin and frowned in thought before saying, "I know the boardin'houses are all full up. Sometimes you can rent the rooms in the back of the Ace-High and Top-Notch Saloons, but with a new batch o' immigrants in town, the gals who work there are gonna be puttin' those rooms to use, if you know what I mean."

Athelstan nodded and said, "Yes, I can make a reasonable guess, Marshal."

Calhoun held up a finger. "But I got an idea, if you ain't too particular about where you sleep."

"Under the circumstances, I don't believe we can worry too much about propriety, although I do draw the line at sharing quarters with the, ah, ladies from the taverns you mentioned."

"How do you feel about horses?"

Athelstan frowned in confusion.

"If you go on along the street here, you'll come to the livery stable. Patterson, the fella who runs it, is a good hombre. If you tell him about your problem, I reckon there's at least a chance he'd make a deal to let you sleep in his hayloft."

"Sleep in a barn, you mean?"

"Well, it's outta the weather, and the smell ain't too bad once you get used to it. I know it ain't anything like what you're accustomed to, back where you come from, but that's a long ways off."

"The other side of the world," Athelstan mused, repeating what Jeremy had said earlier.

"Yep. If you want to give it a try, I'll come along with you and vouch for you to Patterson."

"You don't even know us," Athelstan pointed out.

"Oh, I can size folks up pretty quick-like," Calhoun said with a casual wave of his hand. "Have to be able to do that out here on the frontier. Sometimes you have to make up your mind about folks in a hurry. I think you and your family are all right. You'll do to ride the river with."

"I never heard that expression before," Athelstan said, still frowning. "But it sounds like a good thing."

"It is. Come on. Let's go see if we can get you and your family squared away."

*   *   *

The stocky, red-bearded proprietor of the stable was willing to let the Braxtons and the two servants spend the night in the loft. He even refused to take any payment for the accommodation.

"Can't make a habit of stayin' here, though," he said. "I don't want folks gettin' the idea this is a hotel for people instead of horses."

"If we can stay for a night or two," Athelstan said, "we'll try to make other arrangements."

Patterson nodded. "Sounds good. We'll see what happens."

Theobald and Griggs hadn't taken the bags up the ladder to the loft yet. Before they could do so, a tall, thick-bodied man pushed past them into the livery barn.

"Dick!" he said in a booming voice. "Dick, I have to talk to you. I have troubles. Bad troubles."

Patterson turned to the newcomer and said, "What's wrong, Mr. Deutschendorf?"

"Gabe Hobbs is an idiot, that's what's wrong." The man didn't seem capable of speaking in less than a bellow. "He got in a fight in the Top-Notch just now, and of course Nick Larson had to join in to help him. I cannot fault a man for taking up for his friend, but now both of them are hurt and cannot drive my wagons!"

Deutschendorf yanked his wide-brimmed hat off his head and used his other hand to paw at the tangle of gray hair atop his balding dome. A shaggy, salt-and-pepper mustache hung over his wide mouth.

"And those wagons are full of supplies bound for my trading post on Baron's Creek!"

Athelstan glanced at Jeremy, who looked annoyed at the interruption, and Bodicia, whose face was still pale and strained with grief. Then he stepped over to the newcomer and said, "I beg your pardon, sir. Did you just mention Baron's Creek?"

Deutschendorf frowned at him. "*Ja*, you are familiar with it?"

"I know the name, but that's all," Athelstan said.

"You sound like an Englishman," Deutschendorf said with an accusatory note in his voice.

"Not exactly. My family and I are from the Grand Duchy of Alpenstone."

The man's face lit up with recognition. "I have heard of Alpenstone, of course," he said, "but I have never been there. How in the world did you wind up here in Texas?"

"That's a good question," Athelstan allowed, "and a long story. But we're here now, and before we set sail from Hamburg, I made arrangements with the Adelsverein to claim a parcel of land west of Baron's Creek and north of its confluence with the . . . Pedernales River."

He pronounced the name of the river as it was spelled, which caused Deutschendorf to tip his head back and let out a booming laugh.

"These Texians, they cannot say some words the way you think they would. The river you speak of, it is called the Purr-duh-Nal-iss. Do not ask me why."

"And the people here are called Texians?"

Patterson answered Athelstan's question. "Those of us who came here with Stephen Austin, back when it was still part of Mexico, called ourselves Texicans. After we fought ol' Santa Anna and whipped his, uh, *behind*, and became our own country, we changed that to Texians. Didn't see any need to remind folks we used to be part of Mexico." He scratched his head. "Now that we're part of the United States, the name's liable to change again. I've heard some folks say Texans."

"I am a Texan now," Deutschendorf declared, "but you can call me whatever you wish. As long as you do not call me late to the dinner table, *ja!*"

That prompted more boisterous laughter from the man, but he quickly grew serious again as he turned back to Patterson.

"What am I going to do, Dick? I must get those supplies to the trading post. With Gabe and Nick laid up and unable to drive for a week or more, I cannot afford to wait. And one man cannot drive three wagons!"

Athelstan felt someone looking at him and glanced over to see Theobald regarding him intently. He could tell right away what the old man was thinking. The same thing had occurred already to Athelstan. He nodded to Theobald, who stepped forward and cleared his throat.

"Begging your pardon, Herr Deutschendorf," he said, "but I can handle a wagon team. There has never been a team of horses put together that I cannot handle!"

"I use mules to pull my wagons," Deutschendorf said.

Theobald shrugged. "Mules, horses, it makes no difference to me."

Deutschendorf asked, "Who are you?"

"My name is Theobald, *mein Herr*. I work for these gentlemen and this lady."

"Then you already have a job, *ja*?"

Athelstan said, "I can handle a team as well, sir, and so can my brother. If you're bound for Baron's Creek, we would be happy to help you get there, in return for the privilege of your company."

"You are some of the Adelsverein's immigrants," Deutschendorf said, nodding in understanding. "John Meusebach has made arrangements with the Torrey brothers to transport the newcomers in their wagons. A group of such wagons should be on the way back from their most recent journey by now and will arrive in a week, perhaps two."

"We'd rather not wait. Honestly, it seems like destiny has brought us together, sir. We need transportation, and you need drivers."

Deutschendorf thought it over for a moment and then nodded. "What you say is true," he admitted. "I must get that merchandise to Friedrichsburg if I am to sell it."

"Friedrichsburg is the name of the settlement up there?"

"To call it a settlement is an exaggeration. At the moment, there is my trading post, another store, and a blacksmith shop.

But it will grow rapidly, my friends, I can assure you of that. With good people and such wonderful country, it cannot do anything else!"

"Wonderful country?" Jeremy repeated. "It must not be anything like this around here!"

Deutschendorf's face and voice were solemn as he nodded and said, "You are absolutely correct, young man. I can promise you, the Hill Country is nothing like this!"

Chapter 21

Emil Deutschendorf's wagons had been loaded with crates, bags, and barrels unloaded from the cargo hold of the *Apollo*, which was a trading ship as well as conveyance for immigrants from Europe.

The three large wagons, with canvas tied over the mounds of supplies in the back, were brought from the dock to the wagon yard next to Patterson's Livery Stable. Deutschendorf handled the lead wagon. Athelstan and Theobald drove the other two vehicles, which gave them the chance to demonstrate that they were up to the task.

Theobald had no trouble with the mule team hitched to the second wagon. He used the whip and shouted at them in German, and the large, bulky beasts responded as if they understood every word.

Athelstan had more difficulty with his team. Despite the confidence he had displayed in talking to Deutschendorf, he had never driven mules before. In truth, the most he had done was to drive a two-horse buggy team. The same was true of Jeremy. When Athelstan volunteered for this task, he had assumed they could learn as they went along. He'd never had any trouble picking up skills before.

He had never dealt with such stubborn creatures as these mules, though, and the third wagon, with him at the reins, lagged well behind the other two on the short journey to the wagon yard. Despite that, he got there and tried not to pay too much attention to the skeptical look Deutschendorf gave him. He would do better next time, Athelstan vowed to himself.

The best thing about the experience was that he hadn't caught any sight of the MacLochlainn brothers on the beach when he and Theobald went to the dock with Deutschendorf to retrieve the wagons. Maybe the Irishmen had moved on somewhere.

If he never laid eyes on them again, Athelstan thought, that would be just fine with him.

Deutschendorf planned to leave with the wagons at first light the next morning. Between their grief over Perry's tragic and senseless death, the anticipation of their departure for their new home, and the sheer discomfort of trying to sleep in a hayloft, none of the Braxtons got much rest that night.

But because of that restlessness, they were up and ready to go well before dawn. Patterson, who lived in a cabin behind the barn, shared his breakfast of coffee, bacon, and biscuits with them.

Although it was a far cry from the excellent cuisine they enjoyed back in Alpenstone, Athelstan realized to his surprise that it was one of the best meals he'd ever had.

He and Jeremy and Theobald were waiting next to the wagons when Deutschendorf walked up trailed by three men carrying rifles. Bodicia and Griggs were inside the barn, gathering their belongings.

Deutschendorf nodded to his companions and introduced them as Bob Poole and the Shellabarger brothers, John and Ralph.

"They have farms on the creek north of the settlement," Deutschendorf explained, "and they come with me when I make these trips to pick up supplies. They act as guards."

"Why do you need guards?" Jeremy asked. "Do the Indians we're heard about cause trouble for you?"

Deutschendorf laughed. "One thing Texas has plenty of is trouble! There are outlaw gangs roaming the land, and there is no way of knowing when the Comanche will swoop down on one of their raids. They never come as far as the coast, but one of these days it could happen. They definitely consider the area northwest of San Antonio to be their territory, and we are interlopers."

Athelstan thought back to maps he had studied before setting out on this journey. "Isn't the area northwest of San Antonio exactly where we're going?"

Deutschendorf bumped a fist against his shoulder, grinned, and said, "Now you understand why we have guards!"

Athelstan and Jeremy exchanged worried frowns. Maybe it wasn't a good idea taking their sister into such an untamed region.

On the other hand, where else could they go? This area along the coast offered them nothing, and they would never be comfortable in such a flat, treeless part of the country. It was just too different from their homeland.

Deutschendorf grew serious again and asked, "Do you have any weapons? I should have inquired about that before."

"We have several pistols, as well as powder and shot. Our rifles were left behind in Alpenstone. But we also have three sabers."

One of those sabers had belonged to Perry. The thought of that made another pang of loss go through Athelstan.

"Load the pistols before we depart, and keep them handy," Deutschendorf advised. "We have a plentiful supply of powder and shot. Keep those sabers close at hand, as well. You can never tell when a good sharp blade will come in handy. Among these goods, I have some fine knives in the style made popular by Herr James Bowie. You gentlemen will each want one of those. Perhaps some of Herr Samuel Colt's revolving pistols, as well."

"Is that what the marshal carries? A revolving pistol? I saw his gun but didn't get a close look at it."

Deutschendorf nodded. "*Ja*, Marshal Calhoun is known to be a crack shot with a Colt revolver. It is a fine weapon. A few flaws to be worked out yet, perhaps, but still a huge advantage in the fight against the Indians."

Despite all the emotions still roiling inside him, Athelstan found himself intrigued by the idea of the revolving pistols. If Deutschendorf had any of them in his loads of merchandise, perhaps they would have a chance to try out the weapons during the journey.

If they ran into any trouble, that opportunity would almost certainly happen.

Theobald went into the barn to help Griggs carry out the family's belongings. They placed the bags in the middle wagon. Theobald and Griggs climbed onto the driver's seat of that wagon while Athelstan helped Bodicia get into the back and made a place for her to sit among the cargo. Then he and Jeremy took their seats on the third wagon.

Bob Poole and the Shellabarger brothers were mounted on saddle horses. The brothers would ride on the flanks while Poole, who had been a Texas Ranger before settling in the Hill Country, took the lead and scouted a short distance ahead of the wagon train.

Before riding out to his position, Poole halted his horse beside the third wagon and said to Athelstan and Jeremy, "You boys keep an eye on our back trail. I'd like to have a fella back there bringin' up the rear, but we don't. So it'll be up to you to let the rest of us know if you spot anybody tryin' to sneak up on us."

"Of course," Athelstan said with a nod. "Our pistols are loaded, and if we should come under attack, we'll be ready to mount a defense."

"Fair enough," Poole said. "Just don't go to sleep on the job."

He nudged his horse into motion and loped toward the front of the group.

"Don't go to sleep on the job," Jeremy repeated in an annoyed voice. "What does he think we are?"

"Men who have never little experience of being attacked by hostile Indians or ruthless brigands," Athelstan said. "And that is exactly who we are."

Jeremy shrugged and looked sullen. Athelstan knew he would

have to keep an eye on his brother during this journey, along with everything else.

A few minutes later, Emil Deutschendorf took off his wide-brimmed hat, waved it over his head and swept it forward, and bellowed, *"Hooooo!"*

One after the other, the wagons lurched into motion. They rolled slowly out of Indian Point on a narrow trail that led inland. Up ahead, the trail entered the brush and formed a corridor through the dusty vegetation. Athelstan thought the opening looked rather forbidding.

This close to the settlement, there was no point in watching behind them, so Athelstan didn't remind Jeremy to do that. As Deutschendorf had said, the Comanche Indians didn't raid this far south.

But as Deutschendorf also had implied, there was no way to predict exactly what the Indians might do. Athelstan's nerves were taut already, and he suspected they might well stay that way for the entire journey.

At least, thankfully, the mules were cooperative and plodded along steadily behind the other wagons. The scattered buildings of Indian Point fell behind the travelers.

And because none of them were looking back, they didn't see the haggard, bearded, tangle-haired figure who peered after them from around the corner of one of the shacks. He watched them until the third and final wagon had disappeared along the trail that twisted into the brush.

Then Perry Braxton crawled back behind the stack of crates and other trash where he had hidden all night. He would have to remain there until darkness fell again so that he could avoid being captured and turned over to the law.

Then he would take up the trail of his brothers and sister and not stop until they were reunited.

Chapter 22

By the end of the day, the wooden driver's seat of the third wagon felt like a torture chamber to Athelstan. The trail was rough and rutted, and the vehicle had bounced and rocked until it felt as if every bone and muscle in his body ached—especially those in his backside.

Jeremy was just as sore and uncomfortable, and he made sure that anyone who came within earshot heard about it at length. His unending complaints drove Athelstan almost to the point of distraction.

To make matters worse, the journey was not only physically uncomfortable, it was also incredibly boring. The featureless plain stretched inland from the coast for mile after mile of flat, scrub-covered landscape. Athelstan saw a few clumps of short, twisted oak trees. During one of the stops they made to rest the mule teams, he asked Emil Deutschendorf why the trees were so gnarled.

"It is the wind blowing off the gulf that does it," Deutschen-dorf explained. "The wind almost never stops blowing, so as the trees grow, they have it pushing on them all the time. It makes them lean inland and keeps them from attaining any real height."

That made sense to Athelstan. It also made him miss the tall, stately evergreens that covered the slopes of Alpenstone.

Late in the day, they stopped to make camp on the bank of a

shallow creek. When Athelstan helped Bodicia down from the wagon and asked her how she was doing, she gave him a wan smile.

Instead of answering his question directly, she said, "How many days of traveling like this will it take to reach our destination, Athelstan?"

"Not days," he told her with a weary smile. "At least a week, but probably more, according to Mr. Deutschendorf. Possibly a little longer than that."

"Two weeks of this will feel like a year," she murmured. "There is nothing to see!"

"It will get better," Athelstan assured her. "There will be a few settlements along the way, and the landscape will be more pleasing the farther inland we get."

He hoped that turned out to be true.

Over the next two days, the terrain did acquire a more rolling quality, although Athelstan wouldn't have referred to any of the countryside as hilly. Farther inland, the trees grew a bit taller and straighter, too, and the wagons crossed some broad grassy meadows instead of having to follow narrow, winding trails through thick brush. While it was a far cry from Alpenstone, it was an improvement over the coastal plain.

They forded a good-sized stream that Ralph Shellabarger identified to Athelstan and Jeremy as Coleto Creek. He also told them that twenty miles or so upstream was where the Mexican dictator Santa Anna had had a large group of Texas prisoners massacred during the revolution.

"Wasn't far from the town of Goliad where that happened," Ralph said. "So, to this day, you sometimes hear folks say, 'Remember Goliad' or 'Remember the Alamo.' I was in Sam Houston's bunch, and that's what we was all yellin' the day we caught Santa Anna and the rest of the Mexican army sleepin' at San Jacinto. Sure, we whipped 'em good and won independence for Texas, but scores like that won't never be settled, no matter how many battles you win."

A short time after crossing the creek, they forded a wider

stream that Ralph informed them was the Guadalupe River. The stream bed was wide and sandy, and broken up by brushy sandbars. Bob Poole rode ahead to find the safest route and avoid areas where the wagons might bog down. The river itself flowed in several channels and was fairly shallow, slow-moving, and tinged with green.

Beyond the Guadalupe, they came to the town of Victoria. It was a large settlement, especially compared to Indian Point and the few meager collections of cabins they had passed since leaving the coast.

Victoria boasted quite a few solid, impressive-looking buildings, some even made of brick, and a population numbering in the hundreds. Even though a few hours of sunlight still remained, they would stop for the rest of the day and the night to give the livestock a little extra rest, Deutschendorf declared.

As they brought up the rear of the little caravan, Athelstan glanced over at Jeremy and then looked again as he realized that his brother was staring at something. Following Jeremy's rapt gaze, Athelstan took note of a low log building with a crudely painted sign nailed above its entrance announcing that it was the Matagorda Saloon.

"What are you doing, Jeremy?" Athelstan asked.

"Just taking in the sights," Jeremy replied, his tone casual.

"That's not all, and you know it." Athelstan's voice was sharp now. "You're looking at that tavern and thinking how much you'd like a drink and perhaps a few hands of cards."

Turning a glare toward his brother, Jeremy said, "Do you know how long it's been since I passed any time in any sort of enjoyable fashion?"

"The same length of time it has been for the rest of us. We're stopping here in Victoria to rest the mules and horses, not to drink and gamble."

"I didn't say I was actually going to do anything," Jeremy said sullenly. "You can't blame me for wishing that I could, though."

"Just put the thought out of your mind. We'll all be better off."

Jeremy muttered under his breath but didn't say anything that Athelstan could make out.

When they were on the northern edge of the settlement, Deutschendorf piloted the lead wagon into the shade of some trees beside the trail. The others followed and brought their vehicles to a stop behind Deutschendorf's.

"I've stopped here before," Deutschendorf explained as they climbed down from the wagons. "It's a good place to camp. There's plenty of grass for the animals and it's a comfortable spot. Let's get them unhitched and picketed. And right here by the trail like this," he added, with a smile, "if anyone comes along with news, we can get it first!"

Bodicia insisted on helping tend to the horses and mules. She always wanted to do her share of the work, and Athelstan knew it was a waste of time to argue with her. She heaved a sigh of relief, though, when they were finished and she sat down under one of the trees.

He lowered himself to the ground beside her and asked, "How are you holding up?"

"Thinking about Perry's death isn't such a sharp pain now. It's more of a dull ache." A look of dismay crossed her face as she thought about what she'd said. "Oh, Athelstan, it's terrible of me that I'm getting over it so quickly!"

He shook his head. "It's not terrible at all. It's simply a matter of human nature. We'll always miss Perry, but at the same time, we have no choice but to look ahead. This Texas is a hard land, and it requires our full attention and effort if we're going to survive in it."

Athelstan paused for a moment and then went on in an emphatic voice, "No, not just survive. We are going to thrive here in Texas, Bodicia. I will admit that I was unsure when we first arrived, but the farther we go toward our destination, the more convinced I am that this is where we are meant to be!"

"You can't possibly mean that."

"I do," he insisted. "You can see for yourself how much better the land is. Texas is made for growing crops and raising livestock. And where we are going in the Hill Country will be even better. I'm sure of it."

"I'm glad you're optimistic, Athelstan," Bodicia said with a tired smile. "I'm trying to be. But it's difficult."

"Most things are, if they're worthwhile."

She scoffed. "That's just an old saying."

"Perhaps. But I believe there's some truth in it."

"I hope so."

They sat quietly after that. Jeremy joined them. A few yards away, the Shellabarger brothers stretched out under a tree and went to sleep. Deutschendorf sat down as well and took a small book and a stub of pencil from a pocket inside his coat. He scribbled and figured in the book while Bob Poole smoked a pipe and kept an eye on the trail.

After a while, Poole came over and said to Deutschendorf, "Rider comin' on the Bexar road, Emil. Looks like it might be Tye Salem."

Deutschendorf put his book and pencil away and climbed to his feet. "Herr Salem ranges over most of the country between here and the Pedernales. Perhaps he can inform us of conditions along the way."

The two men walked out into the trail to meet the approaching rider. Athelstan was curious and might have joined them, but he wasn't sure if he would be welcome. Also, he was a stranger, and the newcomer might be reluctant to talk in the presence of someone he didn't know.

Some Texans, Athelstan had discovered, were very talkative, like Deutschendorf, but many of them displayed a tendency toward being tight-lipped.

Deutschendorf raised a hand in greeting as the man on horseback rode up to them and reined in. The lowering sun was behind the rider, casting his face into shadow. Athelstan couldn't tell much about him except that he was broad-shouldered, wore high boots, canvas trousers, a shirt made of some sort of animal hide, and a flat-crowned brown hat with a wide brim.

He also carried two of the revolving pistols in holsters attached to the belt around his waist, and another pair of the weapons rode in sheaths strapped to the saddle. A rifle hung from a sling on the saddle as well. This man, whoever he was, was very well armed.

If he rode alone through the wilds of Texas, he probably needed to be.

Deutschendorf, Poole, and the stranger spoke for several minutes in what appeared to a friendly fashion. The stranger turned slightly in his saddle and gestured toward the northwest, the way he had come from. Athelstan knew that San Antonio de Bexar, the largest city in the region, lay in that direction. They would pass through it on their way to the Hill Country.

After a few more minutes, Deutschendorf and Poole stepped back, and the stranger nudged his horse into motion again, lifting a hand in farewell as they parted. He rode past the trees where the Braxtons were resting, and even though Athelstan still couldn't see his face well, he could tell that the man cast a look in their direction. He was probably as curious about them as Athelstan was about him.

He wasn't the only one taking an interest in the stranger. Bodicia said quietly, "What a dangerous-looking man. Did you see how many guns he carries, Athelstan?"

"He probably needs them to shoot wild Indians," Jeremy said before Athelstan could answer.

Athelstan left that conversation where it was and got to his feet as Deutschendorf and Poole walked over to the trees. He thought both men looked more worried than they had earlier, and that made Athelstan concerned, too. He said, "Were you able to learn anything from that man?"

"*Ja*, it was Tye Salem, just as we thought. Herr Salem is a hunter and a scout. He has worked guiding immigrant parties in the past and also accompanied military surveying parties. He knows the trail between here and where we are going as well as any man alive, I would say, and the area beyond the Hill Country, as well."

"That's Indian country, isn't it?"

Poole said, "Salem's spent time with the Comanche. I wouldn't exactly say that he lived with 'em, but he's been around them a lot more than most white men." He turned his head and spat. "Wouldn't surprise me if he used to have squaws in some of those villages."

Athelstan frowned. He didn't want his sister hearing crude talk like that.

Before he could say anything, though, Deutschendorf said, "There's no need to go into that, Bob. What's important is that Herr Salem knows the Comanche and their ways, even if he is no longer their friend."

"What happened?" Athelstan asked. "Why isn't he their friend anymore?"

"Several years ago, a group of Comanche chiefs came into Bexar for peace talks with the Texans. Herr Salem was one of the men who convinced them to do so, believing an arrangement could be made that might put an end to the bloodshed along the frontier."

Deutschendorf shrugged his heavy shoulders and continued, "Unfortunately, neither side was dealing in good faith, although Herr Salem was unaware of that. The Comanche had agreed to bring in some of the white prisoners they had captured in raids on settlements and ranches, but they brought only one, a young girl who had been terribly abused. They demanded a high ransom before any other prisoners would be released. The Texians were looking for any excuse to exact a bloody revenge on the natives for their past atrocities. So, it came as no real surprise to anyone when a fight broke out and many of the Comanche were killed. A few white men were, as well. But the Comanche regard what happened as a betrayal, and one of the men they blame for it is Tye Salem. He is no longer welcome in their villages."

"What a terrible thing," Athelstan said. "It's a shame a peace treaty couldn't have been worked out."

Poole said, "There have been plenty of peace treaties. The Comanche won't keep 'em. They're happy to agree, but then as soon as the notion strikes 'em to go out raidin' and stealin' and killin' again, they forget all about the promises they made."

Deutschendorf took a deep breath. "At any rate, Herr Salem reports that groups of Comanche had been seen roaming between here and Bexar. It is assumed these are war parties, even though no raids have taken place recently. The Comanche appear to be waiting for the right time and place to strike. They are very strategic fighters and seldom attack unless they're very confident of victory."

"Is it likely that we'll run into any of them?" Athelstan asked.

"Not likely, perhaps, but certainly possible." Deutschendorf smiled. "But don't worry, *mein Freund*. In all probability, the Comanche will leave a party as large and well armed as ours strictly alone."

To Athelstan's way of thinking, a party of six men wasn't that large, although it was true that they had plenty of weapons and ammunition.

"They know we have Colt's revolvers," Poole added. "After what happened at Bandera Pass a few years ago, when they ran into a bunch of Rangers under Cap'n Jack Hays, they've been mighty leery of riskin' another battle like that."

"The Rangers were victorious in that battle?"

Poole grinned. "The Indians had never run up against repeatin' guns before. It must've seemed like the sky opened up and fell in on 'em. They deserved ever' damn bit of what Cap'n Jack gave 'em, too."

Deutschendorf regarded Athelstan curiously and said, "I hope you do not regret offering to come along with us, Herr Braxton."

"We all knew there might be danger along the way," Athelstan said. "I just want to get where we're going."

Chapter 23

Spending long, hard days on the trail as the miles unrolled behind them meant that everyone was always tired by the time they made camp. Today, that respite had come a few hours earlier than normal, but even so, the travelers turned in as soon as the sun went down, grateful for the opportunity to rest their weary bodies.

Usually, Bob Poole and the Shellabarger brothers took turns standing guard, but since they were on the edge of Victoria, Deutschendorf deemed their circumstances secure enough to dispense with posting sentries. Soon after everything had been cleaned up following the evening meal, everyone was rolled in their blankets, sound asleep.

Except for Jeremy Braxton.

He was tired, too, no doubt about that, but he had another urge gnawing at him that was stronger than the need for sleep. He lay silent and still until he heard enough snoring and deep breathing around him to feel confident that everyone else was asleep.

Then he crawled carefully out of his blankets, pulled on his boots, stood up, and started walking toward Victoria, taking pains not to make any more noise than he had to.

The lights Jeremy saw up ahead told him that the taverns were still open. If he had enough time, he would visit all of them, but he would start at the one he had paid particular attention to when the wagons passed through town. The Matagorda, that was what it was called, he remembered. He had no idea what the name meant, but it was memorable.

As he approached the tavern, he heard raucous music spilling through its open door, dominated by the screeching tones of a violin being played at a fast pace. The musician wielding it was really sawing on the strings. Jeremy identified a thumping sound as the stomping of feet in time to the music. Perhaps the patrons were dancing.

No, he saw as he paused in the doorway. The men sitting at the tables scattered around the room were merely stamping out a rhythm on the tavern's hard-packed dirt floor. Only one person was dancing.

That person was a young woman, little more than a girl, really, who bounded and leaped and whirled and writhed around an open space on the far side of the low-ceilinged room.

In addition to stamping their feet, the men watching her clapped their hands. A few were so overcome by enthusiasm that they whistled or shouted encouragement to her.

Jeremy could see why her performance enthralled and excited them. The bright red skirt she wore swirled and lifted with her movements to reveal lithe, muscular, dusky brown legs. Her white blouse left her shoulders and arms bare and dipped daringly low in front. Masses of midnight-black hair tangled around her face as her head jerked from side to side. The dance was a sensuous, uninhibited spectacle designed to strike directly to the heart of a man's most primitive instincts.

Jeremy wasn't immune to that, by any means, but he found his eyes drawn away from the dancer to a table on the far side of the room where four men sat playing cards. A beautiful dancing girl held plenty of appeal, but she didn't match the thrill of wagering victory or defeat on the turn of a card. Not for Jeremy Braxton.

He began making his way around the edge of the room toward the table where the game was going on.

The table was rough-hewn, crudely hammered together. Two of the players sat on crates while the other two perched on three-legged stools. There was an empty crate at the table, and as the hand currently underway concluded and one of the men leaned forward to rake in the pot, Jeremy gestured toward the empty seat and asked, "Do you mind if I join you, gentlemen?"

"That depends," one of the men replied. "You sound like a furriner."

"I came to this country from the Grand Duchy of Alpenstone," Jeremy replied with a note of pride in his voice.

"Never heard of it. But I don't care where you're from, son. I just want to know if you got any American money."

"I have gold coins."

"Reckon that'll do, even though we'll have to guess what they're worth. Pull up that crate and sit down."

Jeremy joined the game, which the men told him was called poker. He was familiar with it. The game was spreading in popularity in Europe, and even though he wasn't all that well-versed in its intricacies, he had a good head for such things and picked up on the play quickly.

He kept his wagers small at first until he was more comfortable and had won a couple of hands. Then he increased his betting but still didn't allow himself to become reckless. None of these men knew just how little money he'd had starting out. He was content to build his stake up slowly.

The lovely young woman continued to dance as a white-bearded old man played the violin and two young brown-skinned men strummed guitars. From time to time, especially between poker hands, Jeremy's eyes were drawn to her. Her hair was wet with sweat and she looked tired, as well she should have. She had been dancing at a furious clip ever since Jeremy had arrived at the Matagorda, and he had no way of knowing how long she'd been at it before he came in.

Her earthy beauty tugged at him, but when the shuffling was

over and the game resumed, he was able to turn his attention away from her back to the cards.

Still, watching her was a nice interlude.

As he played, the old familiar excitement began to grow in him. When he got good cards, he felt the urge to risk more. After all, the greatest rewards came with the greatest risks, wasn't that true? He bet, took cards, bet more. He won—

Then his luck began to turn.

He was confident that he had a good hand, but in the end, it wasn't quite good enough. He leaned back and watched with a disappointed frown as one of the other players raked in the pot to which he had contributed heavily.

He would get that back, he told himself. He would get it back, and more.

But he didn't. He lost the next two hands, and most of the stake he had built was gone. When he bet again, he didn't just wager the last of what he had won, he threw in a good chunk of what he had come here with tonight. But everything would be all right as long as he won.

When the hand was down to just two players, the other man's three sixes beat Jeremy's two pair, jacks and eights. Jeremy stared in disbelief at the cards and burst out, "That's not fair!"

The other men laughed. "This is poker, son," one of them said. "It's fair, all right. You just don't know when to admit your luck's changed."

"If it has," Jeremy said with a scowl.

That made the smiles on the faces of the other players disappear abruptly. A man leaned forward and said, "That sounds mighty like you're talkin' about cheatin'. You ain't tryin' to accuse us of that, are you—you damn furriner?"

Jeremy sneered. "Where I come from, men are honorable."

He knew he was going too far, but he was too disappointed and angry—mostly with himself—to control the emotions raging inside him.

"You sayin' we ain't honorable?" One of the men started to his feet, his hand reaching for the knife at his belt as he rose. "Boy, I'll carve your ears off and make you wear 'em for a necklace!"

Too late, Jeremy realized he wasn't going to get out of the Matagorda Saloon without bloodshed.

The girl had stopped dancing at last, too weary to go on. She sidled up next to Tye Salem, pressed her hip against his, and said, "*Querida*, it has been too long since you came to see Isabel."

Tye took a swig from his cup of coffee and told her, "Isabel, the first time I laid eyes on you, you were draggin' around a rag doll and playin' in the dirt. It's kind of hard for me to think about you any other way."

She leaned forward over the rough planks of the bar so that he had a good view of the smooth brown globes inside her shirt. "I am no longer that little girl. That was a long time ago."

"Seems like yesterday to me," Tye said, with a slight shake of his head.

That was true. His family had come to Texas twenty years earlier, when Tye wasn't much older than Isabel had been the first time he saw her. The two decades had gone by in a hurry. His folks had started a farm down on the Brazos River, and he had grown up half wild, spending most of his time on horseback. He was the youngest, the baby of the family, and his older brothers and sisters had done more than their share of the work. He admitted that. He'd been too fiddle-footed to trudge along behind a plow. The habit just never had taken with him.

But by the time he was half grown, he could ride and shoot like a Comanche, and when he was full grown, as brown and limber as he was, dressed in buckskins and riding bareback most of the time, folks could almost take him for a Comanche.

Yeah, lots of things had happened. Revolution. Massacres at the Alamo and Goliad. The Runaway Scrape. San Jacinto and independence. Afterward, he'd thought about joining the Rangers once they were formed, but even that was too much organization to suit him. He'd ridden away on his own, heading for the tall and uncut, and he'd never been back except for brief visits. All of Texas was his, and he could roam where he pleased, a friend to all he encountered.

The Council House Fight in San Antonio had ended that. The Indians had gone from being his friends to being his mortal enemies as they nursed a blood debt against him. Unjustly, as far as he was concerned, but that didn't change the way they felt. He still rode where he wanted to, but he was a mite more careful about it these days.

Those memories flashed through his mind as Isabel rubbed her hip against his, trying to tempt him into sampling her charms, which was one thing he'd never done. He had no doubt she'd been with plenty of other men, but to his way of thinking, that didn't give him leave to become one of them.

A loud voice from the other side of the room caught his attention. He set his cup of coffee on the bar and turned to see what was going on.

The commotion came from a table where several men were playing cards. He recognized only one of the players, a rough varmint named Hardy Givens. Three of the other men looked like they were cut from the same cloth as Hardy, no better than they had to be and certainly not men you'd trust for a second with your purse—or your sister.

The fifth man was also a stranger, but better dressed than the others, with a slick, handsome look about him. Tye might have taken him for a professional gambler, but he lacked the cool confidence of that profession. In fact, he looked scared as he came to his feet. Hardy was already standing and had yanked a bowie knife from a sheath at his waist. He suddenly lunged at the well-dressed stranger and slashed with the heavy blade.

The stranger leaped back and barely avoided having his guts laid open. He stumbled over something and fell. Men who had been talking and drinking jumped out of his way so that he sprawled on the floor. Shouted, angry curses rose into the pipe smoke that filled the air.

Hardy Givens threw himself after his intended victim, the knife rising high above his head. He swept it down. The stranger rolled aside with a speed born of desperation. The bowie's blade buried itself in the dirt.

Hardy pulled it free, but that delayed his attack long enough for the stranger to roll again and then hurriedly push himself upright. He held out his hands, palms toward Hardy, and yelled, "I'm sorry! I meant no offense! You're an honorable man!"

Hardy was too drunk on whiskey and rage to pay any attention to the frantic apology. Brandishing the bowie, he went after the stranger again.

All the talk inside the Matagorda had stopped as people turned to watch the fight. Pop Hooper had stopped sawing on his fiddle, and the Flores brothers had lowered their guitars. Ed Simmons, behind the bar, might have intervened, but he seemed just as interested in seeing what was going to happen as his customers were.

The only one not engrossed in the fight was Isabel, who pressed her soft bosom against Tye's arm and whined that he should take her out of there, back to her *jacal.*

Tye shook her off. He didn't know what the stranger had done to rile up Hardy Givens, but he probably didn't deserve to get carved up over it. Isabel tugged at the sleeve of his buckskin shirt as he stepped away from the bar, but he pulled loose and kept going.

Hardy had the stranger pinned against the wall now. The mean streak in Hardy was a mile wide. He jabbed one way and then the other with the knife, deliberately missing but making the stranger jerk back and forth to keep from getting cut. Hardy let out a vicious laugh as he toyed with the gent.

It was only a matter of time until he got tired of this game and did some real damage with the blade.

Tye broke stride and caught his breath a little as he recognized the man trapped against the wall. He knew now why the fella had seemed vaguely familiar. Tye had seen him before, sitting under a tree with another man and a beautiful girl, when he stopped to talk briefly with Emil Deutschendorf and Bob Poole.

That girl with her blond hair was one of the prettiest sights Tye had seen in a long time. He'd been too far away to tell for sure, but he'd have been willing to bet a brand-new hat that her eyes were blue, too.

He disliked Hardy Givens just on general principles, and he didn't want to see anybody get hurt, but now he had an even better reason for stepping in. He could have pulled one of the Paterson Colts holstered on his hips and clouted Hardy over the head with it, but the Paterson's mechanisms had a tendency toward being finicky to start with and walloping Hardy's thick skull with the gun might damage it.

So he bent, picked up an empty crate that somebody had been using as a seat, and lifted it as he approached Hardy from behind.

"Hardy, look out!" one of his friends yelled.

Hardy had been coming closer and closer with the knife thrusts and it wouldn't be long before he started spilling blood. At the warning shout, he broke off the attack and tried to turn, but Tye was moving too fast.

He brought the crate crashing down on Hardy's head, splintering the wooden container to pieces.

Chapter 24

Hardy's knees buckled and he folded up, collapsing to the floor with a groan.

His three friends yelled and started toward Tye. One of them gripped the handle of a knife sheathed at his waist. Another clawed under his coat for the barely visible butt of a pistol.

Tye's right hand dropped to his hip and palmed out the Colt on that side. Almost too fast for the eye to follow, he raised the gun and eared back the hammer, dropping the trigger from its recessed position under the cylinder. His finger curled around it but held off on the pressure just enough to keep from firing the weapon.

The three men stopped short as they found themselves staring down the Colt's octagonal barrel.

"I'm sorry I had to do that," Tye said, even though he actually wasn't the least bit sorry. To tell the truth, he'd enjoyed busting the crate over Hardy Givens's head. "But you know good and well Hardy had it coming. If somebody hadn't stopped him, he would've killed this fella."

The man who'd been trying to dig out his gun used that hand to point at the stranger instead.

"He accused us of cheatin'!" the man said.

"Yeah, and he said we was dis—dishonorable," one of the other two added.

Tye glanced at the stranger. "Those are mighty foolish things to say," he pointed out, "unless you know the fellas you're sayin' 'em to really well. And even then, it might not be too wise."

The man swallowed. "I'm sorry," he said. "I was just so upset about losing."

"Man's got to lose some in life to know what it's like to win." Tye used the Colt's barrel to motion to the three men he was covering. "You can pick up Hardy and prop him against the wall. Give him a drink." With his free hand, Tye fished a coin out of his pocket and tossed it on the table. "On me."

"You think you're a mighty big man, Salem, but you ain't," one of the men said with a sneer. "Someday you'll stick your nose in where it don't belong and get it cut off."

"Not by you, mister." Tye jerked his head to the stranger. "Get on out of here."

"I wanted to win back what I lost—"

"You almost lost a heap of blood, and there's not any winning that back," Tye interrupted him. "Now move."

The stranger swallowed and nodded. He edged along the wall until he was closer to the door. Then he broke into a run that carried him out into the night.

Tye followed him, backing away and keeping the Colt pointed in the general direction of the men who began helping Hardy Givens back to his feet. He knew they would tell Hardy who had walloped him, if the brief glimpse Hardy had gotten wasn't enough to identify Tye, and there was a chance Hardy would try to even the score.

Tye wasn't particularly worried about that. Hardy was vicious, no doubt about that, but he was also dumb as a rock. Nor was he the type to face Tye head-on out in the open. Tye didn't think it very likely that Hardy would be able to pull off a successful ambush.

He'd had lots more dangerous folks than Hardy Givens laying for him in the past, and he was still here, wasn't he?

He didn't pouch the iron until he was outside the saloon with the darkness folding comfortably around him. He turned and walked away, figuring he would head out to the camp he had seen earlier and make sure the stranger got there safely.

He hadn't gone very far when a shape loomed up out of the shadows and moved toward him.

Tye put his hand on the gun butt again and said, "Better hold it right there, friend."

"It's just me," the man said as he stopped and lifted both hands. Tye recognized his voice. "Jeremy Braxton. From inside the tavern. You just helped me."

"Yeah, I remember," Tye said dryly. "I figured you'd still be running."

"I thought you might follow me out, and I wanted to thank you. That madman would have killed me if you hadn't intervened."

"He might have," Tye allowed. "Hardy Givens has been known to get carried away when he's riled up. He's not really mad like you just called him, though. Just poison mean."

"I can believe that. If I'd known what was going to happen, I never would have asked to join their game."

"You might want to think about the possibilities next time. And definitely before you start talking like that to men you don't know."

"Yes, of course. I will. Have no doubt about that."

"Best get on back out to your camp now."

Jeremy Braxton started to turn but then paused.

"You know where we're camped?"

"I recognized you from when I rode past there this afternoon. I stopped and talked to Emil Deutschendorf and Bob Poole."

"Of course," Jeremy said. "That's where I've seen you before. I believe Mr. Deutschendorf said your name is . . ."

"Tye Salem," Tye supplied.

Jeremy held out his hand. "It's a pleasure to meet you."

Tye shook with him. "I'll walk on out there with you, just to make sure Hardy and his friends don't decide to follow you."

"Do you think they'd try to cause more trouble?"

"I don't know, but with hombres like that, it's always possible."

They fell in step side by side as they walked toward the northern edge of town. After a few moments, Tye said, "I believe Emil said you and your family are traveling with him to his trading post?"

"That's right. We've arranged to claim some land there in the German colony."

"But you're not German." Tye thought Jeremy sounded more like some of the Englishmen he'd run into. They were more common out here on the frontier than most folks would have thought.

"No, we're from the Grand Duchy of Alpenstone."

"Can't say as I've ever heard of that place."

"I'm not surprised. Alpenstone is a small but sovereign nation bordered by France, Germany, and Switzerland."

"Sort of tucked away in the mountains, eh?"

"That's right," Jeremy said.

"Why'd you come to Texas? Decided you didn't like it in Alpenstone?"

"There were circumstances that made it advisable for us to leave—"

"Hold on," Tye interrupted him. "I'm sorry. It's not considered polite out here to ask a man where he's from or why he left there. Reckon I forgot that for a second, because I've never run into anybody from Alpenstone before."

"That's all right," Jeremy assured him. "Let us just say that we had good reasons to journey to Texas and make a fresh start here."

"It's a good place for fresh starts," Tye said, nodding. "Almost everybody here is from someplace else, although it's getting to the point now where we've got some home-grown Texans, too. I wasn't born here, but I was just a boy when my family moved to

Stephen Austin's colony. I've spent most of my life traipsing around Texas. It'll always be home to me."

"I hope my brother and sister and I come to feel the same way."

"You will. You're headed for the Hill Country, and there's no better place on God's green earth. It's a mite rugged there, mind you, but so pretty it'll take your breath away."

Sort of like Jeremy's sister, Tye thought. But he kept that opinion to himself.

A short time later, they came in sight of the pecan trees where the wagons were parked. Tye didn't see any lights except for some faintly glowing embers where the campfire had burned down. The place was quiet. Evidently, everyone was asleep.

Tye was about to bid Jeremy a quiet good-night and head back into town when a figure stepped out from behind one of the trees.

"Who's there?" a man asked, his voice hard and flat with menace.

Tye recognized the voice. "Is that you, Bob? It's Tye Salem. I'm not looking for trouble."

"Salem? What are you doin' out here? Who's that with you?"

As Bob Poole stepped out of the tree's shadow, Tye saw the rifle in the man's hands.

"Point that thing at the ground," he said.

Jeremy added, "It's me, Mr. Poole. Jeremy Braxton."

Poole lowered the rifle and let the barrel sag toward the ground. "I didn't know you boys were acquainted."

"We just met tonight," Jeremy explained.

"And no offense, Mr. Braxton," Poole went on, "but I thought you was sound asleep in your bedroll."

"I was feeling, ah, a bit restless, so I went for a walk and encountered Mr. Salem."

In the darkness, a smile tugged at the corners of Tye's mouth. Jeremy didn't want the others to know he'd been gambling in a squalid frontier saloon and had come close to getting carved open from gullet to gizzard by Hardy Givens. If that was how Jeremy wanted to play this, that was all right with him, Tye supposed. It was none of his business, even though he had stepped in to save Jeremy's life.

"You're lucky you didn't run into trouble," Poole said in a surly voice. "Just because the Comanche ain't ever come this far before is no guarantee they won't take a notion to. There are white men out there, too, who'd be happy to slit your throat and steal whatever you had on you."

Such as Hardy Givens and his friends, Tye thought.

"What are you doing up and awake, Mr. Poole?" Jeremy asked. "When I left, I thought everyone was asleep."

"You're not the only one who got restless. I'm used to takin' a turn on watch."

"Mr. Deutschendorf said it wasn't necessary to post guards since we're this close to civilization."

Poole snorted. "You can call Victoria, Texas, civilization if you want to, but to my way of thinkin', that's a stretch. I ain't sure anywhere in Texas could be called civilization 'ceptin' maybe San Antonio since it's been there for quite a while. Anyway, no matter what Emil says, I'm in the habit of keepin' my eyes open. So when somethin' woke me up, I figured it wouldn't hurt anything to take a look around and keep an eye on things."

"Probably smart," Tye agreed with a nod.

"I saw you fellas comin' and wanted to make sure you weren't up to any mischief."

"No mischief," Jeremy assured the Texan. "I'm going to turn in now. I think I can sleep this time."

"And I'm heading back into town," Tye added. "Good night, Bob."

Poole hitched at his trousers. "Reckon I'll stay awake a while longer," he said. "If everything stays quiet, I'll turn in, too." He paused, then added, "Salem, why don't you come with us to Friedrichsburg?"

"I just rode in from that direction earlier today, remember?" Tye laughed softly. "Civilization or not, I wouldn't mind spendin' a little time in Victoria."

"Suit yourself."

Jeremy nodded to Tye and said, "Thanks again for, ah, walking with me. Good night."

"Night," Tye said. He watched as Jeremy went over to where the bedrolls were spread and crawled back into his. Bob Poole disappeared again into the shadows under the trees to remain vigilant.

Tye strolled toward town. He wasn't going back to the Matagorda, because he knew Isabel would continue making a pest of herself if he did. A sultry, very attractive pest, no doubt about it, but still a distraction Tye didn't need.

And it was possible Hardy Givens and his friends might be hanging around, hoping for another crack at him. No reason he should make it easy on them, he mused.

As he walked, he considered the invitation Bob Poole had issued. He hadn't been all the way up to the Pedernales lately; his most recent trip in that direction he hadn't gone any farther than Bandera Pass, where the Rangers under Captain Jack Hays had clashed with the Comanche so dramatically and decisively several years earlier.

Something stirred in him, nibbling away at his resolve. When he rode in from the northwest, he'd fully intended to remain in these parts for a while.

But that was before he had seen Jeremy Braxton's sister sitting under that tree. With a muttered curse, he realized he had neglected to ask Jeremy what her name was.

Probably better that way, he told himself. If he'd acted too curious about her, it might have stirred up Jeremy's brotherly defensive instincts. Tye wasn't the least bit afraid of Jeremy, but he tried not to go out of his way looking for trouble, either.

No, it would be better if he just put all thoughts of that little blonde out of his head. In the past, all the dallying he had done with women had been just that: temporary moments of enjoyment that went by quickly. Somebody like the Braxton lass, who had come to Texas with her brothers to start a new life and establish a new home, would expect more out of any fella who tried to court her. She would expect something lasting.

Tye didn't want any part of that.

Even if he had to distract himself with Isabel . . .

Chapter 25

The days and the miles unrolled behind the travelers. Shallow heights that were almost too unimpressive to be called hills broke up the landscape. They were nothing compared to the Alps, but to Athelstan they were better than the dreary, seemingly endless plain along the coast. They at least held the promise of terrain more to his liking.

They came to the town of San Antonio de Bexar, a large but drowsy settlement on the banks of the narrow, twisting stream that gave the place its name. As the little caravan rolled past some old stone buildings that were in a state of disrepair, Ralph Shellabarger nudged his horse over by the third wagon and said to Athelstan and Jeremy, "That's the Alamo. You maybe heard of it."

"Of course," Athelstan said. "The Alamo is famous all over the world as a symbol of courage and the desire for freedom." He cocked his head to the side as he regarded the site. "I must say, it's not very impressive."

"You can see where the cannonballs from Santy Anna's artillery knocked chunks outta the top of the front wall. Most folks figure it'd take too much fixin' up to be fit for use as a mission again. So, it's just sittin' there. Heard some say it might be good for storin' things in."

"It should be a shrine," Athelstan said. "Valiant men fought and died for liberty there."

Ralph shrugged. "Maybe so, but you can't have too many good places for storin' things."

They moved on, crossed the slow-moving river on a sturdy bridge, and didn't stop in the town, even though Athelstan saw Bodicia looking longingly at some of the shops they passed. Things were done differently here in Texas; people had to be practical and concentrate on necessities, not luxuries.

Northwest of San Antonio, actual hills loomed, dark and wooded slopes that made a pang of longing and homesickness go through Athelstan. This was the true beginning of the Hill Country. A few more days of travel and they would reach their new home.

The hills became more rugged the farther the travelers penetrated them. At least there was a decent road leading to the German colony. The route twisted through valleys and over passes between higher elevations. Jumbled piles of boulders topped many of the hills and gave the landscape a forbidding aspect at times.

Early in the morning, thick sheets of mist lay over the valleys. When the sun rose and the mists burned away, this was gorgeous country! Not prime farmland, perhaps, Athelstan realized, although some of the valleys were wide and level enough for crops. The lush grass, though, was made for grazing cattle. They had already seen livestock here and there, great, rangy beasts with curving horns that spread out to an incredible length.

One day when they had stopped for a brief midday meal and to rest the teams, Bodicia went over to John Shellabarger and asked, "Mr. Shellabarger, would you allow me to ride your horse for a while?"

Unlike his brother Ralph, who was very friendly and talkative, John tended to keep to himself and generally didn't speak unless he had to. That might have been because Ralph's garrulous personality overwhelmed his, or it might have just been John's nature.

Or maybe he was just very shy. He looked embarrassed that Bodicia was talking to him.

"I, uh, I'm not sure that's a good idea, miss," he finally said.

"I assure you, I'm a very good rider, and I've watched you ride enough to know that your mount is a steady one."

That was true. The brown gelding John rode was good-natured and had an easy gait. With her riding experience back in Alpenstone, Bodicia probably could manage the horse without much trouble.

John frowned and said, "Sorry, miss, but we don't have a side-saddle."

"Oh, I don't need one," Bodicia said airily, smiling. "I can ride astride."

John looked down doubtfully as the long skirt she wore.

"I'll get a pair of my brother's trousers," she went on. "They fit me well enough—"

She stopped short as she realized she was talking about Perry's trousers, and Perry was dead back where they had landed in Texas. The smile disappeared from her face.

But only for a heartbeat. Then she told herself that Perry had always been one to seek adventure. He wouldn't want anything less for her. She lifted her chin and went on, "Just let me fetch a pair of them and change there in the brush. Please, Mr. Shella-barger. Just for a short time. I'm really tired of riding in the wagon all day, every day."

"I reckon I can understand that. But I got to be sure it's all right with your brother."

Bodicia didn't like that idea, but the Texan was determined to have Athelstan's permission before he would allow her to ride his horse.

To Bodicia's surprise, Athelstan nodded when she asked him.

"I think that's all right," he told John Shellabarger. "My sister is a good rider and has quite a bit of experience. She didn't always use a sidesaddle back home, either." He looked at Bodicia and added sternly, "But you must stay close to the wagons. Don't go any farther ahead than where Mr. Poole is riding. And stay on the road."

"Of course, Athelstan."

He frowned slightly, as if her ready agreement didn't actually reassure him that much. But he made no objection as she dug out a pair of Perry's trousers and one of his shirts as well, took them into the brush, and emerged a few moments later wearing the clothing. The trousers and shirt were a little large. She had rolled up the legs and the sleeves.

As she passed Jeremy, she reached up and took his hat off his head then pressed it down on her own blond curls.

"What are you doing?" he asked. "Give me back my hat!"

"You'll get it back," she said with a little laugh.

She took the gelding's reins from John Shellabarger, grabbed hold of the saddle horn with both hands, and put her foot in the stirrup.

"I don't need any help," she said, as he reached tentatively and awkwardly toward her. To prove that, she swung up onto the horse's back with graceful ease. A smile lit her face again. It felt good to be in the saddle.

A few minutes later, the group got underway again. Bodicia trotted ahead of the wagons with Bob Poole, who didn't look all that happy about having her as company. John Shellabarger had taken her place on the second wagon, sitting next to Theobald while Griggs moved to the back and found a perch on the pile of supplies and merchandise.

Bodicia urged her horse to a faster pace than the one Poole rode. The man said, "Didn't I hear your brother tellin' you not to get ahead of me?"

"I'm not ahead of you," Bodicia said over her shoulder. "Well, not really. I mean, I'm still right here only a few meters away, well within your sight."

"I'd rather you were behind me, miss. That way if any trouble crops up, it'd have to go through me to get to you."

"What if trouble comes from the sides?" Bodicia asked, as she swept a hand at the trees flanking the road. "Then it wouldn't matter whether I was behind you or ahead of you, would it?"

"No, I reckon not—"

"Isn't it more likely that Indians or highwaymen would be lurking somewhere in ambush, rather than approaching directly toward us? Say, in those rocks up there?"

She pointed to a spot about a hundred yards ahead where the road went up a fairly steep slope that formed a pass through a rocky ridge. The ground jutted up on both side of the trail, and a number of boulders littered those rugged upthrusts.

Bodicia dug the heels of her shoes into the gelding's flanks. The horse picked up speed, all but lunging ahead as she rode quickly toward the little pass.

"Miss Braxton, come back here!" Poole shouted after her.

Her voice, full of excitement, floated back. "It's all right! You can still see me!"

He was worrying too much, she thought as she rode ahead. Back with the wagons, Athelstan probably had seen what she was doing and would be furious that she'd disobeyed him, and worried, too.

But after all the unpleasantness and outright tragedy they had endured the past few months, it felt incredibly good to gallop along this frontier trail, the wind in her face, the vast blue sky arching above her, alone for the moment in this beautiful pristine land. They hadn't seen a single Indian since setting foot in Texas. She wasn't sure she believed they actually posed that much of a threat.

She slowed the horse as they reached the foot of the pass. The gelding took the slope easily. Its powerful muscles worked smoothly under the sleek brown hide.

Bodicia looked at the crest ahead of her. When she got up there, she would stop and turn and gaze out over the rolling landscape they had just crossed. She thought the view would be a good one—

Something whipped past her. She felt it brush her shoulder. When she hauled back on the gelding's reins and looked over, she saw the arrow that had just missed her sticking out of the ground where it had landed.

The sight of it was a shock like a physical blow. Bodicia gasped and pulled harder on the reins, stopping and turning the gelding.

Another arrow flew through the air near her. She heard the faint flutter from the feathers attached to it.

The sharp flint head struck the gelding, only a glancing blow but enough to rip a gash in the animal's right shoulder. The horse let out a whinny of pain and pawed angrily at the air as it reared up on its hind legs.

Bodicia almost fell. Instinct made her clamp her knees on the horse's barrel and grab the saddle horn. She hung on. The horse reared up for only a few heartbeats, but it seemed longer.

Then more arrows flew all around her. Shrill cries filled the air along with the deadly shafts.

Chapter 26

Bodicia had never been more terrified in her life. Not even when Jacques LeCarde's men had tried to kidnap her back in Alpenstone.

But despite her fear, a part of her brain was still working. It told her to lean forward in the saddle so that she would be a smaller target. As she did so, she jabbed her heels into the horse's flanks again. This time when the gelding surged into a gallop, they were going down the slope and back toward the wagons.

Those wagons were several hundred yards away, though. Her brothers couldn't do much to help her from that distance.

Bob Poole was closer. He charged along the road toward the pass. Smoke spurted from the muzzle of his rifle as he fired toward the ridge. At that distance, from the back of a galloping horse, it would be pure luck if he actually hit any of the Indians— but luck could kill a man just as dead as anything else.

Bodicia had almost reached the bottom of the slope and was starting to think she might get clear of the ambush when the gelding stumbled. The horse's front legs folded up as it lost its footing. The animal went down hard.

Bodicia wasn't ready for that. She sailed over the gelding's head. The hat she had borrowed from Jeremy came off, letting her fair hair spill around her head and shoulders.

Time seemed to stop while she was in the air, but that frozen instant came to an abrupt and painful end as she crashed on the ground. Momentum rolled her over and over on the trail. She came to a stop on her belly. When she raised her head, her mouth and nose were clogged with dust, and she was choking. It stung her eyes and blurred her vision, as well.

But she could hear just fine. The shrill, excited whoops from somewhere nearby came clearly to her ears. She finally blinked enough that her sight cleared, just in time for her to see the painted, buckskin-clad shapes bounding down the ridges on both sides of the trail.

Comanche, she thought. They were coming for her.

She tried to push herself up so she could run, even though the chances of her being able to get away from them were slim. She had overheard enough talk about what Comanches did to white female captives that she was determined not to let herself fall into their hands. If she had to, she would fight hard enough that she'd force them to kill her.

That was her hope, anyway. Perhaps a forlorn one, because the fall and the hard landing had knocked all the breath out of her body and stunned her. Her muscles refused to cooperate. She made it to her hands and knees, but that was as far as she got. She sobbed in terror as the painted warriors closed in on her.

The swift pounding of hoofbeats made her turn her head. She gazed through dust-bleared eyes toward the top of the pass. A rider appeared with breathtaking suddenness and galloped down the slope toward her.

Even though he wore a buckskin shirt like the Indians, he wasn't a Comanche. The broad-brimmed hat that flew backward off his head, only to be caught by its chinstrap, told her that. So did the thick, light brown hair.

And so did the pistols in his hands that boomed and crashed and spewed smoke and flame as he guided his racing mount with his knees.

Two of the Comanches leaping down the slopes toward Bodicia yelled in pain and spun off their feet as pistol lead tore hotly through them. Others stopped short and scrambled for cover behind rocks as the shots ripped the air around them.

The rider covered the distance between himself and Bodicia amazingly quickly. He had emptied the pistols, so he stuck them back in their holsters strapped to the saddle. When he was close enough for her to hear him, he leaned to his right, thrust that arm toward her, and shouted, "Grab on!"

She tried again to force her muscles to work. This time they did, enough for her to rise on her knees and reach up to wrap both of her arms around his. His fingers clamped around her upper right arm. The jerk as he pulled her off the ground was breathtaking or would have been if she'd had much breath to take.

As it was, she hung on for dear life as he lifted her.

With a grunt of effort—she had always been a solidly built, muscular girl—he swung her up behind him. She tightened her legs on the galloping horse and switched her grip, sliding her arms around his waist and holding on in as tight a hug as she had ever given anyone in her life.

More arrows flew around them. As she peered past her rescuer's shoulder, Bodicia spotted John Shellabarger's horse ahead of them, running back toward the wagons. The fall didn't appear to have hurt the animal badly after all.

Ralph Shellabarger had galloped ahead to join Bob Poole. Both men had dismounted, and as Bodicia and the man in the buckskin shirt raced past them, they fired their rifles toward the ridges.

Up ahead, the wagons had all come to a stop and the men piled off them to grab rifles, as well. They spread out and opened fire on the attackers, being careful not to shoot too close to Bodicia and the man who had saved her. Even young Griggs had a rifle. A cloud of powder smoke rose in the air above the group.

Without loosening her grip on the man's waist, Bodicia turned her head to look over her shoulder. She thought she saw a few Indians vanishing over the top of the ridge as they fled from the withering rifle fire. From the looks of it, they had abandoned their attack and just wanted to get out of there.

The two warriors her rescuer had shot were either dead or seriously wounded. Bodicia had been able to tell that from the way they had fallen. That was as high a price as the Comanches were willing to pay.

The gunfire dwindled away as the Indians disappeared. The rider slowed his horse to a trot and then a walk. He turned his head enough that Bodicia could see the smile on his face as he said, "I'm glad you hung on tight, miss, but I reckon it'd be all right if you let me breathe again."

"Oh!" Bodicia realized how hard she was squeezing him and let go. "I'm sorry."

"It's all right for you to hold on," he told her. "I don't want you to fall off. But the trouble seems to be over now, and we don't have to ride hell for leather anymore."

Something about him was familiar. As the fear for her life receded, she realized what it was. She had seen him only briefly about a week earlier, when he stopped to talk with Emil Deutschendorf and Bob Poole on the outskirts of Victoria.

"You're the man we saw before," she said. "The one who's a scout."

"Tye Salem," he supplied his name. He reined the horse to a stop.

Athelstan and Jeremy were running toward them and would be there within moments. Deutschendorf, Theobald, Griggs, and John Shellabarger hurried not far behind them.

Bodicia started to slide off the horse's back so she could go and meet her brothers. Tye Salem gripped her arm to help her down.

He didn't immediately let go once her feet were on the ground. Leaning over from the saddle, he said, "I told you my name, but I don't reckon I got yours, miss."

"It's Bodicia," she said. "Bodicia Braxton."

"Bodicia Braxton," he repeated. "That's sure a mouthful." He gave her the biggest grin she had ever seen and told her, "I reckon maybe I'll just call you Bodie."

* * *

While Bodie's brothers fussed over—and at—her, Tye rode back to join Bob Poole and Ralph Shellabarger farther along the trail. Tye reloaded the saddle pistols he had emptied at the Comanche war party. The three men, each holding a rifle at the ready, rode through the pass to the top of the ridge. They were alert and poised for trouble, but the Indians were long gone.

"They sure lit a shuck after you tore through 'em like that, Tye," Ralph said with an admiring grin. "That was pretty impressive when you come boilin' down the hill like that, guns blazin', throwin' lead all over the place."

"I was just trying to scatter those Comanche," Tye said. "I promise you, ventilating a couple of them like I did was just pure luck!"

Bob Poole grunted as if he didn't believe Tye's modest statement. He rested his rifle across the saddle in front of him and said, "How'd you come to be in front of us in the right place at just the right time, Tye? Last we saw of you was more than a week ago, down at Victoria."

"And that's where I planned to stay for a while," Tye said. "I honestly did. But I realized pretty quicklike that I'm just too restless for town living. I decided to tag along after you folks and make sure that you made it back to Friedrichsburg safe and sound."

He grew more serious as he went on, "Early this morning, I thought I spotted a rider in the distance. He acted like he was watching something, and I figured it had to be the wagons. He was too far away to be sure, but I thought he might be a Comanch', so I hurried up and made a big circle around you. Didn't think it would hurt to see what I could see. I was working my way back to meet you when I came across that ambush they had set up. They had just sprung the jaws of the trap."

"They made their move too soon," Poole said. "If they'd waited until all three of the wagons were climbing that slope, they could have wiped us out."

Ralph said, "They got too antsy when they saw Miss Braxton. One of 'em didn't want to take a chance of her gettin' away, so he let fly with an arrow. Once he'd done that, the others didn't have no choice but to join in."

Tye suspected that Ralph was right. Seeing Bodie out there ahead of the others had been too tempting of a target for the Indians to resist. They didn't make very many foolish plays, but such things happened from time to time.

Tye was just glad he'd been close by today and able to give her a hand.

Poole said, "Ralph, you ride on back to the wagons and tell Emil it's all clear up here and safe to come ahead." He looked over at Tye. "You gonna stick around for a while?"

"I figured I might," Tye replied with a nod. "Been a while since I've seen the Pedernales country."

"It ain't changed much, except it's gettin' full of people." Poole turned his head and spat. "Hell, it's only a mile from my cabin to the nearest neighbor. Plumb crowded."

They waited there at the top of the trail while Ralph led the wagons through the pass. Bodie was no longer on horseback, although she still wore a man's shirt and trousers as she sat in the second wagon, the one with the old man and the boy on the driver's seat.

Her brothers were on the third wagon. Both looked irritated. The younger one dropped from the wagon to the ground part of the way up the slope and trotted over to the side of the trail to retrieve the hat Bodie had been wearing. He frowned, punched it back into shape, brushed it off, and put it on. Bodie had borrowed it from him, Tye decided, and then lost it in the ambush.

Once the wagons were all on level ground again, Deutschendorf signaled another halt and waved Tye over to him.

"Herr Salem, we owe you our thanks," he said. "If you had not come along when you did, Fräulein Braxton might have been captured or killed. The rest of us might well have been massacred, too, if you had not forced the natives to flee."

"I'm glad I was close enough to lend a hand," Tye responded, with a nod.

The older Braxton brother climbed down from the third wagon and walked ahead. He held up his hand to Tye and said, "Mr. Salem, I want to thank you for saving my sister's life." He glanced toward Bodie. "There's no way of knowing what might have happened if you hadn't come along, but I'm certain things wouldn't have ended well."

"More than likely not," Tye agreed as he clasped the man's hand.

"I'm Athelstan Braxton. That's my brother Jeremy. And of course, you've met my sister Bodicia."

"I've had the pleasure," Tye said.

"I'm sure fighting off a horde of bloodthirsty Comanche wasn't exactly a pleasure."

Tye started to say he wasn't sure about that. Bodie *had* been holding on to him mighty tightly, after all. But probably it would be better not to mention that to the gal's brother, he decided.

"Do you happen to be traveling toward Friedrichsburg?" Athelstan went on.

"I am now, that's for sure," Tye said. "The members of that war party who are left alive will be keeping an eye out for me after today, as long as they're in these parts. I don't figure roaming around by myself is a very good idea. I'd appreciate it if I could ride along with you folks."

Bodie was close enough to hear that. Trying not to be too obvious about it, he watched for her reaction to his answer. It pleased him quite a bit when he spotted a hint of a smile on her face.

"We will be very glad for your company, Herr Salem," Deutschendorf said, "even though it will take only a couple of days to reach our destination from here."

Bob Poole said, "A couple of days can be a long time when there's a Comanche war party helling around the countryside. If we all get where we're goin' with our hair still on our heads, I reckon we'll be doing good!"

Chapter 27

Despite his intentions, Perry Braxton realized pretty quickly that he couldn't keep with the wagons on foot.

The vehicles didn't travel at a very rapid pace; a man could easily walk as fast as one of them But the mule teams plodded along endlessly and a man couldn't do that. He wore down over time.

By the end of the first day on the trail, Perry's feet hurt so abominably that he couldn't keep going. He didn't dare remove his shoes, either, no matter how much he wanted to bathe his burning feet in a stream he found. He knew if he did that, they would swell so badly that he would never get the shoes back on.

Instead, he suffered and tried to sleep on the ground under a bush that night, unsure whether his feet tormented him more from walking or his stomach plagued him more from not eating.

In the morning, he drank his fill from the creek and then followed its banks as he searched for something to ease the gnawing ache in his belly. His feet twinged with every step. Even so, after resting them overnight, the pain wasn't quite as bad as he expected it to be.

He found a bush with some round, dark purple fruit growing on it in clusters of a dozen or more. Closer examination showed him that the fruit weren't growing on the bush itself. Rather, they had sprouted on a vine that had entangled and entwined itself around the bush with such success that the plants almost appeared to be one.

Perry's empty stomach told him to quit wasting time pondering such things. He was well aware that the fruit might not be fit for human consumption. It might make him sick if he ate it. It might even kill him.

But he was hungry. The fruit was here. It was simple enough.

He plucked a handful of the little round things and crammed them between his lips. When he bit down, a slightly bitter taste filled his mouth. It began to sting a little, too, as he chewed.

It was the best thing he had ever tasted.

Perry gathered more of the fruit and ate it. He warned himself to be careful and not indulge too much. After washing down what he had eaten with a long drink from the creek, he picked more of the fruit and stored it in a pouch he fashioned from the tails of his shirt.

So far he felt fine. As fine as was possible, at least, with his feet hurting as much as they did. The primitive meal had eased his hunger and given him some energy. He figured that perhaps he could start after his family again.

If he could figure out which way they had gone.

He soon discovered that when he wandered away from the wagon road, he must have gotten turned around somehow. He couldn't find the trail again.

He knew, however, that the Hill Country lay northwest of where the *Apollo* had landed on the Texas coast. Back in Alpenstone, he had lived enough of an outdoor life that he could tell directions by both the sun and the stars. He wasn't worried about heading in the right direction. Finding his brothers and sister once he reached the Hill Country might be difficult, but he would deal with that problem when the time came.

Perry took a deep breath and headed in the direction he had to go.

* * *

Several days later—he had lost track of how many—he finally admitted to himself that he was hopelessly lost.

It was all well and good to say that he could walk northwest. Unfortunately, obstacles were sometimes in the way. A ridge too steep to climb. A river too wide and deep to cross. A tangle of brush so thick and thorny it would have ripped his flesh to ribbons if he'd tried to force his way through it.

So, he detoured to the west and then to the east and back west again. Sometimes he had to travel due north. He didn't know where he was, and he didn't want to ask any of the very few people he spotted in the distance.

He was still an accused murderer. He would be risking his freedom, perhaps even his life, if he approached anyone and was recognized as a fugitive. That seemed unlikely, but he couldn't risk it.

The only bit of good fortune he'd had was that the vines bearing the fruit he'd eaten on that first morning of his trek were very common here in Texas. He found other berries that had proven to be edible, too. Subsisting on such a diet caused issues that occasionally had him scrambling to get his trousers down in time, but that problem seemed to be getting better as the days passed.

He saw some hares—ugly, big-eared, big-footed creatures that only vaguely resembled the hares he was familiar with—and tried to catch one now and then, but they were too speedy and clever for him. Someday, he vowed, he would eat meat again. However, it might be a while.

His feet still ached and he still hadn't taken his shoes off. The pain wasn't as bad, though. His blisters must be forming calluses, he thought.

He was shocked one day when he came across some ruts left by a wagon. He hadn't seen a road or even a crude wagon trail since the first day of his journey. The only other human beings he had spotted in the distance were men riding on horseback.

Perry still believed it would be safer for him to avoid people.

At the end of these wagon tracks, though, might be real food. Cooked food. Perhaps someone to care for his feet. Surely it would be safe for him to pay a visit to some isolated farm. As bad as he looked, whoever lived there was bound to take pity on him.

He lifted his head, now shaggy and bearded, and peered along the faint tracks.

They led toward a hill with a fringe of trees on top of it, about half a mile away. Perry stiffened as he saw a column of black smoke rising from somewhere near the base of that hill.

The smoke hadn't been there a few minutes earlier. He was certain of that. He would have seen it. Whatever was on fire had just started burning.

Maybe the blaze was deliberate. Someone burning a pile of brush, perhaps.

But then he heard several faint popping noises and recognized them as gunshots.

Whatever trouble was going on over there, it was none of his business, he told himself. He wanted to steer clear of such things.

After the flurry of shots, he didn't hear any more gunfire. Did that mean the fight was over? The smoke column was still rising. In fact, it had thickened. The blaze was getting bigger.

"Damn it," Perry said out loud as he realized he couldn't ignore this. He hadn't spoken in days. His voice sounded rusty and odd.

He started toward the smoke. At first, he was just shuffling along a little faster than he had been walking. After a few steps, though, he began to run. His gait was awkward and made his feet hurt worse, but he kept going.

He stayed out of the wagon ruts because they might have tripped him. They curved to the right, and he did, too. He spotted bright, leaping flames up ahead at the base of that smoke. Some sort of building was on fire.

Mounted figures dashed back and forth between him and the blaze. Perry stopped short and gazed at them.

Then he turned and ran toward some trees to his left. He

darted among them and concealed himself behind one of the trunks.

The riders had feathers in their long hair. He had never actually laid eyes on an Indian, but he had seen pictures of them in books, and he was convinced that was what those men were. Beyond the burning building was a log cabin. This was a farm, just as Perry suspected. The Indians had attacked it and set the barn on fire.

Where were the settlers?

The woods were thick enough to hide him as he stole closer. The idea of being captured was horrifying. He would be fortunate if they killed him quickly. It was more likely they would torture him and make sure he suffered countless agonies before death finally claimed him. If he had a lick of sense in his head, he would turn and disappear deeper into the woods.

Something drew him on. He wanted to find out what had happened to whoever lived here. He didn't dream for an instant that he could help them, but perhaps he might be able to pass along news of this tragedy.

The trees hid him until he was a hundred yards from the burning barn and the cabin. From there, the ground had been cleared. He stopped and knelt in some underbrush, carefully parting it to get a better view.

Two men lay not far from where he was. Neither moved. Nor would they, ever again, Perry thought, because several arrows stuck out of each man's body. They had to be dead.

His eyes were drawn to something on the ground beside one of the corpses. He squinted. He thought the object was a pistol like those carried by the lawman who had come onto the *Apollo* to arrest him. The cylinder that bulged out on the sides was unfamiliar to him, but he recognized the grip and the barrel.

A rifle lay on the ground not far from the other body. Perry assumed the shots he had heard came from those weapons. He wondered if either of them was still loaded.

What was he thinking? He saw almost a dozen Indians riding back and forth in front of the cabin, yipping excitedly and shaking the lances they held. They would slaughter him in an instant if they caught sight of him.

He wondered fleetingly why they hadn't set fire to the cabin yet. He had just noticed that there were a couple of riderless ponies when he got his answer to that question. Two Indians came through the cabin's open door, dragging a woman between them. She tipped her head back and screamed, such a raw sound that it made Perry's throat hurt just to hear it.

Her dark hair had come loose and hung wildly around her head. She jerked and tried to twist away from her captors, but she was no match for the Indians' strength. The ones on their ponies whooped louder at the sight of her.

Perry didn't stop to think for very long. The only thought that flashed through his mind was that if he were to distract them, the woman might be able to get loose and run away. A slim chance, to be sure, but the only chance she had.

He dashed out of the trees. None of the Indians were looking in his direction. Their attention was focused on the woman as the two men dragged her closer. Perry reached the side of the dead man who had dropped the pistol when he was skewered by arrows. He was middle-aged, Perry saw, with silver in his hair and mustache.

He would never get any older.

Perry reached down and picked up the pistol. He held it in both hands. He didn't see a trigger on it, but it had a hammer and when he pulled it back with both thumbs, the trigger dropped down under the cylinder so he could reach it.

He had no idea if the pistol was loaded, but he pointed it at the back of one of the Indians and pulled the trigger.

The booming report slammed his ears like giant fists. The recoil almost tore the gun out of his fingers. If he'd been holding it with one hand, it probably would have.

Through the powder smoke that gushed from the barrel, he saw the rider he had targeted knocked forward on the pony's back. The Indian flung his arms out to the side. Perry was so weak that the pistol's barrel had been dancing around. Luck had guided the shot, and the heavy lead ball had smashed between the Indian's shoulder blades. He slid off the skittish pony and crashed limply to the ground.

The pistol's kick had jerked the barrel skyward. Perry pulled it down and cocked the weapon again as the other Indians screamed in outrage and whirled their mounts toward him. They must have been shocked to see one lone white man standing there. They hesitated.

Perry pulled the trigger again. The roar of the second shot was as loud as the first. This one wasn't as accurate, though. Perry couldn't tell if he'd hit anything.

It didn't appear that he had. Whooping furiously, the war party charged him. He fumbled as he tried to aim the gun and cock it again. He got the hammer eared back and jerked the trigger.

The hammer fell with a metallic click.

Empty.

And those charging Indians, each with blood in his eyes, were only about ten yards away.

Chapter 28

Terror froze Perry's aching feet right where they were. Every instinct in his body cried out for him to turn and run, even though he knew such flight would be futile, but he couldn't force his muscles to work.

All he could do was stand there and stare at death thundering down on him.

The pounding of the ponies' hooves was so loud in his ears that at first, he didn't hear the gunfire that ripped through the warm Texas air.

Then he realized the booming sounds came from behind him and twisted his neck to look over his shoulder. More riders had burst out of the woods. They rode hard toward the Indians. Smoke billowed from the pistols in their hands as they fired again and again.

Perry was between the two forces and in danger of being trampled. He did the only thing he could, putting his head down and running as hard as possible to get out of the way.

When he thought he had gone far enough, he left his feet in a desperate dive. He hit hard, rolled a couple of times, and came up on one knee.

From there he watched as the newcomers swept toward the Indians while laying down a lethal wave of gunfire. Several Indians, as well as their ponies, went down like wheat before a scythe.

Some of them reined their mounts to sliding halts and tried to put up a fight. Arrows whipped through the air around the riders who had come to Perry's aid.

As far as Perry could see, only one man was hit. An arrow embedded itself in his right shoulder. The impact twisted the man in his saddle, but he stayed mounted, switched his pistol to his left hand, and continued firing with barely a break in the assault.

Then the two groups came together in the open area between the burning barn and the trees. What had been a well-coordinated charge turned into a wild melee in the blink of an eye. Riders milled around as swirling dust enveloped them. Pistols roared at point-blank range and blasted Indians from their ponies. One of the savages thrust the lance he carried through the side of a white man.

Perry had had only moments to get a look at his rescuers before dust and powder smoke obscured them, but he had been able to tell they were white men in rough clothing and hats. All of them wielded pistols like the one he had fired at the Indians. Those repeating weapons had taken a terrible toll on the enemy. Only a few Indians were left in the fight. They didn't last long against such a larger, well-armed force.

The gunfire and shouting died away. The riders brought their mounts under control. Once the milling around stopped, the dust clouds began to dissipate in the steady breeze.

All the Indians lay dead or mortally wounded on the ground. None of the newcomers had fallen from their horses, although a few appeared to be wounded.

As Perry rose to his feet, one of the men noticed him and swung a pistol toward him. Perry's hands shot in the air above his head.

That gesture, along with the thick beard he sported, must have told the rider that he wasn't an Indian and, apparently, not a threat. The man lowered the hammer on his pistol and then nudged the horse toward Perry.

"Are you out here alone, fella?" he asked.

Perry nodded and said, "Yes, I—I'm lost."

"I knew you wasn't one of the Jenkinses. Hadn't ever seen you before when we stopped by here."

The man holstered his pistol and thumbed back his hat, which had the brim turned up in front. His hair was white and so was his mustache. Despite his apparent age, he seemed vital and healthy, still in the prime of life.

"The people who lived here, their name was Jenkins?" Perry asked. He wasn't sure why that was important to him, but suddenly it was.

"That's right." A grim look came over the rider's weathered face as he nodded toward the bodies of the two men. "That's Chuck Jenkins and his son, Boyd. Fine hombres, the both of 'em. Good Texans, through and through."

One of the other men called, "Cap'n Sutherland! You'd best come over here, Cap."

Captain Sutherland turned his head and nodded to the man who'd summoned him. Looking back at Perry, he asked, "What's your name, son?"

Without thinking, Perry almost answered with the truth. Then he realized that if this man was a captain, he represented some sort of authority. It was unlikely he was looking for a fugitive and accused murderer named Perry Braxton, but the possibility couldn't be ruled out.

"My name is Smith," Perry said. "Jack Smith."

"Well, come on, Jack. You look a mite on the gaunt and hungry side, not to mention plumb wore out. We'd be happy to share our provisions with you."

Perry had headed for this farm in the first place hoping to get something to eat. Tragedy had taken away that possibility, but fate might have opened another path to him. He nodded and fell into step beside Captain Sutherland as the man walked his horse toward the cabin.

Perry caught his breath when he saw the woman lying on the

ground with the two Indians who had dragged her out of the cabin sprawled in bloody heaps nearby. Several of the white men stood around with bleak expressions on their faces.

The woman—Mrs. Jenkins, she would be—was lying on her back. Her eyes were open wide and stared sightlessly at the sky. The front of her dress was stained darkly with the blood that had flooded from the gaping wound in her throat.

"One o' the devils cut her throat when they saw us comin', Cap'n," a man said. "They were bound and determined she was gonna die."

"With Chuck and Boyd already dead, it might've been a mercy," Sutherland said harshly. "At least she didn't suffer long. That wouldn't have been true if they carried her off." He shook his head slowly and solemnly. "We'll lay her to rest beside her husband and boy."

"What about all these Comanch'?" another man asked.

Sutherland's voice was flat and hard as he said, "Buzzards and coyotes got to eat, too, don't they?"

The other men nodded in complete agreement with the captain's sentiment.

Sutherland went on, "Boys, this here is Jack Smith. He's a pilgrim who wandered up just as that war party hit." He looked at Perry with narrowed eyes. "I heard a couple of shots just before we busted out of the trees and opened up, and one of those Comanche was already down when we started shootin'. Was that your doin', Jack?"

Perry swallowed and nodded. "The farmer—Mr. Jenkins— dropped his pistol when they killed him. I saw it and picked it up. I hoped it was loaded, and luckily it still had two rounds left in it."

One of the men frowned and said, "Now hold on. You're tellin' us you took on a whole Comanche war party by yourself, with nothin' but a gun you picked up from the ground without even knowin' if it was loaded?"

"I thought if I could distract them, the woman might be able to get away." Perry shook his head. "I'm sorry I wasn't able to help her escape."

"Like I said, might've been a blessin'," Sutherland rumbled.

The other man who had spoken to Perry let out a low whistle of admiration. He turned to Sutherland, who was still mounted, and said, "Cap'n, this fella has to have plenty of sand to've done what he did. Might be a good hombre to have ridin' with us for a spell, if he don't have somewhere else he's got to be."

"Yeah, I was thinkin' the same thing. You don't have a horse, Jack?"

Perry shook his head.

"That's all right. We'll have some spare mounts once we round up them Injun ponies. You've already got Chuck's Paterson, and I reckon you can have Boyd's rifle, too. How about it, young Jack? Want to trail along with us for a while? Can't offer you any wages since you ain't an official member of the troop, but we've got plenty o' grub, and you're welcome to share in it. Probably a heap safer than traipsin' around out here by yourself, too. What do you say?"

Perry hesitated. He had gone on the run in the first place to avoid capture by the authorities, not to join forces with them. Also, he wanted more than anything else to reach the Hill Country and be reunited with his brothers and sister.

But this might be a way of doing that, he realized. So far, none of these men had questioned his story, and he couldn't see that they had any reason to do so.

Captain Sutherland looked like he might be getting slightly impatient while he waited for Perry's answer. Deciding quickly, Perry said, "I'm very grateful for your invitation, Captain, and I'll be happy to accept. I'll join your group."

"Well, then," Sutherland said as he leaned down from the saddle to extend his hand, "even though it's on an unofficial basis right now, welcome to the Texas Rangers, Jack Smith."

Chapter 29

As Captain Bert Sutherland had said they would, they buried Charles Jenkins, his wife, Juanita, and their son, Boyd, side by side in the shade of some trees not far from the cabin. The men removed their hats and stood solemnly and respectfully around the graves while the captain quoted Scripture over the dead and finished with a prayer.

The Rangers had already dragged the dead Comanches into the woods on the far side of the cabin and left them there for the scavengers. No ceremony had been involved with that grim task.

They found a couple of mules and a milk cow grazing not far away. The Indians must have hazed the livestock out of the barn before setting it on fire. They would have slaughtered the animals eventually, but they hadn't gotten around to it. They had been too intent on having their fun with Mrs. Jenkins first.

"We'll take the critters along with us and drop 'em off at the Dunnell farm," Sutherland said. "It ain't too far away."

The wounded Rangers had been tended to earlier, as well. Two men had suffered fairly serious injuries, one from an arrow and the other from a Comanche lance, but the considered opinion of Doc Ford, a young Ranger who'd had a little medical training, was that they would recover as long as neither of the wounds festered.

The Indian ponies had scattered, but the men were able to

round up several of them. Captain Sutherland asked Perry, "Can you ride with just a saddle blanket and a rope hackamore?"

"Yes, sir, I can manage," Perry said, even though he had never ridden without a saddle. He recalled some old proverb about necessity being a good teacher.

None of the men wanted to linger around the site of such a tragedy. They mounted up and rode north. Perry didn't have much trouble handling the Indian pony, although it was rather skittish at first. He soon learned how to control it.

He talked to several of the Rangers as they rode, but Doc Ford took the most interest in him.

"Almost everybody in Texas is from somewhere else," Doc said, "but you sound like maybe you come from the farthest away place. I knew a fella from England once. The way you talk sort of reminds me of him."

Perry didn't want to explain about being from Alpenstone. Instead, he said, "My parents were from England. I grew up in Philadelphia."

He plucked that name out of his memory and hoped that Doc didn't know anything about the place. All Perry knew was that he had heard of it.

Doc shook his head and said, "Never been to Pennsylvania, but I'm sure it's right nice."

"Oh, it is." To change the subject, Perry added quickly, "Where are you from?"

"Tennessee." Doc grinned. "Me and Davy Crockett."

Perry just kept a noncommittal smile on his face and didn't say anything. The name Doc had mentioned was familiar, but he couldn't place it right away.

"You know—Davy Crockett," Doc said when Perry didn't respond. "He was at the Alamo with Bowie and Travis and the rest of those boys."

"Of course." The story came back to Perry now. "They were all great heroes."

"Damn right, they were. If they hadn't kept Santa Anna busy

for as long as they did, his army might have caught up with all the folks tryin' to get away, and it would've been a terrible massacre. Of course, if ol' Santa Anna had been even half as smart as he figured he was, he would've left enough troops at the Alamo to keep those fellas penned up inside and just gone around with the rest of his men. Lucky for Texas he didn't think of that."

Perry kept Doc talking about the Texas Revolution. It distracted the Ranger from asking more questions about his background. Also, Perry was glad to learn more about Texas. This was going to be his home, after all.

When they made camp that night, Captain Sutherland noticed the way Perry was limping and came over to him.

"What's wrong with your feet, son?" he asked as he hooked his thumbs in the gun belt around his waist.

"They're just sore from walking, sir. I'm not used to it, and these shoes aren't very good for it, I suppose."

Sutherland nodded, turned his head, and called, "Doc, come over here."

Perry said, "I'm all right, really—"

The captain ignored that and said, "Doc, take a look at his feet."

"Sure, Cap. Jack, sit down on that log over there."

Perry said, "I really don't think this is a good idea."

"I knew a fella once who had to have both feet cut off 'cause he didn't take care of 'em the way he'd oughta," Sutherland said. "You don't want that to happen to you, do you?"

"No, sir," Perry admitted miserably. He wasn't looking forward to having to take those shoes off.

As it turned out, Doc Ford had to cut the shoes off using his bowie knife. He asked Sutherland about it first, and the captain said they could rustle up a pair of boots and some socks for Perry to wear.

"I reckon they better come off," Sutherland added grimly.

It was a miserable ordeal both for Perry and for the men gathered around to watch with macabre interest. The smell that rose when Doc Ford succeeded in removing the shoes made several of the Rangers wrinkle their noses and turn away.

"I grew up sloppin' hogs," one of them commented, "and this is worse'n that!"

"Jimmy, go get a rag good and wet in the creek over there and bring it back to me," Doc said. "We've got some cleanin' up to do here."

Perry swallowed hard and said, "You're not going to have to cut them off, are you?"

The answer from Doc wasn't all that reassuring. "More than likely not."

In the end, Perry's feet were clean and wrapped in strips of cloth. Doc slipped thick socks over those and said, "Stay offa them feet as much as you can until it's time to ride out in the mornin'. I think we're gonna save 'em, but it'll still take some work. Where in blazes were you tryin' to walk to, anyway?"

"The Hill Country," Perry answered without thinking.

"The Hill Country! That's more'n a week's ride from here on horseback. With your feet in such bad shape already, you never would've made it. What's in the Hill Country, anyway, that's so all-fired important you get there?"

Perry just shook his head. He couldn't put it into words, not without going into too much detail and giving away his true identity.

What was in the Hill Country that was so important?

His family—and at this moment, he wasn't sure he would ever see any of them again.

As Emil Deutschendorf had said, Friedrichsburg didn't amount to much as a settlement, just a few buildings scattered along the banks of a creek that flowed into the Pedernales River a few miles to the south.

Even though the settlement was small and unimpressive, Athelstan had felt his excitement growing the farther the group ventured into the Hill Country. The rugged, wooded hills, the

grassy valleys, the streams that flowed swiftly over rocky beds—
everything reminded him so much of Alpenstone.

Different emotions warred within him. On the one hand, seeing this place made him homesick, but at the same time, he had
an overpowering feeling that he *was* home. It was almost as if this
was where he'd been meant to be all along. A beautiful land where
a man could make something of himself, without being surrounded
by all the hidebound traditions of Europe.

There were no grand dukes here. No aristocracy of any kind,
really. Each man shaped his own nobility, if that was what he
chose to do. The sense of freedom that filled him practically took
Athelstan's breath away.

For her part, Bodicia—or "Bodie," as she insisted on being
called these days—seemed to feel the same way. She prevailed
upon the Shellabarger brothers to take turns loaning her a horse.
Wearing Perry's clothes, she rode with Tye Salem on the flanks
and sometimes ahead of the wagons. The exercise seemed to do
her good. Her face was flushed and glowing with health and enthusiasm.

During a halt to rest the animals, she persuaded Tye to let her
shoot one of his pistols. Athelstan wasn't sure that was a good
idea, but when he spoke up, Bodie gave him such a look that he
relented and waved a hand for her to proceed.

"Just make sure you're pointing the gun well away from anything you might hurt," he warned her.

"I'll make sure she doesn't shoot any of us," Tye said. "Nor
any of the mules, either."

Bodie sniffed. "You both act like I'm an infant that can't be
trusted."

"You did go galloping right into the middle of a Comanche
ambush the other day," Tye pointed out with a smile on his face.

"And you're never going to let me forget that, are you?"

"Probably not," he admitted. He extended one of the Paterson Colts toward her. "Here. Be careful, it's heavy."

Soon, the pistol's booming reports echoed back from the rolling hills. Bob Poole shook his head disgustedly and said, "I hope all them gunshots don't make the Comanch' come a-lookin' for us."

Jeremy said, "Wouldn't hearing the gunfire make them more likely to avoid us?"

"They're learnin' how to use firearms their own selves," Poole pointed out. "There are already quite a few old flintlock rifles circulatin' among the tribes. If there's anything an Injun's quick to pick up on, it's a new way to kill his enemies."

"Both hands," Tye said sternly to Bodie as she aimed at a tree limb. "Hold on to it with both hands and you'll be able to control it a lot better."

She muttered something, squinted over the Colt's octagonal barrel, and pulled the trigger again, wincing as she always did when the weapon boomed.

Tye shook his head and said, "I reckon you'll get used to it. Or not."

They had no way of knowing if any Indians heard the shooting, but they didn't spot any more Comanche on the way to Friedrichsburg. When they got there, Athelstan and Jeremy helped Emil Deutschendorf unload the supplies for his trading post, which was a rambling log building with a covered porch and stone chimneys at both ends.

"You can take one of the wagons out to your ranch," Deutschendorf told them. "You have your belongings to carry, and we will leave some supplies in the wagon, as well."

"You don't have to do that," Athelstan said.

"Please. You have been a great help to me, Herr Braxton, and I would return the favor."

"You can start by calling me Athelstan."

Deutschendorf clapped a hand on his shoulder. "Gladly, *mein Freund!* You will need horses, too. Herr Patterson at the black-smith shop also deals in horseflesh."

Jeremy said, "I thought Patterson was the fellow who owned the livery stable back in Indian Point."

"*Ja, ja,* that was Dickie. This is his cousin Joe."

Athelstan said, "I don't know if we have enough money left to buy horses."

"You will be able to strike a deal, I am sure. If you need to, tell Joe that I vouch for you. Later, when you get a chance, you can return the wagon to me. I shouldn't need it in the next two weeks."

"We'll have it back to you within a fortnight," Athelstan promised.

"You called the place we're going a ranch," Jeremy said. "There's nothing there, is there?"

"Not yet, but it will be a ranch, *ja*? There are wild cattle all over these hills. Catch some of them, put your brand on them, and you have a herd!"

"They don't belong to anybody?" Athelstan asked.

"They belong to whoever catches them. They are wild, as I said. What we call mavericks, after Samuel Maverick, one of the early settlers here in Texas. It is said he began the practice of rounding up wild cattle without brands."

Athelstan shook his head. "We don't have a brand. I've never even thought about it."

"That is something you will need to decide, and soon."

"I can see there's a lot to this that we haven't thought about," Athelstan said. "To tell you the truth, I'm not sure we can even find the place."

Ralph Shellabarger said, "My brother and I are goin' part of the way in that direction. We'll ride with you, Stan."

Athelstan smiled. The brothers had started referring to him as "Stan," something no one had ever done before. He didn't like the sound of it, but he didn't correct them. They were just trying to be friendly.

"I'm headed that direction, too," Bob Poole said, "so I'll come along. Ralph and John and I will be veerin' off before you get to where you're goin', though."

"Don't worry," Tye said. "I know these parts pretty well. I'll ride all the way out to the ranch with you and make sure you find it all right."

Athelstan said, "I'm not sure I'll ever become accustomed to calling it a ranch. Back in Alpenstone, we lived on an estate."

Bodie spoke up, saying, "Alpenstone is on the other side of the world. We're in Texas now, and Texas is our home." She tugged on Tye's arm. "Let's go! I want to see the Braxton Ranch!"

A smile appeared on Athelstan's face. He couldn't stop it. "The Braxton Ranch," he repeated. "You know, I like the sound of it."

Book IV

Chapter 30

One year later

Square stone pillars rose on each side of the trail, a dozen feet apart. The pillars were twelve feet tall. An elaborately carved wooden framework ran from the top of one to the other and set into that framework were large wooden letters that read Braxton Ranch. On either side of the words were wooden panels into which were burned the letters *BXT*, the ranch's brand.

There was no fence on either side of this entrance. A man could ride right around it without any problem. But few did. Most visitors followed the trail, which led between pastures of thick green grass and rolling hills topped by magnificent trees.

At the end of that trail stood a large, sturdy log house with a second story in the middle and single-story wings extending out to each side, a porch around it, and a yard bordered by a pole fence.

To the right was a barn with attached corrals, several storage buildings, and a bunkhouse large enough for a dozen men, although only half that many worked on the ranch at the moment. There was a smokehouse, as well, and a building that would be a blacksmith shop when it was finished.

Around on the left were two small cabins. Theobald and Griggs lived in these. They had separate accommodations instead of living in the bunkhouse because they had been with the Braxtons from the start.

Baron's Creek flowed less than a quarter of a mile away, its winding course marked by thick growths of cottonwoods along its banks. Visitors often remarked on what a beautiful setting this was.

The Braxton Ranch was not an empire.

Not yet.

But it might be someday, if Athelstan had his way.

This early morning, he stood on the porch in front of the house with a second cup of coffee in his hand. The crew was already out working under the direction of Frank Schneider, who had immigrated to Texas from Germany and discovered that he had a natural affinity for riding horses and working with cattle. Athelstan had appointed him the ranch's foreman and so far had never regretted that decision.

Athelstan wore canvas trousers tucked into high-topped boots and a brown leather vest over a white shirt. He had grown a mustache since coming to Texas. His face was bronzed from the sun, since he was out on the range doing his share of the work every day. His eyes had begun to develop a permanent squint from the sun and wind.

A new Walker Colt rode in a holster on his right hip. The Walker, named after Samuel Walker, the Texas Ranger who had suggested several design modifications, was a considerable improvement over the Paterson. The trigger was fixed underneath the cylinder and had a guard around it, the cylinder held six shots instead of five, and the mechanism was less prone to jamming.

Athelstan seldom went anywhere on the ranch without carrying the weapon. Big wildcats roamed these hills, rattlesnakes were extremely common, and Comanche war parties still ventured this way on occasion, although the Braxtons had been fortunate. There hadn't been any Indian attacks since their arrival a year earlier.

A familiar step sounded behind Athelstan as he stood there drinking in the glories of the morning.

"More coffee, Mr. Braxton?"

"No thanks, Baldy. What I have will be plenty."

The names were another thing that had changed over the past year. It had taken a while to break Theobald of the habit of calling him Master Braxton. They were in Texas now; "mister" was more fitting. The men who worked on the ranch, in their rough-and-ready fashion, had started calling Theobald "Baldy" almost right away. Athelstan expected the old man to hate the name, but to his surprise, Theobald had taken to it immediately. He was Baldy now to everyone, even Athelstan.

Tye Salem had dubbed Bodicia "Bodie," and that was all anyone called her anymore. Young Griggs's first name was Thomas, so he was Tom or Tommy. He was the wrangler, in charge of the horses on the ranch, just as he had been on the estate back in Alpenstone.

Jeremy, however, was still Jeremy—and Athelstan hadn't seen him this morning, which was a bit worrisome.

He swallowed the last of the coffee in the cup and turned to say to Baldy, "I believe you're going to have to go up and wake Jeremy. He may think he can sleep the day away without doing any work, but he can't."

Baldy hesitated, then made a face and said, "I can't wake him, sir. I already thought about that and went up to give it a try. He's not there."

Athelstan frowned. "Not there?" he repeated. "You don't mean he got up before any of the rest of us and set out to accomplish something, do you?"

Again, Baldy looked like he didn't want to answer, but after a moment he said, "The best I could tell, his bed hadn't been slept in."

Athelstan's jaw tightened. He wasn't the sort of man to curse, but if he had been, some hot words might well have slipped out of his mouth just then. Anger bubbled up inside him.

The swift rataplan of hoofbeats from the trail leading to the ranch house distracted him. He turned back to see a rider galloping between the stone pillars at the entrance, the pillars he had built carefully by hand himself, a stone at a time. He was quite proud of them, even though without a fence they served no real purpose.

The approaching rider wore fringed buckskin trousers and shirt, along with a broad-brimmed brown hat. The hat had slipped back and was held on by its chin strap, revealing blond curls that spilled around the rider's shoulders.

Bodie brought the horse to a swift stop in front of the porch and swung down from the saddle. Her feet were shod in moccasins instead of boots. A belted holster was strapped around her waist. In it she carried a Fifth Model Paterson Colt revolver, the model commonly called the Texas Paterson. Its seven-and-a-half-inch barrel had been cut down to five inches to make it easier for her to handle. The gun weighed less that way, too. The shorter barrel meant its accuracy wasn't as good, but the Paterson wasn't that accurate to start with, except at short range.

Athelstan would have been happy to get Bodie a Walker Colt like the one he carried, but she had learned to shoot using a Paterson and preferred it. In unguarded moments, he still had trouble accepting that his petite, attractive sister, who had been the belle of many balls back in Alpenstone, dressed in men's clothing, packed an iron, as these Texans called it, and galloped around over the wild Texas hills as if she was half Indian.

"What are you doing out and about?" he asked her now. "I thought you were still asleep."

"You're not the only one who can get up before the sun and accomplish something," Bodie said as she looped her horse's reins around the hitching rail in front of the porch. She nodded toward the west. "I went to check on those cows on the other side of the creek. They'd wandered a little too far, so I pushed them back."

"Frank and the other men could have handled that," Athelstan pointed out.

Bodie patted the shoulder of the bay gelding she was riding today. "This old fellow needed to get out and stretch his legs. So did I, for that matter. Neither of us likes being cooped up."

"I'm sure the fact that Tye has been gone for nearly a month has nothing to do with your restlessness."

Athelstan saw the hurt on her features and wished he hadn't made the comment. At the same time, he knew it was true. Bodie wasn't happy when too much time passed between Tye's visits to the ranch. It would have been fine with her if he had just stayed here and rode for the BXT. Then she would have been able to see him all the time.

Tye was too fiddle-footed, as he put it, for that. He was accustomed to ranging all over the known regions of Texas from the Gulf Coast to the upper reaches of the Brazos River, on the edge of what people called Comancheria.

At the moment, he was off guiding a wagon train of newly arrived immigrants from the coast to the settlement of New Braunfels, another German colony just east of the Hill Country. Bodie expected him back soon, but as always, there was no guarantee when he would show up.

"That boy is too blasted undependable," she said as she came up the three steps to join Athelstan and Baldy on the porch. "I've got a good mind to wash my hands of him."

"You do that," Athelstan said, knowing full well there was no chance his sister would follow through on that threat. He went on, "You need to be careful wandering around over there west of the creek. You know some people say the Comanche consider it a dividing line of sorts. Their land to the west, the settlers' to the east."

Bodie scoffed. "And you know it's never stopped them in the past when they wanted to cross it and raid on this side. Anyway, we have cattle over there, don't we?"

"Our claim extends to that side of the creek," Athelstan said with a shrug.

"Then the cattle need to be looked after, and we have a right to be there."

"I just want you to be careful."

She laid a hand on his arm and said, "I know. I don't mean to worry you, Athelstan. Sometimes I just feel as if I have to get out and *do* something, or else I'll go mad." She laughed. "There must be something in the air here in Texas. I never used to feel like that in Alpenstone."

Actually, she had, Athelstan recalled, but not as often. He didn't remind her of that. But she was right in a way. There did seem to be something in the Texas air that prompted a person to get busy and accomplish things.

Those stone pillars at the ranch entrance were visible proof of that.

He handed his empty coffee cup to Baldy, then said to his sister, "I don't suppose you saw Jeremy while you were riding around on the other side of the creek?"

"Jeremy?" she repeated with a frown. "What would Jeremy be doing over there?"

"I don't know, but he's not here, and it appears his bed wasn't slept in last night."

"So, you thought he might be out riding the range and doing some actual work?" Bodie let out a derisive laugh. "You know better than that, Athelstan."

Unfortunately, he did know better. He had tried from the beginning to get Jeremy to handle his share of the load around the ranch, but Jeremy had proven quite skillful in avoiding chores. And when he absolutely couldn't get out of them, he usually did a poor job on whatever it was, to the point that Athelstan had stopped asking him most of the time.

Even so, Bodie's scorn annoyed him. But not as much as he was annoyed at Jeremy.

Bodie went on, "If he's not here, Athelstan, I think we can both make a pretty good guess where Jeremy is."

He looked at her, sighed, and nodded, and then they both said the words together: "King Lothar's Palace."

Chapter 31

Jeremy had to give the Germans credit. They might be a stolid, unimaginative bunch, but they knew how to brew good beer. Even more important, they knew how to have a good time while drinking it.

Even this early in the morning, a group of men at one of the other tables in the *Biergarten* were singing a bawdy song as they waved their steins in the air. They were drunk enough that they were slurring most of the words. Jeremy couldn't make out all of them, but he knew what the song was about.

Lothar Brecht stood behind the bar. His hands, with their fingers resembling the sausages he loved so much, rested on the hardwood. He looked sleepy, as well he should. He had been up all night. The celebration never stopped at King Lothar's Palace, but the saloon's namesake would have to go to bed soon.

He might do that himself, Jeremy thought. He had spent most of the night playing poker, but now he was tired and more than a little drunk. Lothar had some rooms in the back. Jeremy decided he would ask the proprietor if he could sleep it off in one of them.

Or maybe he would just sleep in this armchair near the massive stone fireplace. It was comfortable enough, and he didn't think the singing would bother him enough to keep him awake.

The same couldn't be said of Clara. She squirmed on his lap and did her best to bring him fully awake.

"You can't go to sleep now, Jeremy," she complained as she prodded a long-nailed fingertip against his chest. "You promised me all night that if I let you finish your stupid card game, you would spend some time with me. But now you're half asleep!"

"I'm sorry," he muttered. "I'm tired. We'll be together later."

"That's what you always say! But I need to get some rest, too, you know, and when I wake up, Lothar will expect me to go to work again."

"Well, I can be a paying customer, can't I?"

"Hah! You? Pay? I have never seen such a thing! And Lothar only allows that because of how much money you spend on beer and schnapps. Now you have no money. When Lothar realizes that, he will toss you out on your ear!"

Jeremy winced. Clara was a beautiful girl, but when she was angry, her voice had a strident quality to it that set his teeth on edge.

He also didn't like the reminder that he had lost heavily to Nate Ramsgate during the marathon game the night before. He didn't have enough to cover his debt.

Luckily, Ramsgate had been gracious about it. Before leaving the *Biergarten*, the Texan had told Jeremy he would give him a chance to work off what he owed later on.

Jeremy had no idea what that would involve, but his fervent hope was that the situation wouldn't ever come to that. Ramsgate was a regular at the Palace. Jeremy was sure he would have a chance to win back his money and wipe out the debt. There was no doubt in his mind that he would win the next time.

He tried to shift some of Clara's weight off his lap as he began saying wearily, "Look, if you'll just give me a little time—"

He stopped short as a shadow fell over the chair. Someone was blocking the light from the lamps that hung from the rafters around the room.

Jeremy tipped his head back to look up at the figure looming over him. He recognized the tall, lean shape. He couldn't see the man's face because the light was behind him, but Jeremy knew the hawk nose and the deep-set eyes that belonged to the man. He had looked at that face often enough across the green baize of a poker table, most recently only a couple of hours earlier.

"Time's up, Braxton," Nate Ramsgate said. "I've come to collect what you owe me."

His voice was flat and hard. Jeremy scrambled to sit up straighter. Clara slid off his lap and landed hard on the floor on her ample bottom with an unladylike "Ooof!" But that was hardly the only unladylike thing about Clara.

"What are you talking about?" Jeremy asked as he came to his feet. Standing, he could see Ramsgate better, but that didn't improve the view. The man's predatory face looked like it had been hacked out of stone with a dull chisel.

Jeremy went on, "The game wasn't over until just a few hours ago, and you said you've give me time to pay off what I owe you."

Ramsgate's head jerked in a nod. "That's right. That was a few hours ago. I never said how much time I'd give you, did I?"

"This isn't fair," Jeremy protested. The small shred of self-awareness he still possessed nudged the rest of his brain and reminded him of how often he repeated that same complaint when he landed in trouble of his own making. "I haven't had a chance to do anything since then, even sleep!"

Ramsgate shrugged. "You had time. How you made use of it is your own business. But I've come for my money."

"I don't have it!"

Ramsgate's thin-lipped slash of a mouth quirked faintly at the corners. That was as close as he ever came to a smile. Seeing that, Jeremy realized that Ramsgate hadn't expected to be paid when he returned to the Palace. He was here to demand something else out of Jeremy.

Leaning his head toward the door, Ramsgate said, "Come along with me, then. I told you I'd let you work off the debt. You can get started now."

"Work? Doing what?" As far as Jeremy knew, Ramsgate didn't own a business, nor was he gainfully employed in any other endeavor.

"What I tell you."

Jeremy didn't like this—didn't like it one bit. But Ramsgate had him in the vicelike jaws of a trap. The man carried a pistol and a knife, and was reputed to be deadly with both.

"All right," Jeremy said in a dull voice. "I'll come with you."

Ramsgate gestured toward the table. "Well, get your hat."

From the floor, Clara wailed, "What about me?"

"You're a big girl," Ramsgate told her. "You can get up on your own."

He gripped Jeremy's arm and steered him toward the door. Jeremy glanced toward the bar, hoping that Lothar Brecht might intercede on his behalf, even though he had no reason to think that might happen.

It didn't. King Lothar watched them go without saying anything. The boisterous Germans at the other table had fallen silent and watched their departure with interest, as well.

As he and Ramsgate stepped out into the morning sun, Jeremy heard the obscene song start again behind them.

The horse Jeremy had ridden in from the ranch the night before was tied in front of the *Biergarten*. Another horse was tied next to it. Nearby, four men sat on their mounts. Jeremy recognized all of them as Ramsgate's cronies.

"You ride with us now," Ramsgate said as he unlooped his horse's reins from the rail.

"I don't want to," Jeremy blurted. He might not be the most respectable citizen of the Hill Country, but Ramsgate and his friends had a particularly unsavory reputation.

"Too bad. You should have thought of that when you had all that money riding on the turn of a card." Ramsgate stepped up into the saddle. "Get mounted."

Jeremy swallowed and put his hat on. He rasped his fingertips over the beard stubble on his chin. He knew he looked every bit as disreputable as the others did. He was better dressed, but his clothing showed the ravages of the long night.

"All right," he muttered. He had no choice except to put his foot in the stirrup and wearily pull himself up onto the horse's back after untying the reins.

He turned the horse and fell in with the others as they rode north out of Friedrichsburg. The settlement had grown quite a bit in the year since Jeremy and his brother and sister had first laid eyes on it. Numerous businesses had been established, and a fine-looking church had been built. The place had lost its air of newness. It was a real town now, a permanent town. Many of the settlers had even started calling it Fredericksburg—a Texan name for a Texas town.

Jeremy was only vaguely aware of his surroundings as he rode. His head sagged forward from both tiredness and despair. He kept his eyes on the trail directly in front of his horse, and that was all.

Ramsgate had taken the lead. His men were bunched up behind him with Jeremy in the middle. They were doing that to make sure he didn't try to get away, he realized.

But where would he go if he did? Ramsgate knew where the Braxton Ranch was. Jeremy figured there was no place in this part of Texas where Ramsgate couldn't find him.

He didn't know where they were going and wasn't really aware of how much time had passed when Ramsgate called a halt to the procession. When Jeremy looked around, he realized they had stopped in some trees on top of a hill, overlooking a broad pasture where a small herd of cattle grazed.

"Whose cows are those?" Jeremy asked. For a moment, he thought they might be Braxton stock, but he didn't recognize any of the landmarks he could see, like a pair of hills that rose to the east.

Also, it didn't seem as if they had been gone from Fredericksburg long enough to reach the BXT.

"That's Bob Poole's herd," Ramsgate answered, as he sat easily in the saddle with his hands resting on the horn. "He decided that farming wasn't enough, so he figures to go into the cattle business, too."

Jeremy didn't know that, but he didn't keep up with what Bob Poole or any of the other settlers here in the Hill Country did. Athelstan probably would have known it.

"What are we doing here?" he asked.

Ramsgate chuckled. "Well, you see, the boys and me are sort of the unofficial tax collectors in these parts. Poole's got to pay a tax if he wants to operate, and we figure half of his herd will just about cover it. For now."

"You mean to steal his cattle." Jeremy stared at Ramsgate. "You are"—he searched for the word, then spat it out—"rustlers."

Ramsgate's face hardened. "Now, don't go talkin' like that. I told you, we're just taking our share. What we've got comin' to us for what we do around here."

"You don't do anything around here," Jeremy pointed out.

One of the other men said, "That ain't true. Ain't been no Comanche raids lately, have there? We protect all the ranches in these parts from hostile natives."

"Protect them?" Jeremy repeated. "How do you do that? By hanging around King Lothar's Palace, drinking his beer, and dallying with the trollops who work there?"

Ramsgate crowded his horse against Jeremy's and said, "You let us worry about how we spend our time. What's important is that we're taking those cattle and turning them over to some fellas who'll drive them to San Antonio and sell them—and you're gonna help us."

"Help you?" Jeremy shook his head. "I'm no rustler. I want no part of this—"

Ramsgate's lips drew back from his teeth. "You got a debt to work off, remember? You're ridin' down there with us, and you'll damn well do what I tell you, Braxton." The grimace on the hawklike face became a leer. "Unless you want to settle things some other way, like with a gun or a knife."

"I—I am not armed—"

"Well, hell, we can fix that." Ramsgate reached into one of his saddlebags and brought out a revolver. Jeremy recognized it as a Walker Colt like the one Athelstan carried. A fine weapon—but he wanted no part of it.

He shrank back as Ramsgate extended the gun toward him. "Take it."

"I don't want it."

"Take it, damn your eyes." Ramsgate reached over, grabbed Jeremy's arm and jerked it up, shoved the pistol's butt into his hand. "There. You're armed. What are you gonna do about it? Are you gonna face me like a man, or will you ride down there with us and side our play?"

"I—I . . ." Jeremy felt his determination running out of him like water from a cracked vessel. "I will go with you."

"Of course you will. You've got at least a little sense."

Jeremy wasn't sure about that. This day had taken a turn he never expected, and as the riders heeled their horses into motion and started down the hill toward the cattle they intended to steal, he couldn't think of any way out of this mess.

Chapter 32

As they approached the herd, Jeremy asked Ramsgate, "Aren't you worried about getting caught?"

"Poole doesn't have any hands working for him yet," Ramsgate answered dismissively. "It's just him, and he can't be everywhere at the same time. We've been keepin' an eye on the place. At this time of day, he's usually tendin' to his crops. He still has those to deal with."

"So, what will you do?" Again, Jeremy searched his mind for the right words. "Just round up these cattle and drive them away?"

Ramsgate grinned, but the expression didn't do anything to relieve his face's predatory look. "Well, that makes the most sense, don't it?"

Nothing made sense to Jeremy anymore. Somehow, without meaning to, he was about to become a rustler. A lawbreaker. He was well aware that he had never been the most sterling character and was a disappointment to his older brother, but until now, he had never been an actual criminal.

Maybe he could turn his horse around quickly and ride away before the others could stop him. Then he wouldn't have broken the law—

But he would know that Ramsgate and the others had. They would never allow that. If he tried to flee, they would stop him. They might even shoot him.

One time in the saloon, he had heard a Texan say something about being stuck between a rock and a hard place. That phrase summed up his current position perfectly, Jeremy thought.

Ramsgate lifted a hand and pointed as the men neared the cattle and began to spread out.

"You ride over there," he told Jeremy. "All you have to do is keep those cattle to your left. If any of them start to pull to the right of you, move up, wave your hat at them, and shoo them back. Nothing to it. There'll be another flanker behind you, and we'll keep 'em heading in the right direction. Got that?"

In a hollow voice, Jeremy said, "Yes."

"Don't worry, nothing's going to happen. And your share in what we make out of today's job will be a good start on you payin' off what you owe me."

Jeremy looked sharply at Ramsgate. "I thought if I helped you with this, our debt would be settled."

"You did, did you? Well, you were wrong about that. I'll tell you when it's all square. Now move out there where I told you."

Arguing would be a waste of time right now. Later, once this horrible ordeal was over, he could talk to Ramsgate and try to persuade the man to listen to reason. He was no outlaw. He couldn't continue helping these men steal cattle.

The animals were clustered in several groups as they grazed, but fortunately those groups were fairly close to each other. It didn't take long to push several of them together. Jeremy estimated that they had about forty cattle in the bunch they drove east toward the gap between the twin hills. He had no idea how far they would have to drive the beasts before they turned them over to the associates Ramsgate had mentioned.

They hadn't gone very far when a cry of alarm came from one of the other men. Two more echoed it. Jeremy heard the shouts over the rumble of hooves and turned to look toward the men who had called out the warnings.

In the distance, another rider galloped toward them, leaning forward in the saddle as he pushed the animal on to greater speed. Jeremy could even hear the swift beating of the horse's hooves.

Then a dull boom punctuated that drumming sound. Grayish-white smoke spurted from the gun the approaching rider thrust toward them.

He was shooting at them!

The rider was close enough now for Jeremy to recognize him. Bob Poole wasn't tending to his crops, after all. He had come along in time to see Ramsgate and the others stealing his livestock. Jeremy wasn't surprised that Poole was trying to stop them, even though he was badly outnumbered. The man had always been short-tempered.

Now he was proving to be an absolute fool, charging head-on into six-to-one odds. Well, five to one, Jeremy corrected himself, because he wasn't going to use the revolver Ramsgate had given him. He had thrust the gun into the waistband of his trousers, and it was going to stay there.

Poole was on the far side of the cattle. At that distance, Jeremy wasn't worried about being hit by one of the man's wild shots. Despite that, he didn't like being shot at, even by someone who was in the right, as Poole certainly was. He started to wonder if he might be able to take advantage of the distraction and slip away without Ramsgate and the others knowing.

Then a sharp crack sounded. Jeremy looked at Nate Ramsgate. The outlaw had a rifle snugged against his shoulder. Powder smoke floated over his head.

Jeremy looked back at Bob Poole, only to find that the man was no longer on his horse, which bolted riderless across the field. Jeremy's heart slugged hard and painfully in his chest when he saw the dark shape lying on the ground.

"Damn fool!" Ramsgate yelled as he lowered the rifle. Jeremy assumed Ramsgate was talking about Poole. He wasn't the sort of man who would ever think such a thing about himself.

Ramsgate shouted at his men to keep the cattle moving. He rode over to where Bob Poole lay. The man hadn't moved since

Ramsgate had shot him off his horse a minute earlier. His arms were flung out to the sides, Jeremy noted now.

A ball of sickness rolled around inside Jeremy's belly. He had seen death before, but he wasn't sure he had ever witnessed it being dealt out as swiftly and ruthlessly as Ramsgate just had.

It got worse. Ramsgate drew his pistol, aimed down at Poole, and fired again. Just making certain, Jeremy supposed.

He turned in the saddle, leaned over, and lost what little whiskey and food were left in his stomach from the night before.

His horse never stopped moving while he did that. When he straightened and dragged the back of his hand across his mouth, he discovered that Ramsgate had caught up with him.

"That was a mighty bad stroke of luck," Ramsgate said. He didn't really sound all that upset about what had happened, though. "Poole should have gone to tend his crops like I figured he would. Don't know what he was doing out here at this time of day."

"He's dead, isn't he?"

"What the hell do you think?" Ramsgate snapped. "A man starts shootin' at me, whatever happens to him is his own lookout, not mine."

"I doubt if the law would see it that way."

"There's no law around here," Ramsgate said, scorn in his voice. "The Rangers come through now and then, but they're more concerned with fighting Indians than anything else."

"If the other settlers knew what you did, they might take the law into their own hands."

"What I did?" A grin stretched across Ramsgate's face. "You mean what you did."

"Me?" Jeremy practically yelped. "I didn't shoot Poole. You killed him."

Ramsgate shook his head. "Me and every man here will swear that it was you who blew poor Bob Poole's lights out, if it ever comes to that. You came up with the idea of stealing Poole's cattle and talked us into coming along and helping you, and then when he caught us at it, you put a rifle bullet through him and finished him off with a pistol shot to the head." Ramsgate made a clucking sound with his tongue. "Most cold-blooded thing I've ever seen, and the rest of the boys will back me up on that."

Even though he was sitting on a sturdy horse, Jeremy felt as if he were falling into a deep, dark pit. Every bit of control had been stripped away from him. He was at the mercy of cruel, merciless forces and there was no way he could stop them from treating him like a helpless toy in their vicious game.

After a long, despairing moment, he said, "That's why you made me come along. You wanted someone with you to blame in case anything went wrong."

"You and I might know that," Ramsgate said quietly, "but nobody else ever will. And just imagine how your brother and that sweet sister of yours will feel if you get strung up for murderin' Bob Poole. He and your brother were good friends, weren't they?"

"Damn you," Jeremy whispered.

That brought a laugh from Ramsgate. "I'll worry about bein' damned when the time comes. Between now and then, I'm going to enjoy what we make from the sale of these cows. And the next ones, and the next ones."

"You're going to steal more?"

"There are a lot more in these parts to steal," Ramsgate said simply. "And you're gonna keep on helping us. After today, you're as much a part of the gang as anybody else. Maybe more so, since you're the one with a murder charge hanging over your head."

Jeremy didn't see any way out. Ramsgate and his cronies weren't well liked around here, and the Braxtons were. If it had been his word against Ramsgate's, people probably would have sided with him. Maybe even over Ramsgate and one or two of the others.

But five men swearing that they had seen Jeremy kill Bob Poole—people would have to accept that story whether they wanted to believe it or not.

And Ramsgate was right: it would be devastating for Athelstan and Bodie. After tragically losing one brother already, to have another go bad, turn outlaw and killer—it was too horrible to contemplate.

Ramsgate went on, "In case you're worrying about it, we'll leave your family's ranch alone. There are plenty of cows in these parts besides the ones wearing BXT iron."

Jeremy wanted to believe that, but he couldn't bring himself to do so. Ramsgate and his gang might avoid rustling Braxton cattle for a while, but sooner or later their greed would force them to do so. When that day came, Jeremy would be faced with an impossible choice.

Allow himself to be accused of murder and probably hanged for it? Or hurt his brother and sister worse than he ever had before?

There was one other option, Jeremy realized as his blood seemed to turn to ice in his veins despite the warmth of the day.

As soon as he got a good chance, he could turn murderer for real and kill Nate Ramsgate.

Chapter 33

When Jeremy didn't show up by the middle of the day, Athelstan and Bodie saddled fresh horses and rode out to look for him. They started along the road to Friedrichsburg, or Fredericksburg, as most people called it these days.

Athelstan didn't think it very likely that they would find his brother anywhere on Braxton range. That would require an assumption that Jeremy was trying to help with the ranch work. Athelstan knew how unlikely that was.

There was a much better chance that Jeremy had slipped off to the settlement the previous evening for a night of drinking, gambling, and assorted debauchery.

But even if that was what had happened, Jeremy should have been back by now, unless he was still passed out drunk in one of the back rooms at King Lothar's Palace—if he was lucky—or in an alley somewhere, if he wasn't.

If that was where they found him, Athelstan swore to himself that he would drag Jeremy out of there and dump him in one of the horse troughs in the street. That would sober him up in a hurry.

Athelstan knew he couldn't lock his brother up and force him to conduct himself like a decent human being—but a part of him wished that he could.

They were only about halfway to town when they spotted a

rider coming slowly toward them. Bodie actually saw the man first and pointed him out.

"Is that Jeremy?" she asked.

Athelstan reined in and squinted toward the man on horseback, who rode with his shoulders slumped, leaning forward in the saddle.

"Looks like it might be," he said. "He appears to be not in very good shape. Sick, maybe."

Bodie snorted disgustedly. "Hung over, more than likely, if it's Jeremy. Or still drunk!"

Athelstan hated to admit it, but he knew his sister was probably right.

"Let's go find out," he said, as he nudged his horse to a faster pace.

The other rider must have heard them coming. He stopped and waited for them to close the gap between them. He didn't look up. As they drew closer, Athelstan recognized Jeremy's hat and clothes. It was him, all right.

Jeremy finally raised his head as they reined in beside him. His eyes were red and bleary and had a haunted look to them. Dark beard stubble covered his cheeks, jaws, and chin. His mouth was a thin hard line.

"Where have you been?" Athelstan demanded, without any greeting.

"Hello, brother," Jeremy responded, with an angry twist of his lips. "Good to see you, too."

"Don't act like—"

Bodie interrupted Athelstan. "We were worried about you, Jeremy. We know you went into the settlement last night. That's obvious. Is that where you've been this whole time?"

"That's right."

"At King Lothar's?" Athelstan asked. "I've got a good mind to have a word with Lothar Brecht—"

"I was there last night, but I left early this morning. I needed some fresh air. I rode into the woods and sat down under a tree to rest for a while." Jeremy shrugged. "I fell asleep and just woke up a little while ago."

"You passed out in a drunken stupor, that's what you mean."

"Call it whatever you want, but can we postpone all the chiding and shaming until later?" Jeremy grimaced. "My head hurts, and I'm in no mood for it."

"I don't care what you're in the mood for. Your behavior is unacceptable—"

Hoofbeats interrupted Athelstan's angry words. Another rider was coming quickly along the road from the Braxton Ranch. Athelstan and Bodie turned their horses to face the newcomer. Even Jeremy looked interested.

Athelstan recognized the man on horseback. "It's Ralph Shellabarger," he said. "The way he's hurrying, something must have happened."

"He looks upset," Bodie said.

Ralph's broad, normally affable face was strained as he reined in a few feet away from the Braxtons. Anger and sadness were visible on his features.

"Howdy," Ralph said with a nod. "I stopped at the ranch, and Baldy told me you had started for town, Stan, and Miss Bodie was with you."

Out of habitual respect, Ralph nodded to Bodie and pinched the brim of his hat.

"Miss Bodie. A pleasure to see you, as always." Then he went on, "Glad you're here, too, Jeremy, since Bob was a friend to all of you."

"Bob Poole?" Athelstan asked.

"That's right."

"And you said he *was* a friend." A grim note entered Athelstan's voice as he asked, "What's wrong, Ralph? Something's happened to Bob?"

Ralph sighed. "He's dead. I'm mighty sorry to have to tell you, but he was killed earlier this mornin'."

"By Indians?" Bodie asked, with a slight quaver in her voice.

"No, ma'am." Ralph shook his head. "Although come to think of it, I reckon I can't really say for sure it wasn't Injuns who done it. But poor ol' Bob was shot, and not with arrows. Somebody drilled him with a rifle."

"The Comanche have some rifles," Athelstan pointed out.

"Yeah, but whoever done him in shot him off his horse. And then"—Ralph glanced at Bodie and made a face as if he didn't want to go on with the story in front of her, but he doggedly continued—"whoever done it rode up beside him and put a pistol ball in his head. There's a mighty good chance Bob was already dead or at least dyin', but the killer must've wanted to make sure. Either that or was just pure poison mean."

"That's awful," Athelstan murmured. "And you're right, it doesn't sound like the work of a Comanche. If they'd shot him and then used a knife on him—"

He stopped short. With Bodie here, he didn't want to go into detail about the Comanche's custom of mutilating their victims.

"There's more to it," Ralph said. "Bob's body was found in the pasture where he runs most of the stock he brought in. But the cattle weren't there."

Athelstan's eyes widened in shock. "Rustlers!"

"Looks like it," Ralph agreed.

Jeremy spoke up for the first time, asking, "Who found him?"

"John and I did. We were ridin' over to Bob's place to see if he wanted to throw in with us again on the harvestin' this year, like we did the last couple o' years. As soon as we rode into that pasture and saw his saddle horse grazin' by itself, we knew somethin' was wrong. Didn't take long to find Bob."

"Where's your brother now?" Athelstan asked.

"He stayed to have a look around and see if he could pick up any tracks of the varmints who done it. Told me to ride around to the other spreads and let all the folks in these parts know what happened. Everybody needs to be on the lookout for those no-good—uh, skunks who killed Bob and stole his stock."

Ralph glanced at Bodie again. Athelstan knew he had been

about to express himself with more colorful language than what he'd wound up using.

"We'll certainly keep our eyes open," Athelstan said. "If we spot any of Bob's stock, we'll spread the word and maybe track it back to whoever stole it." He shook his head. "It's hard to believe Bob's dead. He's been a good friend."

Ralph nodded and said, "He sure has. He could be a mite surly at times, but if you needed help, he'd never let you down." He tugged his hat down. "Reckon I'd best go on. Got other places to visit and deliver the bad news."

"Thank you, Ralph," Athelstan said.

"Y'all be careful. Bad things start to happen, sometimes they don't stop."

Ralph heeled his horse into motion and rode on at a fast lope. Athelstan watched him go, then glanced at Jeremy and looked a second time.

Jeremy's face was even more pale and haggard than it had been when they first encountered him a few minutes earlier.

"What's wrong with you?" Athelstan asked.

"What do you think?" Jeremy muttered. "One of our friends is dead."

"You never seemed that close with Bob."

"I still wouldn't want anything to happen to him."

"Of course not," Bodie said. "It makes a shiver go up my spine to think that we have cold-blooded murderers lurking around here."

Athelstan said, "We've always had to worry about the Comanche, ever since we arrived in the Hill Country."

"I know, but this is different. We've always known that the Indians are a threat. And you know if you ever see any of them, they're dangerous and you should get away from them as quickly as you can. But if Ralph is right, if it was cattle thieves who killed Mr. Poole, then it means they were white men and could ride right up to you without you ever knowing just how much danger you're in."

Jeremy suddenly dug his heels into his horse's flanks and made the animal start quickly toward the ranch. Athelstan and Bodie both watched him ride off with surprised expressions on their faces.

"What in the world got into him?" Bodie asked.

Athelstan shook his head. "I don't know, but I don't think he's that upset simply because Bob Poole was killed. That doesn't seem like Jeremy at all."

"Maybe he's afraid the rustlers will come after our stock next."

"I suppose that could be," Athelstan said, nodding slowly. "Not that it would have much effect on Jeremy, since he's hardly ever out on the range."

"It would affect him if we lost the ranch and all our money."

"That's true." Athelstan smiled, but there was no genuine humor in the expression. "He wouldn't be able to afford all his carousing if that happened."

Now that they had found Jeremy, they headed back to the ranch headquarters themselves. As they rode, Athelstan said, "This means that you can't go out riding by yourself anymore."

"Why not?" Bodie asked. "Because I might run into those rustlers?"

"Exactly."

Bodie patted the butt of her holstered Paterson Colt. "I know how to use this gun, you know. Tye says that I've developed into a pretty good shot."

"I've seen you shoot," Athelstan said. "You handle that Colt fairly well, I'll give you credit for that. But it's not very accurate over ten yards or so, and Ralph said that Bob was killed with a rifle, probably from a lot longer range than that. If those rustlers saw you, they might decide it was safer to go ahead and get rid of you before you saw them."

"If I wore my hat back off my head, so they'd know I was a girl—"

"You might be in even more danger that way," Athelstan said. "I hate to speak so plainly, but you know that I'm right."

"I suppose," Bodie admitted grudgingly. "But what do I do the next time I'm restless and want to get out of the house for a while?"

"Ask someone to go with you."

"Everyone's always busy with work."

"Baldy's usually around the house. And Jeremy is, too, for that matter."

"Do you really think Jeremy would be any good at protecting me from rustlers and killers? Any better at it than I would be, by myself?"

Athelstan couldn't bring himself to make that claim. Even without questioning Jeremy's courage, he knew that Bodie was a better shot and quite likely more cool-headed in cases of trouble than their brother.

"Just humor me and stay close to home, all right?" he said.

"All right," Bodie agreed, again with obvious reluctance.

They rode on for a few more minutes before she said, "You know who could track those rustlers and find them? Tye could. There isn't a better tracker in the Hill Country."

"The same thing occurred to me," Athelstan said, with a nod. "As soon as Tye gets back, assuming those outlaws haven't been found already, I'm going to ask him to go after them."

"That can't be soon enough to suit me. Him getting back from that trip, I mean." Bodie grew more serious. "But what's he going to do when he finds them?"

"Men like that aren't likely to surrender and wait for us to turn them over to the Rangers. If Tye can locate them, he'll have to round up the rest of the ranchers to help him, and we'll deal with them."

"By doing what?" Bodie asked.

"By making sure they never steal any more cattle or hurt anyone else ever again," Athelstan said.

Chapter 34

Bob Poole's funeral was held in the Vereins Kirche, the only church in Fredericksburg, and was well attended. Most of the townspeople were there, and many of the ranchers and farmers in the area rode into the settlement, too. Bob wasn't German, but he had been a good friend to the immigrants who had traveled here to make their homes.

After the service, the ranchers gathered outside the church to talk. Athelstan was part of that group along with the Shellabarger brothers.

"I've doubled the number of men riding my range," Jim Niederwald said. "We haven't seen any sign of whoever killed Bob and stole his stock."

"Maybe the thieves have moved on," Hugo Winters suggested. "They might believe that after Bob's death, everyone around here will be on the lookout for them."

Athelstan said, "That's exactly how we all reacted. Now that we're watching for trouble, it won't be as easy for rustlers to operate." He shrugged. "But that will last only for a while. We can't maintain the state of alertness we have now and devote the number of men we have been to standing guard. Work still has to go on, and if the thieves lie low for a while, they'll probably feel as if they can risk striking again."

"What do you figure we ought to do, Stan?" Ralph Shellabarger asked.

Athelstan was aware of the way the other men looked at him as they waited for his answer. Entirely without meaning to, he had become one of the leading citizens in these parts. Many of the settlers in this area came from places where respect for the nobility was ingrained in them. Even though there wasn't any nobility here in Texas, they all knew where Athelstan had come from and what his family represented there.

He would have liked to believe that his intelligence and determined, forthright nature had something to do with how they regarded him, too, but he wasn't sure that was the case.

"Tye Salem will be back soon," he said. "We all know what a good tracker Tye is and how competent he is in a fight. The Rangers would love to have him join them, but he claims he works better alone. I say we give him a chance to do it."

"You mean we should hire him to find the rustlers?" Niederwald asked.

Athelstan shook his head. "Bob was his friend, and I believe Tye might be offended if he was offered wages to avenge Bob's death. As soon as he finds out what happened, he'll probably go after the killers on his own. But we can offer to assist him by providing supplies, perhaps some extra mounts, things like that. And I believe if we post a reward for the capture of those men, Tye would be willing to accept it."

"Assuming he caught them," John Shellabarger said.

"He stands a better chance than any of us," Ralph said.

The men discussed it for a few more minutes and came to an agreement that they would maintain the increased guards on their spreads until Tye got back. Once they had talked to him, they could figure out what to do next.

Athelstan returned to the ranch wagon where Bodie was sitting on the driver's seat with Theobald. She had exchanged her buckskins for a sober gray dress and bonnet. The sight of her like that was somewhat disconcerting to Athelstan. He had grown accustomed to seeing her dressed like "a wild Indian," as Baldy sometimes referred to her usual garb.

Jeremy and Tom Griggs were standing next to the wagon with the horses they had ridden into town from the ranch. Tom held the reins of Athelstan's mount, too, and handed them over as Athelstan walked up.

"What did you and those other fellows decide?" Jeremy asked. If it bothered him that he hadn't been part of the discussion, he showed no sign of it.

"The same thing you and I talked about. We'll turn the matter over to Tye when he returns. He's more qualified than anyone else to deal with it." Athelstan rubbed his chin and added, "Jim Niederwald suggested that we write a letter to the governor in Austin and ask for assistance from the Rangers, but I'm not sure that would do any good. They're stretched awfully thin as it is, just dealing with the threat from the Comanche. Anyway, Jim agreed we should wait and talk to Tye first."

"Maybe he won't want the job," Bodie said. "He's not really a manhunter."

"No one's going to force him to agree," Athelstan pointed out. "And you were the one who said he's the best tracker in the Hill Country."

"That's still true. But those men are ruthless killers. At least one of them is." Clearly, Bodie had been thinking things over during the past couple of days since Bob Poole was shot down. "Trying to find them could be very dangerous. Tye would be risking his life to bring them to justice."

Tom Griggs said, "Tye's been deep in Comanche territory. He told me all about it. That was a whole heap more dangerous than tryin' to round up a bunch of rustlers."

Athelstan had to look down to hide the grin that threatened to spread across his face when he heard Tom's Texas drawl and that reference to "a whole heap." This young man who worked as the wrangler on the BXT bore little resemblance to the stableboy from the Braxton estate back in Alpenstone. Although still in his middle teens, Tom had done a lot of growing up in the past year, Athelstan mused. A whole heap, in fact.

Athelstan looked at his brother and asked, "What do you think, Jeremy?"

Shoulders rising and falling in a shrug, Jeremy said, "What does it matter? You're in charge, Athelstan. Everyone knows that. You'll do what you think is best, and most of the men around here will be quite content to follow your lead."

"I value your opinion."

Jeremy grunted as if he didn't believe that for a second. "My opinion is that between the savages and the outlaws and the rattlesnakes and the mountain lions, there's going to be something that wants to kill you no matter where you turn or what you do. That's just the nature of life in this place."

Athelstan wanted to disagree with Jeremy's bleak assessment, but if he were being honest, he couldn't.

For all the beauty and promise it held, the Hill Country—all of Texas, for that matter—was a dangerous place, so wild it might never be tamed.

The next few days passed uneventfully. Athelstan rode the range every day with Frank Schneider and the rest of the crew, checking on the cattle, moving them when necessary, keeping an eye out for strangers or any other suspicious characters.

He had enlisted Bodie's help in making sure Jeremy didn't try to sneak off to the settlement for another visit to King Lothar's Palace.

"That's just an excuse to keep me here at the ranch headquarters," she said with a pout when he told her.

Athelstan grinned. "I prefer to think of it as being efficient. Two birds with one stone, and all that."

She changed the subject by saying, "I'm starting to worry that something might have happened to Tye. He should have been back before now, don't you think?"

"I don't know. When you start off with a wagon train full of immigrants on a trip of several hundred miles, there are all sorts of things that can happen to slow you down. I'm sure he's just been delayed. He'll turn up any day now."

"And as soon as he does, you'll send him out hunting those rustlers, and I still won't get to spend any time with him." A smile lit up Bodie's face. "I know! I can go with him."

"On the trail of the rustlers?" Athelstan looked and sounded amazed. "You don't honestly believe I'd allow that."

"You're my brother, not my father."

"And I'm still the head of this family."

Bodie, back in her buckskins, snorted, shook her head, and stalked away. All Athelstan could do was stare after her and think about what a profound effect Texas had had on her. She had been reckless and headstrong back in Alpenstone, but living here seemed to have magnified those qualities to quite a degree.

And Texas, he was sure, was to blame for that.

Athelstan had just gotten back to the ranch headquarters late that afternoon when two riders came loping in. One of them was Tom Griggs, who had been sent to Fredericksburg to fetch the mail, if there was any.

The other rider was Tye Salem.

"Look who I found in town!" Tom called happily.

Bodie emerged from the house, breaking into a run as she reached the porch and recognized the newcomers. She hurried out to meet them and caught hold of Tye's left hand with both of hers when he reached down to her.

"You're back!" she enthused. "Finally!"

"I wasn't gone that long, was I?" he asked.

"Forever, it seemed like!"

Tye chuckled. "Best be careful, or you'll give me such a big head this ol' hat of mine won't fit anymore. I'll have to get a new one."

Bodie followed along beside the horse, hurrying to keep up on foot. As the riders reined to a stop in front of the house, she let go of Tye's hand and stepped back.

"Get down off that horse so I can greet you properly," she said.

Tye glanced toward the porch where Athelstan stood resting his hands on the railing.

"I'm not so sure that's a good idea."

Athelstan smiled and waved a hand. "Oh, go ahead," he told the scout.

Tye returned the smile, swung down from the saddle, and handed his reins to Tom Griggs. Then he took Bodie in his arms and kissed her, although to be fair, Athelstan thought, it was almost self-defense. If Tye hadn't kissed her, she would have kissed him.

After a moment, Tye stepped back, rested his hands on Bodie's shoulders, and said with heartfelt sincerity, "It's good to see you again. I'm mighty glad to be back."

Then he looked at Athelstan again and added, "But I hear you've got trouble here. Bad trouble, from the sound of it."

"Bad enough," Athelstan replied with a nod. "Come on in, and we'll talk about it."

A few minutes later, Athelstan and Jeremy were sitting in heavy armchairs near the fireplace while Bodie and Tye shared a settee. Baldy had brought them coffee. Supper wouldn't be ready for a while yet, but a pot of coffee was always on the stove in the kitchen.

"I assume Tom told you what happened," Athelstan began.

Tye nodded. "He filled me in while we were riding out from town. I'm really sorry to hear about Bob Poole. I've known Bob for several years, ever since he came to these parts. We always got along fine. He was a good man. A decent man."

"He certainly was," Athelstan agreed. "But he could be hot-headed, too. When the Shellabarger brothers found him, he had dropped his pistol close by, probably when he was shot. Four of the five rounds in the Colt had been fired."

"So when he spotted whoever it was stealing his cattle, he pulled his iron and charged right at them, throwing lead."

"That's certainly the way it appeared," Athelstan said. "And it sounds like something Bob would do."

Tye smiled faintly. "Yeah, it sure does." He took a sip of coffee and then sat up straighter. "What else did Ralph and John find?"

Athelstan told him about the wounds Poole had suffered and the missing cattle.

"It's rained since then and most of the tracks have been washed away," he said, "but that day it was easy enough to see where the cattle had been driven off between that pair of hills to the east. We tried following them from there, but the tracks all split up and it became impossible."

"I'm not surprised they scattered," Tye said. "That's the easiest way to cover your trail if you're moving a bunch of cattle. I'm sure they had some rendezvous arranged and met up later to dispose of the stock."

"What would they do with it?" Bodie asked.

"Drive it to San Antonio, more than likely. That's a big enough city that there's always a demand for beef. They might have taken the cows down to Mexico and sold them on the other side of the border, but that seems like a lot of work for what probably would be a poor payoff." Tye nodded slowly. "No, I'd say San Antonio is the best bet."

"And I suppose there would be no way of tracing that stock once it was sold," Athelstan said.

"Pretty near impossible. Even if you had an idea who bought it, you'd never be able to prove it."

"So we won't be able to recover Bob's cattle?"

Tye shook his head. "I wouldn't waste time trying to do that. You'd be better off trying to figure out who the thieves are and making sure they don't do it again."

Athelstan rested his hands on his knees and said, "That's what I thought. The other ranchers are in agreement." He gave a firm nod. "We want you to go after them, Tye."

"Hold on." Tye lifted a hand. "I'm not a lawman of any sort. And I don't hire out for jobs like that." His mouth firmed into a grim line as he went on, "But as it happens, as soon as I heard what happened to Bob, I planned to go after whoever gunned him down. A man who'd do that is no better than a hydrophobia skunk, and he's got to be dealt with."

"We couldn't agree more. What we'd like to do is outfit you for the job, Tye. Consider that as our part of the effort to bring Bob's killer to justice."

Tye sat back and considered that. After a moment, he nodded.

"That makes sense, and I can sure understand why you fellas feel that way. I think that'll work out fine."

With a faint tremor in her voice, Bodie asked, "When will you start?"

"No reason to waste time. If I can get those supplies, maybe a packhorse and a spare saddle mount, I'll take a look around tomorrow and see if there's any trail left to pick up."

She sighed. "That's what I thought you'd say."

"But I still plan to have supper with you folks," Tye said, "and if you don't mind puttin' me up for the night, I could use some rest after that trip to the coast and back."

"Of course, you're welcome," Athelstan said.

Tye looked at Jeremy and said, "You're mighty quiet today."

"There's really nothing for me to say," Jeremy replied, with a shake of his head. "Athelstan and the others worked everything out. It's none of my business."

"You don't want Bob's killer to get what's coming to him?"

"Actually, I do," Jeremy said. "I want that very much. But I'm not in any position to accomplish it." He laughed. "You wouldn't want me riding with you."

"Reckon I work better alone, that's true," Tye said curtly. He paused for a second and then went on, "I brought back some news from the coast that might interest you folks. Have you heard about what happened at Indian Point?"

"The place that used to be called Karlshafen?" Athelstan asked. "We haven't heard any news about it since we left there more than a year ago."

"There was an epidemic. Lots of folks got sick, and a bunch of them died."

Athelstan sat forward and clasped his hands between his knees. "What sort of sickness?"

"I'm not a doctor. From what I heard, it was a fever that came on folks suddenly, made their necks stiff and their heads feel like they were about to split apart. They couldn't stand bright light, either. That just made everything worse."

"That sounds terrible."

"It was bad, all right. And most of the folks who got it were the ones waiting by the beach."

"The immigrants?" Bodie asked.

"That's right." Tye was solemn as he added, "You got out of there at the right time, let me tell you. If you'd had to sit around waiting for months, there's no telling what might have happened to you."

"It doesn't seem fair. We came up here and made a home for ourselves, and those poor people who just wanted to do the same thing had to suffer."

"Man is born to trouble, according to the scriptures," Athelstan said.

"There was plenty of trouble, all right," Tye said. "You remember the MacLochlainns? The ones you told me about who were on the boat with you?"

Athelstan and Bodie looked at Jeremy, who shifted uncomfortably in his chair. None of them had forgotten that it was his involvement with Eamon MacLochlainn that had started the chain of events leading to Perry's death.

"What about them?" Athelstan asked.

"They sort of took over while everybody was sick. They hoarded food and medical supplies, such as there were, and tried to make everybody pay for what they needed."

Athelstan nodded. "That sounds like something they would do."

"If anybody complained about what was going on, the brothers would give them a beating."

"And so does that."

"They tried to keep everybody in line by scaring them, but of course, that only works for so long. Eventually, the rest of the immigrants rose up against them. They figured on tar and feathering them, then stringing them up."

Jeremy said, "You mean the MacLochlainns are dead?"

Tye shook his head. "No, they got away. By the skin of their teeth, from what I heard. They took off for the tall and uncut on foot and headed inland as fast as they could rattle their hocks. Nobody ever saw them again."

"Good riddance," Athelstan muttered. "I hate to say it, but Texas is better off without the MacLochlainns. We have enough trouble here without them making things worse."

"I hope they starved to death, slowly and painfully," Jeremy said with unexpected vehemence.

His brother and sister looked at him in surprise, but before they could say anything, Baldy appeared and informed them, "Supper is ready, my friends. Come and get it before, as these Texans say, I throw it to the hogs!"

"But Baldy," Bodie said with a smile, "we don't have any hogs yet."

"That never stopped the Texans from saying it!"

As they stood and headed for the dining table, Athelstan clapped a hand on the old servant's shoulder and said, "Don't forget, Baldy—we're all Texans now!"

Chapter 35

The Texas Rangers lived up to their name. They ranged all over the state, from the thorny chaparral in the south along the Rio Grande and the Mexican border, to the Seven Fingers of the Brazos far to the north, where the forks of the mighty river rose and began their journey southeastward to the Gulf of Mexico. There were only a few troops of Rangers, and they had hundreds of miles to patrol, always on the lookout for Comanche war parties, *bandidos* raiding from south of the Rio, and white outlaws who mercilessly preyed on their fellow Texans.

Perry Braxton loved the life of a Ranger more than he ever thought he would.

When he first started riding with Captain Bert Sutherland's troop, he never intended to stay with them. He would use his time with the Rangers to outfit himself for the rest of his journey to the Hill Country, where he would be reunited with his brothers and sister.

But within just a few days, they had encountered another war party and engaged the Comanches in a running battle that stretched for miles over the prairie. Regular meals and being able to sleep soundly, wrapped in a blanket, had given Perry some of his strength back. During the fight, he had ridden like the wind, his long hair blowing around his head, and fired the Colt at the Comanche raiders, downing at least one of them that he knew of.

It was the most exhilarating experience of his life.

That night, while the Rangers were camped, he had borrowed Doc Ford's bowie knife and used the keen blade to scrape the whiskers off his face. He hacked off some of his hair, too, leaving it shaggy over his ears and the back of his neck.

Then he went to Sutherland and asked, "Cap, how would I go about joining the Rangers officially?"

Sutherland, who was sitting on a rock and eating supper, looked up at him with a frown.

"I thought you figured on headin' up to the Hill Country and findin' your folks."

"I still do," Perry said. "But it may have to wait. I don't own a thing. You've given me the loan of these boots and a gun and let me ride that pony—"

Sutherland held up a hand to stop him. "Hold on," he said. "That pony's as much yours as it is anybody's. We don't have no claim on it. Same's true of the pistol and rifle you been carryin'. They belonged to a good man, and I know he'd be happy you're puttin' 'em to the proper use. As for the boots, nobody else was wearin' 'em."

"They belonged to a dead man, too, didn't they?"

"Well, strictly speakin', yeah, they did. They're yours now, just like the rest of your gear. After the way you pitched in and fought the Comanch' right alongside us today, nobody would think of takin' anything away from you." Sutherland scratched at his jaw. "Fact of the matter is, next time we get into a settlement, the boys and me were figurin' we might get you a saddle. You don't need to be ridin' bareback from now on."

Doc Ford had strolled over and heard part of this conversation. Grinning, he added, "We've talked about outfittin' you with some new duds, too, Jack. Not to put too fine a point on it, but those clothes you're wearin' aren't fit for much anymore except maybe burnin'."

"That would be fine," Perry said with a nod, "but I'd want to pay you back for all of it. I can't think of any better way to earn some money than by—what would you call it? Rangering?"

Doc Ford laughed. "Rangerin' is a good word for it. What do you think, Cap? You reckon ol' Jack here would make a good Ranger? Official-like, I mean."

"The decision's not up to me," Sutherland said. "That'd be up to the commander of the Rangers. But if me and every other man in this troop recommended you, I don't reckon there's much chance he would turn you down. We might even be able to get your wages goin' back to the day we first run into you. You fought beside us that day, too, and ought to get paid for it."

"That would be fine," Perry said. "More than fine. But is it legal?"

"We're Texans, son," Sutherland said. "We worry a heap more about whether somethin's right than we do about whether it's legal!"

From that day on, "Jack Smith" rode with the Rangers, and within a couple of months, he was on the official roster of Captain Sutherland's troop. With a new hat and clothes, and a saddle, he fit right in and was regarded as one of them. He *was* one of them, a Ranger through and through.

But it was only for a while, Perry told himself. He would serve as a Ranger and save some money, so that when he finally showed up at his family's ranch, he wouldn't appear to be some disreputable beggar.

As the months went by and the troop continued its patrols across the frontier, Perry heard more about his brothers and sister. Since everyone believed he was Jack Smith, he couldn't act too inquisitive about the Braxtons who had settled near Fredericksburg, but he heard enough talk to know that Athelstan had established a ranch as he'd intended to do. It was called the Braxton Ranch, although some people just referred to it as the BXT. Athelstan, Jeremy, and Bodicia had all made the journey from the coast and were doing well, although Perry did hear some gossip in an isolated trading post that claimed Bodicia now packed a gun, dressed like an Indian, and rode like one, too. That was difficult to accept, but Perry didn't see any reason why the men talking about it would lie. He looked forward to seeing all three of his siblings again.

He had thought about writing to them, to let them know he was still alive, but it seemed to him that explaining everything in a letter would be too difficult. It would be better, he decided, to wait until he could see them all face to face and tell them why he had made a break for freedom on the ship, as well as everything he had done since then.

And if anything happened to him and he never made it to the ranch, they would never know. It would be easier on them that way. They had already mourned him once; they shouldn't have to do it again.

The troop had camped outside the town of Seguin, a settlement that had been founded less than a decade earlier when Texas was still a republic. Named for Juan Seguin, one of the heroes of the revolution, it had developed into a principal stopover and supply point for the Rangers when they were out on their patrols.

Today, however, only three men were riding into the settlement: Perry, Doc Ford, and a bushy-bearded old frontiersman known as "Bet a Hat" Bates because of his fondness for that phrase.

"I'm so thirsty I could drink ever' saloon in this place dry," Bates declared as they reached the edge of town. "You can bet a hat on that, boys!"

"Cap'n Sutherland sent us to pick up supplies, not to get pie-eyed," Doc said. "You'd best just rein in that thirst of yours, old-timer."

Bates snorted. "You don't tell me what to do, young'un! Why, I was chasin' Comanch' all over Texas before you was even born!

And if my throat needs some lubricatin', you can bet a hat I'll damned well—"

"Hold on a minute," Perry broke in. "Anything strike you boys as unusual about that fella up there on the trading post porch?"

The other two Rangers looked toward the trading post, which just happened to be the trio's destination. A man wearing a long coat stood on the building's porch, his head moving jerkily from side to side as he seemed to be trying to watch in every direction at once. He had his hat brim pulled low and all they could see of his face was a rust-colored beard.

"He seems a mite jumpy," Doc said. "But I don't know—"

"Look at his left arm and leg," Perry broke in. "He's holding something down along that leg and using his body to shield it."

"Dadgum! Is that a shotgun he's got?"

"I think it is," Perry said.

Bates said, "Why would a fella be standin' out on the porch holdin' a shot—? Wait just a dadblasted minute! You think some of his pards are in there robbin' the tradin' post?"

"Sure could be," Doc said.

Bates lifted his reins, evidently intent on charging toward the possible robbery. Doc put out a hand and said, "Take it easy, Hat. You go gallopin' up there, that varmint's liable to blow you out of the saddle with that scattergun. We'll be better off tryin' to take him by surprise."

That was exactly what Perry thought. Carefully, because he didn't want the lookout on the porch to see what he was doing, he slipped his hand down to the holstered Colt on his hip and eased the keeper thong off the hammer. Doc and Bates did likewise. They continued approaching the trading post at an easy, deliberate pace, as if they had no hint anything was wrong.

Seguin was quiet. It was a cloudy day. Some drizzle had fallen earlier, and that helped keep people off the street. A drowsy air hung over the settlement.

A good day to pull off a robbery and maybe get away before anybody else in town knew what had happened.

It was just bad luck that three Rangers had ridden into town at the wrong time.

The lookout had spotted them by now and was watching them closely. Perry tried to appear as if he weren't paying any attention to the man. At the same time, he took as good a look as he could.

As he did that, an odd feeling came over him. Something about the man struck him as familiar. Perry suddenly felt as if he should know him.

The three riders reined to a stop in front of the trading post. The man on the porch had his right side turned toward them. Perry was more sure than ever that he was holding a shotgun against his left leg.

"Store's closed," the man called to them, before they could dismount.

"You don't say," Doc drawled. "Why, I never knew this place to be closed in the middle o' the day like this before." Grinning, he rested his hands on his saddle horn. "Somethin' wrong?"

"Don't know," the man replied curtly. "I think maybe, uh, the owner had a death in the family or something."

"Well, I'm plumb sorry to hear that. Who are you? Friend of the family?"

"No, I just, um, came along, and the fella inside asked me to stand out here and let folks know the trading post is closed right now."

Doc nodded slowly. "So Mr. Milligan is inside?" He started to dismount. "I reckon I'll go in and give him my condolences—"

The lookout made a face and swung the shotgun up from beside his left leg. He wrapped his right hand around the barrels to steady them. The index finger of his left hand was inside the trigger guard.

"It's right there on that horse you'll be stayin', mister!" he said.

Perry was nowhere near as fast as some of the other Rangers when it came to drawing a gun, but he had practiced quite a bit in the months he had ridden with them. The man on the porch was looking at Doc, so Perry took advantage of the opportunity to pull his iron. He eared back the Colt's hammer as he lifted it and shouted, "Drop that gun, mister!"

Grimacing, the lookout tried to jerk the twin barrels toward Perry. He wasn't going to sit there and let the man line up the shot. He triggered the Colt and felt it kick back against his hand as it let out a resounding boom.

The man on the porch twisted under the impact of the heavy lead ball, but he managed to pull the shotgun's triggers anyway. The double blast was deafening, even outside this way. Being hit by Perry's shot had thrown off his aim. The loads of buckshot ripped through the air well wide of the three Rangers.

Doc and Bates were already scattering, spreading out to make themselves more difficult targets. They clawed out their Walker Colts and pointed the revolvers at the trading post as they tried to control horses made skittish by the gunfire and the smell of burned powder.

The man on the porch dropped the empty shotgun and used his left hand to clutch his right shoulder, which was leaking blood where Perry's shot had struck him. He stumbled but stayed on his feet. He had a revolver holstered on his left hip and let go of his wounded shoulder as he tried to draw the gun.

"Don't do it!" Perry shouted at him. The Colt in his hand was already cocked again. "Leave that alone!"

The man's bearded face contorted in a grimace of pain and rage as he drew the gun. The hammer of Perry's Colt fell again before the man could bring his gun up. Perry's gun roared a second time. The ball drove into the man's chest and threw him backward.

As the man landed in the doorway, another figure in a long coat leaped over him, emerging from the building with a gun crashing and spitting fire in his grasp. Three more similarly clad men were right behind him.

Perry yanked his horse around. He felt the wind-rip of a pistol ball as it whipped past his ear. The Colt boomed and bucked in his hand as he fired twice more.

Doc and Bates had started shooting, too. Gun thunder filled the air as muzzle flames a foot long jetted back and forth. Within seconds, the clouds of powder smoke grew so thick it was almost impossible to see, let alone aim. The men on both sides were just sweeping the air with lead and hoping some of it hit what it was supposed to.

The Colt storm slackened as the four men who had burst out of the trading post piled off the porch, two going right and the other pair heading left. They leaped off the ends of the porch and started running, still firing behind them now and then as they fled.

Perry jabbed his boot heels in his mount's flanks and went after the two men who had gone left. The pony leaped forward, nimble-footed, and covered ground quickly. Perry bent forward, low over the horse's neck.

One of the men had pulled ahead of the other; the man lagging behind twisted around and fired practically in Perry's face. Perry sensed as much as heard the hum of the pistol ball not far over his head.

The next second, he pulled his right foot from the stirrup and kicked the man in the chest as he charged past. The kick landed solidly and sent the man flying off his feet.

His companion darted around a corner into an alley. Perry went after him, only to have the pony stumble over an empty barrel the fleeing outlaw had toppled and rolled into the middle of the narrow passage. No matter how graceful it was, the pony had no chance to avoid the obstacle and couldn't escape falling.

Perry flew forward over the pony's head. His hat went flying, too, but he managed to hold on to his gun even when he crashed on the alley's hard-packed dirt floor. He rolled a couple of times and ended up on his belly.

The man he was after had stopped at the far end of the alley. It

was dim and shadowy back there because of the overcast skies.
Colt flame spurted redly in the gloom as the man fired at Perry.
Dirt pelted Perry's face when the ball dug into the ground a cou-
ple of feet short of him.

He had one round left in his Colt, he thought. He tilted the
barrel up and let the hammer fall. The gun slammed out that shot.
The man at the end of the alley grunted, staggered, and then disappeared as he ran off. Perry scrambled up and went after him,
even though he was acutely aware that the Colt in his hand was
now empty.

It didn't matter. When he got to the end of the alley, the man
was gone. Perry didn't know which way he had gone, and there
were plenty of places to hide here among Seguin's back streets.
With a disgusted sigh, Perry went to see if his pony was all right
or if the fall had injured it.

He was very pleased to find that the animal was standing and
appeared unhurt. He caught hold of the reins and led the pony
back to the main street. As he emerged from the alley, Bet a Hat
Bates raced up to him on horseback and brought his mount to a
sliding stop.

"There you are!" the old-timer exclaimed. "Are you all right,
Smith?"

"Yeah, I'm fine," Perry replied. "A little shaken up from taking a tumble off my horse, but that's all. That blasted gunman
got away, though."

"You were right, those varmints were robbin' the store," Bates
said. "Four were inside, and they left that one hombre with the
scattergun to keep an eye on things outside."

"I knocked one of them down with a kick as I went by him,"
Perry said. "Did you get him?"

Bates shook his head. "He must'a been able to get back up
and run off. The others managed to give me an' Doc the slip, too.
But the one you shot on the porch ain't goin' anywhere. He's
dead as dead could ever be, you can bet a hat on that!"

Perry nodded. The thought of killing a would-be robber when

the man was trying to kill him didn't bother him a bit. He had killed several Comanches during battles with raiding parties. This was a white man, but that didn't make a bit of difference as far as Perry was concerned. Anybody, red or white, who threatened the peace and safety of Texas was an enemy to be dealt with as harshly as necessary.

Perry took a few minutes to reload his revolver's cylinder. Having those fresh rounds available was vitally important. Then he walked along the street toward the trading post, leading his pony as Bates rode alongside.

Seguin was a lot less sleepy than it had been a few minutes earlier, before what sounded like a small-scale war broke out. Quite a few people were out on the street now, curious to see what all the shooting had been about.

A good-sized crowd had gathered in front of the trading post, where Doc Ford stood on the porch talking to a portly middle-aged man wearing a canvas apron over his clothes. That would be the fellow who owned the store, Perry supposed.

The bystanders made way for Perry to step up onto the porch and join Doc. His fellow Ranger nodded and said, "Jack, this here is Mr. Milligan. He runs this trading post and store."

Milligan grabbed Perry's hand and pumped it enthusiastically. "Thank you, son, thank you. If you and these other Rangers hadn't come along when you did, those thieving skunks might've cleaned me out! As it was, they were so spooked when the shooting started they ran off without thinking to take any loot with them."

"I'm glad to hear that, sir," Perry said. He reclaimed his hand from the enthusiastic storekeeper.

"It's a shame the others got away, but at least this one didn't," Milligan said with a nod toward the bloody corpse lying on the porch. The dead outlaw had been dragged to one side so he wasn't blocking the doorway anymore.

The man's hat had fallen off, revealing a thatch of rusty hair that matched his beard. Death had frozen a grimace of pain and shock on his face, contorting his features.

Even so, he still looked familiar to Perry, although more so now. That nagging recognition, coupled with the Irish accent that had come out in the man's voice when he shouted in anger, made a jolt of realization go through Perry.

He dropped to one knee beside the body to study the face closer. The action surprised Doc Ford, who said, "What's wrong, Jack? Say, you don't know this son of a buck, to you?"

"Not really, but I know who he is," Perry said. His voice sounded hollow in his ears. His mind was spinning as he tried to get control of the memories that surged up inside him. He had never expected to see this man again, and now that he had, he had no idea what it meant for him.

"His name is—*was* Cathal MacLochlainn."

And Perry couldn't help but wonder if two of the other outlaws who had gotten away were Ronan and Eamon MacLochlainn.

Chapter 36

Cactus Armstrong cursed a blue streak as Ronan MacLochlainn tied up the wounded shoulder. Ronan had to admit that Armstrong's command of the filthiest profanity was admirable.

It was a shame that Armstrong's leadership of this gang hadn't proven equally as admirable. Even if that job in Seguin had gone off without a hitch, it wouldn't have netted them enough cash to do more than allow them to get by for a short time.

They needed something better than these penny-ante robberies Armstrong kept coming up with.

Ronan stepped back and said, "All right, Cactus, I think you'll live. Try not to let that wound fester."

"What do you think I'm gonna do?" Armstrong snapped. "Let it get worse on purpose?"

"I'm just telling you, that's all." Ronan turned to his brother Eamon, who was watching their back trail, and asked, "Any sign of pursuit?"

"No, they didn't come after us," Eamon replied. "At least I didn't see anybody when we were heading out of town, and I haven't spotted any riders since then."

The other surviving member of the group, Al Murphy, was taking care of the horses. He'd allowed them to drink at the stream where the outlaws had paused in their flight. Now he stood holding their reins.

The group was still too close to Seguin to stop for more than a short time, even though the horses and the wounded man could have used the rest. Cactus Armstrong had lost quite a bit of blood.

A pang of loss went through Ronan as he looked at the fifth horse, the one that no longer had a rider to claim it. That bay had been Cathal's mount. Cathal was back in Seguin—dead.

As if the same thoughts were going through Eamon's mind, he said, "We never should have abandoned Cathal like that."

"We didn't have any choice," Ronan said. "Taken by surprise the way we were, all we could do was try to get out of there." He paused and then added bitterly, "He was supposed to warn us if anyone was about to interfere."

"He must not have had the chance. Cathal would never let us down, you know that."

That was true, Ronan supposed. Cathal always did his share of the work, whatever it might be, and if you asked him to take care of something, he did. Until today.

"He might not have been dead," Eamon said.

"He was dead," Ronan said flatly. "I got a good look at his face when we charged out of there. The life was gone from his eyes."

"You can't know that for sure—"

"I'm sure. He was drilled through the heart."

"Who were those damn pelicans, anyway?" the scrappy little outlaw called Murphy asked. "Why'd they ride up and just start shootin'?"

Armstrong said, "Cathal got spooked and started it. I was lookin' out the door and saw him swing that scattergun up. That's when the fella on horseback shot him the first time."

"They were nobody," Ronan said. "Just some short-tempered fellows who happened to be in the wrong place at the wrong time for us."

He wasn't sure that was completely true. Things had been pretty hectic, what with all the guns going off, but for an instant during the battle he had caught a good glimpse of the man who had gunned down Cathal. There had been something familiar about him, a fleeting sense that Ronan had laid eyes on him before, but then powder smoke had obscured his vision and he had never gotten a better look.

It didn't matter, he told himself. Since leaving Indian Point, the MacLochlainn brothers had run into plenty of people as they made their way inland. He could have seen the man he'd noticed today almost anywhere between the gulf and Seguin.

Most of those encounters along the way had been violent, too, and occasionally ended in death, when someone didn't want to surrender whatever it was the MacLochlainns wanted to take. Eamon had no patience for anyone who got in his way and was quick to use a gun or knife.

Of the three of them, Eamon was the one who fit in the most with Armstrong and Murphy, who were veteran riders on the wrong side of the law. Back in Ireland, the MacLochlainns had done plenty of disreputable things, but they hadn't been outright criminals. Since the outlaw life seemed to be their fate here in America, teaming up with Armstrong and Murphy, and taking advantage of their experience, had worked out well for the brothers—until today.

"What are we gonna do now, Cactus?" Murphy asked, still looking to Armstrong for leadership.

"We didn't pick up any loot back there, and we still need money," Armstrong said.

"We didn't get any loot because you panicked," Eamon said, as he glared at the wounded man. "That fellow at the trading post had already stuffed some cash in a bag. You should have grabbed it before we ran out of there."

"For all I knew, the whole place was surrounded," Armstrong snapped back defensively. "I figured we'd better get out of there as fast as we could while we still had the chance."

Eamon snorted, contempt obvious in the sound.

Armstrong flushed darkly. Ronan could tell he was struggling to keep his temper reined in, and he could understand why Armstrong felt that anger. With his blunt arrogance, Eamon had a habit of rubbing people the wrong way.

"Anyway," Armstrong went on, "we'll head on up to New Braunfels and pull a few jobs around there. It's not far. We can be there in a day or two."

"Jobs like this one today?" Eamon asked, his voice dripping with scorn. Ronan wanted to tell his brother to ease off, but it wouldn't do any good. When Eamon was worked up like this, he wasn't one to see reason. "Jobs that won't get us anything but a handful of coins and a chance to get our heads shot off?"

"Well, then, what do you think we should do?" Armstrong blustered.

"I've heard talk that there's a good market in San Antonio for stolen cattle, as well as ranches north and west of there with good herds. It seems to me that getting in on an operation like that would be a lot more lucrative in the long run, and probably less dangerous, too."

Ronan's interest perked up. He had heard the same gossip as Eamon in saloons and taverns and cantinas where men on the wrong side of the law congregated. A few idle thoughts of trying to get some of that profit-on-the-hoof for themselves had crossed his mind. But as long as they were getting by, he had been reluctant to upset things with Armstrong and Murphy.

That was the problem, though. They were just getting by, and when something went wrong, as it had today, they had nothing to fall back on.

Armstrong shook his head. "That's too much of a risk, and it's a week's ride from here to the Hill Country, where those ranches you're talkin' about are located."

"There are ranches around here," Murphy suggested.

"This is mostly farming country," Eamon said. "We don't want to steal a handful of milk cows. Anyway, it's too civilized. Too big a chance somebody would interfere with us. From what I've heard, things are still pretty wild and untamed up there in the Hill Country." He grinned. "Easy pickings for men like us."

Armstrong glared and said, "There's something else you're not thinkin' about. We're almost out of supplies. That's why we needed to pull that job today. We don't have enough food to last all four of us for the time it would take to get to where you're talkin' about."

"Then maybe Ronan and me should go ahead on our own," Eamon said.

Armstrong stood up from the log where he'd been sitting while Ronan patched him up.

"You want to run out on me and Al, is that what you're sayin'?"

"I'm saying maybe we've ridden together long enough," Eamon returned coolly.

Armstrong turned sharply to Ronan.

"Are you gonna let your brother talk crazy like this? We've worked together mighty well, Ronan. No reason to break up the bunch now."

Ronan said slowly, "What Eamon says about pulling jobs that would be more lucrative makes sense, Cactus. If we keep hitting these little stores and trading posts, we'll never grab enough loot to get ahead. We'll just be living from robbery to robbery. I think we can do better."

"By makin' him the boss of the gang?" Armstrong asked as he jabbed an accusatory finger toward Eamon.

"I didn't say that, but a good idea is a good idea, no matter where it comes from."

Armstrong's head jerked from side to side as he glared at the brothers. Then he said, "Look, I'm sorry about what happened to Cathal. I'm just as sorry as I can be. But it wasn't my fault, and it ain't any reason to go changin' things. I say we're goin' to New Braunfels and scoutin' around there until we find a likely place to hold up—"

"If you do, you'll do it without me," Eamon said. "I'm finished with this bunch. Give me my horse, Murphy, and I want my share of the supplies that are left, too."

Armstrong flung out his unwounded arm toward Murphy and said, "Hold on to that horse, Murph. I'm not gonna let some stupid oaf ruin everything—"

"Stupid oaf!" Eamon blurted. Ronan knew what was going to happen next. He couldn't stop it even if he had wanted to.

Eamon yanked his gun from its holster. Armstrong's eyes widened as he reached across his body and fumbled to get his own weapon out. He wouldn't have stood a chance even if he hadn't been wounded.

A shot crashed as flame and smoke geysered from the barrel of Eamon's revolver. Armstrong cried out and clapped a hand to his chest as he took a sudden step backward. He caught himself, took his hand away, and stared down in stunned disbelief at the blood smeared on his palm.

He raised his head to stare at Eamon and said, "You shot—"

Eamon's gun boomed again. Armstrong's head jerked back as the pistol ball slammed into his forehead and bored through his brain. His knees buckled and he went down in a limp, huddled heap.

"Damn right, I shot you," Eamon said as the echoes rolled away over the gentle hills. "Now who's the stupid oaf?"

Ronan had drawn his gun, too, and had it pointed in the general direction of Al Murphy, just in case the man wanted to take cards in this game.

Still grasping the reins of all five horses, Murphy raised his hands and said quickly, "Don't shoot, Ronan. I don't want any trouble. Seems to me that ol' Cactus was just askin' for it by runnin' his mouth like that."

"Don't you believe in loyalty?" Ronan asked in a hard voice.

"Hell, yeah, I do, but I don't believe in throwin' my life away because somebody else got their dander up and started actin' like a damn fool."

Eamon grinned and said, "Now there's a smart man, brother. A man we might want stringing along with us."

Murphy nodded eagerly. "Wherever you boys are headed, I'd be plumb proud to go along and give you a hand. How about it, fellas? The three of us head for—where was it you said, Eamon? The Hill Country?"

"That's right," Eamon said as he slid his still-smoking Colt back in its holster. "I think it's time we take a ride up to the Hill Country and see if our fortune is waiting for us there."

Chapter 37

Athelstan rode with Tye to the spot where Bob Poole had been killed and his cattle stolen.

"That's where the Shellabarger brothers found Bob," Athelstan said as he pointed out the spot. He waved his hand toward a different part of the pasture and continued, "The cattle had been bunched up over there and were being driven toward the hills, by the look of the tracks. The trail led over that saddle between the hills but became impossible to follow on the other side."

Tye nodded. "Rough country east of there. Lots of breaks and gullies. You could drive small bunches of cattle through that stretch but would have trouble with a bigger herd. Splitting up made it easier for the thieves to move that stock, and harder to follow them, too."

"Two birds with one stone, as the old saying goes."

Tye grunted. "I'll take a look around over yonder. There's no point in you riding any further with me, Athelstan."

Many of the Texans in the area had taken to calling him Stan instead of Athelstan, but Tye still used the full name because that was how Bodie referred to her brother.

However, she was adamant that no one call her Bodicia anymore. She had left that name in Alpenstone, she said. Tye thought it had a pretty sound to it and had been teasing when he told her it was a mouthful, but if she wanted to be called Bodie, that was fine with him. She was the same beautiful, fiery young woman either way.

Athelstan said, "I'd really like to go with you and help avenge Bob's murder, but I suppose it makes more sense for me to look after the BXT. It's possible those rustlers could come back and try to hit us next time."

"It sure is," Tye agreed. "I'll feel better about things knowing that you're keeping an eye on the place."

"By things, you mean Bodie. You don't want to be worrying about her while you're searching for those killers."

"Well, sure, but not just Bodie."

Athelstan gave the other man a searching look. "At what point do I need to start asking you about your intentions toward my sister?"

"Not yet," Tye responded with a smile. "Bodie and I are friends. Maybe a mite more than friends, if you want the truth, and I don't feel like lyin' to you, Athelstan. But I'd never do anything improper or dishonorable."

"Maybe it's not you I'm the most worried about," Athelstan muttered.

"I won't let things get out of hand. I give you my word on that."

Tye extended his hand, and Athelstan clasped it firmly. Tye could tell from the look on Athelstan's face that the rancher was reassured. Still worried, maybe, but not quite as much so.

"Good luck in your search."

"Thanks. If I find out where the gang has been holing up—if there is such a place around here—I'll bring word back and we'll put together a group to go after them."

"It's been suggested that we send word to the Rangers and ask for their help."

Tye shook his head and said, "If a troop of those fellas happened to come along and they were willing to pitch in, I'd say, sure, we could use their help. But if we have to send a letter to Austin and then wait for somebody there to respond, the men we're after could be long gone before any Rangers arrived. Better to deal with it ourselves." He chuckled. "Stomp our own snakes, I've heard it called."

"I like that," Athelstan admitted. "Yes, we'll stomp our own snakes."

"But first we've got to find their den." Tye lifted a hand in farewell and rode toward the hills, trailing on lead ropes his spare saddle mount and a pack mule carrying several days' worth of supplies.

"Where are you going?" Bodie asked Jeremy, as he came out of the barn leading a saddled horse.

"I need to get out and move around a bit," he said. "A ride seemed like a good idea."

"A ride into Fredericksburg, you mean? Maybe a visit to King Lothar's Palace?"

Jeremy's face flushed. "Athelstan has made it plain that he doesn't want me going there anymore."

"And you've made it plain you don't care what Athelstan wants."

"That's not true at all," Jeremy said, shaking his head. "Yes, I'm a grown man. I feel I should be able to come and go as I please, wherever I please. But I see no point in deliberately stirring up trouble."

He pointed to the west and went on, "If you must know, I thought I'd take a ride along the creek—this side of the creek—and make sure none of the cattle have strayed across it. The only reason I'll cross it is if they have, and then I'll just drive them back on this side."

Bodie stared at him for a moment before saying, "Why, that sounds like honest, respectable work. The kind that actually accomplishes something."

"You could always be quite a brat on occasion," Jeremy said coldly.

Bodie took a step toward him, her eyes blazing with anger.

"What are you going to do, slap me and prove what I just said?" Jeremy laughed. "Go ahead."

She shook her head, made a scoffing sound, and said, "You're not worth the effort. I'd only do that if I cared what you thought about me."

"You were headed into the barn, too. You know, I could ask where you're going."

"That's none of your business."

"Tye rode out a little while ago, as I'm sure you're well aware. Were you thinking of following him while he searches for those rustlers? I don't think that would go over very well with either him or Athelstan."

She jutted her chin defiantly at him. "If you're a grown man, I'm a grown woman. I don't have to account for my actions to you."

"Let's just leave it at that, then," Jeremy said with a curt nod. He put a foot in the stirrup and swung up onto the horse he had saddled. Griggs had offered to do it for him, but he had stiffly refused.

With a nudge of his heels, he started the horse loping toward the line of trees in the distance that marked the creek's course. He didn't look back. He didn't think Bodie would follow him after that testy exchange, but if she chose to, he didn't really care.

As a matter of fact, everything he had told her was true. He had no secrets to keep from his sister.

No new secrets today, anyway.

His involvement with what had happened to Bob Poole was still known only to Nate Ramsgate and the other rustlers, and it would have to stay that way from now on.

Jeremy would carry that guilt to his grave, as well as the regret that it had ever happened. Confession might have eased the burden on his conscience.

But with Ramsgate and the other members of the gang ready to swear that *he* was the one who had pulled the trigger on Poole, if he tried to tell anyone what actually had happened, quite probably he would wind up putting his own neck in a noose.

Since that horrible day, he had seen no sign of Ramsgate. The man had told Jeremy he would be in touch, but so far that hadn't happened. Maybe it never would. For all Jeremy knew, something had happened to Ramsgate. The circles the man traveled in, it was entirely possible some argument had ended in a fatal exchange of gunfire.

Jeremy could only hope for such a turn of fate.

He reached the creek a while later and turned north. He had seen a couple of riders in the distance and recognized them as members of the BXT crew. At first, he had worried that they might be Indians. Advance scouts for a Comanche war party, maybe. Jeremy knew the family had been exceedingly lucky not to have had any trouble from natives since establishing the ranch. That good fortune couldn't last forever.

He carried a Walker Colt snugged in its holster on his right hip. Another fully loaded revolver was in one of his saddlebags. A Mississippi 1841 muzzle-loading rifle, also loaded and primed so that all he had to do was pull back the hammer, was strapped to his saddle. He had extra ammunition for all the weapons and considered himself well-armed. Also, he had practiced enough with them that he was proficient in their use.

But practice was nothing like engaging in an actual gun battle with someone who wanted to kill him, or fighting off an Indian war party that jumped him. When he thought too much about such things, fear stirred deep inside him. He knew that under the right circumstances, such fear might become hysterical panic.

Despite that, he had grown bored sitting around the ranch house. He had to admit that it felt good to be out riding the range, as Athelstan called it. Maybe someday he would actually get used to such activities.

A rider appeared ahead of him, pushing out of a clump of brush along the creek. It took Jeremy a second to realize what was happening. When he did, he hauled back sharply on his horse's reins and dropped his other hand to the butt of his gun.

"Hold it!" Nate Ramsgate called. "Take it easy, Braxton. It's just me."

Jeremy's pulse hammered loudly inside his head. He had been on edge to start with. The ride hadn't calmed him down after all. On the contrary, thinking about Comanche and all the other bad things that could happen had just gotten him more wound up.

He forced himself to relax and move his hand away from his gun. He swallowed hard, rode closer to Ramsgate, and said, "What are you doing out here, Nate?"

"I came to talk to you, of course," Ramsgate replied as they sat on their horses facing each other. "I've been keeping an eye on the place, hoping I'd get a chance to talk to you alone. I'm glad you finally came out here by yourself."

"I don't think we have anything to talk about."

Ramsgate grinned as he sat slack in his saddle, totally at ease. "What do you mean, kid? We're partners, aren't we?"

"I told you I was done—"

Ramsgate still held himself in a casual pose, but his voice was razor-sharp as he said, "And I told you, you still owe me until I say otherwise. That means we're in this thing together."

"This thing, as you call it, is something I can't be part of—"

Again, Ramsgate interrupted him. "You're already part of it. You killed Bob Poole."

"I didn't, and you know it!"

"In the eyes of the law—if it ever comes to that—you did, and you'd better hope that doesn't come about. Poole had lots of friends around here. I'm sure they'd be happy to put a noose around your neck and let you dance on air for a spell."

That same thought had crossed Jeremy's mind earlier. It put the same bitter, sour taste in his mouth now to hear Ramsgate say it.

"What do you want?" he asked dully. "Are you going to steal my brother's cattle now?"

"What do you mean, your brother's cattle? Isn't this your ranch, too?"

"Legally, it may be," Jeremy said, "but having a ranch was Athelstan's dream, not mine. I'd just as soon leave and go live in a city somewhere—if there was a place in this wasteland worthy of being called a city."

"You'd probably like San Antonio. Lot of folks there, and plenty of places to drink and gamble. Those are the things you like doing best, aren't they, Braxton?"

Jeremy ignored the jeering tone in Ramsgate's voice and said, "You still haven't told me why you're here."

"We made a nice profit on those cows we sold." Braxton reached inside his shirt and brought out a small hide pouch. He tossed it to Jeremy, who caught it instinctively. Coins jingled inside the pouch. "There's your share."

A part of Jeremy wanted to throw the money on the ground in revulsion, but his fist closed around the pouch.

"I don't want this," he said. "And I thought you said my share would go to pay off the debt I owe you."

"I was feeling generous," Ramsgate drawled. He smirked. "Anyway, I kept part of it back on account. But a man's got to have some walking-around money, don't he?"

Ramsgate grew more serious and went on, "That's not all. I wanted to let you know we're going after the stock that the Shellabarger brothers have brought in. We're going to make our move tonight, and you'll be riding with us."

"Forget it. I won't have anything more to do with this. John and Ralph are good friends. I'm not going to see them hurt."

"I don't want anybody hurt. That's why we're going to strike at night this time. We'll get what we want, and nobody'll be any the wiser until the morning."

Jeremy shook his head. "It won't work. After what happened to Bob Poole, everyone around here is expecting more trouble. I'm sure the Shellabarger brothers will be standing guard over their herd."

"Well, then, maybe what we need is somebody to decoy 'em away," Ramsgate said. "If you were to ride up and tell them that Athelstan needed their help on the BXT, they'd head this way in a hurry. That would leave the way clear for us to move in and drive off that livestock."

Jeremy stared at him for several heartbeats, then burst out, "You're mad! I can't do that. It would be the same as admitting that I'm working with your gang."

"Figure out some way to make it all seem like an honest mis-understanding." Ramsgate's voice hardened. "You've got until tonight to come up with something. We're taking those cattle. If we run into trouble, it'll wind up being worse for you. I can promise you that, Braxton."

Jeremy stared down at the ground. He didn't know whether to cry, curse in rage, or scream in sheer frustration. But finally he looked up and said in a voice from which all hope had been drained, "I'll see what I can do."

Ramsgate chuckled. "I figured you would. Good luck, kid. If we pull this off, then maybe—just maybe—I'll consider calling it square between us."

Jeremy knew better than to believe that. Now that Nate Ramsgate had him in his power, he would never let go. Ramsgate would squeeze him and squeeze him and squeeze him—

Ramsgate was turning his horse away when something inside Jeremy snapped. With an incoherent, furious yell, he yanked the Walker Colt from its holster, thumbed back the hammer as he raised the gun, and fired.

Chapter 38

Bodie knew better than to think she could follow Tye, even at a distance, without being discovered. Part of her wanted to try, anyway. But if she did, more than likely she would run into Athelstan on his way back to the BXT after showing Tye where the rustling and the murder of Bob Poole had taken place.

So it made sense to follow Jeremy instead, even though she didn't really want to, because he had practically dared her to do so, and she hated to give him the satisfaction of being right.

However, she liked to ride every day if possible. The exercise was good for her and good for the buckskin mare she had chosen as her primary saddle mount.

Tom Griggs insisted on saddling the buckskin. Bodie didn't put up an argument because she knew it would just waste time. The young wrangler could be stubborn about some things, and treating Bodie in a chivalrous manner, just as if they were back in Alpenstone, was one of them. Even though she no longer liked being fussed over, she supposed it wouldn't hurt anything to let him do so.

A few minutes later she rode out, taking the same general direction as Jeremy had. She could no longer see him, but she figured that if he did what he said he was going to, she would find him sooner or later if she headed for the creek.

She tried to concentrate on how good it felt to be out riding on such a beautiful day. The sky was blue and enormous overhead. A few puffy white clouds hung in the west. A cool breeze blew from the north and caressed Bodie's right cheek. Everything was enhanced. The colors were so vivid they almost hurt the eye—the blue sky, the green grass and trees, the scattered wildflowers with their blue, red, yellow, and white petals. The air was crisp with the smell of evergreens. That was the Texas Hill Country, one of the most magnificent places on earth. At moments such as this, she was truly glad that fate had led them here.

Worry nibbled at the back of her mind, though. Worry about Tye's safety as he searched for those rustlers, for the most part, but she also was concerned that evil might reach out to disrupt what had been a largely idyllic life for her family since they had arrived here.

Day to day, Athelstan was as happy as she had ever seen him. Naturally, he still mourned Perry's death; so did Bodie. But that grief had subsided to a dull ache. Athelstan worried about Jeremy's behavior, too, and his future. So did Bodie.

Those thieves and killers might decide to target the BXT next. An Indian raiding party might show up without any warning. And there was no telling what trouble Jeremy might get into. Any or all of those things could ruin the life they were trying to build here—

She caught sight of Jeremy several hundred yards ahead of her. He had almost reached the creek. Bodie reined in atop a slight rise to watch her brother as he turned north along the stream and followed its brushy, tree-lined banks.

Bodie turned as well and rode parallel to the creek about three hundred yards away. She kept to the trees for the most part. Jeremy might have spotted her if he'd been really looking for her, but he didn't seem to be paying much attention to anything around him.

Then another man appeared without warning, riding out of some brush to intercept Jeremy, who stopped short. Bodie's breath caught in her throat for a second as she thought that this might be a holdup. At this distance, she didn't recognize the stranger who'd confronted Jeremy. He might be a highwayman.

The two men began talking, though, and Jeremy appeared to relax at least slightly after being surprised and possibly frightened at first. Despite that, she could tell even at this distance that he was still tense.

Bodie moved the buckskin deeper into the shadows under a large tree, just to make it less likely either man would spot her if he glanced in her direction.

After a few minutes of talking, the stranger took something out of his shirt and tossed it to Jeremy, who caught it. This encounter was strange and getting stranger, Bodie thought. The conversation between the two men had seemed intense, but now maybe it was over. The stranger lifted his reins and started to turn his horse. Obviously, he was about to ride away.

Bodie gasped as Jeremy suddenly yanked his revolver out of its holster and fired.

Without thinking about what she was doing, she jabbed her heels into the horse's flanks and sent the buckskin leaping forward in a gallop that carried her toward the two men beside the creek.

Something must have warned Ramsgate. With the perilous life he led, he probably never really let his guard down. Whatever the reason, he jerked to the side just as Jeremy yelled and the Walker Colt roared and bucked.

Shocked at his own action, Jeremy peered wide-eyed through the smoke and saw that Ramsgate was still in the saddle and evidently unharmed. He had missed!

Ramsgate's gun came up fast in the outlaw's hand. Jeremy tried to cock the Walker for a second shot, but his thumb didn't want to work right. Ramsgate was about to kill him—!

The hammer on Ramsgate's gun was back, and his finger was taut on the trigger. But for some reason, he held off and didn't fire as he exclaimed in a shaky voice, "You damned fool!"

Jeremy knew he was a hair away from death.

He allowed the Colt in his hand to sag toward the ground. If he continued to point it at Ramsgate, the man would shoot him. He was sure of that. Why Ramsgate hadn't already killed him, he had no idea.

He tried to say something but stumbled. "I—I . . ."

"If you're going to say you're sorry, don't bother," Ramsgate grated. "Hell, it's my own fault. I underestimated you." His lips drew back from his teeth in an expression that was half grimace, half grin. "I didn't think you had it in you, kid. I never dreamed you'd make a try for me."

The swift drumming of hoofbeats drifted to the ears of both men. They jerked their heads around to peer toward the east.

"Bodicia!" Jeremy said.

"Your sister?"

"Yes."

"Pouch that iron, damn you," Ramsgate snapped. As Jeremy holstered the Colt, Ramsgate lowered the hammer of his own weapon and slid it into leather.

As he lifted his reins, he said, "Nothing's changed. You understand me? The job's still on for tonight, and you'd better play your part if you know what's good for you. And in the future, I'll know not to turn my back on you!"

With that, Ramsgate charged across the creek, water splashing up in a silvery spray from his horse's churning hooves. The animal lunged out onto the opposite bank and Ramsgate disappeared between a couple of trees.

With his heart slugging painfully in his chest, Jeremy watched Ramsgate go. Then he turned toward his sister as Bodie galloped up and brought her horse to a sliding stop.

"Jeremy, are you all right?" she cried as a cloud of dust from the buckskin's hooves swirled around them.

"Yes, I'm fine," he told her, even though he wasn't fine at all. Nothing was fine anymore.

"What was that about? Who was that man? Did he try to rob you?"

Jeremy searched frantically for an answer to her questions. He said, "I never saw him before. He stopped me and asked for directions, but I think that was just a ruse. He started asking me questions about the ranch and our cattle." He made himself look as if something surprising had just occurred to him. "He might have been one of those rustlers!"

"I'll bet he was," Bodie said. A puzzled frown creased her forehead. "But I saw him give you something."

Jeremy patted the pocket where he had stowed away the pouch with coins in it.

"Just some tobacco," he said. "I asked him to loan me the makings, and he just gave the whole pouch to me instead. Perhaps he thought it would put me off my guard, so I wouldn't be ready when he tried to kill me."

"But you drew your gun first."

Why was she being so maddeningly stubborn about this?

Because she was Bodicia, he told himself. She always had been maddeningly stubborn about everything. There was no reason this should be any different.

"Actually, I didn't," Jeremy said confidently. "Well, I suppose I might have, what do they call it, cleared leather before him, but he was already drawing his gun when I beat him to the punch and fired first."

He didn't know where she had been hidden while she watched the meeting between him and Ramsgate, but she hadn't been anywhere close, he was certain of that. She couldn't have made out any small details such as whether Ramsgate had been reaching for a gun when he drew his.

"He didn't shoot back at you," she pointed out. "At least, I don't think he did. The hoofbeats were so loud it's hard to be certain, but I didn't see any smoke come from his gun."

Jeremy shook his head. "He saw you coming and you frightened him away. At that range, he couldn't tell you're a girl. Dressed as you are, I suspect he took you for one of our men, or even Tye Salem, who I gather is somewhat well-known around here."

"I'm just glad he fled without hurting you, for whatever the reason."

"I thought you were pretty put-out with me earlier."

Bodie looked intently at him and said, "I may have been angry with you, but you're still my brother, and I don't want any harm coming to you. Don't you ever forget that, Jeremy Braxton."

"How touching," he said. He heard the snide tone in his voice and instantly regretted it when he saw the hurt look on his sister's face. He hadn't been able to suppress his naturally prickly attitude in time.

Without saying anything else, Bodie wheeled her horse and started back toward the ranch headquarters at a fast pace. Jeremy sighed and started after her, moving at a more deliberate speed. He wasn't going to get any more satisfaction out of riding the range today, he thought.

Besides, he didn't know who or what else he might run into. He'd already had one unpleasant surprise today. That was more than enough.

And he had things to figure out, he reminded himself. Criminal plans to further. Friends to betray.

Trying but failing to swallow the bitter taste in his mouth, Jeremy rode on.

Chapter 39

The trail leading to the Cougar's Den was almost impossible to spot unless you knew it was there. Thick growths of seemingly impenetrable brush and trees screened the base of a long, rugged bluff for several miles.

But there was a path through the thicket if a man knew where to look. That path led to a trail that hugged the ridge for a ways and then curved through a narrow passage into a sprawling, amphitheater-like bowl with a grassy bottom. A spring-fed pool provided water. Off to the north loomed the dark, oppressive mass of what the settlers around there called Enchanted Rock. Nate Ramsgate had heard that the Indians considered the huge mound to be sacred ground, the home of the spirits.

Ramsgate didn't believe such superstitions for a second. He believed in gold, silver, lead for bullets, whiskey with a good bite, and warm, willing women. Everything else in life was just a distraction.

The Cougar's Den was empty of cattle as Ramsgate rode in. He and his men had held Bob Poole's herd here for a while until they could drive it out the back door and head south to the rendezvous with the buyers from San Antonio. Soon, though, the Shellabarger brothers' stock would be there, grazing for a day or two to fatten up even more before they put additional money in Nate Ramsgate's pockets.

Some of the men had suggested building a couple of cabins, but Ramsgate turned thumbs down on that idea. The weather was still warm enough for them to sleep in the open. They could rig crude shelters if it rained.

Come winter, he intended to take his share of the loot and head for the border. It could get cold in the Hill Country. Snow and ice even fell at times. He didn't want any part of that.

The Shellabargers were next, he mused, and then a few more of the smaller spreads before he and the others hit the main target: the BXT. They would clean up there, and then it would be time to rattle their hocks out of this part of the country.

The thought that by then Jeremy Braxton would be in so deep he would have no choice but to betray his own family put a cruel smile on Ramsgate's face. The damned fool had it coming.

Ramsgate abruptly slowed his horse and tensed in the saddle as he approached the camp and noticed three horses he didn't recognize picketed with the other mounts. The three strangers who went with the horses stood talking with several of Ramsgate's men. Two were big and burly with dark hair and beards, while the other was on the short and scrawny side. Something about that one was vaguely familiar.

They all turned toward Ramsgate as he rode up. His right hand hovered near the butt of his Colt, just in case. Everybody seemed friendly, though, with no signs of hostility on either side.

The little stranger stepped forward with a grin on his face. He called, "Nate! Hey, Nate, it's good to see you again. You remember me?"

Ramsgate hated it when people did that. Why would anybody assume he'd remember their name?

But in this case, it suddenly came back to him. He reined in, nodded, and said, "Hello, Murph."

Al Murphy turned to his two companions and said, "See, I told you Nate would remember me. We rode together almost four months in a bunch that operated down south of Bexar."

Ramsgate didn't dismount. He leaned forward in the saddle and asked, "What are you doing here?"

"We heard rumors that you'd put together a good outfit and were doing well in these parts. My pards and I are hopin' you can use three more good men."

Murphy had run with a man named Armstrong, Ramsgate recalled. The idiot had called himself Cactus for some reason. Ramsgate didn't see him.

"Who are your friends?"

"The MacLochlainn brothers. This here is Ronan, and the other one is called Eamon. We've been ridin' together for a while now."

"What happened to Armstrong?"

Eamon MacLochlainn said, "He lost his temper and tried to draw on me."

Ramsgate studied the man's brutal face. "Is that so?"

"Yes, it is."

A cold chuckle came from Ramsgate. "No offense, Murph, but old Cactus always did have a habit of doing rash things."

"He did," Murphy agreed. "He sure did." Then the little outlaw hurried on: "So what do you think, Nate? We'd sure admire to throw in with you and these other fellas, if that's all right with you."

"Do you even know what we're doing here?"

"Does it matter as long as there's a good payoff in it?"

Ramsgate shook his head slowly and said, "I don't know. We have a pretty good bunch here. Things have been goin' along just fine. I'm not sure we want to risk upsetting that."

The one called Ronan said, "We can offer more than three gun hands."

"Oh?" Ramsgate cocked an eyebrow. "What can you offer?"

"Information."

"What kind of information?"

Ronan smiled humorlessly. "That would be giving it away, wouldn't it?"

Ramsgate considered and then nodded. "All right. If what you've got to tell me is useful, you can throw in with us."

"Your word on that?"

"My word on it," Ramsgate said.

"All right. We spotted a group of riders about five miles south of here. They looked pretty intent on their business, so we made a wide circle around them and were careful that they didn't see us."

"So?"

Ronan looked at Murphy and nodded.

The little outlaw said, "We were close enough before we spotted 'em that I got a good look at the fella leadin' the bunch. I recognized him from a few close calls in the past. His name's Bert Sutherland." Murphy swallowed. "He's a Texas Ranger, Nate. A captain. And I reckon those fellas with him were a whole damn troop of Rangers!"

On top of one of the cliffs that surrounded the bowl, Tye Salem lay stretched out on his belly between two rocks. His head was edged forward just enough for him to see down into the vast depression hidden beyond the ridge. He had taken off his hat, and he relied on his naked eye instead of using a spyglass. Sunlight might reflect off the lens and give away his position. He didn't want that.

Locating the rustler gang's hideout had presented a challenge, but not a very difficult one. Knowing that they had to have a place to gather the cattle they stole cut down on the amount of territory Tye had to search. From roaming all over this part of the country for years, he knew of several likely spots. This bowl known as the Cougar's Den was the third one he had checked—and sure enough, the varmints were here.

Getting in by using the trail through the brush and then the cleft in the ridge would be all but impossible for a group of men bent on attacking the outlaws. The rustlers would have guards posted, and they could hold off a larger force if they were alerted in time.

Another way into the bowl existed, Tye knew, but using it involved circling all the way around Enchanted Rock and coming in from the north. Easier but still risky, because the gang could have sentries on the rock, too.

Maybe what Athelstan and his friends should do was bottle up both ways in and out, Tye mused, and starve the no-good rats into surrendering. But in this rugged country, a long siege might prove difficult to carry out. The rustlers might slip out of the trap some other way, one or two at a time. They could break up the gang for the time being, but the varmints could just get together again later and go back to raising hell.

They needed some way to wipe out the rustlers, and as long as they were holed up in there, Tye didn't see any way to do it. But at least he knew where their hideout was, he told himself as he crawled backward from the edge of the cliff, and he wanted to pass that information along to Athelstan as soon as he could.

Excitement bubbled up inside Perry Braxton, but he felt dread as well as he and the other Rangers rode along the trail that led north from Fredericksburg. It was the middle of the afternoon, and this was the closest he had been to his brothers and sister in more than a year.

It would be wonderful to see Athelstan, Jeremy, and Bodicia again—but would they feel the same way about him? Would they regard him as a murderer? He had denied killing Ceallach MacLochlainn, but had they believed him? The fact that he had fled might make them think he was guilty after all.

It was even possible they believed he was dead. After diving into the bay, he hadn't surfaced until he was well away from the *Apollo*. Even then, his face had barely broken the water, just enough for him to gulp down some air before going under again and swimming farther.

Later, he had heard talk about how sharks were common in those waters. He knew then he was lucky he hadn't wound up in the belly of one of those terrible creatures. The fact that he had survived such a danger made him feel as if he were destined to escape.

When Captain Sutherland had informed the troop that they were on their way to the Hill Country, Perry had felt a thrill go through him. He still looked forward to seeing his family again, but at the same time, he couldn't help but worry how that reunion was going to turn out.

He would know soon. They were within a few miles of the BXT. That was the brand the Braxton Ranch used and the way everyone around here seemed to refer to it.

"I swear, Jack, you look like somethin's painin' you in the belly," Doc Ford said as he rode beside Perry. "You eat something that didn't agree with you?"

"No, I'm fine."

Since Doc was his best friend in the Ranger troop, Perry had considered telling him who he really was and his connection to the family that owned the ranch up ahead. But he hadn't said anything about it. For all he knew, Perry Braxton was a wanted fugitive, and he didn't want to burden Doc with keeping that secret.

"Well, if you need some o' my special tonic, let me know. I've got a bottle of it in my saddlebags."

Perry laughed. The "tonic" Doc spoke of was whiskey for the most part, mixed with water, molasses, and some herbs. It wouldn't cure anything, but it might make a fellow feel a little better—for a while, anyway.

"I'm all right," he assured his friend. He reached up and tugged his hat brim a little lower to shield more of his face. When they reached the BXT, he intended to hang back in the troop and not let his brothers and sister get a good look at him right away. It would be difficult not to blurt out who he was as soon as he saw them, but it might be better to wait and get the lay of the land first before disrupting their lives—and his own.

Riding in front of the other Rangers, Captain Sutherland slowed his horse and turned in the saddle to signal that the troop should halt. "Doc, you and Jack come on up here," he called with a wave of his arm to summon the two young men.

When they had ridden ahead to join him, the captain said, "We're gonna wait right here while you fellas take a look around. You scout out the area between the creek and those hills over yonder and then ride on to the BXT and let the folks there know we're comin'. I don't like to take a group of men into a place unannounced. Some folks get a mite antsy when they see a big bunch of riders comin' toward 'em. A nervous man's more likely to pull a trigger when he hadn't ought to."

Doc said, "Yeah, but if they see a couple of strange riders on their range, they're liable to take us for rustlers, aren't they, Cap?"

"They might, but once you tell 'em you're Rangers, they probably won't string you up."

"Well, thank you most to death for them reassurin' words," Doc drawled.

Meanwhile, Perry's heart felt as if it had plunged straight to the bottom of his belly. If he and Doc rode into the BXT by themselves, there was no way he would be able to blend into the group of Rangers and conceal his identity. If either of his brothers or his sister got a good look at him, they would know right away who he was.

Or would they? He was a lot leaner and more muscular than he had been when they had left Alpenstone. His close-cropped sandy hair was long, hanging over his ears and nearly to his shoulders. His once clean-shaven cheeks sported several days' worth of beard stubble. He wore range clothes and was well armed. Perry thought he looked like a Texan, through and through.

And of course, he was—as much as many of his companions. They had come to Texas from somewhere else, too. A few were second-generation Texans, even third, but most were immigrants.

You were still a Texan, or so the saying went, as long as you got here as fast as you could.

"Anything in particular you want us to look for?" Doc went on.

"Anything suspicious," Sutherland said. "You've been Rangerin' long enough to know lawbreakers when you see 'em, Doc. Can't rule out runnin' into some Comanch', too. I haven't heard tell of any raids in these parts lately, but those devils can take a notion to come a-lootin' and a-killin' anytime, without any warnin'."

Doc nodded. "All right, Cap'n. If everything looks clear and we make it to the ranch without any trouble, what do we do then?"

"One of you stay there and the other one ride back here to fetch us." Sutherland glared. "Shoot, that's just common sense, Doc."

"Yeah, but my ma said more than once that I was hidin' behind the door when the Good Lord passed out the common sense," Doc replied with a grin. He jerked his head at Perry. "Come on, Jack. Let's get to scoutin' while there's a few hours of daylight left."

Chapter 40

Nate Ramsgate's plans had changed. With a troop of Rangers in the area, the climate around here had suddenly gotten too hot for Ramsgate and the rest of the rustlers. They would have to clear out until the Rangers were gone.

But Ramsgate wasn't going to do that without pulling one last job—and it needed to be a big one.

They would hit the BXT tonight instead of waiting until they had run off the herds from the smaller ranches.

That meant Jeremy needed to know the plans had changed. Instead of decoying the Shellabarger brothers away from their spread, Jeremy would have to draw off the guards on the Braxton herd.

The new members of the gang needed to be familiar with the area before they made their move against the Braxtons that night. Late that afternoon, Nate Ramsgate picked out a couple of men to go with him, then said to the MacLochlainn brothers and Al Murphy, "Get ready to ride."

"Where are we goin', Nate?" Murphy asked.

Ramsgate grinned. "A little tour. I need to run an errand, and I figure I might as well show you fellas around a little while I'm doin' it."

He didn't trust Jeremy Braxton after the young man had some-how found the guts to take a shot at him. He wanted to have another talk with Jeremy and let him know what was going to happen.

He also wanted Jeremy to be fully aware that if he didn't co-operate, it might not be him alone who would pay the price. That pretty blond sister of his might have to help settle the debt.

Ramsgate didn't believe that Jeremy and Bodicia were very close, but hell, they were still blood kin, he thought. With a threat to her to consider, Jeremy would have to fall in line and clear the way for the gang to drive off all the stock from the Braxton Ranch in one daring raid.

The half-dozen men mounted up and rode through the gathering dusk. Once they had emerged from the hidden trail to the Cougar's Den, Ramsgate pointed out various landmarks to them, including the twin hills that marked the eastern boundary of the valley where the creek ran and most of the ranches in the area were located.

They were moving through the saddle between the hills when Ramsgate's keen senses alerted him that riders were ahead of them. He hissed an order to halt.

"A couple of riders down the slope," he whispered to the men who gathered around him. "MacLochlainn—Eamon—you got a good look at those Rangers earlier today, didn't you?"

"Aye," Eamon grunted.

"You come with me. There's still enough light that you ought to be able to recognize them if they're from that troop, right?"

"If 'tis a pair of those Rangers, I think I'll be knowing them," Eamon replied.

"We'll go on foot. Take it slow and easy. We don't want to make a lot of noise. You other boys stay here, but if you hear any commotion, get down there as quick as you can."

Dismounting, Ramsgate and Eamon handed their reins to two of the other men. They kept to the brush and trees as they began working their way down the slope. The steady *clip-clop* of horses' hooves could be heard clearly in the evening air, coming from the base of the slope where the valley flattened out.

Ramsgate put a hand on Eamon's arm to stop him. They both crouched in some thick brush. The two riders were close enough now the outlaws could hear what they were saying.

"Well, there's nothin' goin' on betwixt here and the creek," one of them said in a young man's voice. "I reckon we ought to ride on over to the BXT headquarters like the cap'n told us to, Jack, and let them know the troop's comin' in."

Ramsgate and Eamon grinned at each other in the fading light. They didn't need Eamon to recognize the two men now; what they had just overheard confirmed the riders were Texas Rangers.

Eamon leaned closer and whispered, "We take them and we've whittled down the odds a bit."

"If they don't come back, their captain will suspect something's wrong," Ramsgate replied, equally quietly. "But if we grabbed at least one of them, we could find out what the Rangers are doing around here in the first place."

"They're probably looking for you," Eamon said.

That annoyed Ramsgate, but he kept a tight rein on his temper. "Could be," he allowed. "We'll find out. When they pass us, take the one closest. I'll grab the other one."

"Take them alive, you said?"

"If you can."

The riders were practically on top of them by now. Only a few more heartbeats passed before the men on horseback drew even with the pair concealed in the brush.

Ramsgate burst out of hiding first, lunging out of the thick growth and darting past the rump of the closest horse. Both Rangers heard the crackle of branches and reined in. They started to turn their mounts toward the sound, but Ramsgate was too fast, and they were too late. He reached up, caught hold of his target's arm with both hands, and jerked the man out to the saddle.

At the same time, Eamon MacLochlainn struck. He wrapped both arms around the second Ranger's waist and dragged him from the horse's back.

Ramsgate's foe crashed hard to the ground. The impact seemed to knock the breath out of him. As he lay there, apparently half-stunned, Ramsgate started to draw his gun.

The Ranger acted then. His left foot came up in a surprisingly swift kick. The toe of his boot caught Ramsgate on the wrist and knocked the gun out of his grip. The Colt landed on the ground with a thud.

As Ramsgate reeled back from the unexpected counterattack, the Ranger jackknifed up from the ground and swung his right fist. The blow landed solidly on Ramsgate's jaw and drove him back even more. His bootheel caught on something and he lost his balance. He was already falling backward when the Ranger tackled him.

That accident might have actually helped Ramsgate in this battle. The Ranger seemed to expect more resistance. He lost his hold on Ramsgate and flew past him to land awkwardly. Ramsgate rolled and drove the heel of his boot into the man's side.

Once again, the Ranger seemed incapacitated. Ramsgate reached down, plucked a knife from a sheath inside his boot, and scrambled after his foe. He lunged and brought the knife sweeping down. A red ray from the dying sunset winked off the blade.

The Ranger rolled desperately. Ramsgate's blade missed him and dug into the ground. Ramsgate jerked it up and hacked at the Ranger again. They had rolled and squirmed under the horses, and they both risked a steel-shod hoof crashing down on them at any second.

His heels scrabbling against the dirt, the Ranger pushed himself clear. Ramsgate made it to his hands and knees and crawled away from the horses.

Several yards separated the two men. The Ranger clawed at the gun on his hip and hauled it out of its holster. Ramsgate saw that and did the only thing he could. He reared up on his knees, drew his arm back, and threw the knife at the Ranger as hard as he could.

The man grunted in shock and pain as the blade sank into his chest. He swayed back and forth for a second as he dropped the gun and pawed at the knife's bone handle.

Then he pitched to the side and lay still.

Ramsgate jerked around to see how Eamon MacLochlainn was faring. Eamon and the other Ranger were locked together, wrestling. Eamon seemed to have the upper hand, but suddenly, the Ranger, smaller than Eamon but lithe and quick, managed to get a foot behind Eamon's left knee and tripped him. Eamon went down, landing with a loud "Ooof!" and the Ranger reached for the Colt on his hip.

Ramsgate was on his feet by now. He had spotted his fallen gun lying on the ground. He scooped it up by the barrel, leaped at the second Ranger, and brought the butt down on the man's head. The vicious blow landed with a sound like an ax splitting wood. The Ranger went down hard, either senseless or dead.

Spewing curses, Eamon heaved himself up on his knees, grabbed the Ranger's shoulder, and rolled him onto his back. Eamon's right fist rose as his face twisted in fury. Clearly, if the Ranger was still alive, Eamon intended to beat him to death bare-handed.

"*What the hell!*"

The startled shout ripped from Eamon's throat. The vicious blow never fell. Ramsgate had reversed his gun and held it by the butt again, his thumb looped over the hammer so he was ready to fire. He pointed the gun at the Ranger and said, "What is it? What's wrong?"

Eamon stared down at the unconscious man, whose features were still visible in the rapidly fading light.

"I know this—this—" He added a few obscene oaths to the surprising declaration.

"Who is he?" Ramsgate asked tautly.

"His name is Perry Braxton," Eamon said. "He's part of the family that owns the ranch you're going to raid. But I thought he was dead!"

"He might be. I hit him pretty hard."

Eamon shook his head. "No, he's breathing. I would have sworn he died down on the coast, right after the ship carrying all of us got here. He's supposed to have drowned in the bay, trying to get away from the law."

"What had he done to need to run from the law?"

Eamon chuckled and said, "'Twas believed he murdered a man."

"Then what's he doing riding with the Rangers?"

"I have no idea." Eamon laughed outright this time. "Just like he had no idea!"

"What in blazes are you talking about?"

Eamon shook his head. "It doesn't matter. Is the other one dead?"

Ramsgate turned. The other Ranger hadn't moved. Ramsgate stepped over to the body, reached down, and ripped his knife free from the man's chest.

"He's dead, all right. But we'll take that one with us. He can answer our questions. If he won't talk—"

"I'll make him talk," Eamon said. "I'll take great pleasure in making him talk." He stood up and loomed over the fallen Perry Braxton. "'Tis not a religious man I'm bein', Ramsgate, but I tell you now, I believe in fate!" He threw his head back and laughed again. "And before this night is over, fate will have delivered all of the damned Braxtons into my hands!"

Chapter 41

Having a live Ranger—and evidently an old enemy of Eamon MacLochlainn's—fall into their lap was a boon, Ramsgate knew, but as they headed up the slope to rejoin the others, he realized that he couldn't allow this development to change his plans. He still needed to talk to Jeremy Braxton.

Eamon had the Ranger's senseless form slung over his brawny shoulder. How bizarre was it that the captive was also a Braxton? At least, according to Eamon he was, and Ramsgate had no cause to doubt the big Irishman. MacLochlainn wouldn't have had any reason to make that up.

"Hold your fire, it's just us, boys," Ramsgate called softly to the other outlaws as he and Eamon clambered up the last few feet with their prisoner.

"Was it the Rangers ridin' down there?" Al Murphy asked.

Ramsgate gestured toward the limp form draped over Eamon's shoulder. "Yeah, and we brought one of them back with us. The rest of you take him back to the Cougar's Den and have a nice long talk with him. Find out as much as you can about why the Rangers are here and what they plan on doing. I'm goin' on with the errand I had in mind when we came over here."

"Need any help with that?" Ronan MacLochlainn asked.

"No, I can handle this part on my own just fine."

"I thought you were going to show us around the valley," Ronan said.

Ramsgate shook his head. "Things have started moving too fast. We have to move fast, too, if we want to stay ahead of them. I'll be back and will tell you what to do when the time comes. It won't be a problem as long as you fellas can follow orders."

"You can count on us," Ronan growled.

Eamon threw the prisoner over his saddle, roped the Ranger's wrists to his ankles under the horse's belly, and then climbed up behind him. Ramsgate waited until the men had moved out silently, fading into the dusk on their way back to the hideout, before he swung up into his own saddle and rode at a brisk pace toward the Braxton Ranch.

He wasn't sure how he was going to manage to talk to Jeremy. Athelstan Braxton was sure to have guards patrolling around the ranch.

A grin slowly creased Ramsgate's face as an idea formed in his mind. Maybe the bold approach might be best. Ride right in, claim to be one of Jeremy's friends, and ask to talk to him. Nobody else on the BXT knew who he was or that he was behind the rustling that had been going on in the area.

With that in mind, he nudged his horse to an even faster pace.

A short time later, two men on horseback moved out quickly from behind a rocky knob to confront him.

"Hold it right there, mister," one of them called. "You're on BXT range. Who are you, and what are you doing here?"

"My name's Ramsgate. I'm looking for Jeremy Braxton."

"What's your business with him?"

"No business, really," Ramsgate replied. "I'm a friend of his from Fredericksburg. I haven't seen him for a few days, and I just wanted to make sure he's all right."

"Jeremy's fine," the rider who had spoken said. "He's just stayin' pretty close to the ranch these days. We all are since trouble cropped up."

"Bob Poole gettin' killed is what we mean," the other man added.

Ramsgate clucked his tongue in sympathy. "Yeah, I heard about that. Mighty bad business. You haven't had any problems over here on the BXT, have you?"

"No, and we plan on keepin' it that way," the first man said. "It'd be best if you just turned around and rode on back to Fredericksburg, mister."

"You've got me wrong," Ramsgate said. "I'm not looking for trouble."

The man's voice was thick with scorn as he said, "You don't expect me to believe that story about wantin' to find out if Jeremy's all right, do you?"

Ramsgate stiffened. Anger threatened to boil up inside him. But he controlled it and chuckled instead.

"Well, to tell you the truth, ol' Jeremy owes me some money," he said. Chances were, the members of the BXT crew knew about Jeremy's gambling habit and wouldn't be surprised that he was in debt to somebody. Men like these always gossiped about the people they worked for.

"You can collect on it after things settle down a mite."

"I'd be more than willin' to do that," Ramsgate said, "but as it happens, I owe money to some other folks, and they're not gonna be happy if I keep puttin' 'em off."

The second man said, "Hell, Micah, what's it gonna hurt if we let him go on to the ranch? He's only one man, he can't be up to any mischief."

"You know our orders are to keep an eye out for trouble."

Ramsgate held up his hand, palm out, and said, "I'm not trouble, boys, I give you my word on that. I'll swear on a stack o' Bibles, all I want to do is talk to Jeremy for a few minutes."

The first man said, "If we just turn him loose, some of the other fellas are liable to shoot him."

"I'll go with him," the second man volunteered, "and then I'll hurry right back out here. We won't get in trouble with the boss."

"If we do, I'll take it outta your hide," the first man muttered darkly. "All right, go on."

"I'm obliged to you fellas," Ramsgate said. "Now, which way's the ranch headquarters from here?"

Less than half an hour later, Ramsgate and the man who accompanied him reached the cluster of buildings that formed the heart of the Braxton Ranch. It wasn't quite full night—a shallow arch of reddish gold from the sunset remained on the western horizon—but lamps were already lit inside the main house. Their yellow light glowed warmly through the windows.

Ramsgate and his companion had been challenged a couple of times on the way here, but the other man, whose name was Barney Keller, had identified them and they'd been passed on.

Now, as they reined in, a tall figure stepped out onto the porch and moved quickly to the side so the light wouldn't be behind him, silhouetting him and making him a better target.

"Who's there?" he called.

"Barney Keller, Mr. Braxton. I got a visitor with me."

"Who in blazes comes visiting at this hour?" Athelstan Braxton asked.

"My name's Ramsgate, Mr. Braxton. Nate Ramsgate. I'm lookin' for your brother Jeremy. I need to have a word with him."

Ramsgate saw Athelstan stiffen. "Jeremy's inside," he said. "What business do you have with him?" He paused, but before Ramsgate could answer, Athelstan added, "If this is about a gambling debt—"

"I'm sorry to trouble you, sir," Ramsgate broke in. "If I can just talk to Jeremy for a minute, I'm sure we can straighten everything out."

Athelstan didn't say anything, and for a moment Ramsgate thought his bold plan was going to come to nothing.

But then Athelstan turned his head and called, "Jeremy, get out here. Someone to see you."

Ramsgate heard footsteps from inside the house. Jeremy appeared in the doorway and asked, "What is it?"

"None of my business, so you take care of it," Athelstan said sharply. He jerked his head toward Ramsgate, who sat on his horse in front of the porch. Barney Keller had backed off a mite to allow at least the appearance of privacy, but he was waiting to accompany Ramsgate back off the BXT.

Jeremy recognized Ramsgate in the light that spilled through the open doorway and the nearby windows to create a half circle of illumination in front of the house. For a moment, he looked surprised to see the outlaw. Then he moved to the top of the steps and snapped, "What are you doing here?"

Ramsgate smiled. "Can't a fella pay a friendly visit to one of his amigos?"

Jeremy looked back at his older brother. "I'll handle this," he said. "It won't take long."

"All right," Athelstan said slowly. "If you need any help—"

"I won't."

Athelstan nodded and went back into the house. Ramsgate looked over his shoulder meaningfully at Barney. The rider withdrew even more, definitely out of earshot now.

Jeremy came down the steps. "What are you doing here?" he asked again as he stopped beside Ramsgate's horse and looked up at the visitor.

"I've brought you some good news," Ramsgate said quietly enough that only the young man could hear. "Me and the rest of the boys are pullin' out tonight."

"You're leaving the area?"

"That's right." Ramsgate paused. "But before we go, we have to take care of one last job." He lowered his voice even more. "We're taking all the cattle we can round up in a hurry from BXT range."

"You—" Jeremy started to cry out in shock and anger, but he controlled himself and dropped his tone as he moved a step closer. "You can't do that!"

"We're goin' to. There's a troop of Rangers roaming around somewhere in these parts, and we don't want to tangle with them. But we're not gonna just cut and run without one more payoff, either."

"Athelstan has guards all around the ranch. You're bound to be discovered by some of them if you try to steal any cattle."

"That's where you come in." Ramsgate leaned closer. "Get your brother to pull those patrols in. I want all the guards back here at ranch headquarters and the range wide open in—let's say, two hours from now. It'll be good and dark by then, but the moon won't be up yet."

"That's impossible. It's madness!"

"Maybe, but it's got to be done."

Jeremy shook his head. "There's nothing I can tell him that would make him do that."

Ramsgate thought furiously for a moment and then said, "How about you tell him that while I was on my way up here from Fredericksburg, I saw a bunch of fellas gatherin' a few miles back down the creek. You can say that I overheard them talkin' about how they were gonna attack the ranch headquarters." He grinned. "Why, I think it must have been those no-good rustlers everybody's so stirred up about!"

"I don't understand. You *are* going to raid the ranch—"

"Not this part. There's nothing we want here. The cattle are all out on the range. But if your brother pulls in his men and has them get ready for a big attack from the south, we can move in from the east, gather up as much stock as we can find, and light a shuck back over the hills before anybody knows we've even been here."

As he put it into words, Ramsgate realized the plan, impromptu though it might be, could actually work. All the moving pieces would have to come together properly, but it was possible.

Jeremy was still hesitating. Ramsgate said, "Here's one more thing you need to think about, kid. If we pull this off tonight, you're finished with us. We won't be around these parts anymore, so you won't have to worry about being tied in with Bob Poole's killing. It'd be worth a lot to you to be able to rest easy again, wouldn't it?"

Another long moment went by, and then Jeremy jerked his head in a nod.

"You're leaving?" he asked. "You swear? And everything is settled between us?"

"Settled up one way and down the other," Ramsgate said. "I swear."

Of course, he wouldn't hesitate to go back on his word sometime in the future if it would pay him to do so, but Jeremy didn't have to know that. The young fella always had been pretty gullible.

"All right," Jeremy said. "I'll tell Athelstan what you said. But there's no way I can guarantee he'll believe it."

"Just do your part. We'll trust to luck on the rest." Ramsgate started to lift his reins, then paused. "Oh, yeah. Act like you're handing me something."

"What?"

"Everybody here thinks I came to collect a gambling debt from you. In case anybody's watching from inside, we don't want to make them suspicious, do we?"

"No, I suppose not."

Jeremy pantomimed reaching in his pocket and handing something to Ramsgate, who pretended to stow it away in one of his saddlebags.

Then Ramsgate nodded, said, "Much obliged," loudly enough for Barney Keller to hear, and turned his horse away from the house.

"Are you ready to go, mister?" Barney asked as he nudged his mount forward.

"Yep, I suppose I am." Ramsgate couldn't help but smile as he added, "I got what I came here for."

Chapter 42

Night had fallen, but Tye Salem didn't need light to find his way around in this country. He could have made his way to the Braxton Ranch in pitch darkness if he had to.

He was on his way through the saddle between the twin hills on the east side of the valley when he heard hoofbeats ahead of him, coming toward him. He was too far out for the rider to be one of the guards Athelstan had posted, so he drew off to one side, into the thick shadows under some oak trees, and reined in to wait.

In the Hill Country, it wasn't exactly safe for a man to travel alone by night unless he knew what he was doing. It was better not to meet a stranger if you could avoid it.

The moon hadn't risen yet. The millions of stars spread across the heavens relieved the darkness to a certain extent, but they didn't provide enough light for Tye to recognize the rider as the man moved past him about fifty yards away. He could tell the horsebacker was a man, that was all.

But given that the fellow was headed in the general direction of the rustlers' hideout, Tye wouldn't be a bit surprised if he was a member of the gang. For a moment, Tye considered trying to overtake the man and capture him.

He discarded the idea for a couple of reasons: the rustlers might hear gunfire in the distance and be alerted to the possibility of trouble, and he didn't want to delay passing along what he had discovered to Athelstan.

When the strange rider had gone on past and the sound of his horse's hooves had faded into the distance, Tye rode out of the shadows and resumed heading for the Braxton Ranch.

He heard the swift rataplan of hoofbeats before he got there. Riders were galloping toward the ranch from several different directions, he realized as he stiffened in alarm. Something had to be wrong to have caused such a commotion. He heeled his mount to a faster pace.

The ranch house was ablaze with light. Tye saw men on foot and some on horseback moving around hurriedly. He spotted Athelstan on the porch and swung down from the saddle as he reined to a stop in front of the house.

"Athelstan, what's going on?" he called as he went up the steps.

"Tye! I'm glad you're back. The rustlers have rendezvoused south of here. They're planning a raid on the ranch tonight. This is our chance to strike first, take them by surprise, and put an end to them!"

Tye stood there staring at Athelstan. He was so surprised, he didn't see Bodie until she stepped up to him and put her arms around him.

"I'm so glad you're back," she said, hugging him. She stepped back, came up on her toes for a second, and unashamedly gave him a brief kiss. Then she went on, "Now tell Athelstan there's no reason I shouldn't go along and help deal with those outlaws, once and for all."

"No," Tye said.

"That's it?" She glared at him. "Just a flat no? You're not my husband, you have no right—"

"No, the rustlers aren't south of here," he broke in, talking to Athelstan as much as he was to her. "They're over east a ways, on the far side of the twin hills, at a place some folks around here call the Cougar's Den. It's south of Enchanted Rock. That was one of the first places I thought of that they might be using for a hideout, and it turns out my hunch was right."

Athelstan stared at him. "But we got information they were south of here and planning to strike tonight."

"Maybe they are, although I didn't expect them to make a move against you this soon. But earlier this evening they were all in that hideout I told you about." Tye shrugged. "Maybe they've moved out from there. They've had time."

"It was less than an hour ago we were told they were gathering south of here."

Tye shook his head. "That's just not right. I saw them with my own eyes in the Cougar's Den."

Athelstan's jaw tightened. He turned his head and called into the house, "Jeremy!"

The younger Braxton brother appeared, looking nervous. "What is it?" He sent an unfriendly glance toward Tye.

"Tye says he saw the rustlers well east of here an hour or so ago. Ramsgate must have been wrong when he told you they were going to attack from the south."

"All I know is what he said he overheard," Jeremy replied in a sullen voice. "I can't swear that he was right."

"We should have been more certain before we pulled all the patrols in—"

"It was your decision to do that, not mine. Don't blame me if things don't work out."

"I never would have done it if you hadn't told me what that man said."

The brothers looked angrily at each other for a moment as Tye and Bodie stood to one side.

Then Tye said, "It's all right, Athelstan. Since you've got your crew together, this is still your chance to hit those varmints when they're not expecting it. I can lead you to their hideout. We'll have to circle around and take them from the other side, but it can be done. We need to hurry, though, before they make a move of their own."

"What if they've already started?"

Tye smiled. "Then we'll run into them on the way, more than likely. They'll still be mighty surprised."

Athelstan considered the situation, but only for a moment before he gave a curt, decisive nod.

"All right. The men are ready to ride. I'll give the order to mount up, and we'll go and settle this tonight. Thanks, Tye."

"What about me?" Bodie asked.

"You stay here," Tye told her.

"And Jeremy will stay with you," Athelstan added. "No arguments from either of you."

"I wasn't going to argue with you," Jeremy muttered. "This is a fool's errand."

His face was pale and drawn, though, and Tye thought he looked like the whole bottom had fallen out of his world. Tye didn't know what was going on, but he suspected one thing was true and Athelstan had said it already.

Tonight would settle things.

Consciousness seeped back into Perry's brain, followed by the realization that his head throbbed with thunderous pain at every beat of his pulse, and he was sick at his stomach, to boot. He was in an odd position. It took him a few moments to work out the fact that he was draped face down over the back of a horse.

That accounted for the miserable feeling in his belly. He remembered that he and Doc had been jumped by a couple of men, and during the fight, he must have been hit on the head. That would explain the booming agony inside his skull.

He couldn't move. His hands and feet were lashed together under the horse's belly. Where were they going?

He had no idea, but evidently his captors reached their destination a few minutes later. The horse stopped plodding along. Perry stayed still, sensing that it would be better if the men who had done this to him didn't know he was awake yet.

Somebody cut the rope binding his hands and feet. A strong

hand grasped him and hauled him off the horse's back, only to let him fall. He landed hard enough on the ground to knock the breath out of him.

"If that didn't wake him up, this will," a man said, followed by a harsh laugh. An instant later, the toe of a boot thudded into Perry's ribs, jolting him painfully and rolling him over.

Something had been maddeningly familiar about that voice. Despite the discomfort he was in, recognition crackled in his brain. But he didn't know for sure who the voice belonged to until the man said, "Open your eyes, Braxton, or 'tis kickin' you again I'll be doin'."

Perry's eyelids fluttered up. He saw firelight washing over the ugly bearded face of the man looming above him. He couldn't contain the exclamation that burst out of his lips.

"MacLochlainn!"

"Aye," Eamon MacLochlainn said. "You probably hoped I was dead. I damned sure believed you were!"

Eamon reached down, grabbed one of Perry's ankles, and dragged him closer to a campfire. The light hurt Perry's eyes, but he adjusted to it and looked around. More than a dozen men were gathered wherever this place was. Maybe two dozen or even more, he revised the estimate. They were a formidable-looking bunch, too, roughly dressed and heavily armed.

He suddenly suspected that he was looking at the men responsible for the rustling and killing that had been reported in this area. It came as no surprise that Eamon MacLochlainn would fall in with a group of criminals like that, although it was still beyond him how Eamon had wound up here in the Hill Country.

But *he* was here, Perry reminded himself. There was no reason Eamon couldn't have drifted in this direction after leaving the coast, just as Perry had done. His surviving brothers might be with him.

In that case, a grim reunion between the Braxtons and the MacLochlainns could be in the offing.

As if to confirm that thought, Ronan MacLochlainn strode into

Perry's line of sight. He glowered down at the young man and said, "Ye didn't expect to see us again, did you, young Braxton? 'Tis certain sure we didn't expect to see you!"

Eamon didn't give him a chance to respond to Ronan's words. He dragged Perry well beyond the campfire where the others were gathered before letting go of his ankle.

Eamon hunkered on his heels next to Perry and said, "What are the Rangers doin' here? What plans do they have? Do they know where our hideout is?"

Perry had to try a couple of times before he was able to force words out of his dry throat and mouth.

"You can . . . go to hell," he rasped. "I'm not going . . . to tell you anything."

A cruel grin creased Eamon's bearded face as he drew a sheathed knife and leaned closer over Perry's helpless form.

"Oh, I think ye are," he said. "But you hold out just as long as you can before you talk. Please do. Because I'll purely enjoy workin' on you with this blade. I'll be doin' it anyway. 'Tis the only way of bein' sure that you're tellin' the truth."

"I don't think I want to watch this," Ronan said.

"Go on, then. Join the others. But you'll still have to hear the screamin'."

Ronan shook his head and walked off. The rest of the men were about fifty yards away now, tending to their horses and apparently getting ready to ride somewhere.

To raid the ranch that Perry's brothers and sister had established? It certainly seemed possible.

Eamon put his back to the others and leaned over Perry, the knife poised to begin carving.

"Before we get started good, I want to know how it is that you're alive. Everyone said 'twas drownin' in the bay you were, or that you were eaten up by sharks. How did ye escape death?"

Perry had recovered his breath, and didn't see anything wrong with explaining. Besides, it would postpone the torture Eamon planned to inflict on him.

"I swam underwater," he said. "I'm a good swimmer. I was able to stay below the surface most of the time until I was a mile or more down the coast from where the ship was docked. I was just lucky no sharks noticed me, I suppose. I crawled out, found some brush, and hid there until the next day. I thought about trying to find my family, but they were already gone." Perry sighed. "Just as well. I wouldn't have wanted to inflict having a wanted murderer for a brother on them."

Eamon chuckled. It was one of the most sinister sounds Perry had ever heard.

"About that murder business," he said. "'Tis a bit of a funny joke, Braxton, but I happen to know that you never killed my brother Ceallach. Do ye know how I can be so certain of that?"

Perry just stared up at him numbly.

"I know," Eamon said, "because I killed the little scut meself."

The callous confession surprised Perry so much he couldn't suppress a gasp. Eamon's vicious grin widened.

"Aye, I'm the one who slipped the knife to him," he went on. "The way he kept pesterin' your sister was interferin' with me plans to take your brother Jeremy for every bit of coin he had. All I meant to do was cuff the lad around a bit, but then he had the gall to pull a blade on me. I took it away from him and, well, one thing led to another, as they say. When I saw he was dead, I figured you'd likely get the blame for the killin', but I hid the body anyway, just to put things off for a bit. That way I was able to be somewhere else when Ceallach was found."

Perry finally found horrified words. "He was your own brother."

"Aye, but I never actually liked him. And he was costin' me money—"

Eamon's words choked off as someone jerked him upright with an arm locked around his neck from behind.

"You killed him," a harsh whisper sounded. "Our own brother! And you killed him!"

Ronan squeezed harder. Eamon struggled and tried to reach back and stab him with the knife, but Ronan's other hand caught his wrist and twisted. Perry heard a bone snap with a sound like a small branch breaking. Eamon might have screamed if Ronan hadn't had his air cut off. As it was, he made only a tiny squeaking noise, like a mouse, as the knife fell to the ground.

"Have ye no honor in your soul?" Ronan went on. "Nay, why do I ask that question when I already know the answer? Ye were always an evil man, Eamon MacLochlainn. I'm ashamed to call ye my kin."

Eamon still writhed in Ronan's grip, but his struggle was getting weaker. He was a big strong man, but Ronan was bigger and more powerful. Perry pushed himself into a sitting position and watched as the brutal drama played out.

None of the other outlaws appeared to have noticed what was going on. The shadows were thick here, away from the dying campfire, and they were busy getting ready to move out.

Eamon's feet beat a tattoo on the ground as spasms shook him. He had been pulling at Ronan's arm where it was locked around his throat, but now his hands fell away limply. He had to be on the verge of passing out from lack of air.

Ronan must have gotten impatient. His arms and shoulders bunched and twisted. Perry heard another snap, louder this time but still unnoticed by the rest of the gang.

Eamon sagged lifelessly in Ronan's grip. Ronan had broken his neck, the second case of one MacLochlainn brother killing another.

Ronan lowered the corpse to the ground. He bent and picked up the knife Eamon had dropped. He stepped closer to Perry, who could only scoot away on the ground. His wrists and ankles weren't linked anymore, but they were still tied.

"Let me see your hands," Ronan ordered quietly. "I'm going to cut you loose."

"Why would you do that?"

"That's a foolish question," Ronan snapped. "Let's just say my family has done enough harm to yours. I can't abide a man without honor." He drew in a deep breath. "And I'm afraid I've lost most of mine. But I'll not be plaguin' the Braxton family anymore. I'm goin' to turn you loose. You'll have a chance to slip away. That's all I can do for ye."

"And what are you going to do?" Perry asked as he held out his hands, and Ronan cut the bonds holding his wrists together.

Ronan freed Perry's ankles, too, and said, "I'll leave with the others, then slip away myself once they're on their way to your brother's ranch. I want no part of stealin' his cattle."

"That's what they're going to do?"

"Aye, that's what they plan, as soon as a man named Ramsgate returns. He's their leader."

Perry's head was spinning from these rapid, totally unexpected developments. He glanced toward Eamon's huddled body and began, "Thank you—"

"Don't bother," Ronan grated. "And don't cross my path again, Braxton. Next time might be different."

With that, Ronan turned back toward the other outlaws. Perry climbed to his feet, unsteady at first, because he had been tied for so long. But then he got his legs under him and sneaked away from the camp, deeper under the trees and in the dark shadows. After a few steps, he started running.

He was alone and unarmed, lost in the middle of the untamed Hill Country, but one thing he knew for certain was that he would be better off practically anywhere other than here.

He realized he didn't know what had happened to Doc Ford, and that thought was almost as sharply painful as Eamon MacLochlainn's knife would have been.

Captain Bert Sutherland and the rest of the Ranger troop had been waiting for a long time. Too long. Doc Ford and Jack Smith should have been back an hour or more earlier. Something had happened to the two youngsters. Sutherland was sure of that.

One of the men Sutherland had posted on guard duty called softly, "Cap'n, somebody's out there."

Sutherland strode over to the man and demanded, "Who is it?"

"No tellin', Cap, but I can hear him walkin'. He ain't on horseback. Sounds like he's on foot, and kind of stumblin' along at that."

Sutherland reached down and rested his hand on the butt of his gun. At that moment, a feeble call drifted through the night.

"C-Cap? Cap'n Sutherland?"

"Good Lord," the Ranger captain burst out. "That's Doc Ford!"

Chapter 43

Bodie yelled and even cursed, but Athelstan and Tye stood firm. She wasn't going with the men to attack the outlaw stronghold.

Neither was Tommy Griggs. The young wrangler wanted to be part of the force, but Athelstan drew him aside and told him, "I need you and Baldy to stay here with my brother and sister. Someone has to be on hand to help them fight off any of the rustlers that make it this far." He smiled. "There's no way of knowing that we'll defeat them."

"Of course you will, Mr. Athelstan! They can't stand up to a force of fighters led by a nobleman from Alpenstone."

Athelstan clapped a hand on his shoulder and smiled. "I hope you're right, Tom. I hope you're right."

Elsewhere around the ranch, Bodie and Tye were saying their goodbyes.

"I still don't think it's fair that you're leaving me behind," she said. "You know I can handle a gun and fight."

"There'll be a lot of lead flying around—"

"And it's just as likely to hit you as it would be to hit me, and yet you're allowed to run that risk!"

"That's the way it's always been in history. I'm afraid you're just going to have to get used to it."

Even as he said it, Tye knew good and well that Bodie wasn't going to get used to anything she didn't want to. But that didn't change the facts of what was going to happen tonight, either.

She started to pull away when he put his hands on her shoulders, but then she changed her mind and not only allowed him to kiss her goodbye, she returned that kiss with enough urgency and passion to make him say, "I'll be coming back, I promise you that!"

Jeremy stood alone on the porch, his hands gripping the railing as he watched the preparations for battle. His face was set in bleak lines. This wasn't all his doing, and he knew it. The BXT had been Nate Ramsgate's primary target all along, and the only reason he intended to go ahead and strike at it tonight was because of the arrival of the Texas Rangers. They were the ones who had forced Ramsgate's hand, not Jeremy.

Despite that, he had played a part in the danger that threatened his family tonight. Once again, his fondness for the cheap thrill of placing his fate on the turn of a card had led to misfortune not only for him but for those he cared about.

And hard feelings or not, he *did* care about them. He loved Athelstan and Bodie, and he had come to like and admire Tye Salem. Bodie would be safe here with Griggs and Baldy, well away from the fighting, but Tye would be in the thick of it.

He ought to be, too, Jeremy decided.

But Athelstan had already told him he wasn't coming along.

Once the group rode out, however, Athelstan wouldn't be here to stop him. Griggs and Baldy might try to, but they would back off if Jeremy gave them an order. The habit of obeying nobility was too deeply ingrained in both of them to be ignored.

The newfound determination inside Jeremy made him smile as he watched the men mount up and ride off into the night with a thunder of hooves.

Once a Braxton, always a Braxton. He had forgotten that for a while, but maybe he had remembered it just in time.

*   *   *

Perry stopped when he was about a hundred yards away from the outlaw camp. He found a small rise where he could watch their preparations by the light of the dying fire. A few minutes after his escape, a brief uproar broke out. Perry saw Ronan MacLochlainn standing apart from the others, talking to them.

What was he telling them? He could claim that Perry had overpowered his brother somehow, killed Eamon, and gotten away. The alternative would be for him to admit that *he* had killed Eamon, let Perry go, and explain why.

From this distance, Perry had no way of knowing what Ronan was saying, but the other outlaws didn't pull their guns and riddle him with bullets, so he supposed Ronan had blamed him for what happened. They were clearly upset, but this development wouldn't stop them from carrying out their plans.

He was miles away from the rest of the Ranger troop, Perry mused, and even farther from the Braxton Ranch. If he could have found a way to get there, he would have warned Captain Sutherland about the impending raid. He would have thrown aside his concerns about being reunited with his family and raced to warn Athelstan, Jeremy, and Bodicia, as well. But on foot, there was nothing he could do.

A short time later, a man rode in by himself. Perry heard him shouting angrily after he'd talked to the others. They must have told him about Eamon, and that the prisoner had escaped. The newcomer had to be Nate Ramsgate, the leader of the gang they had talked about. After raging around for a few minutes, the man gave the order for the gang to mount up.

They thundered away from the hideout, into the night.

Perry waited a moment and then ran after them. There was nothing else he could do.

Captain Bert Sutherland leaned over the wounded man and said, "Blast it, Doc, you shouldn'ta gone off and got yourself hurt.

You're the one we count on to patch up ever'body else! What do we do?"

"Keep pressure on the wound, Danny," Doc said weakly to the Ranger who knelt beside him, pressing a pad cut from a clean blanket to the knife wound in Doc's chest. "I'm pretty sure . . . the blade missed my lungs . . . and if it'd got my heart . . . I'd be dead long before now. As long as I don't lose too much blood . . . I ought to make it."

"Who done this, Doc?" Sutherland asked.

"Some of those . . . rustlers. . . . They figured I was dead . . . and I heard 'em say . . . they're gonna hit the BXT tonight. You'd best . . . rattle your hocks . . . on up there."

"What happened to Jack?"

Doc managed to shake his head. "Dunno. I think they must've . . . took him prisoner . . . or else killed him. He wasn't anywhere around . . . when I got enough strength to look for him. Figured I'd better . . . get on back here . . . and let you know what's goin' on."

"You done the right thing, son," Sutherland assured him. "Danny, you stay here and tend to Doc." The captain straightened and addressed the Ranger troop. "The rest of you boys hit the saddle! We're headin' for the BXT, and with any luck, we'll get there in time to catch them dadblamed outlaws in the act!"

Athelstan and Tye rode in the lead of the group from the BXT. When he had first found out about the planned attack, Athelstan had dispatched a fast rider to gallop to the other ranches in the valley and summon help. The Shellabarger brothers had arrived in time to join the force, as well as Jim Niederwald, Hugo Winters, and several men who worked for each of them. The force setting out to stop the outlaws numbered eighteen men.

According to what Tye had reported, that meant they would be outnumbered, but not overpoweringly so. And they had the advantage of fighting for their homes, not out of pure avarice.

Athelstan was cautiously optimistic, but they would need luck on their side, too.

As they rode through the night, listening intently for the sound of approaching hoofbeats, Tye said quietly to Athelstan, "You mentioned something the other day about asking me what my intentions are toward Bodie."

"I did," Athelstan said, "but I *didn't* ask you, as I recall."

"No, you didn't. I'm going to tell you, anyway. I intend to marry that sister of yours, Athelstan, if she'll have me."

"Have you asked her?"

"No, sir. I didn't figure on doing that until I'd talked to you first."

"I see," Athelstan said. "When do you foresee this wedding taking place?"

Tye chuckled. "Shoot, she hasn't even said yes yet. Knowing Bodie, she's liable to tell me to go climb a stump, depending on what kind of mood she's in."

"Yes, I can imagine that," Athelstan responded with a laugh of his own. He grew more serious as he went on: "You should probably go ahead and ask her. If she says yes, then you and I can talk again."

"That sounds like you'd give the idea your blessing."

"Just settle things with Bodie first," Athelstan counseled. "If it's meant to be, then everything else can be worked out later."

"And of course I've got to live through tonight," Tye said.

"Don't even consider any other possibility. I'm not."

Before either of them could say anything else, Tye reined in abruptly. Athelstan followed suit, and behind them, the rest of the group came to a halt, as well.

"You hear something?" Athelstan asked.

"Yeah, and it's even clearer now that we've all stopped." Tye nodded toward the trail in front of them. "There are riders coming this way. A lot of them."

Athelstan turned in the saddle and called quietly to the others, "Spread out! Be ready for anything."

* * *

The ranch house was darkened now, no lights showing anywhere. Bodie came out onto the porch and saw two dark shapes she knew to be Baldy and Tom Griggs. The old-timer and the wrangler held loaded rifles, and several more rifles were close at hand, ready to fire. Each of them wore two holstered Colts as well. They were as ready for trouble as they could be. The air tonight felt as if it were full of something just waiting to happen.

"Have either of you seen Jeremy?" Bodie asked.

"No, miss, I haven't," Griggs said.

"Nor I," Baldy added. "Isn't he inside?"

"I can't find him anywhere." Bodie doubled her right fist and smacked it angrily into her left palm. "Blast him, he's slipped off to get in on that fight and left me here!" She moved toward the steps. "I'm not going to let him get away with that."

Quickly, Griggs got between her and the steps. "Begging your pardon, Miss Bodie, but Athelstan's orders were that you should stay here."

"He told Jeremy to stay here, too, and you can see for yourself that didn't happen!"

Baldy said, "What your brother does has no effect on what you do, miss. Athelstan needs to be concentrating on strategy and not worrying about your welfare. The same is true of young Mr. Salem."

"You're saying I'd just be a burden."

"If you go charging into that fight, that's exactly what you'll be, miss," Griggs said.

Bodie blew out her breath in an exasperated sigh.

"I suppose you're right," she said, "but I sure don't like this waiting."

"None of us do, I reckon," Griggs said, the newfound Texan in him coming out in this moment of stress.

With Nate Ramsgate at their head, the outlaws weren't galloping through the darkness. They rode at a more deliberate pace, and that was the only reason Perry was able to keep within earshot of them. He was already getting tired. His head throbbed with every running step he took.

Over the pounding in his skull, he heard a man cursing loudly and fervently, not far ahead of him. He stopped short and listened.

"Damn saddle cinch would have to break," the man said. "Almost busted my neck when the thing slipped and throwed me off. Come here, blast your hide, you stupid critter! Nate's gonna wring my neck if I don't get there in time to help with the cattle."

Perry eased ahead. The starlight was bright enough for him to make out a man trying to catch a skittish horse. Perry didn't recognize the man, but he had to be one of the outlaws. The saddle mishap had thrown him behind the others, and they hadn't waited for him. Clearly, he was just going to have to catch up once he was mounted again.

Perry wasn't going to let that happen. As the outlaw made another lunging grab for the trailing reins and missed, Perry leaped at him and swung both hands, clubbed together, at the back of the man's neck. The powerful blow landed solidly, the fists crashing against the outlaw's neck with such force that they drove him off his feet and caused him to land face down in the trail.

Moving fast, Perry plucked the man's revolver from the holster on his hip and swung it up and then down. The butt thudded against the outlaw's head. His hat had fallen off, so there was nothing to soften the blow. Perry felt bone give. The man made a noise, shuddered, and then lay still.

Perry knew there was a good chance he had killed the outlaw. He wasn't going to feel bad about that, knowing how the gang had killed and rustled and terrorized this area. He slid the gun in his own empty holster and reached out toward the horse as he spoke softly.

Perry had always had a good touch with animals, especially horses. It didn't take him long to settle this one down and get hold of the reins. He checked the saddle, found that the cinch was broken as the man had said, and finished loosening it so that he was able to haul it completely off. Then he mounted up to ride with just the saddle blanket on the horse's back.

Compared to that Comanche pony he had ridden bareback when he first threw in with the Rangers, this wasn't much of a challenge. Clucking to the horse, he left the fallen outlaw where he was and started off in the direction the gang had taken. He couldn't hear them up ahead anymore, but he knew they were there and hadn't gone too far.

And now, at least, he stood a chance of being able to do something to spoil their plans.

Athelstan's men scattered, moving off the trail into the shelter of trees, brush, and small hillocks. They dismounted and several men were given the job of holding the horses' collected reins and leading the animals even farther back.

Athelstan and Tye remained at the side of the trail, holding their rifles. Athelstan said quietly, "Those riders may not be the rustlers. We don't want to start a battle with innocent men."

"It's not likely a bunch of innocent men would be out and about at this time of night," Tye said.

"We're out and about."

"I reckon you've got a point. What are you going to do, hail them and ask them who they are and what they're doing?"

"We're still on BXT range. I believe I have a right to do exactly that."

"Well," Tye said, "we ought to know pretty quick what's going to happen. Here they come."

The night riders appeared, a dark mass moving along the trail two hundred yards away. Athelstan walked into the center of the trail and stood there waiting for them.

"You do believe in making yourself a target, don't you?" Tye asked.

"Why not? I have you covering me."

"Is this the way folks fight battles in Europe?"

"Not exactly. Over there, armies march out onto the field, face each other, and march directly ahead."

"Sounds like a good way to get shot to pieces," Tye drawled. "No wonder we were able to whip those British boys back during the revolution."

Athelstan laughed. "You can't insult me by insulting the British. I'm from Alpenstone."

Then he stepped forward, thrust his rifle into the air above his head, and shouted at the riders, who were now well within earshot.

"Stop right there, you men! This is the Braxton Ranch. Who are you, and what do you—"

That was as far as he got before all hell broke loose.

Chapter 44

Tye had knelt behind a slab of rock at the side of the trail. A heartbeat after Athelstan hailed the riders, Colt flame bloomed in the darkness like crimson flowers as they opened fire on him. Tye jerked his rifle to his shoulder and squeezed the trigger. He fired by instinct rather than aiming, but it was too dark to aim much, anyway.

And Tye's instincts were very good. One of the riders howled, threw his hands in the air, and toppled backward out of his saddle.

Tye dropped the empty rifle as he stood up. He palmed both Walker Colts from their holsters. Holding the triggers back, he thumbed off shot after shot, back and forth, sending tongues of fire leaping from the revolvers' muzzles and a wave of gun thunder rolling over the hills.

The reports from Tye's guns blended with those from the outlaws' weapons as the riders charged forward. The roar was so loud it seemed as if the very earth itself ought to tremble from it.

The men Athelstan and Tye had brought with them opened fire as well, adding to the deafening racket. So many muzzle flashes ripped through the darkness that the whole scene was lit up like a landscape out of hell.

When the shooting started, Athelstan had sprinted to the other side of the trail and left his feet in a rolling dive that carried him out of the worst of the lead swarm. He came up on one knee, still holding his rifle, and fired into the dark mass clogging the trail fifty yards away. He tossed the rifle aside, drew his Colts, and sprawled forward on his belly as he began triggering the revolvers.

Whooping like Sam Houston's men at San Jacinto as they charged the surprised Mexican army under the dictator Santa Anna, the Hill Country ranchers rushed the outlaws, firing as they ran. The gang's horses were badly spooked, and a number of the riders were thrown.

In a matter of seconds, the battle was a wild melee.

Tye was in the thick of it, emptying his Colts and then using them as clubs until he pouched one of the irons and drew his bowie knife with that hand instead.

The hammers of Athelstan's guns had fallen on empty chambers, too. Recalling the stories Texans told about the Alamo, he picked up his rifle by the barrel and waded in, flailing with it as he had heard Davy Crockett had done at that famous battle.

The fate of the entire state didn't ride on this clash, but to the men in the middle of it, it seemed just as epic—and just as maddening and frightening.

It certainly felt that way to Jeremy Braxton as he forced his horse on and fired the gun in his hand. During the early moments of the battle, the moon had risen above one of the hills to the east and now cast a wash of silvery brilliance over the landscape, so that men could tell friend from foe in the mad jumble of violence along both sides of the trail.

In that moonlight, Jeremy caught sight of a familiar figure: his brother Athelstan battling two outlaws, swinging a rifle at them like a club and holding them off as they darted at him with knives in their hands.

Athelstan was so occupied with those threats that he didn't see the man riding toward him from behind and leveling a pistol at him.

Jeremy jabbed his heels in his horse's flanks and sent the animal leaping ahead. As he closed in, he shouted, "Athelstan, look out!"

Seeing Jeremy charging toward him, the gunman on horseback jerked his weapon in that direction. The gun boomed and spurted sparks. Jeremy felt the solid punch of the ball slamming into his body.

He had already pulled his own trigger when he was hit, though, and as he slumped forward in the saddle, he saw the outlaw slide from the saddle and land in a limp heap on the ground.

The stock of Athelstan's rifle crushed the skull of one opponent, and the other fell to a shot from one of Ralph Shellabarger's guns. Athelstan would have sworn he'd just heard his brother's voice, although that was impossible. Jeremy had stayed at the BXT.

But when Athelstan whirled around, he saw Jeremy swaying in the saddle of a horse that had just come to a stop. Athelstan dropped the rifle and leaped forward to catch his brother as Jeremy finally toppled off the mount. He eased Jeremy to the ground and knelt beside him.

"What are you doing here?" he asked as he propped Jeremy up with an arm around his shoulders. "I told you to stay at the ranch!"

"I'm . . . a Braxton, too. . . . It's my fight . . . as much as yours—"

Jeremy got that much out before his head fell back loosely. Athelstan experienced a moment of panic as he thought that Jeremy had died, but then he felt a pulse still beating strongly in his brother's neck.

That pulse wasn't the only thing thundering. Hoofbeats pounded the ground nearby, forcing Athelstan to realize that a rider was almost on top of him and Jeremy. He looked up, saw the horse looming above them like a mountain, and was about to try grabbing Jeremy and rolling desperately aside when another horse came out of nowhere and rammed a shoulder into the one about to trample them.

Both animals went down in a welter of flailing legs and steel-shod hooves. The second rider had tackled the first one and knocked him out of the saddle. They crashed to the ground, rolled, broke apart, and came up fighting. One of the men held a knife and slashed at the other. In the moonlight, with the battle swirling around them and clouds of dust and powder smoke choking the air, Athelstan had no idea which combatant had saved him and Jeremy and which had tried to ride them down.

He watched the fight go back and forth. The man who didn't have the knife pawed at an empty holster on his hip. The gun that had been in that holster must have fallen out when the men crashed to the ground. Evidently, he was unarmed, but he was fast, which he demonstrated as he dodged the slashes and jabs of the blade the other man held.

Finally, as he darted aside from another thrust of the knife, the man grabbed his foe's wrist and yanked. He had his leg in between the other man's calves. Both of them twisted, went down, and rolled again.

This time, only one of them got up. The other lay there on his back with the knife's handle sticking up starkly from his chest. Almost the entire blade was buried in his body.

The victor turned to Athelstan and Jeremy. Athelstan still couldn't see his face.

Then he asked, "Are you all right?"

The voice struck Athelstan like a bolt of lightning. He was so shocked he literally fell back.

But he could never forget where he had heard it before.

"Perry?" he asked, so stunned that he had trouble forming the name.

The man stepped closer, smiling now, and the moonlight washed over his face enough for Athelstan to recognize it. The features were leaner, more defined, honed down by harsh experience. But the face belonged, unmistakably, to the brother he had believed to be dead for more than a year.

Perry's smile disappeared as he exclaimed, "Jeremy!" He

dropped to a knee on the wounded man's other side. "How badly is he hurt?"

"I don't know. I don't think it's too bad. At least, I hope it's not. Perry—how—? What are you—where have you—?"

A sudden flurry of gunshots broke into Athelstan's questions. He and Perry turned to look as more riders swept up to the battle, firing over the heads of those still struggling and calling for them to surrender. Men threw down their guns, thrust their arms in the air, and shouted that they gave up. The fight was over in moments. The newcomers began rounding up the few outlaws who had survived.

"Who are those men?" Athelstan asked.

"The finest fighting men in the world," Perry said. "But they got here just a mite late this time. That's Cap'n Sutherland's troop of Texas Rangers, Athelstan. The same one I belong to."

Bodie, Griggs, and Baldy stood on the porch listening to the distant gunfire, all of them tense and anxious. Bodie had to fight the impulse to grab a horse and race off into the night toward the sounds of battle. She knew that if she tried to, the two men would stop her. They wouldn't like doing so, especially if they had to lay hands on her in order to make her comply with Athelstan's orders, but they would do whatever was necessary.

Griggs said, "I know how you feel, Miss Bodie. I wish I was there, too. But I know that your brothers and Tye will be all right. They'll beat those outlaws, too, and make them take off for the tall and uncut. The ones who don't wind up six feet under, that is."

"Don't be so bloodthirsty, boy," Baldy said. "Texas is really wearing off on you."

"But they've got it coming," Griggs protested. "This dang Hill Country is going to be settled someday, and there'll be no place for thieves and killers and outlaws."

"That's right," Bodie said. "I just wish I could do my part in getting rid of them."

Baldy harrumphed. "A woman's job in establishing civilization isn't killing badmen," he said. "You should be worried about having children and making a home for your husband."

Bodie swung toward the old-timer and said hotly, "So you think that's all a woman's good for, do you?"

Before Baldy could answer that, Griggs said, "Somebody's coming. I hear a horse."

"Just one horse?" Baldy asked.

"Yes, I think so."

Bodie listened to the slow, thudding hoofbeats and agreed with Griggs.

"You're right, Tom," she said. "It's just one man."

They all relaxed slightly, although a worried frown still creased Bodie's forehead. If a number of riders had been approaching the house, it could have meant two different things: Athelstan, Tye, and the others were returning home victorious—or the outlaws had defeated them and were on their way to loot the place.

She wasn't sure what it meant that only one man was riding out of the night.

"There he is," Griggs said.

"Do you recognize him?" Bodie asked.

"No, miss. The moonlight isn't bright enough. But I can tell you it's not Athelstan or Jeremy. Or Tye, either. Maybe one of the men the other ranchers brought with them?"

"Or one of those brigands," Baldy growled.

"Look at the way he's riding hunched over in the saddle," Bodie said. "He's hurt!"

She started toward the steps, her natural instinct to help coming to the fore, but Griggs blocked her way.

"I'll go see who it is," Baldy said. Carrying the rifle, he went down the steps and walked out to meet the rider, who was only about fifty feet away by this time.

Bodie heard the old servant call out, asking the man who he was and if he was hurt. Suddenly, a flash of gunfire split the night and Baldy reeled backward. The stranger's horse leaped forward and his gun came up and blasted twice more. The balls struck Griggs and flung him backward.

Shocked by the sudden violence, Bodie whirled toward Griggs and saw him sliding down the wall of the ranch house. He came to a stop with his legs splayed out in front of him.

The stranger brought his horse to a stop in front of the porch and leveled his revolver at Bodie.

"Just stand still, girl," he ordered. "I don't want to kill you. You're my safe passage out of this part of the country. But I will if I have to."

"Who are you?" she managed to ask.

"Name's Ramsgate."

"The man who came to see Jeremy earlier this evening!"

"That's right," he said. A chuckle came from him. "Your brother and me, we're partners of a sort, you see."

"That's a lie," Bodie said. "A damned lie. Not even Jeremy would work with a man like you. A man who would shoot down two innocent men—"

"Shut up and come here," Ramsgate broke in and ordered in a harsh voice. "Things have gone to hell tonight, but I'm gettin' out of here, and you're going with me. Nobody's gonna shoot at me when I've got the Braxton girl in front of me."

"That's all I am to you?" Bodie asked, tight-lipped. "The Braxton girl?"

"Well, what the hell else do you figure you are?"

"The girl who's going to kill you," Bodie said.

Her left side was toward Ramsgate because of the way she had turned toward Griggs. He wouldn't have been able to see that she was armed. As the words came out of her mouth, she twisted back toward him and dropped to a knee. Her hand closed around the butt of the Paterson Colt on her right hip as he fired. The ball hummed past her head. The Colt came up, her thumb earing back the hammer as the gun rose, and the revolver boomed and bucked against her hand she fired.

The ball drove into Ramsgate's chest and jolted him backward in the saddle. He gasped in shock and pain and fired another round, but his gun had already started to droop. The ball raked along his horse's shoulder, causing the animal to buck wildly in pain. Ramsgate flew from the saddle and landed in a crumpled pile on the ground.

Bodie was there almost by the time he struck the dirt. Ramsgate had hung on to his gun and he writhed as he tried to bring it up and around. Bodie's Paterson roared again and then again. Ramsgate jerked and twitched, and the gun slid out of his fingers as a final spasm made his heels drum on the ground.

Bodie kicked the fallen gun away and backed off a step. She kept the Colt trained on the fallen outlaw, but when he didn't move, she turned and ran back to the porch to see how badly her friends were hurt.

Chapter 45

Six weeks later

The crowd gathered in front of the Vereins Kirche in Fredericksburg let out a resounding cheer as the newly married couple emerged from the church doors. A few of the men got carried away enough to fire pistols in the air in celebration.

Athelstan had given Bodie away. He had thought she was beautiful in her wedding dress as he walked her down the aisle, but she looked even more radiant and lovely on Tye's arm as they left the church. He had teased her before the ceremony by asking her if she was going to wear her buckskins. She had threatened to do that very thing. But of course, she hadn't.

Tye had dressed up, too, wearing a frock coat over a ruffled white shirt he had gotten somewhere. A silk cravat was tied around his neck.

Perry had served as Tye's best man. The two of them had become good friends during the weeks since Perry's reunion with his family. He followed the happy couple out of the church, trailed by Jeremy, Baldy, and Tom Griggs. All three of them still looked pale and drawn after their recovery from the gunshot wounds they had suffered. Eventually, though, they would be back to normal, Athelstan knew.

When that happened, Jeremy had promised to take a more active hand in the running of the ranch. He claimed he wanted to carry his share of the load for a change. Athelstan wanted to believe that, wanted to believe that Jeremy actually had changed—but he wouldn't do so until he had seen it for himself, with his own eyes.

Tables loaded with platters of hearty German food were set up under some shade trees. The celebration of Bodie and Tye's marriage would continue with a midday feast. A couple of wagons loaded with barrels of beer provided by Emil Deutschendorf were parked nearby, too. Fredericksburg was a happy place today, and would be even happier by the time the day was over.

A couple of men with fiddles struck up a tune, and Tye and Bodie danced together under the trees. Athelstan, Jeremy, Perry, Baldy, and Tom Griggs stood watching with smiles on their faces.

Perry grew solemn as he said, "You know, Captain Sutherland and the rest of the troop will be riding back through here in a few days."

The Rangers had left Perry on the BXT while they continued their patrol up through the Hill Country, but Sutherland had made it clear they would swing by the ranch when they were finished with that.

"Yes, I know," Athelstan said. "Have you decided what you're going to do?"

Perry scraped a thumbnail along his freshly shaved jaw and said, "You know there's a part of me that wants to stay here."

"But you like being a Ranger," Athelstan said.

"I can't deny it. Those fellows took me in and became my friends when I was about as low as a man can get. We've ridden and fought side by side for a year. It's hard to break those bonds."

"The bonds of family are stronger," Jeremy said.

Perry nodded. "They are," he agreed, "and that's why I'm going to be back here someday. I want to help build the BXT into the best ranch in Texas. Just—not yet."

"I understand," Athelstan said. "And I'm sure you'll know when the time is right."

"But we'll miss you," Jeremy said gruffly. "You know, all those months we thought you were dead, I never was able to bring myself to accept it. I kept thinking that I was going to walk around the barn someday, or be riding through through the woods, and I'd look up and there you'd be. And that's sort of the way it turned out."

Athelstan smiled, and said, "You did pick a mighty good time to show up again, Perry. That outlaw's horse would have trampled us into the dirt in another second or two."

"I'm sorry I cut it that close," Perry said. He frowned and went on, "Ronan MacLochlainn's still out there somewhere, you know. I don't know how much ill will he bears our family. He did help me escape, but he also warned me not to run into him again."

"You think he might show up around here and cause trouble?" Athelstan asked.

"I suppose it's possible. At this point, I don't see any way we can know for sure what he's going to do."

Jeremy said, "You mean he's just as unpredictable as the Comanche."

Tom Griggs spoke up. "Tye says that another war party is bound to come raiding this way sooner or later. The Comanch' aren't going to give up this country without more of a fight. He knows them better than anybody else around here, so I believe him."

"So do I," Athelstan said. He stood there musing, as unwanted scenes of terror and bloodshed played through his imagination. He hoped those bad days wouldn't come—but he was almost certain that sooner or later they would.

They were the price of civilization.

Baldy got all their attention by saying, "Look there. Wagons coming."

Athelstan turned to gaze along the road leading into Fredericksburg from the south. Half a dozen covered wagons were indeed rolling slowly toward the settlement.

Finished with their dance, Bodie and Tye came over to join

the others. Athelstan asked, "Do you know anything about those wagons, Tye?"

"Another immigrant train, I'd say," the groom replied. "From what I've heard, they're leaving Indian Point on a more regular basis now, some of them heading here and others over to New Braunfels." Tye grinned. "This whole Hill Country's going to be full of German folks pretty soon."

"Don't forget the ones from Alpenstone," Bodie told him.

Athelstan said, "I suspect we'll be the only ones to hail from there."

"Let's go over and meet them," Bodie suggested. "There's enough food here to feed the whole crowd three or four times over. We should invite these newcomers to join the celebration."

"That's a kind thought," Tye said. "It's all right with me."

The seven of them walked toward the wagons, which had come to a stop along the road in front of Emil Deutschendorf's trading post. Men were climbing down from the vehicles and then turning back to help women and children disembark.

Athelstan drew a sharp breath as he thought he recognized a man and woman who had just gotten down from one of the wagons. It couldn't be—

Then they turned, and it was them. With a huge smile on his face, Charles Edgerton hurried forward to throw his arms around Athelstan in a back-slapping bear hug. When he stepped back, he said, "It's really us, cousin. I know, you can't believe it, can you?"

Athelstan said, "I didn't know—never expected . . ."

Charles's sister Claudia, as beautiful as ever despite the hardships they must have endured on the way here, moved up to Athelstan and put her hand on his arm.

"Did you miss me?" she asked softly.

Athelstan couldn't find the words to answer. He was too busy looking at the devils lurking in her eyes and dancing as merrily as ever.

Texas, 1875

The old man's still-keen ears heard horses moving around in the trees. Those bushwhackers were probably getting impatient. His instincts told him they were going to charge him again. They outnumbered him, after all.

The memories that had occupied his mind while he lay behind the rocks began to fade. There were plenty of other memories in his head. So much had happened since the day Bodie and Tye had gotten hitched. So much tragedy and grief and loss, so much blood and fire and death.

But so much life, too. The beautiful moments that made it all worthwhile, when a man could stand and look around at his family and home, and realize he had done something, by God. All flesh was dust, as the Good Book said. Memories didn't last. Someday, he and all his accomplishments would be forgotten.

But in that day, people would walk this land and live their lives because of what he and all the men and women like him had done. Forgotten their efforts might be, but those efforts would carry on, rippling through time for all the days to come.

The old man squinted. Dust rising to the north. Dust coming from the hooves of horses ridden by hombres who'd come to look for him. And they were headed this way.

So were the bushwhackers, who burst out of the trees yelling and shoot-

ing as they galloped toward him. He thrust the rifle over the rock in front of him. If he fought them off for long enough, he would live. Simple as that.

"Come and get me, you scoundrels," Athelstan Braxton said through gritted teeth, as he peered over the Winchester's barrel.